AJ AIKENS

Published in Australia by AJ Aikens in 2026

AJ Aikens acknowledges and pays respect to the past and present Traditional Owners and Custodians of Country throughout Australia and recognises the continuation of cultural, spiritual and educational practices of Aboriginal and Torres Strait Islander peoples. This book was written on Turrbal and Jagera land whose custodians never ceded their sovereignty.

Structural editing by PS Editing: psediting.com.au

Copy editing by Words on Words: wordsonwords.com.au

ISBN: 978-1-7643972-0-9

Disclaimer

This book is intended for adults and contains sexually explicit content, graphic language and drug use. Sexual abuse, domestic violence, loss of a parent and suicide are mentioned. The author's intention was to handle these topics sensitively and respectfully. While this book discusses these themes, it is ultimately about resilience, loving yourself and recognising the good around you.

Survivors deserve their happy ending.

Please read with care.

For anyone who was made to feel like they were weird or 'a bit much'. Being weird or a bit much beats the shit out of being a boring cunt.

Chapter 1

Fridays are for the boys

Kirra decided that her last billing cycle would finish on time at five o'clock this Friday. Many of her clients had not yet returned after the Christmas break, and she was already way ahead of the monthly target set for her by Kensington Menschel, a global law firm where she was a partner in the Brisbane office. She was one of the few people back at work – her colleagues were set to return on Monday. She would spend the rest of today's minutes as she deemed fit. She shut her laptop down and flipped over her personal phone.

She had dozens of notifications across multiple apps, the siren song of friends and lovers who wanted to debauch with her this sticky, steamy January eve.

Her dealer had sent her a single snowflake emoji in WhatsApp. The man made her feel like Alan Turing – communicating through a heavily encrypted app with an almost indecipherable pictographic code, but she had the brains to crack it. Kirra rolled her eyes. She smirked at the thought of him probably making more money than half of the twats she worked with. The smirk faltered when she considered that it was a twat like her that kept him rich too.

A group chat she had with Joel and some of the other boys was filled with incessant chatter and several pointed @s to Kirra asking for her commitment to dinner, drinks and dancing.

Zoe was heading out to be wooed by a new fellow she was head over heels in love with after two dates and had messaged Kirra a picture of her outfit for approval.

"Hot, gorgeous, stunning – but would swap out those pumps for something open and strappy. Closed round-toe is giving 2010s business casual," she messaged back.

Zoe reacted with a heart instantly, clearly too short on time before her date to respond with anything more. Kirra scrolled back and reread the conversation where she had strongly advised Zoe not to introduce Holding a Fish in Tinder Pic to her daughter, Kirra's goddaughter, yet. It was way too soon. Zoe had taken her advice at that point, but Kirra decided to add Hattie meeting some random jerk to the list of things that she would need to worry about.

It was a long list.

Dan was working away this week and wouldn't be back in town until Monday, but he had messaged her a few hours ago asking what she had planned for tonight and to say he was thinking of her. The rush of love Kirra felt at the mere thought of Dan squeezed her heart like a vice. He was the human equivalent of a piece of toast and a cup of tea – his presence, even via text, warmed her from the inside out. She responded that she was thinking about him too, and that she was leaning towards heading out with the boys.

"Be good Kiz, remember your New Year resolutions xx."

"Do lots of drugs and humiliate myself, got it!" she'd replied.

"I don't remember that being on the list, but you have fun anyway, tell Joel hi for me x."

While Dan was in fact gay, he wasn't in her mind one of *the boys*. He would come out to drink and dance regularly but, given all his commitments to his very large extended family, he wasn't chronically out like they were.

When out with the boys, she had so much fun that she forgot what time it was. She felt free to go on side quests, meeting up with other friends or men. The group all tended to peel off and pursue their own pleasures at some point in the evening. The Boys were also always out Thursday through Sunday, so she knew that if she wanted to party with them, the offer was basically always on the table.

She entered the group chat and said she would meet them wherever they were after she had gone to the gym, showered and reapplied her makeup. There was much cheering and merriment at her commitment to the cause, making her giddy with excitement. She opened up Tinder.

A torrent of dicks greeted her.

Mostly they were top-down points of view, a sucked in and or tensed abdomen above a fully or partially hard member jutting this way or that. Sometimes it was a mirror selfie – cock in hand and camera in front of his face for some semblance of deniability. The particularly artistic ones might even send a short movie of them wanking or a voice note describing what they would do to Kirra once they got her alone.

But what did they do to her once they got her alone? Generally, nothing particularly memorable or satisfying. By the time she eeny-meeny-miney-mo'd who she would be meeting up with, any physical sensation the encounter offered was felt through the thick blanket of whatever substances she had imbibed earlier that evening. While she wasn't particularly discerning in her choice of guys, she had rules. She never took anyone back to her house where they would meet her dog Gus, and she never stayed the night. Regardless of how wasted she was, she would slip out and skulk back to her renovated worker's cottage in Paddington or Dan's Woolstore apartment in Teneriffe.

She responded to the thirteen dick pics with a nude of her own, faceless of course, and the same one for all thirteen, accompanied with a devil emoji. To the six messages from more well-meaning guys who were inviting her to dinner or a drink, she sent a copied and pasted "Maybe later, just heading out with friends x".

To her dealer, she sent the *100* emoji indicating that yes, she would be buying from him.

Tonight is a very special night that deserves celebrating.

It's Friday.

Chapter 2

Tall, dark and handsome

Kirra was fucked up and more than $1,500 poorer.

She and the boys were dancing, sweating and screaming on the dancefloor of a rooftop bar, freshly out of drugs and completely out of their minds. She retreated to the bar for a drink then took it outside to cool off and regain her balance.

She looked down at the winding brown snake that was the Brisbane River to the distant blinking red lights atop Mount Coot-tha, hovering above the peak like fireflies, as her head swam. She closed her eyes and tilted her head back to let the gentle breeze waft over her overheated skin.

"You looked like you were having fun in there," a voice said from somewhere to her left.

She turned towards it, her vision a few seconds behind her movement, and rallied her focus to take in the body attached to the voice. An older guy, maybe in his late forties or early fifties, tall with a dark short-back-and-sides greying above his ears, was walking towards her. He was well-dressed in clean RM Williams boots, light-coloured chinos and a long-sleeved shirt rolled halfway up his forearms – the classic Queen Street cowboy. When Brisbane's winter struck, with blistering lows of 20 °C, a black puffer vest would inevitably be added to the ensemble to make it a year-round look.

"Shiiiit …" She quickly realised how drunk she sounded and focused on getting her tongue operational in her mouth. "That, good sir, is a very nice watch."

She placed her drink on a table and stumbled forward, taking his big wrist in her hands, turning it over to admire the watch.

"You've got a nice one too, it would appear," he said, returning the gesture and wrapping his hands around her wrist to inspect her Carrera. He rubbed his thumb along the back of her hand. His hands were warm and huge; the pad of his thumb on her skin left her tingling. The feeling of his touch mixed with the humidity and assorted chemicals flooding her nervous system made her want to skip her usual pleasantries.

"What's with the wedding ring tan?" she said, staring him directly in the eyes and removing her hand from his grip.

Even in her state, she had spotted the lighter patch of skin while she was looking at his watch. She wasn't a homewrecker. She despised unfaithful men and had a keen sense of when someone was lying to her, the latter of which helped make her an excellent lawyer.

He looked shocked, clearly taken aback by the accusation. After a moment's pause, he responded. "I'm recently divorced. We've been separated for a while, but it was finalised this week. I've only just taken my ring off. You can ask those guys in there if you don't believe me." He gestured to a group of similarly dressed men sitting at a table near the bar.

"As if they would tell me if you were," she replied. She wasn't sure where this was going or whether she wanted to fight with this guy or fuck him. Maybe both.

"Yeah, you're probably right," he said, with a small chuckle. "Look, I'm not going to try and convince you I'm single, that feels desperate. I was just coming over to say hello. You have a nice night with your mates."

He gave her a smile, a very attractive one, Kirra quickly noted, then turned to walk away.

"Why'd you guys split?" she called out to the back of his head as she flopped down on a vacant chaise lounge and picked up her drink. She still wasn't sure what she was looking for from this guy, and she now had several unanswered calls and messages from the slew of men she had texted earlier.

He paused, turned around and sat down with her.

He explained that he and his wife of twenty-eight years had drifted apart, that they were probably never really suited for one another to begin with. They had kids, who had grown up, they paid off the house, and they even got the holiday house in Noosa (it was a *really* nice watch). Life had become so comfortable and easy that there was no hiding from the fact they were living separate lives, like acquaintances or roommates, in their own huge, beautiful home. Homes, plural.

Either this guy was an Oscar-award winning actor or Kirra had killed the last of her brain cells tonight, maybe a combination of the two, but she believed him.

He asked her about herself and seemed genuinely interested in her answers. He never took the conversation anywhere sexual, as men tended to at this time of a night … or morning, as it was. She explained she was a lawyer, lived in Paddington and that, if you cut her, she would bleed maroon for her beloved Broncos. They chatted about footy and her work while she inched closer to him on the chaise lounge they had semi-reclined on. She was close enough to smell his spicy cologne and feel the warmth coming off his body.

Without warning, she leaned in and kissed him. After a moment's shock, he kissed her back while bringing his hand to the side of her face, the other hand carefully placed on her knee. He was much taller and broader than Kirra, but she was in charge, determining the pace and depth of their kiss. She brought one hand up to his jaw and across his stubble, the other down his lower back, dragging her fingernails, while she pushed her tongue further into his mouth. He groaned and tilted his head to kiss her more deeply. Just as suddenly as she had kissed him, she pulled away.

"Can we go back to yours?"

His lids were heavy with lust, and his look bordered on dazed. Clearly lost for words, he nodded his head.

"Do you have condoms?" She wasn't ever backwards about coming forwards.

He shook his head but quickly added, "Get some on the way?"

He said a brief goodbye to his friends, who Kirra sheepishly waved at as she stood next to him. They were clearly trying to play it cool, but one of them gave a thumbs up when they thought she wasn't looking. Kirra found the boys, who gave her a far less subtle send-off.

"Bubbye ya big SLUT!" Joel screamed as he kissed her on both cheeks, blowing a kiss to her new friend as he strutted back on to the dancefloor.

"Love you, babe; have fun climbing that man mountain!" Finn screeched at her from several metres away, poking the index finger of his right hand into the O-shape made by his left.

***

Back at his rented apartment in Spring Hill, Kirra dimmed the lights and climbed on top of him. The apartment was sparsely furnished, and the sofa smelled new, further corroborating his story.

She kissed down his neck while she squeezed his shoulders, rocking back and forth on his lap. Her tiny scrap of a dress had ridden up to her waist, revealing her arse and G-string.

He placed his hands there and groaned. "Holy fuck, your body," he whispered into her hair as he tightened his grip on her cheeks.

She moaned into his neck too; his hands were huge, and the pressure he applied to her skin was perfect. Kirra could feel he was as hard as a rock beneath her. Her breasts fell free of her dress, which was now bunched up around her middle. He leaned back to take one into his mouth, sucking deeply and swirling his tongue around her nipple, taking hold of her hips and grinding her down on his erection. Her head fell back. She gasped as the sensation shot straight down to her pussy. It felt so good, and she briefly wondered how much better it would be had she not spent the first part of the evening numbing her senses to near-oblivion.

He continued sucking on her for a while longer before he stood up with Kirra wrapped around his waist and spun around. He gently lowered her to the sofa and dropped down to his knees, nestling between her legs. He kissed her, starting with her neck, then her stomach, pausing with his hands curled in the waistband of her underwear. Even in the dim light, she could see how turned on he was, his dark brown eyes boring into her.

"May I, please?"

Holy fuck, why was the word 'please' so fucking sexy?

She nodded, clearly beyond speaking English.

He dragged her underwear down slowly then threw it aside, following with featherlight kisses from her navel down to her mound. Kirra whimpered, her feet coming up to rest on his back. He separated her folds with his hand and dipped his head to take one long lick, groaning into her.

"Fucking hell, you're so wet," he whispered. He continued dragging his tongue over her clit, winding her up tighter and tighter. He squeezed her arse with his free hand and took his time, savouring her, but Kirra was impatient.

"I want to fuck you, right now." She moaned, pushing him back and standing up, her dress falling to the floor.

On shaky legs, she walked over to the kitchen bench to the box of condoms they had purchased on the way back to his place. He stood up and followed her to the kitchen counter, placing an arm each side of her. He was still fully dressed, and the contrast of his still-clothed arms around her completely naked body made her jittery with anticipation. He kissed down her neck while she opened the box and removed a condom.

She spun around and pulled him free from his pants and briefs. All of a sudden the big hands made sense. She let out an appreciative whistle as she admired him, running her hand up and down his rock-hard length.

Kirra rolled the condom down, and he scooped her up in his arms to carry her back to his bedroom.

There was a king mattress on the floor with fresh bedding, the packet it came in discarded to the side of the room. He laid her on the mattress and stood up to step out of his pants. He unbuttoned his shirt and took it off. He had a scattering of dark chest hair and muscles that looked useful, not just pretty.

"You're so fucking sexy." She smiled up at him from the bed as he towered over her.

"So are you." His eyes raked over her from head to toe, intent on taking all of her in.

He knelt down on the mattress and started kissing her again, more forcefully this time, his tongue deep in her mouth while his cock butted up against her entrance.

"I want you to take me like this." She lightly pushed him back and rolled over flat on to her stomach, poking her behind up at him.

"Fuck, that looks good," he groaned, gently running his hand over her arse and squeezing it before he moved. He placed his knees on the outside of her thighs and ran his cock up and down her folds, making sure she was soaking wet and ready for him. She whimpered into the pillow and raised her rear higher in invitation.

He slowly inserted himself into her, holding his breath as he did, before letting out an "oh fuck" on an exhale once he was almost all the way inside her. She couldn't stifle her moan at the sensation of being stretched open and filled with his thickness. He started gently, easing back out of her in one slow, steady pull before pushing back in, and then again. He kissed down her back and took his time enjoying every inch of her.

It wasn't fast or hard enough.

"Deeper," she croaked out.

Clearly intent on giving her everything she wanted, he obliged and buried himself all the way inside of her, his abdomen pressing into Kirra's arse. She cried out and arched her back even further.

"Is that good?" he asked, voice deeper than before, withdrawing almost entirely then slowly sliding back in all the way.

"Fuck yeah. Harder, faster."

After he was satisfied she was enjoying herself, he wasted no more time and slammed into her with everything he had. She screamed out in pleasure as he hit her innermost walls. Her screams seemed to spur him on, and he fucked her deeply, gathering pace as she continually begged him to go harder and faster, her cries partially muffled by the pillow. Stomach to the mattress, she reached out for one of the arms he had propped beside her for support and guided his hand to her throat.

"Choke me," she squeaked while he pounded into her relentlessly. He applied gentle pressure around her neck. She placed her hand over his and showed how hard she wanted to be squeezed, which was hard enough to hurt and make her feel lightheaded.

"Sorry, I don't want to do that, baby," he panted, leaning down to kiss the side of her face and loosening his grip. A little dejected, she decided to tease him by clenching her inner muscles around him as tight as she could.

"Fuck, don't do that. I won't last much longer," he said in a strained whisper, reaching under her front with the hand he just had on her throat to find her clit. He started making circles on her with his fore and middle fingers, but Kirra knew it was pointless. She never came after a night out. She appreciated the effort and tenderness he had shown her in *almost* giving her exactly what she wanted. She knew making a new woman come after so long with another would be a huge deal to him, so she put on her best performance.

"Oh daddy, fuck, I'm going to come, yeah just like that." She increased the volume of her moaning, rising up on her forearms and knees and pushing back in to him. His pace grew uneven, and he pumped into her faster and harder than before. After a few minutes of relentless pounding, he let out a shout and gave one last almighty thrust as he finished in her. Panting and dripping in sweat, he kissed down her back, still inside her.

"Jesus Christ," he let out on an exhale, still panting. "That was amazing, you're so fucking gorgeous." He slowly pulled out and lay down next to her. He wrapped her up in his arms and dragged her on to his chest where she listened to his heartbeat as it slowed.

She looked up at him as he looked out the window, his face illuminated by the moonlight. He was dripping in sweat and had the sexiest smirk on his lips, clearly quite pleased with himself. They lay there in silence for a few minutes, basking in the afterglow when he jolted gently, as if remembering something.

"I feel like such a jerk only asking you this now. What's your name? Mine's Ben." He smiled down at her, stroking her hair.

"Jane," she answered and pretended to fall asleep in his arms.

Chapter 3

Saturdays are for the girls

When her peers at UQ were getting part-time jobs in hospitality or, if they had the right parents, in legal firms as paralegals, Kirra got a job at Tweetie Pies, a gentleman's club a short walk from Roma Street Train Station. Kirra justified that this was the best way to support herself through her studies using several lines of logic.

Firstly, the pay was better than anything her friends were making working regular day jobs. Given she was a natural raconteuse who could sweet-talk even the most I'm-just-here-with-my-friends of patrons out of their hard-earned Australian dollars, she felt a sense of control and agency in her work. The flirtier and more attentive she was to the gents in the room, the more money she made. She ate what she killed, so she killed a lot and remained well-fed while her other uni friends risked starvation week to week.

Her peers were content with a set hourly rate, but not her. After doing some shifts in a café – waking at an ungodly hour to handle sticky coffee cups and customers' crusty morning breath – she decided she preferred sleeping in, handling sticky booths and clients' whiskey breath instead.

Secondly, working at Tweeties afforded her the luxury of hanging out almost exclusively with other girls, something she was in dire need of in her family of only men.

Thirdly, it was a shit-tonne of fun, no matter what anyone else said.

***

The girls sat around the circular table at their favourite Chinese restaurant in Fortitude Valley on Saturday night. Earlier that morning, she had waited for Ben to fall asleep then snuck home. While she'd had fun with him, she couldn't believe she'd broken one of her New Year's Resolutions in record time.

No more random hook ups.

She could have got Ben's number, but instead she acted on an impulse, as she always did. Was this year actually going to be any different? After escaping her hook up, she had been in her own bed by four o'clock in the morning and slept the entirety of her Saturday away, as per usual. Fourteen hours of sunshine passed by while she lay in a darkened room, comatose, too useless to even care for her dog Gus who was next door with Geoff, her neighbour.

The girls had caught up here at least twice a year since they had stopped working together at Tweetie Pies almost sixteen years ago. Kirra was still hungover from yesterday, today, whatever it was, but had dragged herself out as cancelling on the girls was tantamount to treason and punishable by death.

Tamika heaped honey chicken and fried rice on to her plate. She had high cheekbones, cat-like eyes and strawberry-blonde hair that hung in huge waves around her face. Her striking elegance was offset by a thick, loud bogan accent that made Kath and Kim sound like British royalty. Tamika had stripped for fun and extra money while working as a hairdressing apprentice and now owned a chain of successful hair salons throughout Queensland. She had worked her arse off and had a dogged determination Kirra hadn't ever seen in anyone else. There are few people in the world who could cut hair all day and dance all night then rock up the next day to do it all again. Although Tamika could afford Bollinger, she insisted the girls washed down their Chinese with BYO Passion Pop for 'old time's sake'.

Severely hungover Kirra took the Passion Pop like medicine, hair of the dog with a side of nostalgia. She sipped it at room temperature out of a mirky, chipped glass and watched with roiling nausea as Zoe plopped fluorescent pink sweet and sour pork on her plate.

Zoe was a firecracker, and her and Kirra would often kick on into the wee hours long after they had put Tamika to bed. Zoe continued to dance at Tweeties for a few years after the other two. She had a baby at twenty-three to her then boyfriend, which ended the dancing. Zoe and Michael were in love and, while unplanned, they were the most perfect little family Kirra had ever seen.

Kirra vividly remembered laying eyes on Harriet for the first time. She felt as if her heart had both stopped and started beating all at once. The instant, intense sense of love she felt for her was like nothing she had ever felt before or since.

Initially, Kirra was shocked at the classic private school name, considering Hattie's mum was a stripper and her dad was a diesel mechanic. Game of Thrones was in its third season when Harriet was born, and Kirra thought Zoe and Mick would have chosen an edgy, albeit not future-proof, name for their daughter like Daenerys or Melisandre.

Instead, Harriet Anne Nguyen was born to the two most doting parents one could wish for.

Zoe and Mick eventually grew apart and divorced but remained friends. They couldn't have had a more amicable co-parenting arrangement. Despite not being in attendance for the christening, citing fear of her skin peeling and blistering upon entry to a church, Kirra was Hattie's godmother. Kirra took this duty seriously and was as utterly besotted with Hattie now, at almost fourteen, than she had been at zero, staring down at her in her pram in this very restaurant.

God, she can't be fourteen so soon, she was only just born. Hattie being fourteen also brought with it the sombre thought that Kirra would be thirty-five this year. How could she be thirty-five this year, *she* was only just born?

Hattie reached out and piled some chow mein noodles on to her plate, picking the chicken off, a dedicated vegetarian since she had watched Charlotte's Web when she was four. Kirra was transported back to Hattie asking a myriad of questions after she had connected that Wilbur was bacon, bacon was Wilbur.

"How old are they when they get turned into bacon?"

"Can you have a pig as a pet?"

"How smart are they? Do they actually talk to other animals?"

"Why do we eat pigs and not koalas?" and so on and so forth until Kirra had almost gone vegetarian herself.

Hattie was beautiful, smart and kind, and Kirra was sure she worried about her as much as her own mother did. Maybe even more. Not that there was anything specific to worry about, other than being a young girl in a world filled with predators, double standards and being attached to a device that keeps you miserable twenty-four hours a day – just that whole thing.

"Aunty Kiz, what music did you and mum dance to when you worked together?" Hattie asked through a mouthful of noodles.

"Well, back in our day," Kirra intoned in her best old lady voice, "we didn't have your Maggie the Stallions or your Cardigan Bees to shake our rumps to, twarting or whatever you call it."

Hattie's eyes were rolling back in her head with embarrassment while she simultaneously fought a smile.

"We used to dance to, what was it again, love?" She was screeching at this point.

"We used to do the can-can with a real-life brass band playing," Zoe shrieked back in her even-louder old lady voice.

"Yes, yes, used to give the fellas a thrill when we'd lift up our petticoats and show them our stockings."

"Alright, alright! Forget I asked!" Hattie was in hysterics. "I was just trying to make conversation, fucking hell."

"Watch your language, young lady!" Zoe snapped, still in the voice of an octogenarian.

"We had our own songs." Kirra was back to using her normal voice. "I was always partial to a bit of R&B, sometimes hair metal like Poison or Skid Row."

"I was always an Acka-Dacka, Cold Chisel girlie myself," Tamika added.

"Your mum could, and still can, dance to anything. She's got great rhythm – that's where you get it from, sweetie," Kirra said to Hattie, taking a big swig of her now warm cat's piss.

Hattie was a dancer, and Kirra hadn't missed a performance since she started at three years old. Her dance school did everything from hip hop and ballet to contemporary and tap. Hattie couldn't choose what she wanted to focus on and would move between styles, a natural regardless of the music or genre.

Kirra was obviously exceptionally biased, but Hattie was growing up to be a beautiful young woman. Zoe was fair and petite with big hazel eyes, and Michael's parents had come to Australia from Vietnam during the war. Despite having two short parents, Hattie was inexplicably taller than Kirra and Zoe.

"How about you Hattie-Bonna-Pattie, what's news? Whatcha dancing to these days?"

"Um, I've been doing a lot of contemporary lately. My teacher's choreographed this beautiful piece I'm performing with a partner at the next showcase." Hattie blushed and looked down into her noodles at the word *partner*.

Kirra's buzz was instantly killed. She was on high alert in a moment. Before she could ask any follow-up questions, Zoe piped up.

"Oh, you should see this kid, Kiz. He and Hattie are the most beautiful pair when they practice together, like they're gliding on air—"

"Is he straight?"

The light-hearted tone had disappeared completely from Kirra's voice as she interrupted Zoe.

"Jesus, Aunty Kiz, I don't know," Hattie replied, cheeks flushed and still looking down.

"I reckon he's pretty keen on you though, woooooo," Zoe chided her daughter, oblivious to Kirra's alarm, and Tamika joined in, their volume reaching ear-splitting levels.

"Hattie's got a crush!"

"Is he cute, do we have a picture?"

"HATTIE'S IN LOVE!"

Kirra's vision blurred, and the squawking dulled to a ringing in her ears. She was acutely aware she had gone quiet but couldn't bring herself to join in the incessant but light-hearted ribbing, so she forced her dinner and drinks down instead.

When it came time to say goodbye, a process that took anywhere from thirty minutes to three business days, the group stood on the street, prolonging the conversation before walking back to their cars. Tamika and Zoe were in a heated debate over a ghastly reality show that Kirra couldn't stand when Hattie gave Kirra a hug.

"Are you okay, Aunty Kiz?" she asked, looking slightly down at her and making Kirra feel like the child in the situation.

"Yeah, I'm fine, sweetie. I just … You're growing up so fast. I feel like I was changing your nappies yesterday."

"I'm fourteen in a few weeks. Most of my friends are madly in love with someone."

"And … are you? This dancing partner of yours?" Kirra ventured, quietly terrified of what Hattie's answer would be.

"Um, no, he's really nice, and a really good dancer, but we're just friends at the moment."

The 'at the moment' sent Kirra's heart jackhammering. She remembered how hard it was to act nonchalant when someone would mention *his* name. Was Hattie doing that right now?

"I'm kind of surprised you care so much about that sort of thing. I thought you'd be carrying on like these two," she gestured to Tamika and her mother who were still animatedly talking about which C-grade celebrity would be leaving the island next. "You know, 'cause you are quite keen on the fellas yourself," she added, eyebrows raised.

"Well fuck me – my own goddaughter slut-shaming me, after I just paid for her noodles too," Kirra shot back, which made Hattie laugh hysterically, Kirra's favourite sound in the whole world. In Hattie's defence, Kirra had literally been begging a stranger to choke her in the wee hours of that same morning, so her comment wasn't exactly baseless.

"No, I just …" she went on, not really knowing how to put into words just how dangerous falling in love could be when you're young and stupid. "I just feel old. That's it, mostly. I can't wait to see you and lover boy dance next month."

Hattie beamed – Kirra's favourite sight in the whole world.

"I love you, Aunty Kiz."

"I love you so much, Hatts."

Chapter 4

Kirra, fifteen years old

She saw him for the first time in the passenger seat of her dad's white Hilux, and he was beautiful.

Being a self-employed chippy, her father had turned their carport into a warehouse of sorts, all manner of tools and building materials stored on rickety shelving. On this particular afternoon, he brought home several lengths of timber, a few panels of plywood and Chris, his new nineteen-year-old apprentice.

She watched as he hopped out of the ute to help her dad unload the supplies, towering over him by at least a foot. He easily carried twice as much as her dad could, and as he reached overhead to straighten the lengths of wood on the top shelf, his white T-shirt rose up, revealing a V of muscles that disappeared into the waist of his thick cotton work pants.

Kirra was fifteen, turning sixteen in September, and up until that exact moment thought she was either gay or asexual. Her friends were fiending over anything with an Adam's apple, and she couldn't have cared less. Not being keen on any of the boys her friends seemed to be obsessed with, she thought she may have been in love with Katie, the captain of the under-17 soccer team.

Katie was the coolest person Kirra had ever met, a talented athlete who coached the younger girls at her club, and had the nicest pair of boobs Kirra had ever laid eyes on. Upon reflection, Kirra realised she probably wasn't gay either, she merely had a respect-crush on Katie and coveted her own pair of nice boobs.

The moment she laid eyes on Chris, however, she realised she was hopelessly straight.

He caught her looking at him and waved up at her.

She hadn't realised she had stopped eating her plate of Doritos covered in microwaved cheese (an after-school delicacy) as she gazed down at him. The plate was balanced on the edge of the brick wall that boxed in the balcony, and when she waved back, she awkwardly smacked the plate down to the ground level. Chris quickly looked up at her mortified face and ducked to grab it. He dashed up the stairs, taking two at a time with his long legs, and held out the empty, cheese-encrusted plate to her.

"Sorry, the nachos couldn't be saved," he said, smiling. He had a deep voice, a man's voice, which rendered an otherwise overly talkative Kirra completely mute. She blinked at him once, twice.

"Ah thanks," she mumbled as she snatched the plate back off him with greasy, yellow fingers. I probably have cheese in my teeth and Dorito dust around my mouth, she thought – stricken and mortified.

"I'm Chris – your dad's taken me on as his apprentice. Him and my dad used to work together. He spent all day telling me about you and Nick. You must be Kirra."

He spoke clearly and looked into her eyes, not at his feet or her chest like the boys at school usually did when they spoke to her.

"Yeah, I'm Kirra," she replied. To avoid further embarrassment, she turned and scurried back to hide in her room.

If her life was a bookshelf, there would be a book for each part of who she was. There had been a tome each for school, soccer, family, movies, bands, videogames, holidays, thoughts of the future, friends, teammates, cousins, dreams, fears and hopes.

On the day she had knocked her plate off the balcony, she had gone back to her room, grabbed the bookshelf and tipped it forwards, spilling all those books into a great pile on the floor. She stepped on top of them, those unique parts of her world that made her Kirra, curling their pages and breaking their spines. On the now empty bookshelf, she placed one new book and decided that it would be all she would read ever again – an all-consuming story that made all others seem boring and insignificant in comparison.

She placed Him on the shelf, and everything was different.

Chapter 5

Self-care Sunday

The alarm went off at quarter to six in the morning, and Kirra rolled out of bed. She ran a brush through her long dark hair and scooped it up into a high ponytail before washing her face and applying her sunscreen. After dressing into her Sunday uniform of black leggings, joggers and a cropped white tee, she grabbed her shopping bags, popped Gus on his lead and headed for the Milton Markets.

She was determined to sort her life out this week, once and for all. No more partying, hooking up with complete strangers or wallowing in self-loathing while wasting entire days of her life in bed. She and Dan had set New Year's resolutions, and she had fucked them up in record time. Rather than dwell, she vowed to get them back on track. She was a doer, a doer of mostly dumb shit, but still a doer.

Once at the markets, she grabbed an iced latte. She almost made good on New Year's resolution number four: to order her drinks with oat milk. The thought of the thin, watery swill that would befoul her caffeine hit made her gag, so she ordered it on good old-fashioned cow pus instead. But as she really did think about ordering it non-dairy for a second or two, she awarded herself points.

Drink in hand, she hit her usual stalls to stock up on meat, fruit and vegetables, all organic, grown and harvested in the beautiful sunshine state of Queensland. She stuffed her bags with spinach, cucumbers and carrots for her salads; berries, bananas and granola for her smoothie bowls; and a pig's ear for Gus who carried it home like a prize. Her body would be a temple this week, filled with nourishing food and not assorted party drugs or the penises of strangers.

At home, she proceeded to wash her produce and prepare her meals. She created perfectly balanced bowls of protein, fat and carbs that fit her carefully planned macros to ensure she was fuelled and thriving for the work week ahead. While meal-prepping, she listened to a podcast on setting intentions and raising your vibrations, or some similar nonsense, which made her feel like she had ascended the summit of spiritual wellness despite not understanding a single word of it.

After her meal prep was complete, she sat down on her deck with her journal and wrote down everything she was grateful for, like the podcast told her to do. *I am grateful for my beautiful Gus, the best boy who ever lived.* Gus, her small Staffordshire terrier, paused chewing on his treat to snap at a fly before returning to his task. *I am grateful for Dan, the most beautiful man on planet Earth.* She gazed at the picture of her and Dan on her fridge, her best friend of almost 15 years, atop Mount Ngungun after a hike. *I am grateful … to be here.* She ran her fingers over the long, crooked scar across her stomach. *Very fucking grateful.*

Her Self-Care Sunday was reaching its crescendo: the Everything Shower.

The Everything Shower is a transformative, religious ritual that has been performed by women all around the world since the beginning of time. When a gal steps into her shower, she is not simply cleansing the day away: she's cleansing the week away. She's casting off the week's failures to make space for all the blessings the universe will bestow upon her in the next seven days. She's a snake shedding her old skin, and on the other side of the shower she will slither out into the world anew: a fresh, exfoliated, moisturised she-snake, ready to swallow possums and do whatever other cool snake-shit she pleases. Kirra was washing off the money she had wasted on drugs, the precarious situation she had put herself in by going home with yet another stranger and getting so fucked up she had lost an entire day of her life. Again.

Kirra began her ritual by combing through her hair and dry brushing her body from head to toe to stimulate blood flow and encourage skin cell turnover. She washed her hair with a clarifying shampoo twice. She lathered herself up and shaved every hair the laser had yet to permanently remove. After this, it was time to apply a hair masque and let it sit for fifteen minutes. This portion of the ritual took place in front of the mirror where she tended to other matters. She plucked stray eyebrow hairs and applied a dark tint to fill in any gaps. She lubricated her face with an oil and swiped a thin blade across it, removing a fine layer of fuzz, before wiping off the brow tint. She returned to the shower to rinse off the hair masque and lathered herself in a shower oil, restoring moisture to her freshly shaven skin.

Out of the shower, she blow-dried her hair, a gargantuan task for locks that fall almost to her elbows. Hair dry, she wrapped herself in a light robe, donned a sheet mask and moved to the loungeroom to watch The Wedding Singer for the four-hundredth time: her emotional support movie. During the film, she gave herself a full manicure and pedicure, snacking on a dinner of cheese, crackers and grapes. After her toenails and fingernails were cut, filed, polished and dried, she peeled off her face mask and rubbed in the leftover serum. She scraped her tongue, flossed, brushed her teeth and applied a near-lethal dose of active ingredients to her face and décolletage so that they could erase the damage almost thirty-five years under the harsh Australian sun has done to her fair skin.

With Gus fed and in bed, her house cleaned and orderly and her body smooth and fresh, she downed a cocktail of temazepam and melatonin at the most respectable hour of nine in the evening before drifting off into a deep, restorative sleep.

This week will be different.

She will be different.

Chapter 6

Jane

With the renewed sense of discipline that a well-spent Sunday brought, she would enact number two of her New Year's resolutions:

Do not make any more professional enemies
Be more collegial

Kirra was on her best behaviour whenever she bumped into colleagues, hitting them with a "How was your Chrissy?" and some "Bet the kids were spoilt!" followed by "Me? Caught up with family, time at the beach, it's just not long enough, is it?!" Fake smiles and forced laughter ad nauseum. She thought she was doing a great job so far. Her first real challenge would be the Welcome to The New Year speech the lead partner of the firm would undoubtedly give his underlings, which was about to be held in the large communal dining area next to the kitchen.

Nathaniel Dabbs-Pearson was the biggest wanker Kirra had ever had the displeasure of meeting, and that's saying a lot having only ever worked with lawyers and strip-club patrons. She'd had her fair share of dealings with scum, but NDP took the cake. Not only was he completely incompetent but he was also a vicious misogynist. He would routinely find subversive ways to manage women who dared go on maternity leave out of the firm. On top of all of that, he was also gifted his position in the practice by his father (and grandfather, and probably that guy's fucking grandfather too). He was an insufferable stain of a man, and that was putting it lightly.

Nathaniel's assistant, an equally insufferable brat with a familial connection to the firm, had rounded up the staff and had them standing shoulder to shoulder waiting for his lordship's address. Kirra's colleague Paul sidled up to her with raised eyebrows and a colluding look. Paul was also a partner in the firm, and her favourite. He too thought Nathaniel was a huge piece of shit.

"I wonder what wisdom our liege will bestow upon us today, milady," he said, doffing an invisible cap, emulating a Dickensian orphan.

"He's going to double our rations and chase the rats out of our sleeping quarters, methinks," Kirra returned in a similar accent, earning a low chuckle from Paul. "Honestly though, fuck this cunt," Kirra whispered, probably not quietly enough.

Be collegial, you wrote it down! It's a resolution, where's your resolve? It's only quarter past nine, and you've already said cunt out loud. So long as she hadn't called anyone a cunt to their face directly, surely the resolution remained intact and was salvageable? Paul snickered as Nathaniel made his way to the front of the group.

"Good morning colleagues, and welcome back! Wow, what a year we've got ahead of us ..." He continued prattling about just how amazing the firm was.

Kirra had built a steady stream of clients in the healthcare industry that refused to deal with anyone but her, and she loved the work she did. Her workload had grown exponentially since the pandemic, and she had been begging Nathaniel for a second paralegal to help her, which he had repeatedly denied her.

"We also have a new partner joining us from our Sydney office. Everyone, this is David Waters," he boomed, gesturing to a man Kirra hadn't even noticed standing next to Nathaniel.

"Hi, everyone. Pleasure to be up here working with you all," he said, extending a small wave as a greeting to his new colleagues.

"I didn't know we were getting a new guy," Kirra whispered to Paul.

"Me neither. What desk do you think he's working?"

"He's probably brought his own clients up here with him."

Nathaniel cleared his throat, "David will be joining Jane in healthcare, sharing the portfolio and expanding on the amazing work she's been doing in that space."

A dozen sets of eyes turned to Kirra. The bottom of her stomach felt like it had given out.

"The industry is just getting so big, too big for one person, an extra partner to share the workload will help us capitalise …" he droned on about the amazing new strategy he alone had come up with before introducing a new paralegal working for a different partner. A male partner, obviously.

Un-fucking-believable, but also, very fucking believable. Kirra's thoughts swirled. She had asked for help, something she was loathe to do, and had received this instead. Was this even legal? Unethical and disrespectful clearly, but those were Nathaniel's double-barrelled middle names. Could he actually make Kirra give up her clients?

After the meeting, the crowd dispersed with more than a few pointed looks in Kirra's direction. If her colleagues could write her a report card, she imagined it would most likely read 'does not play well with others'. NDP had returned to his corner office and shut the door behind him. She skulked to the kitchen for a glass of water, to catch her breath, to calm her thoughts. What would Dan do in this situation? she asked herself, and the answer appeared in an instant. Take a minute, play your cards close to your chest and don't do anything you'll regret later.

But she was not he.

She crossed the floor at pace and stormed into her boss' office. Without knocking, she swung the door open and charged forward. He looked up at her in surprise as she slammed both her hands down on his desk, leaning forward and glaring at him.

"What the fuck are you playing at? I ask for administrative help after running the most profitable desk in this whole fucking place completely on my own for the last however many years, and this is what I get? You expect me to hand my clients over to some cunt from down south?" she spewed, barely breathing between words.

It was at this point she acknowledged the other man sitting in the room.

"No offence," she said to David Waters.

"None taken," he responded quietly, avoiding her eyes.

Well, there goes that part of the resolution.

"Look there's no need to get hysterical Jane, particularly not in front of our new colleague," Nathaniel cooed through fresh veneers two sizes too big for his tiny rat mouth. "As you said, you've managed so many clients on your own for so long. We see the hours you do. You're still working as if you're a graduate trying to make a name for yourself, but you don't need to anymore. All of Brisbane knows you're Jane McNamara, and they want to work with you. David's here to start with some of your smaller clients, which will free you up to go for new ones for us," he explained, the smoothness of his delivery a stark contrast to Kirra's high-pitched curses from seconds prior.

She turned from Nathaniel to David. He was white, in his late thirties or maybe early forties, and wearing a baggy dark navy suit and a light pink shirt underneath. He wore glasses, was clean shaven, and was still looking down at the ground.

"What have you been told about this arrangement then?" she asked, hands still on her hips.

"That's what Nathaniel and I were just in here discussing. We were about to come get you," he said, offering her a small smile.

"There's nothing to discuss. My clients won't want to work with anyone but me, and I'm not working with anyone else either," she spat, wiping the smile from his face. "I said I needed a second paralegal, Nathaniel, not someone to steal my clients."

"Jaaaaane," Nathaniel said. "How about we pick this up again tomorrow. You're busy, and I've got a bunch of onboarding stuff to go through with David anyway. Take some time to calm down, then you can come back to the table with some fresh eyes."

Never in humanity's history have the words *calm down* calmed anyone down. She was just about to tell NDP to go fuck himself, and that David from down south could give him a reach-around while he did so, when they were interrupted by Nathaniel's assistant carrying a tray of coffees. There were three in the cardboard carrier, so the story about coming to get Kirra might have actually been true. She turned on her heel, snatched her iced latte off the tray and stormed out.

Chapter 7

Kirra is a stripper's name

Growing up, Kirra had never given her name a second thought. In fact, she kind of liked it. It was unique and had a story.

Her dad had fought to name her after his favourite Gold Coast beach against her mother's wishes, but the pair had had an arrangement; Lisa had picked the name for their firstborn, and Steve their second. Steve had desperately wanted to name his son after his own father, who had only just passed away, but Kirra's mum said there was no way she was dropping a *Mervyn* off at footy practice when all her friends were naming their sons Corey and Ryan. It would be Nicholas Steven, and two years later, Kirra Jane that completed the McNamara family of four.

At school, she took legal studies because some of her friends did, and it was her favourite. Arguing was already a hobby of hers, and the thought of arguing for a cause appealed to her more than anything else. She also loved how impactful either winning or losing a big case could be – setting a precedent for other lawyers to use some day, like laying the slab for a house that will be there for years to come.

In year 12, her mum died suddenly from breast cancer. Kirra worked her arse off at school to avoid thinking about it, to avoid grieving. She couldn't and she wouldn't.

She was accepted into a Bachelor of Laws at the University of Queensland. Her first year was tumultuous. She was commuting hours to uni each day and pushing herself on all fronts to achieve top results while surviving off Centrelink and two-minute noodles. But her hard work paid off, and she got straight sevens for all eight of her subjects.

Buoyed by success, Kirra overloaded subjects in her second and third years and was set to finish her degree a full twelve months earlier than her peers. By that point, she was dancing at Tweeties in the few hours she could spare from her studies and crashing at her filthy share house in Saint Lucia the remaining hours of the day. Life was intense and busy, but she fondly remembers those years as the best of her life.

While leaving the law library one evening, a flyer caught her eye – an application for the Rhodes Scholarship, a two-year program where you were paid to study at Oxford University, England. Students who were finishing their undergraduate degrees and looking to study further were invited to apply. The program was exclusive: only nine young scholars from the entire continent would be successful. After experiencing the thrill of academic success, a growing savings account and a whole new group of friends, she already felt like the world was hers for the taking.

It's easy to overanalyse and justify why you won't get something you desperately want. You'll say things like 'I'm throwing my hat in the ring' and 'we'll see what happens' and then, the big one, 'I'm not getting my hopes up'. You might go so far as to list the myriad of reasons why the thing you're pursuing is never going to be yours and that you don't care that much anyway, you're just 'having a crack'.

Kirra never bought any of that 'don't get your hopes up' nonsense. She had watched her mother shrivel and die before her eyes and was terrified that same illness would one day claim her. All she had was hope. All anyone has is hope. Someone is going to get what you want, so why shouldn't it be you? She thought of the other applicants, probably all saying the same things, giving up before they even applied. She might not have the pedigree or private school education a lot of the other up-and-coming lawyers in Brisbane had, but she had smarts, hunger and work ethic in abundance.

She applied.

She was successful, obviously.

At Oxford, Kirra met Dan, another Rhodes Scholar from New Zealand, and they had been inseparable since.

During her studies, Kirra had met Jeannine Klemmens, a powerhouse of a woman who was still Kirra's mentor after all these years. Jeannine was a Barrister, now in her late-fifties, steadfastly childless and on her way to becoming a judge. Jeannine projected a masculine energy, but Kirra felt a motherlike attachment to Jeannine almost instantly. The connection was probably more intense given the loss of her biological mother and Jeannine's heavy involvement in Kirra's professional world, something a lot of mothers probably don't share with their daughters.

"Lose the name," Jeannine had told Kirra when she returned from the UK.

Kirra had been surprised at first. Admittedly she was studying with a lot of Charlottes and Amelias at UQ and Victorias and Josephines at Oxford. Kirra did kind of stand out.

"Kirra's a stripper's name – you're a Rhodes Scholar and a lawyer now. Use your middle name instead," Jeannine had advised her.

At twenty-three with an LLB with first class honours from UQ and an MSc in Criminology and Criminal Justice from Oxford (fuck that looks good on paper), Jane was quickly snapped up by Kensington Menschel where she completed her PLT's and was finally admitted as a lawyer by the Supreme Court.

Pretty good for a stripper from Caboolture.

Chapter 8

Dr Dan

Kirra stormed out of her office building while hyperventilating. She slipped down the side of the building where the smokers congregated, pulled her vape from her pocket and took a massive drag. It wasn't even ten o'clock and she had already screamed at her boss, called a new colleague a cunt and vaped, the latter another resolution on her list that had already been broken. She hurriedly bashed out a message to Dan.

"Are you free for lunch? I'm spiralling."

"Sure, babe. Meet you at Figaro's in ten," he replied almost instantly.

Dan was a psychiatrist who worked in policy for the Department of Health in a building three city blocks from Kirra's. By the time she made the quick journey to Figaro's, their favourite hole-in-the-wall café, Dan was standing there, two grease-stained sandwich bags in hand. They found a quiet spot to sit, and Dan talked Kirra down.

He opened their unofficial therapy session, as he always did, asking if she wanted a solution or someone to vent to. She went with the former and, after twenty minutes, Kirra and Dan had constructed a plan for how she would handle her own professional version of the Red Wedding from Game of Thrones.

She was to head back to the office, avoid NDP and the new guy and complete her workday as per usual. After work, she and Dan would do a spin class at the gym, go back to hers for dinner, put Kirra's resumé together and start the hunt for a new job.

Kirra couldn't move past the betrayal and public humiliation of having her hard-earned desk chain sawed in half by the most useless twat in the southern hemisphere. She would have to move on to a new firm after twelve years with KM: a fresh start. Dan made Kirra promise she wouldn't do anything brash and that she wouldn't resign until she had a new role to move on to.

"Anyway, enough about work, tell me more about Daddy with the Submariner," Dan said. Joel had clearly mentioned Kirra slutting off on Friday.

"Not much to tell. It was fun, he was nice, didn't get his number." Kirra relayed a few other details she could recall.

"That's the type of guy you should probably go for, Kiz – the man who will complete New Year's resolution number one."

Find someone, enough with the hook-ups.

"He sounds perfect – already had kids so won't want any out of you, presumably wealthy, hot, nice guy with a huge dick. Why didn't you get his number? What if he had a gay twin brother for me?"

Dan shared the goal of meeting someone and leaving the hook-up culture they were fully entrenched in and made completely miserable by. Dan said he wanted to fall in love, adopt kids and build a life and a future with Mr Wonderful.

Kirra wanted to hop off the carousel that was meaningless sex, but she didn't know what that would look like in practice. She had decided long ago to never have children, much like Jeannine, and loved her life exactly the way it was, for the most part. She wasn't sure how a relationship was going to fit in, and it was the resolution she was the least excited about.

"I don't know, maybe I should have."

"Have you looked him up?"

"I can only remember his first name and I blacked out a bit on the way to his place in Spring Hill, so I don't know his address either. Anyway, I'm not about to Cinderella my way through Brisbane trying to find this guy."

"I mean, of course, that would be stalkerish, but we could go get a drink at the bar you met him at. Maybe it's a regular thing he does after work on a Friday."

"Um, yeah sure, let's see at the end of the week."

As Kirra and Dan walked arm in arm in companionable silence back to their offices, Kirra imagined seeing Ben again. She would be sober, or close to, but then what? He could be embarrassed to see her, maybe even on a date with another woman by that point. Even admitting she wanted to see him again seemed desperate. She had no experience in romance and felt embarrassed to admit that, at her big age, she had no idea how to tell a man she liked him enough to see him a second time. A lump began to form in her throat, and she could feel her eyes burning.

"Oh Kiz, what's wrong?" Dan said, stopping in front of her and taking her face in his hands.

Kirra couldn't contain her tears any longer and let them flow in the middle of the Queen Street Mall.

"Fuck Dan," she choked out. "I'm thirty-five this year and have no idea how to get an actual boyfriend, or if I even really fucking want one for that matter. I've just had all my hard work ripped away from me, and there's nothing I can do about it. My life's a joke." She wept openly, gushing snot down her white linen shirt. She was an ugly crier, and a loud one too. "I used to do brave shit like hop on a plane to England by myself to study and now I'm too scared to try and get a fucking boyfriend. Manfriend? What do you even call them when you're in your forties?"

"Kirra Jane McNamara, look at me right now," Dan commanded. Her head snapped up to look at him. "You're turning thirty-five. Stop saying you're in your forties. We're the same age and *I'm* not in my fucking forties." He had taken a tissue out of his pocket and was cleaning up her running mascara. "I know you don't really think that about yourself. You're indulging in a bit of self-made misery, which is fine in small doses." He had finished with her eyes and held her by the tops of her shoulders, lowering himself to be at eye level with her. "You are stunning, exceptionally smart, hilariously funny and financially independent. You're an amazing friend, the most generous, hard-working person I know, and you have an arse you could bounce a coin off."

Kirra chuckled, sniffing up the last of her snot.

Dan continued. "The guy you deem fit enough to be your partner is going to be the luckiest man alive," he said with conviction. "You're Kizrat, and there's no one else like you."

***

Kirra executed their plan as discussed. She kept her head down and powered through her work for the day while successfully avoiding David and Nathaniel.

At her place, she made Dan a saucy pasta dish that they mopped up with a loaf of homemade focaccia she'd had rising in the fridge all day while she was at work. Dan's eyes rolled back in his head as they always did at Kirra's cooking.

"Consider our therapy session paid for."

They formatted Kirra's CV, signed her up for some job mail alerts and looked on LinkedIn, the most cringeworthy website on the entire internet.

"Let's take a look at this new guy. What's his name?"

Kirra had enjoyed her evening so much – exercising, cooking, being with Dan – that she had almost forgotten the reason she was even looking for a new job.

"David Waters," she told him. Her stomach churned when they found his profile at the top of all the David Waters of LinkedIn.

"I know you don't want to hear this Kiz, but he's kind of hot," Dan said, grimacing.

"You're right. I don't want to hear that."

"Look here, he's been at KM Sydney for like twenty years. He's got to be at least forty-one if he started there as soon as he graduated. Why would he come up here anyway? Did you ask?"

"Nah, I was already a little, shall we say, flustered by that point." Kirra stared at the profile picture of the man who was about to rob her in broad daylight.

He looked younger in his picture than he did in real life, the same as everyone on LinkedIn, and Kirra took in his features in more detail. He had dark hair that was swept back off a smiling, rather unremarkable middle-aged face, his most prominent feature a pair of pale blue eyes that seemed to bore into her from her laptop screen.

"Look at this, he does a bunch of volunteer work too," Dan commented, scrolling down the page.

Most of Kirra's male connections on LinkedIn would say they were advocates for men's mental health by growing a moustache in November. They would arbitrarily post a picture of the growths on their top lips and ask for donations before promptly shaving it off December first, their civic duty done until the following year.

David's online activity showed he regularly contributed to discussions on mental health charities' pages, he had authored and co-authored articles highlighting the prevalence of suicide in Australian men in their forties and fifties and had several heartfelt pleas for donations of both time and money to Beyond Blue on his page.

"I suppose he does, and now he's banking on my charity to fund his new job up here."

"Yeah, maybe so, but I mean – he seems genuinely dedicated to helping people. Not everyone is 100% bad, babe."

Kirra slapped Dan on the arm. "Okay, he's 99% bad and this is his 1%. Why are you on his side?"

"I'm not, Kiz! He's the antichrist, and we hate him!" Dan said, giggling with his hands up defensively.

"That's right. He's the antichrist, and we hate him," Kirra agreed.

Chapter 9

Tuesday blues

Rallying to present an 'everything's okay, I love it here' front at a job you have decided to leave is a soul-draining experience. Pair that with the three-day-comedown that accompanies the consumption of some of your friend's ecstasy on a Friday night, and you've got yourself a real waking nightmare.

Kirra arrived at work before anyone else as usual, turned the lights on in her office and stashed her lunch in the fridge. She sat at her desk and fired her laptop up.

"Good morning."

Kirra yelped and spun around in her chair.

David Waters was standing there, smiling and extending an iced latte to Kirra.

"You scared the shit out of me. What are you doing here so early?" She shot at him, not taking the coffee, clutching a hand to her chest.

"What are you doing so early in here?" he replied calmly, setting down the coffee she was quite obviously refusing to accept next to her laptop.

"I get here around now every day," she said. With that, she turned her back on him and returned to her computer screen.

After a minute of him awkwardly standing in the entrance to her office, he propped himself on the edge of her desk, clasping his hands together at his waist and staring at her for what felt like a further minute.

She snapped.

"What?"

"I would really like to have a chat. I'm sorry you didn't know I was coming up here before yesterday, I thought Nathaniel would have told you."

"Yeah well, he didn't. What is this arrangement supposed to be anyway, what were you told?" Kirra couldn't be bothered to mask the hostility in her tone.

"I was told by my managing partner down in Sydney there was a gun of a partner up in Brisbane who was billing more hours on her own than me and my whole team of five were down there. They said KM has bigger plans for her, to put her meticulous knowledge of the pharmaceutical and medical implant industry to use on new clients looking to establish themselves in Australia, and that I was to go and help make that happen."

"That's bullshit, so what – I have to chase these new clients down and then you just take my book off me?"

"They told me they were going to keep me on my base salary and let you keep the lion's share of whatever I bill on your clients, freeing you up to make more on the new ones, which they've already got leads on."

Kirra was stunned. She had no clue KM thought so much of her that they planned to let her keep earning on her current clients while bringing in newer, seemingly bigger ones. She was simultaneously gobsmacked at how they had treated this guy. He must be really shit at his job.

"I must be really shit at my job, you're thinking, to get handed a deal like this?" He interrupted her thoughts with freakish accuracy.

"Well, it does look like a demotion – what about your clients down in Sydney? Who's going to look after them?"

"I was in the wrong sector at the wrong time. All those construction firms that went insolvent?"

"Oh, fuck, okay," Kirra generally kept to her own part of the world and didn't know or care what the other partners did, but even she knew the industry David had been working in had suffered a massive downturn. Many of his clients were non-existent now. It would have been a shit few years leading up to this point too, the claims he would have had to handle, including the poor families who had put everything in to building their dream homes and been left with nothing. "Could you not have looked for new clients to bring back into KM? Or even found a different job down in Sydney?" Kirra was still suspicious about the way this whole situation had unfolded, but he did seem genuine. A splash of curiosity was diluting the rage coursing through her veins.

"Truth be told, I was looking to move up here anyway for a fresh start. This deal, which obviously doesn't seem amazing, might suit me for a while. I don't really have that killer instinct I think KM values. I never have," he replied, sounding earnest.

At this point, Kirra took the iced latte and had a sip. She had a lot of new information to process, and a dull headache was forming behind her eyes.

"So, what are we meant to do, me and you?" Kirra asked.

"D-P was going to share the plan with you, but essentially, I'm just going to follow you around like the stray dog I am and hopefully you will both introduce and endear me to your clients. We're not going to say that I'm taking over, just that you and I are partnering to cover the market more effectively."

The combination of her comedown, the upset to her morning routine and the overall strangeness of this arrangement had Kirra feeling lightheaded.

"I need some painkillers and a sausage roll. Do you want to come for a walk to 7-Eleven with me?" she asked.

"I'd love to."

***

Sausage roll in hand and having washed down three times the recommended dose of ibuprofen with her iced latte, Kirra walked back to the office with David where they would shortly meet with their eminent leader and finalise the plan of how the handover was to work.

Kirra was still resolute in her decision to leave the firm, even if it meant a pay cut and starting over. The way it was sprung on her seemed like Nathaniel was trying to upset and get a reaction out of her, and she was still deciding on whether she completely believed David's version of the story.

"I'm sorry I called you a cunt," Kirra offered, gingerly squeezing tomato sauce on her breakfast.

David chuckled, showing off the smile she had seen in his LinkedIn photo last night, the corners of his eyes crinkling.

"All good. I appreciate the genuine reaction. Now that I know you had no idea why I was up here, it makes perfect sense."

"I'm sure some of the guys in the office have already told you I'm a bit unstable," Kirra said, unsure why she decided to blurt that out.

She pictured the faces of Ken and Patrick, Nathaniel's lackeys, nasty old sleazebags who had made Kirra feel unwelcome ever since she started at the firm. They found her self-confidence abhorrent, her lack of breeding and family name unsavoury, and had fought her making partner with all they could. She would never win them over, but she knew screaming in the office only proved their point that she was trash. They were why she had made the resolution to be more collegial; she didn't want to give them anything new to work with.

"Kerry spoke very highly of you, said you're an actual genius. Paul said you'd chew me up and spit me out and that you take your iced lattes with an extra shot."

Kirra laughed – Paul was one of the few partners Kirra had shared her real name with, as she had with Kerry, her paralegal. Kerry was in her sixties with a perm she had maintained since the eighties, and she was the calm constant to Kirra's chaos. They made an excellent team.

"That's nice of them."

She wondered if the other pricks had pulled David aside yet and whether he was just being polite by keeping that to himself. They wouldn't have been so flattering in their description of her.

"You don't seem unstable at all to me," David said. "I don't know how someone who makes millions of dollars a year for the business could be."

The compliment seemed genuine, and Kirra felt her face warm ever so slightly.

Chapter 10

Partner

Kirra had worked her arse off and made partner after only six years at the firm.

Her coworkers joked that she gave off a bit of a Mike from Suits vibe. She liked to think the comparison came from having an almost photographic memory (when sober) and how she could draft up a bulletproof case before her contemporaries had even fired up their laptops. She became obsessed with learning the ins and outs of how something worked, studying deeply and retaining almost all of what she read. This applied to anything, but in her job, she applied it to learning new industries and the acts they were governed by.

In reality, the similarity between her and the fictional lawyer probably arose more from the fact she didn't act like someone who had ever been to university, especially given how into rugby league she was and her frequent coarse language. She had only recently had her Southern Cross tattoo lasered off, the hint of it still visible in the right light.

She had started the same way all graduate lawyers did, being drip-fed bits and pieces of work from her superiors and drowned in administrative work she hadn't just studied five years to do. Kirra had dutifully done all she was asked for the first year but was itching for autonomy and to show everyone what she was capable of.

She was repeatedly told to wait her turn when Ken, Lord Sauron himself, had tossed her a client he didn't have time for. It was a software developer who had created a cloud-based patient-management system. Ken intimated to Kirra this guy was a nut and wouldn't be a long-term client as no one was going to buy his software. The ball was in Kirra's court, if she wanted to work with him then Ken would allow it, but if her main role as an indentured slave suffered, the client would be cut loose.

The developer believed his system was going to fundamentally change the way people received medical treatment in hospital, where even small mistakes in how information was shared could cost a life. Kirra was instantly enamoured by her client's vision; his passion was contagious, and he spent hours explaining to Kirra how it all worked. While the technology did seem risky and far-fetched, this young guy wouldn't have scraped all this money together to come to the best law firm in town to patent and protect something he wasn't one hundred per cent sure was going to work. Kirra believed in him.

Within months, the software was picked up by Queensland Health, with other states and territories following suit shortly thereafter.

Kirra knew the business and software inside and out and had been with them the entire way while they scaled up, expertly managing all their legal matters along the way. The founder had begged Kirra to come work for him as in-house counsel, but at this stage she still felt gratitude to Kensington Menschel for giving her a chance.

Ken would never admit it to himself, but there is no way he could have done what Kirra had: he was too old and out of touch. He still took all the earnings from the deal, profiting off Kirra's hard work, but that would only last for so long. Lucky for Kirra, her first client wasn't a fluke, and she had stumbled into a niche that would make her an indispensable part of the firm. She chased down new clients with as much enthusiasm as she had shaken money out of men back at Tweeties, and they all fell in love with her, barely batting an eyelid at the top-of-the-market, thirteen-minute-rate they paid for her time.

Her early success and innate talent made her colleagues sick with jealousy and had placed a huge target on her back.

Back at the office, Nathaniel and Kirra discussed how the transition would work. Kirra's stomach was in knots for the entire meeting, but she bit her tongue and listened. *I'm not staying anyway, just smile and nod.*

The firm was already dealing with several healthcare technology clients in London and New York who were looking to establish themselves in Australia. They were offering her a thirty per cent pay rise on her base salary. It was a brilliant deal. She knew she deserved it, but it still felt too good to be true.

She had so many questions about why they had decided to tell her the way they did and why David was the one to replace her. But, as she had decided she was leaving KM, instead of asking these questions, she signed her new contract and said she would start the handover with David tomorrow.

That evening, she journalled, dumping her thoughts and worries on paper, an exercise prescribed by her very own Dr Daniel Manaaki to help free her anxious mind of intrusive thoughts: *You will find a new job and it's going to feel amazing to tell Nathaniel, Ken and the rest of those pricks to shove it up their arses.*

Her mind wandered to something else that had been gnawing at her since Saturday. She added to her journal: *Hattie is a smart girl – she's not going to get herself into any sort of trouble with this dancer boy. Zoe will tell you straight away if something happens, then you can go and kill him yourself. Hattie is fine, Hattie is safe. There's nothing to worry about.*

Hattie is not you.

Chapter 11

Kirra, fifteen years old

It started small. It always starts small.

Nothing noticeable to the casual observer. Time had become dichotomous to Kirra: there were the moments she was with Chris, and the moments she wasn't, the latter of which were spent thinking about him and nothing else.

When her father had shared a tin with Chris, he had introduced himself to Nick too, and the two had become fast friends. This was a blessing as that meant Kirra got even more chances to see Chris when he was at her house to see Nick. The three would sometimes play video games together when Nick would allow it, but Kirra was usually banished from hanging out with any of Nick's mates. Kirra would watch Chris while he and Nick worked out in the backyard. Nick had taken an early interest in being a huge, dumb meathead, and Chris was his de-facto personal trainer.

In the early stages, Kirra was convinced her love was unrequited. Although she would give her right arm to talk more to Chris and show him how funny and clever she was, she thought it was safer to view him from a distance or exclusively in the company of Nick. That was until one day when Nick was held up on a job site as part of his school-based apprenticeship, and Kirra was already home from school.

She was in the backyard hanging out laundry. She had changed out of her school uniform and was wearing mini denim shorts and a white spaghetti-strapped camisole that showed off the beginning of her curves. She heard a car pull up and, thinking it was Nick, was getting her most cutting insult ready to hurl at him. He had gotten into personal grooming and, after finding some copies of Men's Health around the place, she had much fodder to insult him with.

She heard the crunching of gravel underfoot and called out from behind a sheet she was hanging up, "Finished your back, crack and sack wax so soon?"

Her heart dropped down her chest and straight out her arse when it was Chris, not Nick, who poked his very beautiful head from behind the sheet.

"I've never had one of those before. Is that what you're into, Kiz?" He smiled his radiant smile that showed off his perfect teeth.

"Oh, um, no. Sorry, I thought you were Nick. He spends a lot of time looking at himself in the mirror, and I figured he'll go full dolphin-smooth one of these days."

A genuine laugh erupted out of Chris. Kirra's heart fluttered in her chest at the sound. He looked at her for a moment, then another one.

It was then that she saw his eyes take her in, her bare legs, her shoulders and collarbones. She hadn't taken much notice of the camisole she had thrown on and was too self-aware to look down now, but she was sure he could see the outline of her nipples through the sheer fabric. She was a late bloomer and hadn't got her period yet, but the curves, extra hair and mood swings had been in full flight for years now. Her mum had told her that although all the sport she played may be delaying the actual visit from Aunt Flo, she was a 'young woman' now.

The phrase made Kirra gag. A woman? What, with periods, a job, kids, stretchmarks and responsibilities? No thank you, she was quite happy being a kid, a teenager at most.

However, the way that Chris was looking at her right now made her want to grow up in an instant. Conscious thought had vanished from her brain, and in its place was a swirl of feelings she didn't have words for.

"Hey, Kiz. I hope you don't mind me saying this, but I think you're the most beautiful girl I've ever seen."

Kirra thought she might die.

He liked her back.

Chapter 12

Wednesday afternoon

Kirra had spent the morning handing over everything she had built to David from Sydney. To his credit, he had been a dutiful student, taking detailed notes and listening intently. He never interrupted her and handled the thinly veiled insults she threw at him with good humour without biting back.

Kirra had set a face-to-face meeting with a client to introduce David. They were an ASX-listed company that developed diagnostic tools to detect and monitor cancer and other serious diseases. Their CEO was a former country GP from a small western Queensland town who had found herself in the big smoke managing a business turning over millions of dollars a year. She had previously told Kirra she enjoyed doing business with another 'salt of the earth' woman like herself, which was code for 'a little rough around the edges' or, more pointedly, a bogan.

"And you're a man, from inner-city Sydney, wearing a four-thousand-dollar suit," Kirra told David in the cab on the way to the meeting. "I'll be honest, I don't know how she's going to warm to you."

"I won't mention I went to Glenmonte then," he offered dryly.

"No fucking way, did you?" Kirra gawked.

He nodded.

"Isn't that the one where you get shipped off to the bush for half of year nine? Parents get to offload their hormone-addled, smelly sons at the peak of their teenaged angst?"

"Yep, that's the one," he chuckled, looking out the window of the taxi.

Kirra wanted to make a cutting remark about David's parents not getting their money's worth out of him but thought better of it. He wasn't exactly bragging.

"Yeah, maybe don't mention that. You might also want to consider changing your clothes a bit. We don't really do suits up here, only when we're in court."

"I'd noticed that I was a bit overdressed. You'll have to give me a Queen Street cowboy makeover."

She laughed. He had heard the term too, then. He turned from the window to look at her. She looked back, taking him in, maybe for the first time since they had met. His eyes were a pale blue and fanned with thick dark lashes. She found it criminal how men generally had the thickest, darkest natural lashes, meanwhile she spent ages each morning applying mascara to the few sparse spider legs in her own lash line.

He had a sharp jawline, his face made up of elegant angles in his arched brows and perfectly straight nose. He had a slight build, lean, and maybe four or five inches taller than Kirra's five foot four. His hair was perfectly styled each day, and he wore expensive-looking dark framed glasses and a vintage Rolex.

"Sure, we'll get you some RM Williams and you'll fit right in."

***

Kirra explained that David Waters would be their main contact, and the client seemed okay with it. To his credit, David had handled himself exceptionally well. Unbeknownst to Kirra, he had done his own research and was across all of the work she had already done with them, where the business was heading and how he planned to work with them. He was charming without being overly slick and he asked thoughtful questions. Kirra could tell her client was comfortable with him.

"You did well there," Kirra said in the cab back to their office. "I wasn't embarrassed by you."

"High praise, McNamara," he returned, eyebrows raised.

"That didn't sound good. I'm actually trying to be nice." She paused, choosing her next words more carefully. "They liked you because you sounded like you knew what you were talking about. Thanks for taking this whole thing seriously."

"Of course, I know how hard you've worked for these guys."

They sat on their phones in silence and were almost back at their office when he spoke again.

"I don't think Nathaniel was trying to wrong you, by the way. I think he would have given you the promotion first before introducing me. He just got my start date wrong."

"He is incompetent, so that's plausible. But they've made attempts to get me fired in the past, so there's history there."

"Oh really, what did they do?"

"I won't go into detail, but it has been made very clear to me that the rules that apply to them don't apply to me, and vice versa."

Kirra considered that enough information. He didn't need to know everything.

"Okay, that's fair. You didn't like how it was delivered, but are you happy with the deal?"

"Uh, yeah. It's pretty good."

Kirra had been considering the deal, and her decision to leave. She hadn't applied for a job since she was a graduate and had no idea what to expect. She knew that if she did make it official that she was looking for a new firm, half of Brisbane would find out the minute she sent an email. Nothing's truly confidential in a small major city. Her mind swirled and she knew she needed advice, if leaving was still the right call. She would see Jeannine tomorrow and ask her what she should do.

The cab arrived back at their office building. Through the floor-to-ceiling glass walls, Kirra could see Dan waiting in the foyer for her. They were going for a mid-week dinner to celebrate hump day. Kirra normally worked until close to ten each night, but she figured she had earned herself a few early marks.

"I'm not coming back up, Daveo. I'll see you tomorrow," Kirra shot over her shoulder as David headed for the elevators. She sauntered over to Dan's hulking figure. He scooped her up and spun her around while she squealed with delight, and she had the distinct feeling that David was still looking their way.

Chapter 13

Tell me what to do

Thursday went much the same as the previous day had gone. Kirra handed her client notes to David and set up handover meetings. She was also given the names of the companies she would be targeting as part of her new deal and spent some time researching them.

Jeannine had agreed to meet her for a coffee.

Kirra made her way to a café near Jeannine's chambers. She was seated with Kirra's coffee waiting for her by the time she arrived. Jeannine was an imposing figure, both physically and professionally, close to six feet tall with her silver hair perfectly toned and cropped to a bob just below her ears. She wore simple, dark colours and understated jewellery.

In the twelve years Kirra had known Jeannine, she had never heard her say "um" ever. Not once. Kirra was painfully aware of how much she said 'like' in her presence, which made her nervous, so she would do it even more. She sat down, and Jeannine took her time finishing the email she was drafting on her phone before she acknowledged her coffee date had arrived.

"You should stay," she said, placing her phone down and looking up at Kirra all in one fluid motion.

"Wha … how could you possibly know what's going on already? It happened on Monday."

"You know why."

Of course she did – she was Jeannine Klemmens.

She had paved the way for women in law since the eighties, busting up the boy's club and advocating for equality. She had shaken Queen Elizabeth's hand and was on her way to becoming a Supreme Court judge.

"Why do you think I should stay? I mean, did you hear how he did it?"

"I did. You're interpreting it with your feelings that he's spiteful and has an agenda, but you need to interpret it with your brain that he's incompetent and lacking interpersonal skills. None of which is news – everyone knows Dabbs-Pearson is a twat."

Kirra let Jeannine's words sink in while she sipped her coffee. Her mentor was speaking the truth and always had Kirra's best interest at heart, but she still felt let down and empty somehow. She wanted validation, words of kindness, a hug perhaps. Times like this made her miss her mum desperately, but she squished that thought tightly back in its box.

"As to why I think you should stay," Jeannine went on, "you have the drive and tenacity to take on bigger and better things. While you've got that hunger and ability you should use it, a lot of your peers simply don't have it."

A picture of David's profile, head turned looking out the cab window in silence, came to Kirra's mind.

"If they compensate you fairly, and I'll make them if they don't, you need to cut your emotions out of it and take their money. You could be mortgage-free by the time you're forty if you play your cards right. Think of that freedom. Take their money, play nice and do what you do best."

Kirra had been mortgage-free since last year, but she didn't see the need to correct Jeannine. The words meant a lot coming from her. She was fierce and at the top of her game and, most importantly, she truly believed in Kirra. You only ever need one person to believe in you, and Kirra's one person was powerful and influential. She could sook and whinge about growing up working class and not being gifted her job by birthright, but there weren't many people Jeannine gave this much time and attention to, which was its own form of privilege. Sometimes Kirra needed that chip knocked off her shoulder and a wake-up call as to how lucky she really was.

She felt an odd surge of emotions she couldn't quite articulate. She was moved by her mentor's kind words but also believed Jeannine didn't really understand how this industry had often made her feel: always one step behind, on the outside of an inside joke, never one of *them*.

Her treacherous bottom lip began to tremble, and she felt her eyes begin to burn. The thought of crying in front of Jeannine made her quickly don her sunglasses and take a sip of her coffee to hide her mouth.

"Thanks again for your time Jeannine, I really appreciate it," she quickly muttered, shoving off from the table in a hurry.

***

She skulked back to work and busied herself building a case she would be in court for next week. The company she represented was headquartered in Brisbane, but the case was being heard in Perth as that's where their supplier, who was refusing to honour several elements of their contract, was based. David would fly over with her and also attend the hearing.

The long flight, how much time she was going to have to spend with someone she barely knew, being away from Gus for even longer than usual, being undecided about what she was going to do with her career, worrying about Hattie at dance practice with this boy … it was all too much.

"Are you okay, Jane?"

David's voice snapped her out of her reverie. He was standing in her doorway with a look of concern on his face.

"Oh, hey. Yeah, I'm fine. Why?"

"You were really still – you're normally always moving."

"I am?" She was at a loss for words. What an odd thing to notice.

She had decided that while David's interference with her working life wasn't ideal, she didn't dislike him as a person. She

56

had been deliberately unpleasant to him all week, and he had been nothing but gentlemanly in return. While she still didn't completely trust the reason he was in Brisbane, she trusted him, oddly enough.

"Yeah, you're always tapping your foot or rolling a pen in your hand, even when you're typing or reading something. I came in here and it was the first thing I noticed – you were really still."

"Jesus, I didn't realise I did that. Sorry, sitting next to me all week must have irritated you."

"I didn't say that, just wanted to check you were okay."

He stood there awkwardly for a moment, looking at Kirra who was still a bit offput by his concern.

"Did you need something?" she asked.

"Just that it's almost ten, and I'm heading home now."

Kirra looked at her phone and was shocked at the time. This happened to her a lot. She would get so engrossed in a case she would forget to eat or go to the bathroom. Normally Paul or Kerry would throw a screwed-up piece of paper at the back of her head as a signal to go pee and make herself a cup of tea.

"Oh fuck, you're right. I'll head out in a tick too."

David hesitated a moment, drumming his fingers along the door frame.

"Does your partner have a similar job? Is that why he doesn't mind not seeing you some nights?"

"Bit homophobic of you to assume my partner is male, isn't it?"

Kirra wished desperately to be a lesbian. Surely all straight girls do at one point, for many reasons, but one of her main ones would be correcting people when they asked her what her hypothetical husband did for work. She could then reply that her hypothetical *wife* was an architect. She had even rehearsed how she would say wife out loud a few times.

"Ah, I was referring to the guy in the lobby last night, the All Black," he said, not exactly avoiding Kirra's eyes, but not meeting them either.

Kirra smiled at David's description of Dan. He was built like a brick shithouse, towering over Kirra at six foot five.

"Oh! That's my mate Dan. We're soul mates but platonic ones. I'm not his type."

"Ah okay, my bad then. None of my business anyway."

"I don't have a partner," she blurted out. "Which is surprising, because the dating pool when you're in your thirties is amazing," she added, trying to make light of the admission.

"It's even better in your forties," he added before quickly wrapping up the conversation. "I'll see you tomorrow, feel better."

Chapter 14

Friday afternoon, again

The usual buzzing of her phone began again around four in the afternoon. Dan reminded her that they were going to have one drink at the rooftop bar where Kirra had gone home with Ben the previous week. If they saw him, great, if they didn't, they would both go back to Dan's and watch a movie. They had imposed a curfew on themselves – if there was no sign of Ben by eight o'clock, they would head home. They were to imbibe no illicit substances, consume minimal alcohol and keep their bodies and minds in fit states so they would be fresh for their beach trip tomorrow.

But we all know how those promises go.

It was almost midnight, and Dan and Kirra were wasted. They had moved on from the club they had met at. After three margaritas, they had forgotten why they were there and met up with some of Dan's work friends. Dan's friends had begged Kirra to hook them up with something 'a bit more', but her repeated messages to her dealer were unusually ignored. Then Dan's social battery ran out and he tried to get Kirra to come home with him, but she was having too much of a good time with the crew they were with.

She staggered to the bar and was trying to order another round when a man in his late thirties, heavily tattooed and with a long, dark beard, approached her. He was flanked by two other guys with tattooed faces and knuckles. Kirra took him in through blurry eyes, clutching the bar to stay upright. He glared at the bartender, who swiftly turned away from Kirra and served another customer instead.

The bearded man approached Kirra and grabbed her roughly under the elbow, hauling her out of the bar. No one tried to stop him, and she was dragged out on her shaky legs, his lackies clearing the floor ahead of them as they went. He took her out to the balcony where it was less busy. The guys he was with stood a distance away, waiting for him. The man roughly pushed Kirra down in a chair before taking a step back and glaring at her, arms crossed across his broad chest.

"You're fucking wasted," he seethed, staring down at her.

She looked up at him, returning his disdain.

"It's nice to see you too, Nick," and promptly blacked out.

Chapter 15

Kirra, fifteen years old

A week after Chris had told her she was the most beautiful girl in the world, Kirra was home alone on a Friday night. She was excited at the prospect of time alone and planned to finish an entire box of Roses chocolates and watch the footy when there was a knock at the front door. Anticipating that her parents may have bailed on the Eagles cover band show at their local RSL, or that Nick was popping back to change for the party he was heading to, she didn't hesitate in opening the door wide open. It was him.

"Oh, hey!" she said, shocked and instantly tingling all over. Her hair was still wet after hopping out of the shower, and the dress she had thrown on barely covered her bum.

"Oh, hi Kiz," Chris said, looking down at the floor quickly. "Is Nick around? We were meant to be working out today." He looked genuinely uncomfortable and kept his eyes down.

"No, he's at a party on the southside. The moron's probably forgotten, sorry."

"Yeah, ah fuck, um okay – I'll text him." He paused, briefly looking into her eyes. "I'll see you later. You have a nice night."

He turned to head back down the stairs. In a moment of hormone-fuelled madness, Kirra called after him.

"Hey, uh, did you want to watch the Bronco's game and have some pizza?"

Who the hell was she, asking him in like that? Forming words that expressed her innermost desires? What if he said no? Or worse, what if he said yes?

"Are you sure? That wouldn't be weird?" he asked, looking at her through long, dark eyelashes that made his big brown eyes even bigger.

"I mean, I make most things weird, why should this be different?"

She put a frozen pizza in the oven, poured them both some colas (RC cola, not Coke, she cursed her tight-arse parents for bringing such shame upon her) and sat down to watch the game with him. They chatted, her heart fluttering uncontrollably at the admiration and reverence in his eyes as she spoke animatedly about the Bronco's current lineup. He was a massive rugby league fan too and played at their local club. She had gone with Nick once to watch him, and he was pretty good. He also looked fine as hell in his uniform.

Over the course of about an hour, they slowly edged closer to each other, and Kirra was bold enough to prop her legs across his lap and rest her head against the arm of the couch. For an agonisingly long few minutes, he had kept his hands at his side. Just as she was about to move away, he laid his palm on her knee. He kept his eyes fixated on the game.

He lightly ran his hands from her knees to her ankles then back again, an absent-minded, friendly gesture. Kirra thanked God she had decided to shave her legs for the first time ever that evening. His lightly calloused hands caused a sensation that ran all the way up to between her legs that felt *different*. He was only going as far as her knees, his eyes glued to the TV screen, as were hers, but she was silently willing him to go further, further. As if picking up her signal, he did, travelling past her knees to stroke her thighs.

If the sensation from his touch on her shins created a buzz of electricity, this was a lightning bolt. The sensation was so strong she was sure he could hear the blood pumping between her legs in time with her racing heart. The feeling was alien, and terrifying, and exhilarating.

She dared to look at him and saw a bulge in the footy shorts he was wearing. She was naïve but knew enough to recognise what was happening. Her brain short-circuited. The tiniest moan escaped her mouth involuntarily as he continued to stroke her legs. She was immediately brought back to her body with embarrassment. It had been her plan to let him keep touching her so long as it wasn't acknowledged or until she spontaneously combusted into a pile of dust.

At the sound, he turned and looked at her fully, his hand on the inside of her upper thigh, and she brazenly returned his stare. The lids of his eyes were heavy, his jaw tight, and he had a pained look on his face like he was struggling to control himself.

"Kiz, can I kiss you, please?" he asked with a choked voice.

"Yes," she got out in barely a whisper.

He quickly crawled over the top of her, propping his hands on either side of her head and looking down at her for a moment. The height difference was significant, and he lurched over her, hovering inches from her face.

"You are so very fucking beautiful," he almost whispered, then he kissed her.

Kirra floated in and out of her body. His lips felt so good, his body warmth, his sheer size. He gently pecked at her lips, and she didn't dare try and kiss him back. She had no clue what he was doing and even less clue of how to reciprocate. She lifted her hands up and ran them under his shirt. His stomach and chest were smooth and hard. She wanted to touch him everywhere all at once and couldn't decide where to put her hands next. He pulled back for a moment to look at her, his eyes roving over her face, her neck, her chest.

He was leaning back down to kiss her when the headlights of a car reflected on the wall of the loungeroom; someone was home. Chris shot off her in an instant, and she bolted to her room without a word to put on more clothes, returning just in time to plonk herself on the couch in her much more discreet PJs seconds before the door opened. Chris had either lost or concealed his erection somehow and was in the recliner in the corner of the room, leaving Kirra on the couch by herself.

The door opened and her dad stumbled in, chuckling. Pissed on RSL pots, and with a brief nod to both his daughter and apprentice, he plonked himself next to Kirra on the lounge, instantly absorbed in the last ten minutes of the game.

"We started watching it down the club. How good is Locky tonight?" he said excitedly, patting Kirra on the knee.

With a rush of shame, Kirra thought about where her knees had been mere minutes prior and how gross it was her dad was sitting where he was. She came up with a quick response about the footy and acknowledged her mum who was watching the game from the doorway. Her mum looked at her, smiled at Chris then went to the bathroom. Her dad was clearly oblivious to what had just happened, and who knew what her mum thought.

Chapter 16

Saturdays are for hating yourself

Kirra woke in her makeup and shoes at eleven the next morning. She groaned as the sunlight poured through her window. Her mouth was lined with sandpaper, and she had the distinct sense she wasn't in her house but rather on the First Fleet, being thrown around in wild seas where several of the other convicts had already gone overboard.

She ran to the bathroom and vomited, violently, her hair sticking to her sweaty forehead and cheeks. She felt the humiliating sensation of peeing her pants as she heaved, unable to control her bladder. She slid to the floor of her bathroom and hugged the bottom of her toilet, placing her burning cheek to the cool porcelain, laying in her own urine. She desperately wanted to stand up and have a shower, clean up the pool of pee, but the message she was sending to her legs wasn't being received. Hangovers in your thirties are no joke.

After what seemed an eternity, ground control finally reached Major Tom and she stood up. She looked at herself in the mirror with disgust.

"Kirra Jane McNamara, you are thirty-four fucking years old and covered in your own piss. Grow up, bitch!"

She cleaned her bathroom, removed her makeup, showered and got into clean clothes. The entire process took three hours as she had the balance of a newborn foal and had to stop to spew several times. She turned her phone over to several panicked messages from Dan last night.

"You still out?"

Several missed calls, back-to-back.

"Max said some guy grabbed you – are you okay?"

And some time later: "They said he put you in an Uber, had a beard and a tonne of tatts. Did you know Nick was up from Byron??"

More missed calls this morning, then the message: "Guess the beach is off then, talk later."

God she was a piece of shit.

She limped next door to Geoff's. He was out in his backyard, picking cherry tomatoes and cucumbers that had grown over a rusty archway. Gus was rolling in the grass, enjoying the sun, and didn't even notice Kirra shuffle over and sit on the old wrought iron bench beneath the canopy of vines.

"You look fresh," Geoff greeted Kirra.

She tucked her knees up to her chest. "Sorry I'm so late getting Gus. My church service went a little over this morning," she deadpanned back at him, plucking a tomato off the vine over her head and popping it into her mouth.

Geoff wheezed a laugh and stopped his work to look at Kirra.

"You alright, darl?" he asked, leaning against the archway to support himself.

No, I'm not.

"Yeah, just getting old."

Gus finally noticed Kirra and leapt up next to her. She put her nose against the top of his head and breathed in his wet-dog-freshly-cut-grass scent.

"Don't talk to me about old, young lady," he intoned seriously, taking a seat next to Kirra and Gus.

"How was Gussy last night? I'm so sorry I was out so late, I didn't mean to be. Was he any trouble?"

"You know he's never any trouble, Kizzy." He scratched Gus under his chin. "He's my best mate, aren't you Gus-Gus?" Gus' tail wagged enthusiastically. The love the two shared was mutual and unconditional – it almost made Kirra feel better. "You got lots to do darl, and I'm just here on my lonesome. I love having Gus over. Anytime, for however long, until I'm dead."

"Don't say that Geoff, you're going to make 100 and get a letter from the King."

"Yeah, don't know about that, love."

Kirra sat with her eighty-seven-year-old neighbour in familiar, friendly silence, letting the filtered sunlight shine through the canopy of hanging vegetables and warm her face.

***

A few hours later, Kirra stood in the middle of Macquarie Street, Gus' lead in one hand and a bag in her other, screaming.

"Daniel Manaaki! Let me in, please! I'm sorry, Dan. I'm so sorry I ruined our beach day!" She yelled at the top of her lungs to the second-storey window she knew he was on the other side of. There was no response, echoing the silence of the messages and calls she had made before travelling to Teneriffe.

"But if you recall, Daniel" – she paused a second to catch her breath before returning to shouting – "Kai Manaaki, thirty-four years old, son of Hemi and Naomi Manaaki, that you too have piked on our plans before—"

A neighbour of Dan's opened their window.

"Will you shut the fuck up?!" a man in his early fifties shouted down at Kirra.

"No sir, I will not shut the fuck up, until Daniel Kai Ma—"

Another window slid open in a rush.

"Christ woman! Come up then!" Dan bellowed back down at her.

***

She hadn't come empty-handed. Knowing Daniel would be nursing a hangover too, Kirra had assembled a gigantic pile of greasy KFC chicken alongside an almost-as-gigantic pile of salty chips to reline their stomachs with. To wash down their dirty bird, she had brought two large post-mix Sprites from Maccas. For dessert she placed two Magnum Double Caramel Ego ice creams in Dan's freezer, to be consumed only once they were reclined and watching RuPaul's Drag Race.

He had forgiven her for ignoring his messages last night and this morning, saying he was hoping she would want to cancel anyway as he felt like shit too.

"How random of Nick to pop up like that in Brissy. Was he up seeing your dad?"

"Not that I was aware of, but I haven't spoken to Dad in a week or so."

"Was Bree with him?"

"Nah just a couple of his juicer friends, probably just up for a night out."

"Hmmmmm," Dan trailed off, stroking Kirra's hair while she lay sprawled across his lap, savouring the last of her ice cream, Gus curled into her side.

"What's hmmmmm?"

"Nothing Kiz – who do you think's going to win this episode?"

"The same queen who's won it the last six times we've watched this exact episode, probably."

Chapter 17

It had been a long-arse day, and Kirra and David were checking in to their hotel for the evening. They were required back at court the following day, but it was looking like they should be done by then and Kirra would be back in her bed by tomorrow night, early Wednesday morning at worst if Nathaniel's assistant booked them on the cursed redeye.

David had been useful without getting in Kirra's way, and things were looking like they were going in their favour. The day had been long but successful.

David had swiftly taken Kirra's wheeled suitcase and wouldn't let her carry it herself even after she tried to snatch it back off him. They were getting checked in, the concierge taking an agonisingly long time to find their details and check their ID. After what seemed like an eternity of him muttering to himself, clumsily smashing every key on the keyboard thirteen times, he let out a loud tut, shaking his head.

"Oh, I'm so sorry, you've only been booked one room! The last vacant one too." He looked up into Kirra and David's bloodshot eyes.

"No fucking way," Kirra said, monotone, her patience completely gone. She turned to David who looked equally as dead inside.

"Aaaah no need for that, just having a laugh! Here you go." He handed them two separate keys to two separate hotel rooms. Very fucking funny.

David carried Kirra's bag up to her room. After a day full of travel and talking, they were spent. He said he would take care of the arguments for tomorrow morning and that she should get some sleep. Too tired to argue, she bid him good night and retired to the room opposite.

***

Later that evening, Kirra knocked on David's door. He opened up, and she barged past him, looking wildly around his hotel room.

"Where's your charger? I need it, urgently," she said, clutching her laptop in one hand, her phone in the other.

"Laptop or phone?"

"Both!"

He led her to the coffee table in front of a small sofa in his hotel room, unplugging his own laptop. He plugged in her phone and laptop and retreated to a desk on the other side of the room.

She knelt down in front of the coffee table and returned to the video call she'd been on.

"It's going to be okay, Tim," she reassured the man looking back at her. He was in front of a plain grey wall, wearing a white singlet and third degree-sunburn. He had two full-sleeve tattoos and next to no neck, his trap muscles almost swallowing his head.

"What should I do?" he asked, panic lacing his voice, "there's no interpreter and none of them speak English. They've got the fucking death penalty here Kirr—" but she cut him off before he could use her first name, aware that David could be listening from across the room.

"Tim, point to the screen and say *pengacara saya*."

He did, and the screen was turned by a pair of until that point unseen hands. A middle-aged man wearing the dark blue-grey uniform of the Indonesian police looked at the screen.

Kirra explained in fluent Indonesian that Tim Genrich was her client, and that he was entitled to an interpreter, and that detaining and or questioning him for longer than twenty-four hours was unlawful by their civil laws. She asked a barrage of questions. By the end of the video call, Kirra had arranged that

70

Tim would spend the night in his villa under police guard until an interpreter and a local lawyer were appointed to him. She got the contact information for the station and told Tim she would call him back in the morning to make sure they had come through on their end of the deal.

The video call went dead, and Kirra shut her laptop screen.

She rolled her shoulders and let out a sigh. She had been running on adrenaline since she received the desperate call from Tim, one of Nick's oldest friends, and tried to recollect her thoughts.

She heard a polite cough from behind her.

"Oh, hey – thanks so much for letting me use your charger, I live my life on 2% battery at any given moment."

"Friend of yours?" David asked, placing a cup of tea next to Kirra.

"Ah thank you." She sipped the drink. It felt good on her strained vocal cords. She hadn't spoken that much Indonesian since she learned it at high school, and it had completely exhausted her already tired throat.

"No, one of my brother's dickhead mates. Wrong place, wrong time."

"Like Schapelle Corby," David offered, smirking.

"Eh, not quite. It wasn't a boogie-board bag full, and he wasn't trying to board a flight. I can't say much, but I don't think they have much of a case." She took another sip.

"You speak fluent Indonesian." It wasn't a question.

"Oh, I don't know about fluent."

"You know Indonesian laws."

"I remembered some important ones, I guess."

"You successfully negotiated a drugs charge in another language and convinced them to let him go back to his villa over a video call."

He was clearly impressed.

"I suppose so." She drained her cup of tea and felt the warmth spread across her face. She came back to the present moment, trusting that Tim was going to be safe for now and that she could relax.

It was at that exact moment that she realised she wasn't wearing pants.

She leapt up, grabbed a pillow off the lounge and took three steps away from David, pillow over her crotch and arse facing away from him. She had been getting out of the shower when the call came through and had quickly thrown on her underwear and a T-shirt, but she hadn't worried about the bottom half considering it wasn't visible on the call. That was before she had noticed her battery had almost gone flat and charged across the hallway in a rush.

She had been kneeling at that coffee table for almost forty-five minutes with her arse hanging out of a pair of cheeky-cut briefs.

"I am so embarrassed," was all she could spit out. "I, uh – I better go back to my room right now."

David was clearly mortified. "Look, I wasn't ogling you the whole time. I did spend a lot of time making that cup of tea, like a really long time looking for a cup, then looking at the cup once I found it, the teabag, the kettle and uh, not you," he blabbered, eyes decidedly on his feet.

Kirra took some steadying breaths, trying to keep from making matters worse. She had just shown up at her new colleague's hotel room half-naked. Wouldn't Ken and Nathaniel love this story when they heard it. Fuck. Double-fuck.

"I won't say anything to anyone. I know you didn't mean to come in here to show me your arse – you were busy and doing something important and got distracted. It's all good, Jane." David ventured a look from his feet and into her eyes.

This man was clearly a mind-reader, or she just had an exceptionally readable face. She had made a fool of herself but believed he wouldn't share what had happened with anyone else. He had class.

After a minute, her heart had finally stopped trying to break out of her chest. "Thanks for making me feel better about it, I just …" she stopped for a second.

"Go on." David sat down on the chair next to the desk.

Kirra sat down on the lounge facing him. "I just, I do dumb shit like this all the time without thinking. Then when I have a quiet minute to myself, I'll replay it all over in my mind and worry that everyone thinks I'm a total idiot," she confessed.

David was silent for a minute. "Jane?"

"Yeah?"

"Literally everyone over the age of eight does that."

She scoffed.

"You're so hard on yourself, crazily so."

"Yeah, maybe, with some things."

"You don't need to be, you know. I kind of thought you were taking the piss with the whole self-deprecating thing, to seem more personable."

Kirra huffed a laugh, taken aback. "What do you mean by that?"

"Well, just …" he paused again, like he was at pains to say what he was about to. "You are undeniably brilliant. In the week I've been working with you, I've seen you speak three different languages like it's nothing. Everyone in the office comes and asks for your advice on everything, all day, and every time you know exactly how to help them. You're never condescending about it or make them feel like they're putting you out; you just help everyone without question. I feel like the minute I get my head around something for work, it's changed and redundant, but your mind is like this bottomless pit."

Kirra sat, a little dumbstruck, but didn't interrupt. She was aware her heart had started beating faster again.

"And it's not just your memory, it's how quick you are, with everything. Like how funny you are, I don't think I've laughed this much at work with you and Paul since I was a graduate and still had some semblance of a soul left."

She laughed, and her face started to feel hot.

David's mobile started buzzing.

Oh no, he's going to stop talking.

He quickly declined the call, put his phone on Do Not Disturb and placed it face down on the desk.

"You're so quick-witted and magnetic. Your clients have been okay with me to my face, but you can tell they're pissed they're not going to get to talk to you as much." He paused, considering his next words. He opened and closed his mouth. "I hope you don't mind me saying this, but I'm already rambling. On top of all of that, you're stunning."

The bottom of Kirra's stomach gave way, adding to the trifecta of overwhelming bodily sensations that had begun since David started telling her how amazing she was, in her underwear, in his hotel room.

"When I've got your full attention, I can barely talk sometimes. I've got into this habit of focusing on your nose or ear when you're talking, or deliberately not wearing my glasses sometimes, so I can think enough to string a sentence together."

He was looking at her directly, with his glasses on, and she returned his stare, stunned and expressionless. His open laptop started chiming, a Zoom call. Kirra glanced over and saw it was Nathaniel. It wasn't unusual for him to disrespect professional boundaries and call his staff late into the evening.

David snapped the laptop lid shut.

"So yeah, I kind of thought, this woman isn't real. So, when you'd speak ill of yourself or downplay what you're capable of, which is very often, by the way, I thought it was an act to make people feel more comfortable around you or something. But it clicked for me just now that you don't think that highly of yourself, which is ridiculous, because you're perfect."

She was at a complete loss for words. She didn't know what shocked her more; the fact he thought all these lovely things about her or the fact he had noticed how lowly she spoke of herself.

"My name's Kirra," she said in almost a whisper. "Jane's my middle name, and I use it professionally, but my first name's Kirra."

"Kirra," he repeated back, a smile tugging at his lips like he had just been given the best news ever. Kirra *really* liked hearing him say her name.

At that moment, the hotel phone blared behind David. It was a shrill sound that filled the whole room. He didn't turn to answer it, clearly hoping it would stop, but after almost ten rings he swung around in his chair and picked up the receiver.

"Yes," he said, the frustration evident in his voice. "Yeah, put him through …"

There was a pause, and then he started speaking twice as fast as he usually did, answering Nathaniel's questions, pointedly reminding Nathaniel his update on how court had gone was in the email he'd already sent some hours before. He turned to Kirra and rolled his eyes before turning back to the phone, desperately trying to finish the call.

Kirra's head was spinning. She felt like she had been truly seen by someone who was essentially a stranger to her. She hadn't shared her first name with anyone at work since … she couldn't remember when. Kirra had a core group of people she deemed friends and family, but that group was static. No one else outside that circle really knew her at all, had really seen her for who she is.

She had known this man for a week.

She had known that David was a gentleman in the old-fashioned sense: his manners, the way he spoke, his treatment of her and those around him. What she hadn't known was how much he had noticed about her, things she hadn't even really noticed herself. Had she really spoken three different languages? She practised Portuguese with the barista in the foyer of their building as she was learning it on Duolingo. She had also signed in Auslan at one of their meetings to translate for a deaf client, so it was three, after speaking Indonesian tonight. He had also noticed her physical tics and quirks, enough that he noticed her stillness when she would disappear into her head.

Her initial embarrassment at being truly seen dissipated quickly into something else, because she had seen him too.

Kirra had noticed David didn't like the elevator. Every time they went up to their offices on the twenty-third floor, his jaw tensed and he would clench and unclench his hands. He already felt comfortable around most people in the Brisbane office – he was a chatty, friendly guy – but she could tell there was something about Patrick, one of Ken's old cronies, that bothered him. Patrick was originally from Sydney too, and she would see an almost imperceptible change in David's posture when Patrick spoke to him.

She had also noticed his smile.

It was beautiful. It transformed his whole face, not just his mouth. He had a serious-looking face normally. If you didn't know him that well, you would assume he was a miserable bastard. But when he smiled, it lit up his eyes, their cool blue turning warmer.

He also smelled amazing, all the time. She had smelled his cologne walking to the bus one afternoon and had been disappointed when she turned, expecting to see David, but it had been someone else.

All this flashed in her mind while David was trying everything to get Nathaniel off the phone short of hanging up on him. Would she share what she noticed about him when he was free? She could just leave now, while he was on the phone, and pretend like this conversation hadn't happened. They would go back to court in the morning, and things could go back to the way they were before.

Or she could do what she did best – act now and worry about the consequences later.

Chapter 18

Different time zone, different rules

Without giving her rational brain a second longer to tell her to stop, she stood up and crossed the room to beside where David was sitting at the desk. He noticed her movement and turned his head to give her a polite 'I'm really sorry about this' smile, and she smiled back at him. She had left the pillow she was covering herself with back on the lounge.

She drew her black T-shirt over her head and dropped it to the ground, exposing her breasts.

David's face turned from a polite smile to a look of deep shock in half a second.

She smiled as seductively as she could and shimmied her underwear down her hips and kicked them off next to her shirt. While the room was only lit by a floor lamp, she was conscious it was bright enough to show the crooked scar on her lower abdomen. When she was still dancing, she'd leave her underwear on where it remained concealed. She had always dimmed the lights whenever she hooked up with someone, but she figured David had already seen so much of her already.

She could hear Nathaniel's voice through the phone, growing louder on the other end at David's silence, asking if he was still there.

"Yeah, still here," he offered, eyes fixed on Kirra's, searching for understanding as to what she was doing.

Kirra slowly walked back to the lounge and dragged over the coffee table. She laid back on the lounge and propped her feet up. David turned in the chair, facing her directly, with the phone to his ear.

She spread her legs wide and ran a hand slowly down from her neck, to her breasts, to her clit.

David let out an involuntary "oh fuck" into the receiver and was quickly jolted to his senses by whatever it was Nathaniel had said in response. He was done trying to be polite and cut Nathaniel off with a curt "Have to go – bye" and slammed down the phone, quickly pulling the cord from the wall.

He stood up and took a step closer to where Kirra was spread out before him, touching herself.

"You look even better than I imagined, and I've been imagining it, a lot," he stammered, his eyes raking her whole body from her feet to her face, his hands running through his hair as if in frustration. He clasped them behind his head, looking on with a focus so intense she almost felt it touch her skin.

She let out a breathy "Yeah?" before continuing to touch herself for him. While the objective of her display was for his gaze, his enjoyment, it still felt so good. She hadn't made herself come in weeks, and her skin felt like it was on fire. She didn't need to fake anything.

"Does that feel good?" he asked her, eyes falling to where her hands were working between her legs. She breathed an "uh-huh" as a small moan escaped her. She stopped circling her fingers and instead dipped them inside herself, thrusting once, twice, before dragging her wetness back up to her clit where she resumed her slow circles.

"Fuck, Jane – Kirra I mean, can I … Can I please make you come?" The desperation in his plea was palpable, and she could see he was hard through the gym shorts he was wearing.

She didn't speak, just nodding and putting both her hands behind her head in invitation.

He kicked the coffee table to one side and knelt in its place. He dragged her body to the edge of the lounge by her hips, placing her legs over his shoulders and wasted no time in burying his face into her. He hungrily lapped at her, groaning into her as he tasted her for the first time.

"Oh fuck, you taste even better than I imagined too."

The desire in his tone had a multiplying effect on the physical sensation of his tongue across her clit, and she gasped with pleasure. He licked her in long strokes up and down, gently running his nose across her clit before starting a slow spiral on her with his tongue. She was beside herself with how good it felt and wanted more. As if reading her mind, which he had been doing for a week now anyway, he slid a finger inside her. She moaned a deep, guttural sound. He curled his finger and started working her. She already felt close to coming twenty seconds after he had started.

"Please, put another finger in," she gasped.

He obliged, the sensation almost tipping her over the edge. He stopped licking her for a moment to look at her while he slowly pumped his fingers in and out. She opened her eyes and the way he was looking at her, his desire to make her feel good, made her ravenous. He reached up with his free hand, his shoulder under her thigh, and massaged her breast, never looking away from her.

"That feels so fucking good," she moaned, digging her heels into his back and driving herself down on to his fingers. He was beyond words and could only manage a "holy fuck" while she rode his hand before returning to licking her.

The sensation of his hand on her breast, his fingers, his tongue was so intense, so pure, her abs had tensed to a point of pain. She told him not to stop, that she was coming, and he maintained his rhythm. Her thighs trembled and her inner walls clamped down on his fingers while the dizzying relief of the exploding tension swept over her. He didn't stop throughout her climax, his fingers pumping in and out of her, tongue swirling. She let out a cry that she was sure the people in the neighbouring rooms could here as she finally reached her peak.

Her consciousness floated back down into her body, and she was aware of a fresh tear that had rolled down her cheek and a soreness in her throat from screaming so loudly. The next thing she knew was a fathomless dark as she fell into a dreamless sleep instantly.

When she awoke after the most deep and restorative sleep she'd had in months, she wasn't in her own bed. Not in her bed in Brisbane, nor her hotel room bed. She was still in David's room, on the sofa, with a pillow propped underneath her head and a blanket wrapped around her. She snapped up, alert as she heard the beep of the hotel key on the other side of the door. David stepped in, fully dressed for court, holding two coffees.

She was mortified on several fronts.

"What's the time?" she blurted out by way of a good morning.

"It's eight-fifteen. We're due in court at nine, our cab's picking us up in half an hour."

"Fuck! I fell asleep so early, I didn't even finish our arguments. Shit, we're going to be fu—"

"I said I was going to do that, and I did. Here, take this." He handed her a coffee, which she clutched at involuntarily. "I'll meet you downstairs at eight forty-five. I'll lead – if I fuck anything up, you call a recess and correct me."

She went to stand up and realised she was wearing the black T-shirt and underwear she had entered his room in.

He had given her the best head she had ever received in her life. She had passed out, and he had dressed her and put her to bed. She had known him a week, and worked with him, and he could still potentially be part of Nathaniel's plan for her to be moved on from the firm. Even by Kirra's standards, this was all a bit fucked.

He averted his eyes as she quickly balanced her coffee and belongings and ducked across the hallway.

***

Kirra had put herself together and was down in the lobby just as their cab pulled up. Her mind raced on the way there. In almost twelve years of practising, she had never shown up to court as woefully unprepared as she had today.

"Do you trust me?" David asked, snapping her from her head and back into the cab.

She thought about it for a second.

He had proven himself capable of handling her clients well to this point. He was an experienced lawyer, more experienced than her, even. She had also let him see her scar and masturbated in front of him while he was on the phone to their boss. If that wasn't trust, she wasn't sure what was.

"Yes."

"I've got this. You don't need to worry."

He was right.

David closed the proceedings confidently, and the judge ruled in their favour. The company had been spanked hard and would think twice before fucking with Kirra's, well, David's client, ever again.

They had another rushed end to the day and were in the cab on the way to the airport with barely a word exchanged. David had been on the phone with Nathaniel the whole way in the cab and in the airport, and Kirra had been handling Tim's case in Bali too. She hadn't had a chance to look at him properly, let alone talk about what happened last night.

Chapter 19

They were finally seated on the plane, so they would have five hours to talk about it now. Kirra knew they had to clear the air, but she was scared. She didn't know what was going to be worse: him telling her to forget about it or him telling her that he wouldn't forget about it.

Just as he turned to speak, a larger lady in her sixties interrupted them.

"You're in my seat, K11," she snapped down at David. There were only three seats in the configuration, and Kirra's was definitely K10; she was still holding her boarding pass. David took his pass out of his pocket: K12.

"Here, you have the window seat." Kirra smiled and got up to move but I-need-to-speak-to-the-manager bob cut stopped her.

"I don't want the window seat, love. I want my seat."

"What, between us? Really? Who would ever want that?" Kirra argued while David sat in stunned silence, looking between Kirra and The Karen.

"Move!" she barked at David, who dutifully stood up and waited in the aisle while Karen plonked herself in the middle seat, David returning to the aisle seat a moment later.

Karen took up a lot of room, and Kirra was squished up against the window. She chanced a peek over at David, and he was angled away, into the aisle, not looking in her direction. For a while after take-off, Kirra and David sat in silence, separated by their grumpy travel companion, who was playing Candy Crush at full volume on an old Samsung phone.

"Do you want to talk about last night, Kirra?"

The sound of her actual name coming from him did things to her.

She turned from her cramped position against the window, and saw David was hunched forward, his head almost touching the seat in front. His words travelled across The Karen's sizeable chest. His eyebrows were raised with a hint of mischief, and his eyes darted to Karen for a second, then back to Kirra. She picked up what he was putting down.

"You mean you giving me earth-shatteringly good head and me passing out in your hotel room, is that what you wanted to talk about?"

Karen's head snapped towards Kirra.

"Do you mind? What an inappropriate conversation to have in public!" she scoffed.

"Well, can we swap seats then please?" David asked. "I really need to talk to my colleague, who I went down on, who's sitting just there." He pointed to Kirra and was speaking at least fifty per cent louder than usual. "See, I made her come, hard and in my mouth, and we just need to talk about that as a matter of urgency, please," he finished, in a perfectly friendly, albeit loud, voice.

Kirra fought to hold back her tears of laughter on the near-silent flight. David had spoken loud enough that several other passengers had chanced a glance at their row and were exchanging looks with one another.

Rather than be reasonable, Karen dug her heels in. She fished headphones out of her handbag, plugging them in to her phone and wrapping a travel pillow around her neck. She crossed her arms over her massive jugs and formed an almost impenetrable wall between the two.

Guess 'the chat' was going to be had back in Brisbane.

***

The minute they had dislodged themselves from The Karen, who huffed loudly and took her sweet time getting her bag down from the overhead compartment, David moved in closer to Kirra.

"Can I take you to dinner on Friday night, please?" he asked, hefting both travel cases down and carrying them out as they disembarked the plane.

"Yeah, I'd like that," she responded, instantly second guessing herself. "Wait, is this a really bad idea, going on a date with a colleague?"

For someone who made exceptionally dumb, quick decisions all the time, she struggled to make them for important things. Usually, she deferred a solid yes to anything until she'd had a chance to ask Dan, Zoe or Jeannine for advice.

"Yeah, maybe it is," David responded thoughtfully. Kirra noted, with interest, how the idea of David rescinding the invitation made her want to throw up. "Well, how about we don't call it a date. We can call it a meeting, an exchange of information over a meal," he added, to her relief.

"Alright, sounds like a plan." She smiled, trying to sound confident while they made their way through the airport.

"Did you mean what you said on the plane, or were you just trying to rile Candy Crush up?" he asked, avoiding her eyes, "the bit about it being 'earth-shatteringly good'?"

They were at the cab rank now.

There was a lot that hadn't been said. He had eloquently shared the subtle nuances he had noticed and admired about her, and she had acted like a baboon, showing her genitals in a rudimentary display of returned feelings. The fact that he wanted to ask her to dinner after that was surprising, even knowing how he felt about her.

It was also endearing that he wanted to know if he had done a good job. He was ever so slightly blushing, and Kirra fought the sudden urge to reach out and touch his face.

"It was amazing. I don't come a lot of the time if I've been drinking, so that in itself was crazy." Kirra wasn't normally one to mince her words but saying 'come' out loud felt like crossing another line.

"Wait, what – you'd been drinking? When?"

"I ordered a few shower beers on room service; it helps me unwind after a long day. I also knew the trip was on Nathaniel's card, and I have a compulsion to spend his money. I wasn't pissed by any means."

David laughed, shaking his head and looking down at the ground.

"What's funny?"

"Oh, just that if you were to write down the events on paper without context – sober male performs sex act on intoxicated female colleague – it sounds awful."

Their cab pulled up, and they hopped in. It had gone midnight. It was now Wednesday, and Kirra was exhausted. David opened her door then went around to the boot to load their bags before taking his seat next to her in the back.

"I wasn't intoxicated," Kirra argued, her words slightly slurred as she began to feel the effects of the previous twenty-four hours.

"Still, doesn't look great," David said, although his tone was light-hearted.

Their driver wanted to ask them a thousand questions, and David, being too polite, couldn't give him the short, curt answers Kirra normally gave to people as a warning that she didn't want to talk. Their chatting about AFL put her to sleep.

***

She awoke to David's hand lightly on her shoulder in the back of the cab. David walked her to her front door, carrying her bag for her while the cab waited to take him to his apartment in Kangaroo Point.

"Wow, your house is beautiful," he said, admiring the stained glass of her front door and the ornate woodwork in the architraves.

Oh fuck, now he knows where I live too.

Kirra snapped to her senses. She had agreed to a date with David, but this felt like too much. Geoff would be asleep with Gus next door, but she needed to keep some parts of herself guarded. Maybe being in a different time zone had scrambled her brain. She needed some quiet and time alone to get her thoughts in order.

"Thanks for walking me in. I'll work from home tomorrow, today, whatever, but I'll see you Thursday," she said in a rush.

He took the hint and, with a tight-lipped smile, bid her good night.

Chapter 20

Depressed? Go get a blow-dry

Tamika had messaged Kirra for a catch up. She lived on the Sunshine Coast but was in Brisbane seeing her accountant. Kirra said she felt like shit and didn't really feel up to lunch, and Tamika had bribed her with a shampoo and blow-dry at one of her city salons. She said she would even get back on the tools and do it herself to cheer Kirra up. Tamika gave the best head and shoulder massages in the world, something she often used on punters back at Tweeties, so Kirra couldn't say no.

Reclined, head in a basin, Tamika worked her magic on Kirra's scalp.

"What's up, babe? Tell Auntie 'mika."

She was digging her long acrylic nails into Kirra's pressure points, and she could feel the tension leaking out; the woman was a witch. She had been wearing the same sickly-sweet perfume since she was in her early twenties, and it brought back such fond memories of dancing on stage together for Kirra. The combination of smells and sensations made Kirra feel like she had been drugged with truth serum.

"I have a date tomorrow night."

"Ooh yeah, is he hot?"

"He's good-looking, not my usual type."

"What, he's not big and dumb?"

"Yeah."

"Where'd you find him?"

"At work."

"He's not a crim is he, Kiz? A defendant?"

"I don't do that type of law." Except for Nick's dumb friends. Tamika didn't really get what Kirra actually did at work.

"No, he's a colleague. He's actually stolen all my clients and forced a weird sort of promotion on me."

"Oooookay, so you're telling me, that you, Kizrat, who barely goes on actual dates, is going on one, with a guy she works with, and who's stolen from her?"

"It's a bit more nuanced than that, but yeah."

"Don't use big words like that, mate. I'm a hairdresser."

"You're a millionaire."

"Yeah, that too."

Tamika took Kirra back to the chair and set to work blowing out her wavy, near-black hair. Kirra stared at her reflection in the salon mirror while Tamika's high-pitched voice battled over the hairdryer.

Kirra looked tired. She had faint purple bags under her dark, grey eyes, and her skin looked dry and patchy, her makeup clinging in chunks after some of it had washed off in the basin. She tried to listen to her friend, but it was too hard, so she just responded with an 'absolutely' or a 'oh, a hundred per cent' every so often while she disassociated.

She wondered how many women in the world were doing the exact same thing as her right now: sitting in a salon chair, silently criticising their own appearance while spending hundreds of dollars on a hairstyle they probably couldn't really give a shit about to be deemed moderately fashionable or attractive.

She guessed at least a few thousand.

"Babe, where are you?"

That actually cut through to her.

"Sorry, I'm feeling a bit off. I'm so tired. I've been working my guts out and I'm a bit all over the place. Moreso than usual. Nick randomly popped up in Brissy last week and dragged me out of a club, literally threw me in a cab. And I've got this fucking date tomorrow night with this guy, who by the way, went down on me on a work trip two days ago, and—"

Tamika was laughing now.

"What's so funny?"

"Oh mate, I just … your life. It's so hectic, and I love hearing about it. I've been rabbiting on about the boys' soccer and tennis and here you are living an actually interesting life."

So that's what Tamika had been talking about. Her boys were eight and ten years old now and were experiencing a far different upbringing than she or Tamika had had. Tamika, the stripper-hairdresser, raising sons whose future high schools have rowing and fencing as extracurricular activities. There's some upward mobility for you.

"I don't know if you'd call it interesting – it's more just a fucking mess."

Tamika then launched into one of her famous pep talks. She was telling Kirra how much she had going for her and that the universe was on her side. Kirra knew she was lucky to have such good people behind her. She wished the voices of the people who hated her were quieter than the ones of her loved ones, but unfortunately it was the former that kept her awake most nights.

"So anyway, back to the task at hand. Your hair's done and looking GORGEOUS. Do you know what you're wearing tomorrow?"

Holy fuck. She hadn't even thought about that. There was no way she could make that decision on her own.

After leaving Tamika's salon, she created a new group chat with Joel, Finn, Dan and Zoe asking for advice on what she should wear on her date tomorrow night. Tamika was a huge fan of Camilla kaftans and animal print, so she was allowed to sit this one out. Kirra answered all their opening questions then gave them the location and time of the date and a brief description of David. She realised she didn't really know anything about him, but she supposed that was what the date was for.

A slew of conflicting information was sent in rapid fire.

"Little black dress, why are we even having this conversation?" Zoe offered. "She's got a killer body, and it's simple, timeless, elegant."

"I concur," added Dan. "Wear it with those heels with the strap." He really was a straight man who happened to be attracted to men; that description matched about fifteen pairs she had in her cupboard.

"He means the Zanottis you wore to Finn's birthday," Joel translated.

"I think a little black dress is too predictable and not Kiz enough for this date," Finn added. "This guy is super keen on her. He wants to know her outside of work … it needs to be bold and more on-brand than that. You should wear that Zimmerman set, the floral one with the big skirt and the matching bralette – super sexy and flirty …"

"That's too day-at-the-races for an evening date, Finn – and she also doesn't have any shoes to go with it," Joel countered.

"Yes I do! The ones I wore with it to dinner that time."

"Oh babe … no, that didn't work."

God, these guys don't hold back.

"Well, it needs to be something sexy."

"Elegant"

"Hot"

"Demure"

"Classy"

This had not helped at all.

She thanked the crew for their valuable contributions and promptly left the chat she had started. She knew they would find that funny and not bitchy.

When she left the chat, she was almost back at work.

Kirra had an important first meeting tomorrow morning with one of the new clients Ken and Nathaniel had bought on. Kensington Menschel had worked with them in Europe and the US, and they were now setting up in Australia. The French pharmaceutical giant was coming Down Under for the leading-edge medical research being conducted in Queensland.

David had enough work to do on his own now, and as she had walked to Tamika's salon, she realised with unsettling certainty that she was going to miss chatting to him in her office.

She had been working on her own for over a decade and was disappointed he had been given his own office earlier that day. It had been one week, what the fuck.

David was returning from a meeting as Kirra entered the foyer of their building. "Hey Ki—" She saw him quickly look around as if to see if anyone had heard him. "Jane! Wait up." He jogged to catch up with her.

"Oh, hey," she replied as they walked towards the lift together. She stood to the side and let him in. She was acutely aware a smile had erupted on her face at hearing David's voice. She chanced a look up at him and noticed he was also smiling, still catching his breath from running. The doors closed.

"I'm so excited about tomorrow night. I can barely think about anything else," David blurted out.

"Yeah, really?" Kirra was mortified about how high-pitched that had come out and how her smile had instantly stretched even wider. She cursed her treacherous body. *Get it together woman, it's just a date — be cool.*

"Absolutely, I'm also super nervous too." He had caught his breath now and was looking straight at her, with his glasses on, so he could see her. His tone was even and matter of fact.

She had never had a man be so direct with her. Even the few men she went on 'speaking' dates with could only talk about themselves or how they found her attractive. It was all very surface level. They clearly liked her enough to text her and buy her dinner, but they never communicated their feelings. Admittedly, neither did she. David spoke so earnestly, honest and direct. No fluff.

It was equal parts refreshing and unsettling.

"Me too," she admitted.

"Which one?"

"Both."

His smile broadened even further, and she was aware he was looking from her eyes to her lips to the freshly blown-out hair draped over her shoulders. They were almost at their floor, and she glanced down at his hands and noticed they were relaxed at his side, not balled up in fists. The lift doors opened, and they walked in separate directions back to their offices.

Kirra sat at her desk with a fluttering in her stomach that felt different to her constant caffeine jitters and IBS. She was, in fact, very excited to go to dinner with David tomorrow night too. He had texted her yesterday to tell her where he was taking her, a very nice steak restaurant on James Street, and the time he had ordered an Uber to come and pick her up. She was surprised he had managed to get a reservation at the restaurant given how popular it was and the short notice. Her anxious mind started spinning up a story; what if he'd had the reservation for someone else, and she had cancelled on him?

Her butterflies quickly shrivelled up and sank to the bottom of her stomach.

The thought that her feelings could be even slightly affected by someone she had known less than two weeks made her feel sick. She barely knew David. She hadn't anxiously anticipated a meeting with someone like this in a very, very, long time. Memories were being churned up and brought to the surface, and she busied herself with work in the hopes of banishing them back down to where they belonged.

Chapter 21

Kirra, fifteen years old

After almost getting caught making out, Kirra and Chris avoided each other … until it happened again.

Kirra was home alone after finishing school early for the day, and Chris told her dad he was sick so he could leave the site to drop in. After some initial pleasantries and awkwardness, Chris brought up The Incident.

"Um, I'm really sorry if I came on too heavy the other night. I'm not a creep, I know you're only fifteen, but it's just I really like you. You're funny and smart and fun to hang out with. But yeah – sorry about that."

Kirra's heart was pumping at a wild rate, as it always did in his presence, but this was next level.

He liked her, actually liked her.

"I really like you too," she said, her words spilling out of her before she had a chance to reel them back in, "and I really liked kissing you."

Her brazenness surprised her. A few weeks ago, she hadn't ever shaved her legs and thought she may be asexual, and now she was here, telling a grown man she had liked him on top of her. Her voice didn't sound like her own, but it was – a new version of her.

He locked his eyes on her.

"Your dad's not back from the job for at least two hours, your mum's at school until three and Nick is at TAFE until late. Can I show you something else that I think you'll really like?" He smiled, and the smile was sinisterly beautiful. He had dark, shoulder-length curls, and towered over her, she had to crane her neck up to look into his eyes.

She nodded, and he took her by the hand and led her to her room.

He took her face in both hands. Craning his neck down, he planted a kiss on her lips so soft that she barely felt it, but it put every nerve ending in her body on high alert. He gently walked them back to her bed until the backs of her legs bumped into her mattress. He laid her down on the bed and sunk to his knees.

He slowly unbuttoned her shorts and shimmied them down her hips and onto the floor. He looked at her underwear, then back into her eyes.

"Can I take these off?"

Kirra was vibrating with excitement and frozen stiff at the same time. She nodded.

After their last encounter, Kirra had been possessed by the idea that her pubic hair needed to go, that it was gross. She had almost chopped her labia off in the process and shuddered at the thought of having to try and do that forever once it grew back. He removed her underwear and gazed down at her appreciatively.

"Who did you do this for?" He ran his hands up and down her hips.

"You," she responded breathlessly.

He smiled in approval and kissed his way across her stomach, each hip, to the top of her mound, delicately placing featherlight pecks here and there. She whimpered with the sensation, her whole body quivering. He finally lowered his head and kissed her down there. She saw all white for a moment, and her head spun. He kept using his tongue on her until Kirra felt the unusual sensation of something coiling up within her, washing over her in waves. The waves grew closer and closer together until she felt an explosion of something from deep within her, making her cry out.

Chris lay with her for a moment longer before helping her get dressed and kissing her goodbye. She was in awe of what he was able to do to her, how he got her body to respond to his touch like that when she couldn't even do it to herself. The experience left her reeling, not knowing who she was or what had happened to her.

Chapter 22

Big Pharma

Kirra was at work by her usual six in the morning, fuelled by anxiety and adrenaline at meeting with her new client. She, along with Nathaniel and Ken, would meet Guerír at their offices. She had researched them extensively, poring over recent disputes they had settled, lost or won across all the continents they operated on, and had stalked the two gentleman she was meeting on social media for good measure. She couldn't be more prepared if she tried.

She sat in the front of the cab while Nathaniel and Ken had the world's most boring conversation about golf in the back, not acknowledging her once, which was how she preferred it.

When they arrived, she thought she might be sick.

This was a pattern for her – the grandiose, heady feeling of being prepared and confident then a second later a panic attack over the imminent promise of embarrassment in front of colleagues who already hate her guts. She often swung between feeling she was the most intelligent, talented woman in the room back to feeling like a dumb, unpolished bogan who wasn't meant to be in meetings like this. She just needed the pendulum to swing back in her favour before she sat down in a meeting with some of the biggest names in Big Pharma.

The trio found their way to the boardroom where the meeting would take place.

"Jane," Ken said, "Nathaniel and I will lead this meeting. You can answer any questions they ask of you but otherwise don't interrupt."

The condescension and disrespect were nothing new, and as Kirra was still feeling sick with nerves, she decided she would let it go to the keeper. Mostly.

"Ja, mein Führer."

She smiled sweetly at him. Nathaniel quickly swivelled his head around to see if anyone had heard while Ken rolled his eyes and checked his watch.

The doors opened up, and two of the most well-dressed men Kirra had ever seen entered the room. They shook her hand first before shaking Ken and Nathaniel's, then they both offered her an introduction and a kind smile. She was instantly at ease at their warm welcome and felt the pendulum swing back in her favour, right on cue.

Thank you, nervous system. Next time don't leave it until the last minute.

Ken opened up by bragging about how KM had worked globally with Guerír's competition when he was interrupted by Big Pharma Frenchie Number One.

"We already know this. Thank you, Ken," he said in a heavy accent, "it's on your website. We want to talk to Jane about a patent case she won last year for one of your other clients when we hadn't had any success in Europe on an almost identical case. How did you do it here, when we lost ours there?"

Kirra knew exactly what he was talking about and launched into a detailed recount of how the laws in France differed from the one she had built her case on here in Australia.

She kept her explanation simple. She would often hear Ken and Nathaniel spew the most overly complicated bilge to clients and colleagues alike to bamboozle them in to thinking they were smarter than they really were. No one liked that, it was alienating and self-serving, like enjoying the smell of your own farts while everyone else gagged. Her colleagues were dutifully silent while she spoke, but she could feel the rage rippling off Ken at being ignored.

"You'll be dealing mostly with our new Australian CEO who is based here in Brisbane, he's only been appointed this week.

He'll be here in a moment," Kirra's new client explained before Ken and Nathaniel discussed the contract details.

Kirra heard the door to the boardroom creak open. As she turned to get up out of her chair in greeting, the CEO was introduced to the group.

"Jane, Ken, Nathaniel – this is Ben Andrews."

The bottom of Kirra's stomach gave way almost immediately as she stood, but her body kept moving as she reached out to shake Ben's hand. It was the same hand he had wrapped around her throat while he fucked her from behind two weeks ago to the day.

His eyes lit up in recognition immediately, and he stuttered before pretending to introduce himself to Kirra for the first time. He was clearly as shocked as she was. He shook Ken and Nathaniel's hands too, muttering his name while learning theirs.

Kirra's ears were ringing. She needed to get out of here, out of this room with Ken and Nathaniel's eyes on her, before anything seemed wrong. This meeting had gone so well, and now this. Why him? Why here, of all places? Brisbane really was a small fucking place.

Ben had regained his composure and sat down opposite Kirra and her colleagues to continue the meeting, apologising for his late arrival.

Ben's French colleagues reiterated his role in the business, then he explained how KM would complement the in-house counsel they already had. Frenchie Number Two added, "Jane will be your main point of contact, Ben. She's very skilled in our industry and has a great track record here in Brisbane too." If Kirra wasn't ready to throw up, she might have felt flattered at the compliment.

"That's great, it'll be a pleasure working with you, Jane." He smiled sheepishly at her, and she could tell he was just as keen to get out of this room as she was.

She chanced looking at him directly.

He was exceptionally good-looking, maybe even better than she remembered him through her substance goggles. He was in a dark suit this time, rather than the chinos and boots, and he towered over his petite French colleagues. He was broad and had his huge hands clasped together on the table they were sitting at. With a rush of shame, lust, who knows what, Kirra remembered how easily he had scooped her up in those big arms and laid her down. How he had felt in her hands when she had taken him out of his briefs—

"Well, we must be off, here's my card." Frenchie Number One offered Kirra his first, and his colleagues followed suit. Ken and Nathaniel returned the gesture, and Kirra thought she had better too, offering a card to each of them. Ben pocketed Ken and Nathaniel's but kept Kirra's in his hand.

"Jane McNamara," he read her name out loud, a faint smile on his lips. "Is that Irish?"

"Yes it is. I come from a long line of convicts."

Ken shot her an almost imperceptible *shut the fuck up* look that she caught in her periphery as Ben chuckled. He was staring down at her card, with her email, phone number and work address, then back to her, tapping it against his other hand.

The French group walked Kirra and her colleagues back to reception. Ben turned to shake her hand one last time, ever so gently running his thumb over the skin of her knuckles as he did. It sent a shiver down Kirra's spine.

"I'll be in touch soon."

***

He texted her as she hopped in the cab downstairs.

That was quick.

"Not to sound like a stalker, but I've been trying to find you for two weeks." Thirty seconds later came, "This is Ben Andrews, by the way."

"I figured as much."

"I get if you regret the other night, but I don't. It was amazing. Can I please take you to dinner? Nothing 'more' – just dinner."

Kirra was blushing in the front of the cab, grateful Ken and Nathaniel were in the back and ignoring her as they usually did.

He had found her, or she had found him, and she would have to deal with him professionally too.

She gazed out the window, more detail of her and Ben's night coming back to her. Their conversation had flowed so easily on the rooftop before they had gone back to his and, once there, he had been attentive, gentle and really, really fucking hot. She remembered that much. Kirra had always had a thing for guys like Ben: tall, older, confident and powerful physically as well as professionally.

"You're the Australian CEO for the largest pharmaceutical company in the world," she messaged him back, ignoring his question. He would be on an astronomically huge salary. He had given her the impression when they had met that he was comfortable in life, but she hadn't gauged just how comfortable.

"You're a gun lawyer for one of the largest law firms in the world," he retorted. Touché. "Who is stunning, and funny," he quickly added. "Dinner? Tonight?"

Tonight.

David.

His face came flooding back to her, and she felt a rush of guilt at the messages in her phone from Ben, like she should delete them. She chatted with dozens of guys, often not even the same ones week to week, without so much as a scrap of guilt. So why did she feel like she was going to be sick at the mere thought of David when Ben was messaging her?

"I'm busy tonight," she responded. "We'll need to meet soon to discuss when I can work with your in-house folks, anyway."

"Coffee, Monday morning?" He was persistent. And hot. And as tall as Dan. Dear lord.

"Message me Monday, will make some time."

Regardless of whether he wanted to take her on a date or not, he was critically important to her career. If he decided he didn't want to work with her, the client was lost to KM. Nathaniel, Ken, Patrick and the rest of the bastards would make it all her fault without any other information. She hadn't decided whether she would go on a date with him, but she knew she couldn't avoid him.

"Will do, have a nice weekend."

The dots of another message came up and went down three, four times, then one last message came through.

"I can't believe I found you."

Chapter 23

Date night

Kirra sat in the Uber on the way to her date with David, her stomach in knots for the second time that day. If she didn't die from breast cancer like her mum did, she was sure there was a stress-related tumour growing somewhere else in her body.

What a morbid fucking thought, a little voice in her head chided her.

The outfit she had chosen in the end was nothing like what any of the brain's trust had suggested. David had been open and honest with her from the very start, and she owed him the same. Showing up to their date dressed in anything that she hadn't picked herself felt wrong. She had bought the set on a whim and against the vehement wishes of Joel who was shopping with her at the time.

"Babe, no – it's like, Wiggles performer but somehow slutty, like Emma Wiggle had a huge rebrand and then went on Love Island."

The outfit had been stashed in the back of her wardrobe for months. It was a hot pink bandeau top that tied with a bow across her back with spaghetti straps. It was low enough that it showed the tops of her breasts, completely exposed her back, and came down to a V at her waist, showing the sides of her abs. It was essentially a bandanna.

The top came with matching bottoms made out of the same silky material that hugged her arse and thighs, flaring out over the pair of strappy Zanottis Dan had suggested she wear, showing off pedicured red toenails. Her blowout was still fresh, she barely had any makeup on and she had spritzed herself with her favourite perfume. She took a glance at herself in the mirror and felt beautiful for the first time in weeks, maybe months.

As her Uber pulled up outside the restaurant, she felt faint with nerves. The minute she stepped out, she regretted her outfit, feeling painfully exposed. She should have just gone with a stupid black dress. Kirra chastised herself for not putting on more makeup too, what had she been thinking?

"Holy fucking hell," she heard from across the street.

She turned around, and David was standing there with his mouth agape, looking her up and down like he had never seen her before. The well of worry and regret she had been bathing in dried up the instant she saw him.

He crossed the road and kissed her on the cheek. "You look so gorgeous." He stood back and took her in, his hand lightly on her elbow. He was genuinely so excited to see her even though he had seen her three hours ago.

When she had returned to the office after the meeting with Ben, she had barely had a chance to talk to him. Although they were both busy, he had silently left her a cup of tea on her desk as he left for the evening, texting her a 'see you soon' as he did.

He was wearing a white shirt and sports jacket, the perfect balance of well-dressed without looking pretentious. He had a different antique watch on to the one he usually wore, and he wasn't wearing his glasses, his serene blue eyes on full display.

He offered her his arm, and she looped hers through as they walked into the restaurant. Once inside, he pulled out her chair for her and waited for her to sit down before he did.

"I've been wanting to come here for ages. How'd you get a reservation on such short notice?" Kirra asked.

He had been so honest with her in the past, maybe he would just say, "My other date ditched me, then you showed me your puss in Perth and I didn't want to pay the cancellation fee."

"I know the owner. We went to school together, and I've done work for him for his Sydney venues. He cancelled a reservation when I called in the favour."

"Oh, that's sad! They must have been so disappointed." Kirra instantly felt bad for the couple who had probably been waiting to come here for months.

"No, they were obnoxious influencers who routinely ask him not to bill them in exchange for the publicity. They come here all the time."

"Oh, fuck them then."

"That's what I said."

He smiled at her, opening his mouth to say something before shaking his head and looking away, pretending to read the menu.

"What is it?" she asked. He smelled so good Kirra wanted to lean across the table and take a bite out of him.

He looked up at her.

"Just, I shouldn't have put my contacts in. I can see you too well and I want to be impressive and witty, not a gibbering idiot." He smiled, looking back down at the wine list. "Can I please show off the little French I can speak by ordering us a bottle of champagne?"

"Uh, I didn't want to drink tonight, actually."

Kirra had made the decision to be stone-cold sober for this entire evening.

"Oh yeah, absolutely. Can I ask why?"

"I just … well a few reasons. I've been feeling like shit lately. I think the partying has caught up to me at my big age. So, health, reason number one. And, um …"

Goddamn Kirra, be brave, go on.

"I want to remember tonight," she continued. "I want to know more about you and, if I get wasted, I'll miss things."

See that's nice – he'll like that. Maybe don't say the rest.

"Also, I am very attracted to you, and if we have sex tonight, I'd like to not be drunk during it." *Probably didn't need to say that, but okay.* "And on that subject …" *Oh my god, shut up, shut up!* "Do, uh, normal people who go on dates have sex on their first one?"

"What do you mean, normal?"

She appreciated that he focused on the normal part and less on the awkward declaration that she would like to have sex with him. "Like, I don't know, people who date normally?"

He looked at her, mild confusion on his features.

"I've never been in a relationship," she added.

"Oh really? I find that so hard to believe. I feel like you'd have a lot of people in love with you."

"That's nice of you to say but, yeah, I'm not really experienced in this …" She finished by gesturing at the air between the two of them.

"Well, I don't think there really is a 'normal' date, but I guess knowing what the other person is looking for is a good start. Do they just want to hook up, be open or have a closed relationship?"

"What do you want?" Kirra felt like she'd already broken a 'rule' asking him that so soon. She wished she could suck the words back.

"A closed relationship … with you, ideally," he said in his matter-of-fact tone. He must have already thought about it, because he answered quickly. "Not to tell you how to suck eggs – how gross is that saying by the way? – but I guess the ball's in your court. You decide what you want then let me know, given that you know what I want now."

"Oh, okay, yeah." She was a bit floored. This guy didn't mess about.

"No rush to decide what you want, by the way. I just want to get to know you better tonight, Kirra." He smiled at saying her name, her real name, out loud. He said it like it was a grand secret he had been lucky enough to be trusted with.

The waiter arrived and took their order. While they waited, their conversation flowed just as easily as it had done the past fortnight. Kirra had so many burning questions for David, but she was acutely aware she had already told him she wanted to fuck him and revealed she had never been in a relationship, so she figured she would save them for another time.

David spoke animatedly of his family, all of whom were still in New South Wales, but particularly his teen nephews George and Edward, whom he loved dearly. He disclosed that their mother, his older sister, was a bit unpleasant.

"She hates me, truly, madly, deeply."

"A Savage Garden lyric to describe familial hatred, interesting. We have that in common – my brother hates me too."

They then compared notes as to why their sole sibling despised them.

David went first, explaining that his sister Catherine (don't dare call her Kate, and your days are numbered if you utter Katie) was icy and that while he loved his nephews, she was making some very interesting parenting choices.

"She has constructed this whole universe for those two where they are always right, no matter what. I was at one of their soccer games recently and a call went against George. Catherine was up in the ref's face arguing with him, saying George would *never* do an illegal tackle. The kid's sixteen, it was mortifying,"

"Did he do the illegal tackle though?"

"Absolutely he did, but it's not just that. No one is allowed to share a joke with the boys or take them anywhere fun without her present. She's exceptionally controlling, and her poor husband, Christ."

"What was she like before she had kids?"

"Exactly the same, controlling, jealous, frosty. She had all these issues at work with her colleagues, always in fights with someone. She's been a stay-at-home mum since she had the boys … a stay-at-home mum with an au pair, cleaner and chef. But even when we were kids, she was hard work. She couldn't stand not being the centre of attention. I swear she broke her arm on purpose on my tenth birthday. I'd gotten the bike of my dreams, and we had this big party. Next minute, she's thrown herself down a flight of stairs and needed to go to hospital. Party over."

"Shit, you really think that she did that on purpose?"

"Look, who knows? But it tracks with other stuff that happened, so maybe." He quickly turned the conversation back around. "Tell me about Nick – why does he hate you?"

She hadn't told anyone why Nick really hated her, and she wasn't about to tell David on a first date either.

"I don't know why he does, but he does. He's a bit of a meathead and constantly has this huge crew of idiots around him. I was bailing one of them out when we were in Perth, actually." Kirra's mind flashed back to that evening, David's head between her legs.

She cleared her throat and went on.

"He's a tradie, an electrician, and he's done very well for himself. He's got this crazy beautiful house down in Byron with his wife Bree, the most stunning woman on planet Earth, who is at least ten times too good for him. Nick's not much of a talker, but when he speaks to me, it's vile."

Nick had famously announced one Christmas to a group of extended relatives that Kirra had had more dicks than she'd had hot meals. He also often insinuated her drug use to their father, who would laugh it off as harmless ribbing. Their father handled all awkwardness the same way, a giggle and an 'oh well', never stepping in to defend his daughter.

"He's just an angry, moody bastard who only smiles for Bree." That last part was true and one of Nick's redeeming qualities. He was the most devoted, in-love husband Kirra had ever come across. He worshiped the ground Bree walked on, as he should. She, unfortunately and to her detriment, was madly in love with him too.

They had been married for almost ten years and were desperately trying for a baby. Kirra had lost count of how many rounds of IVF they were up to. Seeing her close friend in pain over their repeated failure to conceive was heartbreaking. Bree deserved her baby, her happy ending, more than anyone she knew.

Their meals arrived, and Kirra sliced into her steak. Her eyes rolled back in her head, and she let out an involuntary moan of pleasure.

"Oh my god, that's good," she said around the hunk of meat in her mouth.

"It seriously is," David concurred, his mouth also full. "Can I be honest with you, Kirra?"

"Christ, you've been pretty honest so far, so now I'm scared." David snorted a laugh.

"I seriously haven't been able to think about anything else since Monday night in Perth with you."

Kirra blushed instantly. Her mind had been awash with so many competing thoughts this week, but what he had done to her body had often risen to the surface when she was trying to focus on something else.

"Uh, I'm sorry about how I did that, by the way," she interrupted him. "I didn't get to say anything nice back to you, and I also didn't give you a chance to say no to seeing me in the nude. If the roles were reversed and I was a dude and just pulled my jocks down and started wanking in front of you, I'd be sacked and maybe in handcuffs."

"That's very progressive of you Kirra 'Red Pill' McNamara, but I could have quite easily said no and helped you back to your room. Instead, I begged you to let me go down on you and almost came in my pants."

"Yeah?"

"Yes, it was the hottest thing I've ever seen or done. You passed out immediately, and I thought you might have been faking it to get out of saying no to anything more, which, you wouldn't have had to, by the way. But you started snoring almost immediately, so I knew you were really out."

"Oh my god, that's absolutely mortifying! I snored?!" *This is why you don't stay the night.*

"I took it as a compliment that you'd enjoyed yourself," he said, smiling at her again.

Her face was warm from laughing and chatting with David and not from booze, for a change. She felt relaxed, and reminiscing about Perth was making her undeniably horny.

"You didn't answer me before about if you're supposed to have sex on a first date." She was leaning into the table. She was fixated on the strip of exposed chest under his open collar; she wanted to lean in and smell him, touch the skin on his neck and feel his body warmth. He mirrored her stance and placed both his forearms on the table, wrapping one hand around her elbow. "Does it ruin anything? Like is there a certain number of dates you're supposed to wait?"

She was seeking approval and confirmation from David, as she often did from her friends and Jeannine, but she had already made her mind up.

"I don't think those rules exist anymore," David said. "You do what you want to do."

"What do you want to do?" she asked him, the feeling of his thumbs rubbing both her elbows now sending a signal to her heart, which had quickened its pace, to send a steady throb between her legs.

"Honestly, anything and everything. Most importantly, I'd very much like to kiss you" – there was a pause – "on the mouth." She snorted a laugh, aware she was biting her lower lip and running the backs of her hands over his jacketed forearms.

"Yeah?" she said, leaning in closer.

"Yeah," he replied, looking down at her mouth and leaning forward.

Just then, the waiter brought their bill over.

What fucking timing. Read the room, mate.

David quickly straightened up and placed his credit card on the book, flashing a look over at Kirra. Within minutes, they got up to leave, David taking Kirra by the arm and leading her out into the evening.

They took two steps towards the street before David pulled Kirra into an alcove next to the restaurant, spun her around so her back was up against the brick wall, and took her in an urgent kiss, his hand wrapping around the back of her head, the other resting on her hip.

Stars instantly burst behind Kirra's eyes, and she melted into his embrace, both of her hands spearing up to the back of his head and to his scalp. His hair was soft and smooth, and the smell of his skin enveloped her. He hungrily kissed her and lightly groaned into her mouth as she pushed her body up against his, her breasts flattening against his chest.

The kiss was unlike anything she had experienced, and she had the distinct feeling her feet weren't touching the ground anymore. He gently tilted her head to the side to deepen the kiss, pushing more of his tongue into her mouth. She moaned, and at the sound he broke the kiss off immediately, a cool breeze replacing the enveloping warmth that was there a moment prior.

"You keep making those little noises, and I will actually come in my pants like a fourteen-year-old boy," he warned her. A group of women on a girl's night out started furiously catcalling the pair from across the street.

"Yassssss girl, get iiiittt!"

Kirra sheepishly looked from the group to David, who was staring at her, clearly desperate to return to kissing her, his hands resting on her hips.

"Do you want to come back to mine?" The words escaped her before she'd had a second longer to think about it. Gus was home – David would meet Gus and maybe even Geoff if he popped over for anything. This was dangerous, but the hunger she felt needed to be sated immediately or she would lose her mind.

"Yes please."

Chapter 24

Breaking the rules

As they walked up the pathway to her front door, she could hear Gus' nails sliding over the polished wood floors in anticipation of his mum's arrival. She opened the door, and his body tossed back and forward in a happy dance, tail wagging and tongue lolling out of his gigantic, smiling mouth. David was on his knees in a second, Gus abandoning Kirra to aggressively lick his new guest.

"Aaaand who are yoooou, young man?" David asked Gus while being furiously slobbered on, Gus' tail threatening to whip a hole in the floor.

"Oh Daveo, your shirt!" Kirra cried. "Gus-Gus, get down." She clicked her fingers and Gus backed off, still wiggling with excitement.

David straightened up.

"This is my boy, Gus. Gus, this is David." Kirra made the introduction and looked to David, who was beaming.

"Isn't he just the most perfect boy ever," David said, still looking at the nuggety Staffy. "Does he like being picked up?"

"He loves it."

David picked Gus up and rocked him back and forth like a baby.

"When you've got a minute, I can show you around." Kirra offered. David followed her, not putting Gus down.

"This is Casa De Kiz. I renovated this place almost entirely on my own – it's my favourite place on Earth," Kirra said, walking through the living room and out onto the back deck that looked out to her small, quaint garden. The deck had a hammock and small wooden dining set. Festoon lights criss-crossed the deck's high roof and cast the place in a soft, warm glow.

"It's beautiful, Kirra, and exactly what I expected it to look like too."

"Yeah, and what's that?"

"I don't know, it's just very you. Hasn't your mum made a nice place for you to live, mate?" he said down to Gus, who was calmly reclining in David's arms still, relishing the attention.

David gently placed Gus down, who went and plopped himself on his dog bed tucked away in the corner of the deck. David crossed to where Kirra was standing and wrapped her in his arms, kissing her on the forehead. She breathed him in, a mix of David's skin and cologne and Gus' shampoo. She melted into the embrace.

He tilted her head back and kissed her again, the same way he had at the restaurant. She ran her hands down his chest, down his front, resting them just above the waistband of his pants. She was admiring how hard his abs were, running her hands back up to his chest and resting them on his shoulders, squeezing them as she did. He was far more muscular than she had anticipated. The suits he wore hung off him and made him look smaller than he was.

"Jesus, you're really fit," she sighed, pulling out of the kiss.

"So are you. Strong too — when you came you almost crushed my skull with your thighs." His head was tilted on an angle, and he was looking down into her eyes, his lids heavy with lust.

"Like Xenia Onatopp," she let out on a breath, taking him by the hand and walking him silently back to her loungeroom.

***

She pushed him down lightly on to her sofa. He smiled up at her while she stood over him. She reached behind, took her top off and threw it down next to him, leaving her completely exposed from the waist up. Her pants were high cut enough that her scar was hidden.

"God you're so beautiful." He looked up at her reverently. She climbed on top to straddle his lap, and he ran his hands up from her waist up her bare back and back down again. His hands were warm and smooth, and his pressure was perfect. She closed her eyes and dropped her head back, moaning with how good it felt. He took one of her breasts, sucking her nipple into his mouth. She moaned even louder as he alternated between sucking and circling his tongue around her.

She could feel he was as hard as a rock beneath her, and when she looked down as he was switching from one breast to another, the sight almost drove her mad.

"You're really good at that," she sighed as he got to work on her other nipple. He hummed a response around her and gripped her arse with both hands. She wanted to make him feel as good as he was making her feel. She took his face in her hands, guiding him away from her breasts, and kissed him deeply, rolling and swivelling her hips as she did.

She shuffled back off his lap and kissed down his neck. His skin was smooth, and warm, and that smell …

"What is that cologne? It's so fucking sexy," she interrupted herself, and he laughed at her exasperated tone.

"Aventus," he groaned as she lightly bit his neck where the smell was the strongest.

"No way, I know that fragrance, and you smell" – she licked where she'd just been biting, he was barely breathing – "so much fucking better than that."

She continued kissing his neck, unbuttoning the top of his shirt to kiss along to his shoulder, keeping a steady rhythm with her hips as she ground down on the erection straining through his pants.

It was almost imperceptible, but his breathing stilled and his hands loosened on her for a split second. It was enough for her to know something had changed.

She snapped up immediately, taking his face in her hands. "Are you okay?"

"Yeah, why?" He seemed a bit shocked at her sudden question, his eyes opening wide.

"Just … I felt you hesitate. Do you want me to stop?"

"Uh, wow. I didn't know I did," he paused, collecting his thoughts. "I guess I'd gone in my head a little bit, actually, now you mention it."

She made to hop off him, but he lightly held her in place by her hips.

"Please don't, I just … I'm really nervous. I've been thinking about this since the minute I met you."

"What, after I called you a cunt?"

"Yes, right after that. We've had this nice night and now I'm worried that I'm going to ruin it by either coming in thirty seconds or going soft or just not being what you expected. I want you to be thoroughly impressed by me."

She was touched by the admission. It was nice to have someone share their unfiltered thoughts as much as she did. His were a lot less sweary and aggressive than hers, but they were still real.

"I am thoroughly impressed by you; you don't need to worry about any of that. And, I have a plan."

His eyebrows shot up. "A plan?"

"A plan."

"Okay, tell me."

He was smiling again, running his hands from her arse up to her lower back and down again while she was speaking. His hesitation from before had disappeared.

"I'm desperate to suck your dick to even the ledger from Perth."

"The earth-shatteringly good head," he smirked, quoting her own words back to her.

"Yes, that, so here are the options. You come in thirty seconds, great – we can watch a movie and I'll feel like I'm really good at giving head, win-win. Or, you go soft, and that's fine too – I don't have to brush my teeth twice tonight."

"You have it all figured out, but there's no ledger between us, nothing needs to be reciprocated." He seemed back to his old self. She could feel he was still hard.

"I know that. I really, really want to though." She rolled her hips on him again, earning another groan out of him.

With that, she slid to the floor and undid his belt, unzipping his pants and shimmying them down. She ran her hands up and down him through his briefs, and he was watching her with a focus so intense it made her pussy throb. She reached under the waistband and pulled him free, letting out a quiet scoff of laughter as she held him.

"You've got my cock in your hand and you just laughed. Should I be worried?"

"Oh, it's just that you're physically perfect." She ran her hand up and down him, and he groaned, resting his head back against the headrest of the sofa. "Your smile, your eyes, the way you smell, your hands, and then this." She rounded her fist around his tip, twisting lightly as she did, and he sucked in a sharp intake of breath. "You literally have the perfect cock – you're actually fucking beautiful," she said on an exasperated laugh. Then she ran her tongue from his base all the way to the tip before circling his head with her tongue. She was done talking.

"Oh, fucking hell," he groaned, his voice strained. She lowered her head and took as much of his length as she could, stopping as he hit the back of her throat. She let out an appreciative moan as he filled her mouth and started working him, her hand following her mouth in a coordinated stroke.

He scooped up the hair that had fallen over her face into a makeshift ponytail so he could see what she was doing, and the light pressure at the nape of her neck drove her even wilder. After a few long, slow passes, she quickened her pace and hungrily swallowed him down.

She withdrew her mouth from him, and while her hand continued to stroke him, she lowered her head and gently sucked each of his balls into her mouth, one at a time, swirling her tongue around before popping them out and returning to his shaft.

He was reduced to quietly swearing, barely managing to keep hold of her hair while she worked him, his head lolling back.

"I'm close," he warned her, but there was no way he was finishing anywhere other than the back of her throat. She was a woman possessed and gave it all she had, producing the most porn-like sounds as she came close to gagging with each pass. His groaning quieted for a second and he stilled before shooting into her mouth.

She made a huge show of gulping down every last drop, eventually removing her mouth from around him after she was sure she had gotten it all. She ran her fingers along the outside of her mouth and licked them clean too.

He gazed down at her. Her eyes were burning embers staring back at him. He was utterly spent and looked dazed bordering on shocked.

"Um, holy fuck," he muttered, running his hands through his hair, his cock still out and gleaming with Kirra's spit. She was soaking wet, and the satisfied look on his face made her feel like she was about to split out of her skin. In fear of humping his leg like a dog, she quickly excused herself.

"I'm going to go pop on something a bit comfier. Feel free to get a drink out of the fridge if you need," she said, rising from her knees and staring down at David, who was still dumbstruck.

"Uh-huh," he replied, staring back up at her, mesmerised.

***

Kirra retreated to her bedroom where she hung up her outfit and looked in her drawers for something to wear. She wanted to wear something comfy, not *slip into something more comfortable*. David had been so upfront with her about being nervous – walking out in lacy lingerie would set too much of an expectation. Also, her G-string had ridden up while she was grinding on his lap, and her labia deserved a break.

She slipped on an oversized grey T-shirt and a pair of lounge shorts. Walking into her ensuite, which had a window that opened out on to the deck, she fished out her toothbrush. She heard the door to her deck slide open, then she heard David talking in a hushed whisper to Gus.

"Hey buddy." She could hear the familiar thwacking of Gus' tail on the deck. "Sorry if you saw that through the window. Your mum and I were just, uh, having a cuddle."

Kirra snorted a laugh and set to brushing her teeth slowly and quietly so she could still eavesdrop on their conversation.

"Put in a good word for me with her, would you mate? I'll get you a treat next time if you do, deal?" She could hear Gus loudly licking David's face. The throbbing in her nether regions had eased off, replaced with butterflies in her stomach and an odd sort of heaviness in her chest.

She heard some shuffling. She was curious about what it was, but if she moved the window's louvres, the light from the bathroom would give away that she was spying, so instead she decided to take the last of her makeup off. She applied a moisturiser, deodorant and some lip balm, washed her hands and piled her hair up in a bun. Feeling fresh, relaxed and free of the burning urge to jump her colleague's bones, she walked out and around the corner to the deck.

David was reclining in the hammock with Gus curled in a ball under his arm, the pair of them staring out at the stars. Another uncontrollable smile split Kirra's face as she approached them.

Gus wiggled excitedly for Kirra, and David awkwardly stumbled out of the hammock.

"Probably didn't need to see me flop out of a hammock on a first date."

"Better exiting a hammock than watching you eat a criss-cross cut mango."

"Oh my god, now you mention it, that probably would be an instant ick," David said, pulling a face.

"It absolutely is. It's on par with seeing someone in bowling shoes."

Kirra offered him a cup of tea, and they both walked into her kitchen.

"Your house really is stunning. The deck's amazing."

"Thank you. It was pretty dilapidated when I got it. The previous owners had renovated it by covering all the hardwood floors with this hideous lino and the walls with wallpaper, which hid the beautiful original VJs."

"You'll have to translate that for me. I've never done a hard day's work in my life."

Kirra chuckled – his hands were incredibly soft, so that checked out.

"Vertical joints, the wood panelling. I excavated all of her charm then added back in all the brass finishings and stained glass she would have had in her heyday."

"Well, you did an amazing job. One more thing you're good at, well, two considering … uh," he gestured to the sofa where she had just blown him, "your other talents. It's getting a bit obnoxious actually."

"Why thank you. I love making those around me feel inferior, it's kind of a kink."

He laughed, and she realised just how much she enjoyed the sound.

The kettle had boiled, and she made them both a cup of tea. She could feel his eyes on the back of her from the other side of the kitchen. She had her hair in a blob atop her head and was wearing the most shapeless shirt in the world, but when she turned, his gaze made her feel the most beautiful she had in a long time, even more so than when she was all done up earlier in the evening.

"Kirra, I'm about to say something not often uttered by men in their forties."

"What's that?" she asked warily.

"I'm good to go again." With that, he crossed to where she was and hoisted her over his shoulder.

She erupted into giggles. "What about this tea I've just made?" she managed to get out between fits of laughter.

"Iced tea for later," he replied, rounding the corner and flopping her down on her bed.

He backed off her and took off his jacket and shirt. He draped them over a lounge chair in the corner of the room, his pants still on but his belt discarded in the living room, and looked down at her.

She had propped herself up on her elbows and was admiring him in the warm light of her bedside lamp, which cast him in a rosy glow.

"I don't know if anyone's told you this recently, but you're jacked bro," she said. His dark, navy pants hung off his hips, the taper of muscles she hadn't noticed when he was sitting disappearing into the waistline of his pants.

He laughed, shaking his head. "I don't know about jacked."

She crawled to the edge of the bed and knelt up, placing her hands on his chest and drinking him in with her eyes.

"I particularly like this part here," she said, placing a kiss on the expanse of skin between his neck and shoulder. He let out an appreciative *mmmm* while she dragged her nails down his chest. He had some seriously nice shoulders, and she had never appreciated a man's neck as much as she did his.

"I like every part of you," he returned, his hands grabbing both of her arse cheeks through her shorts, "but I must say, you have an absolutely breathtaking arse. I didn't get to see enough of it in Perth. Also, your lips ..." He lent in while pulling her against him, his hardness pushing in to her middle, and kissed her, slowly and deeply. She moaned at how good his mouth tasted, how warm his skin was against her. He bit her bottom lip lightly as he pulled back. "Your lips are so fucking perfect. You're the most beautiful woman I've ever seen."

She couldn't handle just looking at him one minute longer.

She reached down to rub him through his pants, and he mirrored the gesture, reaching down the front of her shorts and finding her clit. He began slow, light circles while she struggled to remain focused enough to undo his fly and relieve him of his pants. They kissed while working each other, and it quickly became a game of who would give up pleasuring the other first.

"Does that feel good?" His voice was deeper and ragged. She had never heard it like this before.

"Yeah," she let out on a sigh, wiggling out of her shorts. "How about this?"

"Uh-huh, but you're going to stop doing that in a second so I can focus on this."

He slid his fingers down her folds, inserting two into her in one smooth action, his thumb taking over the work of rubbing her clit. The sensation, the command in his voice … she only realised after a few swirls of his fingers inside of her that she had let go of his dick. She was clinging on to his shoulders for balance while her knees threatened to give out.

"Oh my god," she moaned into his shoulder, biting him lightly.

"Fuck you're so tight … and wet." He quickened his pace, managing to bring her close to coming with one hand while he supported her from toppling over with the other. The obscene squelching sounds he was getting out of her bordered on embarrassing, but she was beyond caring. The tension in her lower abdomen was building to an almost painful degree, her eyes rolling back in her head.

"I'm going to, I'm going to …" she squeaked as the intense release of pressure made her legs give out. A warm gush of liquid splashed the inside of her thighs and down David's wrist.

She collapsed on to his shoulder, and he slowly withdrew his hand after the tremors of her orgasm had subsided. After a few seconds of lying limp across him, she opened her eyes and looked at him. He was trembling with restraint, his cock jutting out, jaw tight. His intense look was a stark contrast to what she imagined hers looked like right now, a melted pile of goo barely clinging to her skull.

"I'm not a squirter," she let out on a breath, willing her eyes to focus.

"What's this then?" He gritted out as he licked down the side of his hand and fingers, which were glistening with her release. It was now her turn to look mesmerised and dumbstruck.

He climbed up onto the bed with her and lowered her on a pillow while he climbed over her. He leaned down to kiss her, and she could taste herself on his tongue. The throbbing within her kicked back up almost immediately, and she needed him urgently.

"Top drawer," she managed, inclining her head to the left. While she never had guys over, she kept a pack of condoms in there, decanting its contents into her bag when she'd head out. He shot up to the bedside table. He let out an appreciative whistle at the contents of the drawer.

"I am going to have to use some of those on you another time." He was, of course, referring to the assembly of toys she had in there.

"Oh sorry, I forgot. That's awkward," she said, covering her face with her hands. She hadn't even thought – she had never had a man in her home before.

He had unwrapped a condom and rolled it on himself then he was back, resting over the top of her.

"No, it's not, its fucking hot. I'll be picturing you using them on yourself for my foreseeable wank future."

She giggled, and he kissed her again deeply, his cock nudging against her.

The familiar urge to flip over and have him take her from behind arose. She pushed him back by the chest to swivel around. He lightly held her by the hip and turned her back to look up at him so she was on her back again.

"I don't mind if you want to be on top, but I need to be able to see your face, please." His eyes were sincere, and his gaze was darting from her eyes to her mouth and back again.

Her brains were still scrambled from the orgasm she'd just experienced, and his focus made her feel light and tingly all over.

She wrapped her legs around his lower back and reached down between them to guide him into her. He kissed her again, sliding inside of her in one fluid movement and groaning into her mouth as he did. She gasped at the feeling of him, and his eyes snapped open, boring into hers in an instant.

"Is that okay? It doesn't hurt?" he asked quickly, making to back out, but she tightened her legs around him and shook her head.

"That feels so fucking good. I feel like I'm about to come again already," she moaned.

He stopped kissing her for a moment, watching her intently while he withdrew and re-entered her at a painfully slow pace. She felt nothing but pleasure, his weight suspended above her so she could breathe easily and watch as his abdomen tensed on each thrust. He had started circling her clit with his free hand while bracing himself above her with the other.

Kirra knew she wasn't that easy to make come. If she didn't fake it, most guys would get frustrated with how long it took her. David was making her reevaluate that. She chanced a look down between their bodies, and the sight of him sliding back into her, rubbing her in slow circles, almost made her come then and there.

"I can't believe how good that feels," she said, unable to hide the surprise in her voice. It was good ol' fashioned missionary, but she felt that familiar sensation coiling up within her again.

"I know," he concurred. "I'm trying not to think about it too much."

He enveloped her mouth again in a devastating kiss and picked up his pace, angling his body so that he was grinding up against her clit as he did, removing his hand from her front and instead lightly squeezing her throat.

The kiss and the pressure of his hand on her throat made her feel like she was going to die from pleasure, like her body didn't know what to do with how perfect it felt.

He broke the kiss to ask, "Is my hand okay there?"

She nodded before begging him, "Faster, please, deeper." Her bottom lip had started to tremble uncontrollably as she got closer. He did as she requested, thrusting into her hard and at a furious pace, burying his face into her neck and kissing and biting her lightly. He kept a perfect, unbroken rhythm, and Kirra felt like she could cry.

"Kirra, I'm going to come, you feel too good." He groaned into her neck.

"Me too," she whimpered as she started feeling the familiar waves washing over her, her body trembling as it took her completely. She cried out as she felt her orgasm come to a peak. David fucked her through it. Her inner muscles clenched around him, and he followed her with his own release a moment later.

They stayed there like that for a moment, him still inside her, both reeling from their climaxes. After what seemed like forever, he slowly withdrew from her and looked down at her. He wiped his thumb across her lip then wiped tears from the corner of each of her eyes. She hadn't even realised they were there, yet another thing only he seemed to be able to do to her.

He rolled over to rest beside her, his head propped up on his hand looking down at her. They had been in such a rush she hadn't taken her shirt off, but it was rolled up to under her chin, her breasts exposed. When she could control her limbs again, she mirrored his stance, putting her shirt to rights and looking back at him in silence.

They were both smiling, lost for words, staring at each other for what seemed like an eternity. Her body felt lighter, energised and completely satisfied. Kirra didn't have the right words to describe what she had felt just a moment before. She wanted to say something, and it seemed he had a similar idea as they both said in unison:

"That was fucking amazing."

"Jinx, buy me a Coke," Kirra got in first, out of habit. She immediately regretted spoiling the moment, but David laughed.

"Sure, will do." He chuckled and traced the outline of her lips, which were still sensitive from being kissed so hard only moments prior. "I think making you come has become my soul mission in life, Kirra Jane McNamara," he said, staring at her lips with those fathomless blue eyes.

"I'm okay with that," she replied dumbly, having had her wittiness apparently fucked out of her. "Do you want to have a shower?"

***

Inside the small shower, there was barely enough room for the pair of them, but she lathered them both up in a subtly sweet shower oil, and he wordlessly took responsibility for washing her. She got to feel him up and was embarrassed by how much she liked the way he looked, her stupid satisfied grin erupting into a giggle every so often. She kept looking up at him, and he seemed to be feeling the same way, laughing whenever they caught each other's eye.

"I think my boobs are done now, Daveo." She feigned a serious voice, fighting against how good it felt. "You've been lathering them up for about five whole minutes now."

"Can't be too thorough with these things," he deadpanned, staring at her breasts while he slowly massaged them, running his thumbs over her overly sensitive nipples. His cock was thickening again, and she ran her soapy hands up and down him.

"You're not up for round three, are you?"

"Absolutely not. He might be, but I can barely stand up right now."

He did look spent, and it was after midnight. Kirra's mind snapped back to reality, and she realised she would have to find a kind way to send him home once they were out of the shower. She hoped he would see himself out once they were dry and save her the awkwardness.

David shut the water off and hopped out, handing Kirra her towel before he dried himself with another.

As she dried herself, David silently dressed back into what he was wearing at dinner

"I can tell you want me to leave. You did that quiet-still thing in the shower. I'm not taking it personally," he said, not unkindly, putting his clothes back on.

124

"It's not that I want you to leave, it's just I've never… I don't—"

"You don't need to explain yourself to me," he said, underwear back on and doing up his pants while she stood there wrapped in a towel staring at him.

"Do you want to stay the night?" she asked.

"I don't want to pressure you into doing anything you don't want to do."

"But do you want to, honestly?"

"Of course I do, I've had the best night ever and I don't want it to end." His shirt was back on. "But I'm going. I'll text you tomorrow, okay?" He crossed to where she stood, wrapping his arms around her in a firm hug. "Good night, Kirra," he murmured into her hair, and turned back to the living room to go find his belt and shoes. She followed him out, watching him thread his belt through and kick his shoes back on.

"Tell Gus I said good night, please," he said with a small smile then made for the front door.

Kirra knew it was for the best – she had already broken so many of her rules. She had let him in to her house, and he had met Gus. She worked with him – she would have to share a lift ride on Monday morning with a man she had squirted on, a man who made her come hard enough that she cried. Twice. She was confused enough already without even taking those very complicated factors into consideration.

Where to from here? She wasn't even sure what to do after you'd hooked up with a person you really like. This wasn't something she could study, like an act or law, but she knew there were unwritten rules on how you're meant to act in this situation that every adult seemed to understand intrinsically, except for her. She felt embarrassingly inexperienced and unsure about how to handle any of this.

She was, however, sure of one thing. The rules she'd been living her life by weren't keeping her safe, they might have even been keeping her miserable. She knew the pit forming in her stomach wasn't for letting David into her house, it was from watching him leave it.

"Dave!" she called out, rushing to her front door. He was out on the street with his phone in hand ordering an Uber. He turned towards her voice, his face illuminated by his phone screen.

"Stay with me."

Chapter 25

A sleepover

She had found him a pair of old stubbies Dan had left at hers that were way too big on David and one of her favourite shirts from Retro Metro, a vintage shop around the corner. It was a customised buck's night T-shirt from *Barry's Weddin' in '07*, the screen printing peeling off and the hem stitching loose in places.

"Do you think Barry's still married?" David asked, sitting down on the sofa next to Kirra, holding one of the cups of tea she had remade for them.

"Statistically, no. Also, his mate didn't even want to keep the shirt from the night, not even as a rag to clean the car with – he was probably a bastard."

Kirra stretched her legs out and rested them in David's lap while she propped herself up and enjoyed her tea. He lightly traced her shins with the fingers of his free hand, his eyes roving from her feet to her face and a smile tugging at his mouth.

"I'm sorry if I keep staring at you – I genuinely can't help myself."

"That's okay, I like it." And she did.

She'd had guys leering at her for a long time, but she knew there was so much more behind David's stare than just lust or conquest. It also helped that his eyes were beautiful, and it gave her a chance to look back into them.

"Thanks for letting me stay tonight. I know it's a big deal to you."

"Has anyone told you that you sound like a book? Non-fiction, specifically."

"If you meant that as a compliment, I'm not sure I'm flattered," he said, squeezing one of her toes a little too hard.

"Ow! No, I mean, you just say exactly what you've got to say without any fluff. I really like it, actually. Reminds me of my mentor."

"Jeannine Klemmens," David offered.

"Yeah, how'd you know that?"

David broke his gaze from Kirra for a moment.

"Did Ken say something?" she asked.

"Yeah, said she was really fond of you. Which is obvious, bec—"

"Can you tell me what he actually said? I can take it – I'm a big girl."

David hesitated. Kirra could see that he didn't want to hurt her feelings, but he also didn't want to lie to her.

"He said you were protected by her, that the firm can't get rid of you because Jeannine would make their lives miserable if they did. Which is obviously bullshit. Jeannine wouldn't make their lives miserable; their wives would. Their fat, old, lazy husbands wouldn't be making as much money if you weren't there."

"I appreciate you saying that." She felt bile rise in her throat. "Did he tell you why they want to get rid of me?"

Kirra knew all of this already, but it sickened her to know that Ken had tried to poison David against her so soon after his arrival. She had the ghoulish desire to add more detail to the negative perceptions others held of her so she could dwell on it and let it fester. Her conscious mind didn't care what a crusty old prick like Ken thought of her, but a deeper part of her wanted to hear all the ugly things she already thought about herself. It was as if hearing it from someone else gave you permission to keep thinking it about yourself.

"I won't repeat it, Kirra. I obviously don't believe it, and he's clearly very jealous of you. I'm sorry if I've upset you."

Kirra felt tears pricking her eyes, her throat closing up and her chin beginning to tremble. David was up in an instant, setting his tea down and cradling her face as the first tear fell.

"Oh fuck, fuck – I'm so sorry, I can't believe I've upset you after you let me stay. Jesus, I've fucked this ..." He was desperate, wiping her tears, angling her face so he could look at her.

"You didn't upset me, I just ..." She sobbed, embarrassed that she had started crying so easily. "I have always," she started to say, but her crying had picked up steam, the snot trickling out of her nose. "I just ... it doesn't matter how many nice things I hear about myself, I just" – her shoulders were shaking uncontrollably – "don't believe them. Whatever Ken said about me, he's right."

After a while, her sobbing turned into silent shudders as David wrapped his arms around her, enveloping her on the couch. He didn't try and stop her or quiet her – he just held her until she was done.

After a while, he spoke. "You already know this, but I think you're wonderful."

"Thank you." She sniffed into his, her, shirt. "You've made that very clear."

"I've now got a second mission in life, on top of making you come."

She laughed, leaning back and wiping her tears. She knew her face would be blotchy and red, and her eyes bloodshot and puffy, but David was looking at her the same way he had a few hours earlier when she had hopped out of the car for dinner.

"Yeah? What's that?"

"To make you see yourself the way I see you."

***

After she had calmed down, the pair brushed their teeth. Kirra offered David a spare toothbrush. She had brought Gus inside to his bed at the foot of hers, and he was genuinely excited to see that David was still there.

"Can he please sleep up here with us, pleeeease," David begged, feigning a pout while rubbing Gus' belly.

"Will you clean the sheets if one of his anal glands leaks?"

"You make a good point. Good night, mate."

Gus took the signal to hop down onto his own bed.

They turned the lights off, and Kirra could make out the lines of David's face as he reclined on her pillow and looked up at the ceiling. She mulled over the events of the last fortnight and thought about how strange it all was. David Waters, the cunt from down south, was in her bed, wearing her clothes, and it appeared her dog was a little bit in love with him.

He rolled over and kissed her, slowly and gently, his hand running down her side and pulling her close to his body. Even after showering using her soap and wearing her clothes, he still had that undeniable David scent that she was quickly becoming addicted to. She buried her head into his neck and took a deep inhale.

"Are you sniffing me right now?" he asked into the darkness.

"Yes," she let out on her exhale.

"Good, keep doing it."

She did, wrapped in his arms, nestled into his neck, the slow steady pulse of his heart and the warmth of his body putting her at ease.

Chapter 26

Saturdays are for shopping

When her eyes opened, he was gone.

The early morning sun filtered through the high glass windows of her bedroom as she realised she was alone in her bed. She reached over for her phone – it was just before eight. Her vision was clear, and the contents of her stomach were quite happy to stay where they were.

She had woken up on a Saturday without a hangover.

She called out for Gus, but he didn't come.

Panic gripped her just as her front door rattled open. David walked in, still in the same clothes from last night, with Gus on his leash. He was carrying two coffees and his phone. After dropping Gus' leash, who ran to jump up into his mum's arms, David crossed to where Kirra was and leaned in to kiss her hands-free while he held the coffees.

"You've got morning breath, here." He handed her the coffee. "Have something to make it worse."

They sat on the bench on Kirra's front deck.

"I hope you don't mind that I took Gus for a walk."

"He would have loved it. That's what we usually do when I'm up at a reasonable hour."

Which is never.

"He did love it. I asked him not to shit on the way as I didn't have any bags, and he complied. He really is a very good boy. Also, that curly-headed guy at that café with the green chairs out the front is quite clearly keen on you."

Kirra choked slightly on her coffee.

His name was Jed, and she had been shamelessly flirting with him since he started working there. He hadn't asked for her number, but he flirted back with her each time.

"He recognised Gus, and the shirt. He was trying to make light chit-chat with me while he was doing our coffees but was clearly trying to suss out who I was to you."

Did this man ever make small talk? A comment on the weather or gossip about someone they worked with? She had only just woken up.

"Um, what did you say?" she asked.

"Nothing really, fobbed him off." He paused, smiling to himself. "I was on a bit of a power trip though, knowing he was pissed I was wearing your shirt and taking Gus for a walk."

This was moving way quicker than Kirra had the faculties to deal with. She had worried briefly that someone might have seen them at dinner last night. The outfit she was in would have destroyed the 'after-hours business discussion' story they had agreed on if they'd been busted by someone from work. Now David was in her neighbourhood, showing off the fact he'd slept over last night to people she had to see every day. All of this was slipping out of control faster than she'd anticipated.

"I'll head home soon. I was going to go shopping for less pretentious clothes today anyway."

Kirra was aware of the heat in her hands. She had clearly been squeezing her coffee cup while lost in thought.

"I'm really sorry I'm so weird about everything. I had an amazing time with you last night, and I liked that you stayed over," she said in a conscious effort to recognise David had feelings too.

"You don't need to apologise to me for anything – I get it. I didn't even think of being discreet when I took Gus for a walk this morning, I just wanted to get you a coffee. I know Brissy's a small place. I shouldn't have put you in an awkward position."

"I don't want you to have to worry about being discreet, either."

"Well, whatever happens, we'll need to be discreet at work. There's a non-fraternisation clause in our contracts."

"They're hard to enforce, particularly as you're not my manager," Kirra countered.

"Still, KM wouldn't approve. It'd also make our colleagues uncomfortable. No one likes that shit."

That was true. Kirra had watched many workplace romances, often extra-marital, bloom in the office over the years. In one particularly self-righteous move, she had anonymously posted details of one of her male colleague's glaringly obvious affairs on a Brisbane gossip Facebook page. His wife had found it and divorced him, and both he and his work-wife had been 'performance-managed' to the point of resignation shortly thereafter.

Would she be a huge hypocrite if she kept seeing David? If not that alone, she knew she was playing with fire pursuing anything with him. One misstep and Nathaniel, influenced by Ken, would send her packing.

She might not need to worry about it anyway. Kirra hadn't yet shared her plan on leaving KM with David and was less serious about resigning in general.

Jeannine had explicitly told her not to, and she had followed basically everything else her mentor had told her to do up until this point. The name change, getting her tattoos laser removed, losing the acrylic nails. Jeannine had been telling her to cut her hair to a more 'professional' length for a long time too, but Kirra had been resistant. She was almost thirty-five and wasn't going to be bullied into a bob.

"I need to get my goddaughter a birthday present – she's fourteen tomorrow. Did you want to go shopping together?"

A huge smile split over his face.

"I'd love that."

***

Kirra drove them down to Pacific Fair, which took just over an hour. She figured it was safer, less chance of bumping into someone they both knew. She was also buying Hattie a pair of Gucci slides because 'Gucci Flip Flops' by Bhad Bhabie was their unofficial theme song, and the Gucci store was better down there anyway.

"This car is also very you," David commented, dressed in the same clothes he wore to dinner last night in the passenger seat of Kirra's blacked-out M2 coupé.

"What do you drive?"

"An E-Class."

Classy. That tracks.

"Do your Glenmonte mates let you park it near their S-Classes?" she responded in mock disgust.

"No, I have to park in the bushes when we're at the country club."

They shopped together for a few hours, David's hands never far from her – on her lower back, holding her hand, twirling the ends of her hair. He bought more casual clothes, which he changed into to shop in, and they procured him some more Queensland-appropriate work attire.

Kirra had got Hattie her Gucci slides, and they had lunch together. She was shocked it was only one o'clock. She was sickened by the thought of just how much time she had wasted spending her Saturdays hungover. Adding it up, it would be in weeks – months, even.

They decided to head back to Brisbane. David was having dinner with Paul at Felon's under the Storey Bridge, the pair having struck up a bromance, and Kirra was going over to Zoe's to celebrate Hattie's birthday.

"Before we head back, can we swing past Kirra, Kirra?"

"How long have you been waiting to say that?"

"About three hours."

***

On the way to the shopping centre car park, Kirra felt around in her bag for her keys and there was a small, lumpy shape attached to them that hadn't been there before. Fishing them out, dangling from the end of her key fob was a matte black figurine of a dog next to a silver charm of an S overlapping an L: the Saint Laurent logo. The dog had a stocky little body and compacted snout, maybe a Frenchie. She looked to David.

He grinned at her. "Do you like it? Not as cute as Gussy, but close."

"You're slick. I didn't even see you buy it or put it on."

"I bought it when we split up and you got Hattie's present, and I attached it when you were in the ladies."

"Oh, David, that's too much, really." She was aghast at how much the keyring would have cost. She held it in her hands, rubbing her thumb over the tiny muzzle.

"You don't like it? You think it's tacky?"

"No, no I love it! Thank you so much, it's perfect."

David's smile was so infectious that she couldn't help but beam back at him. He backed her up against her car and took her in a slow, deep kiss, pressing his body into hers. They had been restrained in Pacific Fair, keeping it to some light touching, but she'd been desperate to kiss him the entire time they were out.

His hands cradled her face, and she melted into it.

"I'm glad you like it."

***

A few hours after walking along the beach, they had made their way up to Kirra Hill Lookout. Holding on to the railing and looking out at the beautiful blue of the Pacific Ocean, David wrapped his arms around Kirra. Last night had been almost perfect, except the whole ugly crying inches from his face and admitting she hated herself to him. Saturday, however, had been perfect.

They got back to his building in Kangaroo Point, and Kirra carried some of his shopping up to his apartment. It was a stunning modern space with sleek finishings and huge glass windows that looked onto a beautiful view of the Brisbane River.

135

It was the perfect spot for someone new to the city who wanted somewhere central.

"Whoa, this is nice," she said, placing the bags down on his sofa and gazing out at the view.

"Not halfway as nice as your place though," he said, coming up from behind and holding her to him. "It does have a very cool infinity pool on the roof though. I can take you up."

"No, sorry. I've got to dash and wrap Hattie's present before I head over."

"Oh, okay, you're in a rush?"

"Yeah, they live a good half hour from me."

He paused for a moment, looking down at his feet.

"Look, um, I've had a really nice weekend with you," he started.

Oh great, he's going to tell me that's it, no more, already. I suppose that's a good thing, it was going to be awkward as fuck on Mond—

"And I'm really keen to keep seeing you. I won't say anything about you to Paul tonight, so you don't have to worry about that. But I just wanted to be upfront with what I want."

"Uh, okay."

"You don't have to say anything just now. I wanted to, though. I've made mistakes in the past where I've assumed things or kept them to myself until it was too late. Bit of a New Year's resolution to be more open."

"I have some resolutions too."

"Yeah? Like what?"

Have a relationship with someone.

"Cut out dairy."

"Oh yeah, that's a good one. I've been on the long blacks for a few years now." He looked a little dejected at Kirra's obvious attempt at a topic change.

"I appreciate you being so upfront with me, David. I've had a nice time with you too. I really like you, but I'm still figuring some stuff out." She figured she could return his honesty, even if it was just admitting she didn't know what she was doing. It was all moving so fast, and while she had grown close to David in the last two weeks, it had still only been two weeks. Is that long enough to decide you want to be exclusive with someone? Or had she already made her mind up about him, but admitting she wanted the same thing too daunting to say out loud? Once she said it, he might lose the thrill of the chase and move on, or worse, he might stick around long enough to realise she's too much hard work, and not good enough for anything long term. She couldn't make sense of her own thoughts.

"Like I said, there's no rush. You know where I stand."

He leaned in and kissed her goodbye. While she didn't know what she was doing; she knew she wanted to be kissed like that, by him, more. A lot more. She wrapped her arms around his neck, and he held her in place by her hips, giving everything to her in that moment. The kiss was devastating, slow and passionate, and made her feel faint in the best possible way. It was Kirra who broke away, begrudgingly, conscious of the time.

When she did, she saw something different in his eyes that she couldn't quite place. It was like he already missed her, even though she was still there.

"I'll see you Monday," she got out quickly, then turned and left.

Chapter 27

Gucci flip flops

"GUCCI FLIP FLOPS!" Hattie squealed at the top of her lungs at opening the gift, and her and Kirra screamed the rest of the line from the song in unison.

"Jesus, Kiz, how much did you spend on those?" Zoe was shaking her head as Hattie popped the platform sandals on and ran to look at herself in the mirror.

Kirra could hear her squeals of delight from the next room and more lines from their favourite song. She thought her heart may actually burst from how much she loved seeing her very own Hattie so happy.

"Zoe, she's my one and only goddaughter, let me spoil her on her fourteenth birthday for fuck's sake." Kirra rolled her eyes, exasperated.

There was a knock at the door, and Zoe hopped up from the couch to answer it.

"Oh, is Mick coming over too?" she called out after her.

It was technically Hattie's birthday tomorrow, and Kirra hadn't asked for details about who would be here tonight. Hattie's dad had remarried and had two kids with his new wife, and Hattie was as much a part of that family as she was when it was just her and her mum. Mick's new wife and Zoe got on exceptionally well, unnervingly so for two women who'd had kids with the same guy, and the mixed crew would often celebrate milestones together.

However, it was not Mick who walked in the loungeroom behind Zoe.

A tall, skinny boy of about fourteen stood awkwardly with a bunch of flowers and a gift bag over his arm. His Adam's apple bobbed in his throat as he tried to say hello to Kirra.

"Kiz, this is Hattie's friend Harrison. Harrison, this is Hattie's godmother, Kirra. HATTIE, HARRISON'S HERE! Jesus, that's a mouthful, isn't it?" Zoe chuckled, looking between the boy and Kirra.

"Harry, come here! Look what Aunty Kiz got me!" she called from her room. Harrison smiled and nodded at Zoe before heading down the hallway.

Kirra glared at Zoe.

"What?" Zoe asked.

"You're letting him go into her room?" Kirra said in a dangerously cautious monotone. She was aware she hadn't blinked in a few seconds.

"Kiz, they're mates. The door is always open."

"It better fucking be!" Kirra snapped.

"Hey, hey – you need to calm down. You're not Hattie's mum, I am."

Zoe was clearly upset, and Kirra took a minute to still her breath. She bit her tongue, to the point of tasting blood, so that she wouldn't say anything she would regret later.

"Kiz, it's all good, trust me. I know how much you love Hatts. Harrison is just a friend – he's a lovely kid too."

They always seem lovely, at first.

"I'm … I'm sorry, Zoe. Honestly mate, I just—"

There was another knock, and Zoe gave Kirra another meaningful look before turning to answer the door again.

Moments later, another random male appeared in the room.

"Kirra, this is Jason. Jason, this is Kirra – the one I was telling you about."

"Hattie's lawyer godmother! So nice to meet you, Kiz." He crossed the room and stuck his hand out, a huge grin across his ginger-bearded face.

"It's Kirra. Nice to meet you too," she said, reaching out and shaking his hand twice as hard as she probably needed to. He winced a little. She looked to Zoe, who was shaking her head slightly in warning.

"Where's the birthday girl then?" he said, looking around. Jason went looking for Hattie, gift in hand.

"I'm just going to go grab some air. Be back in a tick," she spat out quickly and made for the back door.

She walked all the way down to the back fence of Hattie and Zoe's townhouse courtyard, finding a dark spot where the outdoor spotlights couldn't shine on her. She fished around in her bag for her vape and couldn't find it. Her pulse quickening at the thought of having nothing to take the edge off her anxiety.

She was madly rifling through her bag, checking all the pockets, when she brushed her fingers over another small, lumpy shape. She gripped the dog keychain in her hands and brought it out of her bag, holding it up to the moonlight. Kirra ran her trembling fingers over the little dog and immediately thought about the man who had given it to her. She wished he or Dan were here with her right now to help her come back to reality.

She heard the door slide open.

Zoe crossed to Kirra's hiding spot, handing her a cigarette. Kirra took it silently, Zoe popping one in her own mouth and lighting them both up. Kirra looked back to the house. Through the back window she could see Jason, Harrison and Hattie, who had moved into the living room. Hattie was opening the presents they had brought her. If Kirra didn't have direct view of Hattie, she wouldn't have been able to stand outside knowing Zoe wasn't in there with her.

"I know some shit happened to you, Kiz, but it's not happening to Hattie. I won't let it."

Kirra had never told anyone the story of Him, but her friends weren't idiots and she wasn't one to mask her emotions. Dan had probed on multiple occasions, but she was not a willing patient, although he'd had some success in getting her to talk about her mum.

The box that held the grief of her mother's death had airholes stabbed in it for oxygen, but what was inside was never allowed to see the sunlight. The box for Him, however, was a vault wrapped in chains, weighed down with bricks and sunk to the bottom of the ocean.

"You're the best mum in the world, Zo-Zo, I know that," Kirra said, taking a drag on her smoke. "Anyway, I thought you'd quit." She knew Zoe had given up so she could put 'non-smoker' on her dating profile.

"Yeah, I did. I have – just had this packet in case of emergencies."

"Like after two glasses of wine, that kind of emergency?"

"Yes, like that."

The pair laughed, enjoying their lung lolly in silence for a moment.

"They're both good guys, Jason and Harrison. Do you trust me, Kiz?"

That was the second time she'd been asked that question this week.

"I trust you, but I don't trust them. If anyone hurt you or Hattie, I'd have to kill them."

"You don't have to worry about me and Jase, I've got him wrapped around my little finger. Hattie wouldn't do anything with Harrison either, she's not interested," Zoe replied, conviction in her voice.

"Girls get horny too, Zoe, earlier than I think the world would have us believe too. Don't you remember being a teenager?"

"Yeah, but – maybe like when I was sixteen? She's turning fourteen."

"Look, I trust you mate, I do. But just … please be vigilant with those two, for me?" Kiz tried to hide the desperation in her voice.

"Of course, but do you really think I'd let anyone fuck with my Hattie? Remember when I glassed that guy at the club for pulling Tamika's hair?"

Kirra snorted.

"Yeah, I do. Good times."

"Our girl is safe, and I'm good too," Zoe said, butting her cigarette out on the fence and wrapping her hands around Kirra.

"She's safe," Kirra repeated, squeezing one of her oldest friends back tightly.

She had to be safe. Kirra couldn't handle it if she wasn't.

Chapter 28

Kirra, fifteen years old

She knew she should try and appear outwardly 'normal' to her friends and family, but it felt fake and inconsequential as her thoughts inevitably refocused on him – his next text message, if he was thinking about her, when she would finally get him alone again. She would see him at her house each morning as he left to travel to a job site with her father, or when he was lifting weights with Nick of an evening, but they couldn't exchange more than a passing greeting for fear of arousing suspicion. It was torturous.

It was two agonisingly long weeks until they saw each other alone again.

He had collected Kirra from school, picking her up around the corner so no one saw her get into his car, and taken her back to his house. He lived two suburbs away at home with his mum and dad. His older sister had just moved out. His parents were away up the coast, and he had the place to himself. Kirra had told her family she was staying at her friend Kristy's house, and they had believed her.

Of course they had. She had never given them any reason to doubt anything she said, until that point.

The chat in the car ride on the way was innocuous. They laughed together like they always did, and while the atmosphere in the cab of his unroadworthy Jumbuck was anticipatory, it was still great just getting to hang out with him.

While what he could do to her body was unbelievable and addictive, she also craved his attention. The thought he was into her stroked her ego like nothing else. *I am old for my age, no one would suspect I was only fifteen* and *I'm basically sixteen* cropped up in self-defence whenever the age gap came to her mind.

The car ride ended. He walked around to get the door for her and led her into his house.

He gave her the grand tour of the modest lowset brick home and its inground pool. He offered her a drink but she declined, suddenly anxious and wanting to touch him, to be touched by him. When he was sure no one was home and the front door was locked, he lent down and kissed her, slowly and deliberately. Kirra tried to kiss him back, their tongues working together. He broke the kiss to lead her back to his room.

It was clean and tidy, by nineteen-year-old boy standards. It only smelt vaguely of pot and body odour, largely masked by Lynx Africa. His sheets were clean and soft when he laid her on them. He lay on top of her and continued to kiss her – deeply, slowly and passionately – until she reached for his zipper.

"Are you sure you want to do this? I know it's your first time." He sounded hesitant, like that was a big responsibility he wasn't sure he wanted to carry.

"I'm sure, I'm just a bit nervous. I have no idea what to do."

"Well, how about we start like this …"

He lay down next to her, unbuttoned his jeans and pulled his penis out of his briefs. He was big and hard. The sight made her heart race even faster and the spit dry up in her mouth.

He grabbed her hand and wrapped it around his shaft, then put his hand on the outside of hers, showing her how to touch him. After a while, he took his hand off hers, and she continued the rhythm on her own. He groaned while she stroked him, encouraging her to keep going. He slid his hand down the front of her school shorts. The combination of feeling him grow even harder in her hand, his groans of appreciation, and his hands on her made Kirra want to jump out of her skin.

He rolled over, reached into his bedside drawer and knelt above her with a condom in his hands. She watched with fascination as he unrolled the condom along himself then climbed between her legs.

She felt frozen. Her heart was thundering in her chest and her body felt simultaneously soft and fuzzy but rigid with overwhelm. The throbbing between her legs told her she wanted the same thing he did, but the rest of her body didn't know what it wanted.

"I'll be gentle," he whispered as he nudged himself into her.

It hurt. It hurt a lot. She immediately let out a hiss of pain and scrunched her face up.

He stopped immediately.

"Oh god, Kiz, I'm so sorry." He backed away, but she held on to him by his shoulders.

"It's okay," she panted. "Can we try again really slowly?" She was close to tears, but the desire to show him she was a woman compelled her to keep going. He seemed close to saying that they were done for the day, but then he knelt back down between her legs. He pushed in again, little by little, and the burning pain was intense. He kept asking her if she was alright, and she kept saying yes, so he kept going. She could feel herself being stretched, torn as he advanced and retreated little by little.

She focused on her breathing as he picked up pace a fraction at a time. She willed herself to open her eyes and look at him. He was staring back at her, completely transfixed and unblinking, making sure she was okay. She managed to control her breathing and tried to ignore the pain. The realisation that this is what sex was, and that she was having it with a boy, made her feel like a different person, like the pain was being experienced by someone else.

After a while, he thrust into her harder, all the way, and she felt a different, duller pain in her lower abdomen in addition to the burning and stretching of her vagina. His pace became feverish and uneven as he pushed into her one last time. Then he collapsed on top of her, sweating and panting, and Kirra realised that it was over.

She had bled, a lot, and was in pain afterwards. He helped her up out of his bed and took her to his shower where he gently washed her body while he washed his own. He dressed her in one of his clean shirts, which hung on her like a nighty, changed his sheets and placed her back down in bed. He kissed her gently all over and told her how beautiful she was and how bad he felt that he had caused her any pain at all.

But the physical pain was nothing compared to the gaping wound she felt opening up in her heart. She wasn't just infatuated with Chris anymore – she was completely in love with him.

Chapter 29

Integrity

Kirra was the first person in the office, as per usual, and set to task on developing training she was to deliver to Ben's recently appointed in-house legal counsel later this week. She had been so focused on David, how to act at work, Hattie having a boy in her room and Zoe introducing someone new into her goddaughter's life that she hadn't really considered what she would do about Ben Andrews, particularly after the weekend she had shared with David.

Kirra logically knew that this was what dating was; that she was allowed to spend time with someone and not have it turn so serious so quickly. Her doubt came from trusting herself to manage the situation the right way, to not hurt anyone, or herself, for that matter. She was having dinner with Dan and Joel after work to get their advice on how to casually date people the 'right' way.

"Morning, Jane." She jumped at the intrusion and turned around. David was standing in the doorway to her office, bag still over his shoulder.

"The new clothes suit you," she said, commenting on the outfit they had purchased together on the weekend. Her *there he is* smile threatened to tug at the corners of her mouth, but she clamped it down by biting her lip. *Come on, we need to keep this slow and casual, remember.*

"Thanks," he said, his lips closing to a straight line too.

He briefly checked over his shoulder. Once he was sure the coast was clear, he took a step further into her office. His cologne was fresh on his skin, and she could see more of his body now that he wasn't wearing a jacket or such dark colours. The urge to stand up and touch him was so powerful that Kirra gripped the arms of her chair for strength.

"I'll keep my distance today, I've got a lot to do anyway, but I just want you to know I haven't stopped thinking about you since we said goodbye on Saturday," he said in a low voice.

"Me too." Not casual, woman. Not casual at all.

At that, he let more of his smile through. "I'll call you tonight, but you won't see me today," he said, politely nodding at her and walking over to his office.

Kirra had managed, somehow, to refocus and continue working when her landline rang.

"Ben Andrews, the CEO of Guérir, is here to see you," the firm's receptionist James informed Kirra.

"Oh, what, like here here?" Kirra's heart leapt up into her throat.

"Yes, are you available to meet with him? I've got Integrity free right now," he said, referring to one of their meeting rooms. Kirra said she would be there in a moment.

She walked around the corner, the journey feeling like it took a year, her stomach churning and pulse quickening. He said he would be in touch today, but she hadn't expected this. She willed her heart to stop thumping and her feet to keep moving. She paused at the glass sliding doors to reception, swiping her access card for them to open.

Ben was standing there in his more casual clothes, like the night she met him. He was imposingly tall and broad. She did her best to convey confidence as she crossed the room to greet him.

"Hi Ben, so nice to see you again." She smiled, shook his hand and looked to James. "Thanks for Integrity, I'll take us through."

"No troubles," said James, shooting Kirra a catty glare over the top of his glasses.

Ben followed her for a few metres. She was acutely aware of his presence close behind her. On the way, she passed David, who was talking with Kerry at her desk. He turned towards her and their eyes met for a second before Kirra turned and entered the meeting space, leaving the door open behind her. She offered Ben a seat, and he closed the door as he entered.

"I'm sorry I just popped in. I hope you don't mind."

"It does look a little odd," Kirra said, "given your seniority at Guérir."

"Well, we need to talk about the setup anyway, and I was obviously desperate to see you in person again," he said, smiling. He had warm brown eyes with crow's feet and had leaned forward in his chair towards Kirra.

"Are you seeing anyone?" he asked her, direct. "Has anything changed since we," a decided pause, "met?"

Fucked.

"I am, sort of," she admitted before she could think of anything else to say.

"Exclusively?" he responded without a second's pause.

His eyes were searching her face for answers.

He was persistent and direct, but Kirra didn't feel intimidated or uncomfortable. She could see how he got to where he was – his presence and demeanour demanded attention without being aggressive, a natural leader. Her face was definitely heating up, and her heart threatened to shoot out her arse.

"Uh, it's kind of new. That hasn't been discussed yet." She had no intention of saying anything about David, but her mouth and brain weren't working together today.

"That doesn't sound like wedding bells yet. Can we go to lunch? We'll need to meet to sort work out, so why don't we do it today?"

Nathaniel and Ken knocked on the door and let themselves in. Ben's presence had clearly been announced around the office. She was ambivalent about the intrusion. On the one hand, she was relieved she could take a minute to think. On the other, she was worried that a lunch date may now be off the table, or worse, that Ken and Nathaniel would invite themselves along.

There was the normal hand shaking and small talk before Ben cut it short, addressing the room.

"Gents, I need a policy finished to get the regulator's sign-off and start operating. It's critically important that it's done today, and I was hoping Jane could come and meet with my guys now, if that suited everyone? Jane?"

Ken and Nathaniel turned their eyes on Kirra, and she wished she could read their minds. Ken's lip curled ever so slightly with disgust, as it always did when he looked at her. Nathaniel's look was more imploring – she should ask their client how high seeing as he just told her to jump.

"I'm free, I'll grab my things," she said, ducking out to get her bag and laptop. She looked around, but David was nowhere to be seen.

Ben and Kirra were alone in the lift when Ben spoke.

"I know I've been really forward, but a woman like you doesn't stay single for long," little did he know, "and when you want something, you've got to go for it with everything you have. We'll have lunch and then you decide whether our relationship is purely professional or something else. Please, if that's okay," he added, for good measure, remembering his manners.

He was clearly used to getting what he wanted.

His overt masculinity and directness was, much to Kirra's shame as a card-carrying feminist, a huge turn-on. She was already feeling a deep sense of guilt at having left David up there to come down with Ben, but she wasn't sure if the guilt was justified. She was, technically, single and had in fact met Ben before David. Had slept with him first, too.

"Sure, let's do lunch then."

They travelled further away from Kirra's building to avoid prying eyes. They walked past Guérir's building.

"Aren't we going up there to see your guys first?"

"No, the policy's already done."

Damn, he really did get what he wanted.

Chapter 30

Another first date

They took a seat in an Italian restaurant, and Kirra tucked her laptop away now that she was under no illusions a business discussion was to be had. While being seriously attracted to both men, she felt different around Ben, bolder somehow. It was a vibe only at this stage, but she felt like David's feelings were very close to the surface of his skin and bruised easily whereas Ben's were buried a little deeper. Maybe he could handle a bit more of her Kirra-ness.

She genuinely didn't have a clue as to which she preferred. She was swinging between labelling herself a two-timing-whore and an independent woman, weighing up what worked best for her.

"How old are you?" she asked as the waiter brought them their menus.

"Not here to fuck spiders, are you, Jane?" he said, eyebrows raised but smiling. "I just turned fifty. I was actually having birthday drinks when I met you. How old are you?"

"You're not meant to ask a lady that."

"You just asked me, and I'm a gentleman."

"Take a guess," she ventured, eyes widening in an obvious dare.

"Well, if I said you don't look a day over twenty-five, I'd sound like a paedophile wouldn't I?" he said, hailing the waiter. "I'm having a beer, what would you like?"

"I'll have one too. I'm thirty-four, thirty-five in September."

Ben ordered the pair their drinks and some olives.

"Shit, that's a bit of an age gap," he said. "For context, my ex-wife and I are the same age, I'm not like a—"

"Leonardo DiCaprio?"

"Yeah," he laughed in agreement. "I'm not even on any of these dating apps my mates are trying to get me to sign up to. Apparently you put in an age range."

Kirra's was twenty to fifty-five, but she only went on actual 'speaking' dates with guys a bit older than her. She found dating guys her age or younger often ended up as one-sided interviews – they had no banter. Depending on how she was feeling of a Friday or Saturday night, she would trade potential erectile dysfunction for shit chat. The dating pool needed some chlorine.

"Does the age gap bother you?" she asked him as the waiter quickly returned with their drinks and snack.

"No, it doesn't bother me, but it's not a kink to me either. I like you because you're funny, smart and were easy to talk to that night. You're also very attractive, obviously."

"Thanks, you're pretty hot too." She smiled at him, which he returned. She felt a pang of guilt at complimenting him, but she reminded herself she didn't owe anyone anything; she was a free agent. They ordered their lunch, a pizza to share.

They chatted over their food. He was funny and down-to-earth for someone who owned at least two fifty-thousand-dollar watches. He was wearing a different Submariner to the one he was wearing the night they met.

"So, how do you get to be a CEO anyway?"

"Uh, I guess you're on the tools and then jobs in management open up. You go for it, get it and, if you're not a total idiot, it just keeps going on from there."

"On the tools? What did you do to begin with?"

"I'm an ortho, by trade."

"As in—"

"An orthopaedic surgeon."

Kirra choked on her pizza a little bit. "Holy shit, so you're Dr Ben Andrews."

Kirra prided herself on judging someone by the way they treated others foremost – she wasn't interested in braggards or show-offs. But she would be lying if she said she wasn't just the tiniest little bit impressed that he was a doctor. A well-hung, rich doctor.

"I haven't practised in ages. I had a bunch of old injuries from playing footy back in my youth, and surgery was killing me. Being in management was the easier option."

Ben was definitely more *salt of the earth* than David too. He had gone to a boarding school in regional Victoria as his family were farmers, and even though he was from down there, he agreed with Kirra that AFL was the lesser football code. They had finished their pizza, and Kirra declined a second beer.

"What kind of relationship do you want, Jane?" he asked, leaning into the table. "I know you want one, because you've started seeing this other guy, but what's it look like to you?"

"To be honest, I'm kind of still figuring that out," she answered in earnest, her eyes snagging on some of Ben's exposed chest hair. Her mind flitted back to when he scooped her up and lay her down on his mattress.

"How about you?" she asked, swallowing and getting her eyes back on his face.

"I'm open to anything, really. I'm not having any more kids, but ideally I'd like to have something serious, someone to share my life with." He paused, searching her face for evidence that she was looking for the same thing. "I'd also be keen on something else with you. Even if it was just another chance to make you come without you having to fake it," he added with a smirk.

Kirra's eyes bulged for a second.

"Fucking hell, I wasn't—"

"You quite clearly were. You're a much better lawyer than you are an actress. You were trying to spare my feelings, but you didn't have to."

Kirra was reeling at Ben's forwardness, and a little embarrassed he had figured she was faking. She had never uttered the word *daddy* out loud before that night and, in retrospect, was mortified that she thought that it would be hot.

"I also wanted to apologise for that night. I should have got your number and let you go back to partying with your mates then messaged you the next day. I honestly didn't think you were that drunk after talking to you, but now that I've seen you sober in broad daylight, I know that you were. I'm sorry about that."

David and Ben had a few things in common, it would appear, and being straight shooters didn't begin to describe it.

"I was wasted, but I was consenting, and it was a fun night," she replied sheepishly.

"It was a really fun night," he said, looking a little embarrassed for the first time since they had sat down to their meal. They finished their drinks and food and actually talked about work for a while until the waiter brought their bill over.

"Let me walk you back to your office," he offered as he paid.

They walked back in the direction of their offices for a while when he stopped.

"Can I kiss you, please?" he asked, hands at his side and looking down at her. She looked up into his face for a moment, mind racing, before nodding her head ever so slightly.

He leaned in to her, taking the back of her head with one hand, and she raised on to her tiptoes to meet his lips. He slowly kissed her, and she sighed at how the chemistry that had been building between them over the past two hours at lunch exploded. She reached her arms around his lower back and ran her hands across the muscles there. His free hand came up to cradle her face, his thumb lightly dragging across her cheek. They stayed there for what felt like five minutes, but it might have only been one.

He pulled away first, and Kirra dizzily opened her eyes.

He looked at her for a moment, and slowly shook his head, as if in disbelief. "Ah shit, I'm in trouble."

***

Nathaniel was on her in an instant as she arrived back at the office, grilling her about what she had discussed with Ben's team. She prattled off some points she had worked on in her plan, failing to mention that they were still just a plan at this stage. Nathaniel seemed convinced, but he was easily convinced of everything.

She walked back to her office, stopping at Kerry's pod to ask if anyone had tried to reach her while she had been out. Kerry looked up at her over the colourful rims of her huge glasses.

"In your office now, miss," she whispered, making her way ahead of Kirra.

She closed the door behind them.

"What's wrong?" Kirra asked, worried.

"He's bloody smitten with you," Kerry whispered. Kirra paused for a second, about to ask who, and the pause was enough for Kerry to fill in the gaps.

"David!" she exclaimed, quickly swivelling her head around to see if she had been heard, before continuing on in a whisper, "but there's something going on with that big fella too!?"

"No! Why would you say that?" Kirra attempted to defend herself, her lips still tingling with the kiss they had shared after lunch.

"Oh darl, you're a shit actress."

That was the second time today she'd had that allegation made against her.

"Look, whatever, none of my business, but just so you know – when David watched you walk that bloke into the meeting room, I knew. He didn't have to say anything. He basically stopped breathing."

Kirra was panicked in an instant. She had thought she would have more time before whatever was happening with David and Ben had to be decided on. She realised in that moment she couldn't have picked a more complicated pair of guys to choose between, and she'd have to make the choice sooner rather than later. If she was smart about it and wanted less trouble, she'd pick neither of them, but that wasn't exactly her style.

"Sweetie, I won't say anything to anyone. You're a big girl, and you know I love you," Kerry said, placing a hand on Kirra's arm. "Just be careful, alright darl? I'm here if you need me."

***

As she left for dinner with Joel and Dan after successfully avoiding David for the rest of the day, she said a polite goodbye to James on her way out of the office.

"There's a package here for you – courier just dropped it off a second ago," James said, eyeing Kirra suspiciously and pointing to a small rectangular box. "Hope the 'training session' at Guérir went well," he said, making air quotes and levelling Kirra with a knowing look.

"It did, thank you James," she smiled sweetly back at him, swiping the package off the counter and shoving it in her bag.

In the lift alone, she opened it. After removing the brown cardboard outer, she held an olive-green box with golden lettering across the front, a brand name she didn't recognise. After the elevator deposited her in the foyer, she sat down on one of the lounges and lifted the lid of the green box. Inside was a smaller white box tied with a silk bow in the same olive-green of the outer box. She untied it and lifted the lid.

Inside was a thick gold bracelet, inlaid with five shapes that looked similar to four-leaf clovers. It glittered under the lobby lights, the light catching and reflecting off the strikingly beautiful green stone. Kirra took it out of its box and laid it across her wrist without fastening it. It looked beautiful against her fair skin. She noticed there was a note in the box and opened it up.

Something to remind you of your Irish criminal ancestry.
B.A.

Holy shit.

156

Chapter 31

Sage advice

"Kirra, this is a fucking Van Cleef Alhambra bracelet," Joel said, his eyes wide with shock, holding the bracelet in his hands as they sat down for dinner.

"It's really pret—" she started to say, but Joel cut her off with a shriek.

"Pretty!? It's ten fucking thousand dollars! We don't even have a store in Brisbane … we're not fancy enough! He would have had to pull some strings to get it up here this quickly!" His exasperation at Kirra's cluelessness had reached a fever pitch.

Kirra hadn't recognised the brand when she opened the box, but her knowledge of designers came exclusively from old rap songs; Gucci, Louis, Fendi, Prada – does anything even rhyme with Van Cleef? Beef? Queef?

"Whoa, Kiz – this is that guy from the rooftop bar the other week?" Daniel was clearly as shocked as her at how much Ben had spent on the gift.

"Yeah, him," she said. Her heart was racing. She needed to take the edge off her nerves immediately. She fished around in her bag for her vape, dumping out her phone and keys as she did.

"Well look at you Miss I-don't-know-any-designers, you've got a Saint Laurent keychain now too?" Joel snatched up the mini-Gus David had bought her on the weekend and was inspecting it closely. He was already wearing the bracelet.

"Uh, funny story about where that came from too," she said, taking a hit of her vape and blowing the smoke over the balcony.

Joel and Dan sat on in rapt silence while Kirra told them what had happened with both men, sparing no detail. After she had finished, they both looked at each other.

"Kirra, drop this David guy and let Ben buy us, I mean you, more goodies," Joel insisted, taking a picture of his wrist and uploading it to his Instagram.

"You take that off. I'm not keeping it," Kirra warned Joel, who sullenly slipped the bracelet off his wrist and back into the box.

"Oh okay, so you've chosen dog keychain boy then. I mean that little thing is like four hundred bucks." He shrugged.

"No, well, I don't know – I do know I don't feel comfortable with the bracelet though." Kirra carefully slid the box back into her bag.

"Are you sure, Kiz? He did say he wants anything with you, maybe you could be his sugar baby? I had a sugar daddy for a while," Joel patted his Louis Vuitton bag.

"I mean, I'm not really a baby though, am I? I don't think that really suits me, no offence."

"None taken, the guy that bought me that bag constantly smelled like onions. It was barely worth it."

"What's your heart say, Kiz?" Dan asked. Joel made a fake vomiting sound.

"It says I want both of them, and neither of them." Her mind was spinning. "They're both quality dudes who I probably don't deserve."

"Oh, shut the fuck up, Kiz," Joel said. "Both of these guys are crazy about you, Miss Good Puss!"

"Yeah girl, cut that shit out. They've both told you they want something with you. They've tried to spoil you, given you space, been upfront. I think they both seem like great choices. You need to do what you want to do."

Dan was such a good friend and counsellor – a mirror that showed you what you already wanted rather than a compass pointing you in one direction.

Kirra, however, was still lost as to what she was going to do, what the smarter choice would be. Maybe making the 'smart' choice wasn't the right thing to do here, she had to quieten the noise in her head and let her heart make a choice for a change.

Chapter 32

Phone voice

Kirra was laying down in bed scrolling when David called. She hesitated. What would she say if he asked her about Guérir and where she went today? She didn't want David to think she was avoiding him, so she decided to pick up.

"Hey."

"Hey, now a good time to chat? You're not about to go to sleep?" He sounded nervous.

"Yeah sure, I'm awake. How are you?"

"Good, good," he trailed off awkwardly. "And you?"

"Yeah good." Kirra's stomach was doing butterflies, the bad kind, with how uncomfortable this phone call had started. If he asked, would she tell him she had kissed someone else today? Did she need to, was that the right thing to do?

"I can't stop thinking about you," he said, sounding more like himself.

Small talk didn't suit him, and hearing his normal, assured tone made Kirra loosen up a little.

"Yeah, I've been thinking about you a lot too, actually," she said, unable to keep the smile out of her voice. Thoughts of Ben receded.

"Yeah?"

"Yeah."

"What are you doing right now?" he asked. It was such a simple question, but somehow it felt naughty. It was like being twelve and talking to your crush on the landline for the first time.

"Laying down, just hopped out the shower."

"Yeah? What are you wearing?" His voice sounded different, deeper.

"I was actually just laying here in the nude, letting my moisturiser sink in." She heard a slight groan from the other end of the phone. "How about you?"

"Paul and I ended up going for a ride up Mount Coot-tha, so I'm clad in Lycra and sweat, baby."

She snorted.

"Oh no, you're a MAMIL?" she groaned – a middle-aged man in Lycra.

"I am, I'm afraid. Spent a tonne on a road-bike within minutes of turning forty. It's a rite of passage."

Kirra was laughing, feeling relaxed and a surprisingly turned on at the thought of David in a skin-tight onesie clip-clopping around in a pair of cleats.

"You have a really nice phone voice, by the way," she said, a little breathless.

"I was just about to say the same thing to you too. It's making my Lycra tight."

She huffed a laugh.

He groaned a little again, sounding frustrated that he wasn't there with her in the flesh.

"Can you do me a favour, Kirra?"

"Uh-huh." Hearing her name in his sexy-slightly-deeper phone voice lowered her IQ dozens of points.

"Reach into that bedside drawer to your left and grab that white and blue lightsaber."

"The magic wand," she giggled, reaching over to grab it before returning to her reclined position.

"Yeah, that thing."

"What do you want me to do now?" she asked, her pulse kicking up, keen to hear whatever he had to say to her. She despised being told what to do in the real world, but the idea of being bossed around by David via a phone call turned her on to the point of distraction.

"I want you to turn it on and tell me what it feels like when you're using it on yourself."

She turned it on to its lowest setting and started by rubbing it around her clit, a little moan escaping her throat. She heard him quietly curse to himself at the sound the toy had elicited from her.

"It feels good," she sighed. "I wish you were here using it on me."

"I do too. What else would you do if I was there right now?"

"Ummmm, I'd want you to suck on my nipples." She was holding the wand directly over her clit now, imagining David knelt over her and touching her, "and I'd want your fingers in me, like on the weekend."

"When you squirted for me?" His voice was setting her nerve endings on fire. He sounded so different on the phone that it was like talking to a new version of him. It was hot as fuck, and she wanted more of it.

"Uh-huh, what would you do if you were here right now?" She responded, her breath catching in her throat as the wand worked its magic, tension already building up inside her.

"I want to do about three hundred things to you, but if I was there right now, I'd have you sitting on my face with my tongue deep in your tight pussy."

"Holy shit," *holy shit*, "and then what?" Kirra already felt close to coming. She struggled to hold the wand and the phone at the same time, quickly putting David on loudspeaker so she could focus more on his voice and the waves of pleasure sweeping over her. She had debated spending so much on this toy, but it was *effective*.

"Then I'd drag you down onto my cock and have you ride me like your life depended on it, with my hands wrapped around your throat until—"

Kirra let out a cry as she came, her orgasm rocking through her in waves. She lay there in silence, basking in the afterglow for a second before remembering David was still on the phone.

"God that sounded so hot," he groaned into the phone. "Did that feel good?"

Kirra laughed, slightly embarrassed. "Um, yes it did. God, the way you talk is so sexy. I've blasted myself with that thing a hundred times, but I've never come like I did just then," she confessed.

"Can I come over tomorrow night, bring you dinner? Maybe afterwards you sit on my face, maybe you don't, no pressure."

She could hear the smile in his voice. The thought of sitting on his face was already getting her horny again, seconds after coming.

"Yeah, I'd like that."

"Well, I'll let you get to bed. To paint another sexy picture for you; I'm going to go peel myself out of my Lycra and have a wank in the shower."

"Will you think of me?" Kirra asked, a huge dumb smile plastered across her face.

"Obviously I'll be thinking of you. I'm always thinking about you."

"Good night, David 'Dirty Talk' Waters."

"Good might, Kirra Jane McNamara."

Chapter 33

A gut feeling

After actually delivering the training to Guérir's in-house counsel in their offices the next day, Ben invited Kirra into his office. She had asked to speak with him privately, saying it was to do with billing.

She couldn't shake the feeling she was leading both Ben and David along. Her stomach churned with guilt, and she wondered how people who 'dated' multiple people at the same time could enjoy each partner without feeling like they were wronging the other. Power to them, she supposed, but her brain didn't work that way.

Kirra had been trying to figure out what kind of relationship she wanted so that she could figure out who would be the best choice to have it with. She had even started a pros and cons list in her journal, weighing up her options, but that exercise had left her feeling sick to her stomach. Human beings can't be boiled down to a series of pros and cons. Ben and David were both great guys. She ultimately realised, even with her minimal knowledge of how relationships worked, that you don't pick someone based on their pros alone.

In the end, she let the little voice in her head, and the little keychain in her handbag, make the decision for her, not her rational brain. Dating David was going to have its own consequences, but the way he made her feel was unlike anything she'd experienced. He was gentle but forthright, decisive but accommodating, and when he touched her, it was as if the rest of the world disappeared. She'd called him a cunt and he'd seen her ugly crying on their first date, and yet he still wanted more of her. Being wanted, being seen, being appreciated for her tics and quirks; she didn't want to risk losing that while she made the 'smarter' choice. Kirra also got the distinct impression that Gus wouldn't forgive her if he never got to see David again.

"I've started seeing someone else. I can't accept this, I'm sorry," she said, sliding the bracelet back across Ben's desk. He looked down at the box.

The people-pleaser in her wanted to apologise for him having wasted so much money on a gift that had been rejected, but her conscious-self reminded her that she didn't ask for it and that she had absolutely nothing to be sorry for.

"I appreciate you being upfront, Jane." After a moment of looking at the floor, he stood up and crossed the room, leaving the box where it was.

"Can I kiss you goodbye?" he looked down at her mouth then back to her eyes, "Just one more time?"

Kirra's heart raced, but she didn't hesitate in her response.

"No, thank you." She extended her hand for a handshake.

He nodded, a tight-lipped smile on his face. He took her hand and shook it. He didn't rub his fingers along the back of her hand.

"Purely professional," he nodded again, as if trying to convince himself, "but I obviously hope this guy's a dud – don't lose my number."

***

Back at the office, Kirra and David worked together for the afternoon.

One client had given a blanket *no* to not working with Kirra anymore but said they would stay on if David worked alongside her. They had a dispute to settle over an accusation of wrongful dismissal.

One of their client's employees had been accessing the HR database and stalking one of his much younger coworkers. He was found out when he sent flowers to her personal address, which she had never given him. It was an open and shut case of harassment, but he had been close to retiring and getting a huge payout, so he lawyered up to try and protect himself and get his money.

"We're going to squash this creepy old cunt," Kirra advised David in a tone far too collegial for the choice of words.

"I'm looking forward to it." He smiled back at her.

It was nice sitting next to him again in the office. After working almost completely on her own for so long, it was still surprising to her how much she had missed working with him.

"I'm looking forward to tonight, too," he added quietly.

"Me too." She fought to hide her smile.

He had deliberately sat opposite her, far away enough that they couldn't touch. How strange to be working on a case in a small office with someone you'd had phone sex with the night prior. The tension was still palpable.

She debated whether she should tell David about Ben, the bracelet and the kiss or whether any of that was really necessary. Again, the rules of how people acted in relationships were a mystery to her. She had resolved to admit she had kissed someone, once, since she had met David, if he ever asked. She didn't want to know if he had hooked up with anyone else since he had been in Brissy, so she wasn't going to ask either.

Kirra had felt some of the stress release from her once she had decided she was going to date David and let Ben get on with his life. Her stomach had been churning since the beginning of the year almost constantly with anxiety. She would frequently throw up – before court, after court, or after a particularly awful interaction with Nick or Ken – from stress and worry. Dan had given her some cognitive behaviour therapy tips to help quieten her mind. So far, they hadn't worked once. Admittedly she had never used them, but both statements were logically true.

She knew she wanted to change so many things about her life and was, in principle, committed to making it work. She wanted to be nicer at work and date more seriously, like someone her age should be. She should be spending less money on illegal substances and also giving up dairy, which almost seemed like a no-brainer for someone whose stomach was a washing machine on the most violent part of its cycle almost constantly. Hell, her mother had died of cancer at forty-two, yet Kirra still vaped. Change is hard for most people, but it felt almost impossible for her.

She had kept such a tight lid on the grief at the loss of her mother and her memories of Him. If things changed, even if they were for the better, could that lid come loose? Habits, even if they're killing you, still felt safer than the unknown. Opening herself up to David felt dangerous, but the pull she felt towards him stopped her from making any other choice.

She knew pursuing David wasn't the smartest thing she could do; she worked with him, for fuck's sake. But she couldn't discount an undeniable feeling in her gut, a new one on top of the churning and butterflies, that told her something else. She didn't know what it was, but she could feel it there, growing.

Who knows, maybe it was a big fat tumour?

She remembered New Year's resolution number five:

Stop making morbid jokes about dying of cancer – from Dan.

Chapter 34

What's wrong with you, exactly?

There was a knock at her door later that night. She had worked out and showered, and now she was wearing a light purple matching lounge set that clung to her breasts and arse, showing off her curves. It was a soft, light material that made her feel sexy. She was more than a little excited for David to see her in it. Gus made it to the front door before she did and was skidding around, sensing who was on the other side.

She opened the door, and David was in a plain white T-shirt and dark workout shorts, looking even sexier than he did in a suit or dressed up for dinner. He was holding a brown paper bag.

She was doing her best to push her chest out and *may* have even teased her nipples a little on the way to the door so that they would be standing to attention by the time he saw her. She had run the straightener over her hair, going for an *I don't even need to try, I just look this hot all the time* look, which she thought she had nailed – but David's attention was wholly elsewhere.

"Gusssyyyyyy." He handed Kirra the bag without looking at her and knelt down to cuddle Gus, whose tail was helicoptering at a dangerous speed.

Kirra couldn't even feel rejected. The pair were so happy at being reunited after two days. After Gus had let David stand up, he looked her up and down, drinking her in with his eyes and lost for words, his gaze snagging on her breasts.

"My eyes are up here, Waters," she said as seriously as she could.

Then he looked at her eyes, his pale blue stare taking in all of her features. God, he was beautiful, even when he wasn't smiling.

He leant in to kiss her and pulled away after a little more than a peck.

"Despite your best efforts to seduce me, I would very much like to eat some Thai," he said, then marched past her in the direction of the dining room.

The pair shared some pad thai and washed it down with sparkling water that David had also brought with him, a tradition in keeping with their sober first date. They chatted about how their weekend had finished up rather than what had happened that day, so Kirra didn't need to lie about going on a date with Ben.

"I didn't want to assume you were drinking again. I'll bring wine next time," he said as he refilled her glass of sparkling water, emphasising the *next time*. His eyes searched Kirra's face for some sign of what she wanted with him.

At least she hoped that's what that look was, otherwise she was about to make a colossal fool of herself.

"Waters, I want to be in a relationship with you. A closed one, please."

"Really?" he asked quickly, his eyebrows shooting up and a huge grin splitting his face.

In her head, she had wanted to make David see that she was a serious, grown-up woman who felt that he was worthy of her time and attention.

Instead, she said, "You still keen?"

He quickly rounded the table and threw her over his shoulder, much the same way he had on Friday. He marched her to her bedroom, placing her back on her feet at the foot of her bed and kicking the door shut behind them.

"Yes, of course I want to date you exclusively. But first, you," he pointed to her, then back to his own head, "on my face, now."

***

After having *her* face melted off, they sat down on the sofa on her back deck, Gus nestled between them, and enjoyed the balmy evening together while they chatted.

Without asking directly, Kirra calculated David was turning forty-three by the year he had finished high school, and Kirra offered that she remembered the Sydney 2000 Olympics as an almost-nine-year-old, subtly giving her own age. She was surprised this hadn't come up on the weekend, but they had somehow had too much else to talk about.

"So, I'm eight years older than you. Is that a bit weird?" he asked.

"I don't think so. Do you feel like you're babysitting me?"

"Absolutely not. You're multilingual, make more money than I do and can renovate a house on your own. You have far more life experience than I do."

He stared up into the night sky as if lost in thought for a moment.

"What are you thinking about?" she asked him.

"Just that … it's a little interesting you've never had a boyfriend or a partner. You're gorgeous, funny, smart, financially independent—"

"You're wondering what's wrong with me?" she said, smirking. "Couldn't I say the same thing to you, David Waters? Why does a good-looking, professional man like you not have a partner or children by your age?"

"You could ask that, sure. Are you asking that?"

"I don't want to be rude, but I am curious. You go first, then I'll tell you what's wrong with me."

"I mucked around a lot as a young guy," he said. "My gap year turned into a gap three-years, so I rooted half of Western Europe."

"Such a rich kid thing to do. Kids from Caboolture don't do gap years," Kirra snorted, "unless it's a year of playing video games and smoking pot on your JobSeeker payment."

"You're right, but you know, I had worked *so* hard at high school, I'd earned the time off." His ability to laugh at his own privilege was quite endearing.

"Then you're back in Australia," Kirra steered him back to his story while laughing.

"Did uni, started working at KM straight out, got my first serious girlfriend when I was in my mid-twenties. We were together for six years. Things were great for ages, then she was pushing me for a ring and I felt like I wasn't ready, like a big dumb baby. I broke it off."

"Shortly after that, my best friend killed himself."

Kirra's mind went back to the mental health charities on his LinkedIn page that she had stalked with Dan when she still thought David was a cunt.

"It messed me up in a massive way. I've had my own struggles with head stuff over the years, and to see it take him was too much. I've had a few semi-serious relationships since then, but they'd always get sick of my bullshit eventually, or I'd push them away."

Kirra was listening so intently that she had stopped breathing. She had so many questions as to what his 'head stuff' was. She was curious, and appreciative of his honesty, but she would be lying to herself if she said she wasn't at least a little worried too. He hadn't been able to keep a long-term girlfriend, and he had, or has, mental health problems. She was a little ashamed that she wanted to judge him so quickly when she herself had been so worried about being judged by him.

"Time passed, quickly actually, as it does when you get older, and it reached a head. I was drinking heavily and snorting tonnes of coke. I'd put on a heap of weight and was really unwell."

That explained the old suits that hung off him.

"Then, to top it off, I turned forty."

"Whoa, and you were already in crisis," she said.

"Yep, but my midlife crisis was a good one, in comparison. I decided to sort my health out and started giving back to mental health charities that could have helped Harry. After a few years, I was feeling good and like things were moving in the right direction. The move to Brisbane was meant to be a fresh start too. New faces, new people."

He smiled, looking into Kirra's eyes for the first time since talking about himself. It clearly made him uncomfortable, but he had persisted for her benefit.

"That, and I was kind of forced up here because I'd been so shit at work for so long. I'd fucked up a few big cases even before all my clients went broke. They felt bad for firing me."

That struck Kirra as odd.

"Why would they feel bad for firing you? KM cut the slack for fun up here. I could imagine it's even more cutthroat down there."

"Um, you'll love this – it's because of my father and grandfather."

Oh no, he's not …

"The Waters have worked for KM since the firm first set up in Australia."

Kirra's mouth opened and closed a few times before she could speak.

"I get the distinct impression you despise nepo-babies," he said, grimacing at her.

"It's not that I despise nepo-babies, it's just—"

"It's all good, it is pretty obnoxious." He smiled at her, the soft lights warming his face. "To summarise, I'm a silver-spoon underachiever reinventing himself in the sunshine state. But enough about me, how about you? I don't want to interview you, but I do have six thousand questions."

"I wouldn't mind the interview. Go for it." She had propped her legs across his lap while they reclined together. He began rubbing her feet.

"Where are you from?"

Kirra had alluded to being from the wrong side of the tracks to David on the weekend but hadn't gone into detail.

"Caboolture. It was a shithole then. Might not be these days with property prices, no one can afford to buy in even 'undesirable' suburbs now, but I haven't gone back there, so I wouldn't know, my dad lives further up the coast now. It's surprising how much it comes up, even now. You get asked about where you went to school, even in your thirties, so much around here because they want to size you up, see if you know the same people. I always pretend I don't know they mean high school and say I went to Oxford to shut them up."

He listened to her every word, massaging her feet and taking her in like he was trying to remember every line on her face and the way every letter sounded as she spoke it. His attention was intense. After a pause, his interview continued.

"I still don't really believe you've never had a boyfriend." It wasn't a question, rather a leading statement. "Nothing even in school, a fling?"

"I've had flings, a few repeat dates here and there, I just – I don't know. I love my life as it is, and until recently I didn't think I wanted it to change."

"What made you want it to change?"

"Um, well …"

The crushing realisation that at almost thirty-five you don't understand what a romantic relationship is, that you're burnt out and tired from an industry that you've never felt a part of, that you party so much you have huge holes in even your sober memories and your body count is in the hundreds? And the question of if not now, then when will you ever actually grow the fuck up? Are you going to be vaping, doing drugs and sending nudes to random men when you're forty? Fifty, you silly cunt?

"New year, new me, you know."

They sat in silence for a while, the only sound Gus' loud snoring.

"What do you think a relationship will be like?" David was still massaging her feet, looking at her under the warm glow of the string lights, a burning citronella candle keeping the bugs at bay.

"I don't know, what's a good one look like?"

She appreciated him not belittling her lack of knowledge. She was embarrassed by it, and he was being nothing but kind. He pondered the question for a moment while his hands expertly worked over her tired feet. God his hands – whenever he touched her anywhere, she felt it all through her body.

"Maybe it's like building something new together, sharing the good times and the bad, although it shouldn't be hard work most of the time. You're both better off because you've got each other. It's not a give and take, but rather a give and give."

Kirra let his words sink in.

"That sounds really nice, I want that."

"Me too."

They smiled at each other for a moment in the silence, then Kirra checked her phone. It was after eleven.

"Oh shit, it's late," she said.

"You're right, I'll head home." He let go of her feet, and she missed his touch instantly, the warmth draining from her like an unplugged bathtub.

"Uh, you don't need to. Do you have clothes for tomorrow?"

"I do," he said, smirking at her. "I didn't want to be presumptuous, but I chucked them in the car just in case."

"Hmm, quite a presumptuous act in itself," she said with a sly smile.

They made their way inside to take a shower. Kirra piled her hair high on top of her head and put on a shower cap to keep it dry.

"Ooh, sexy." David chuckled, pointing to the cap.

He was already in the shower and opened the door to let her in. Once she had stepped in, he tilted her head back and kissed her deeply. She moaned into his mouth, the sensation of his touch and the hot water hitting her skin waking up all her senses at once. She ran her hands up his chest and wrapped them around the back of his neck. He looked good soaking wet.

"Damn, if I'd known you liked shower caps so much, I would have worn it earlier," she cooed, his burgeoning erection pushing up against her as they held each other under the hot water.

She wrapped her hand around him, his head fell back on a groan, and he let her stroke him a while longer before he held her lightly by the arm.

"Sorry McNamara, not tonight. You've got to remember I'm an old man, I'm tired. Turn around so I can wash your back."

They finished showering, dressed for bed and made sure Gus was comfortable. David told him a bedtime story of the three little pigs, which Gus actually seemed to be listening to, much to Kirra's delight. She had talked to Gus for hours on end but never told him a fairy tale.

As they hopped into bed, Kirra felt immediately sleepy, which struck her as unusual as she hadn't had anything to drink or taken sleeping tablets. She had been battling insomnia for months now, so it was novel to feel like she might fall asleep without a struggle. She let out a massive yawn.

"My life story bored you to death, I get it." David wrapped his arms around her, and she could hear the smile in his voice.

"The opposite, actually. I am surprised by how much I like sharing a bed with you. I'm a touch particular about a lot of stuff," she nuzzled into his neck, "but it's better with you here."

"It's better with you too, Kirra."

Chapter 35

It's official

After shutting off her alarm, she could smell coffee and hear David talking to Gus in the kitchen. There was a knock at the door, and David popped his head back into her room.

"Did you want me to get that?"

"It'll be my neighbour Geoff coming to collect Gus. I'll grab it."

Kirra threw her robe on and went to the door.

She said good morning to Geoff and let him through; they often shared a coffee before Gus went back home with him, Geoff an early riser too. She led him into the kitchen to where David was standing.

"Geoff, this is David, David this is Geoff – Gus' grandpa."

David crossed the room and took Geoff's hand. Geoff looked a little shocked at first but then smiled and shook David's hand back.

"It's lovely to meet you. It's great Gus has someone to keep him company during the day," David said, beaming down at Gus and back to Geoff.

"He's the one who keeps me company, mate." Geoff chuckled. "Is that your Mercedes out there?"

"Yeah, sorry. It's not too close to your driveway, is it?"

"Nah, beautiful car, I used to have a ..." The pair engaged in a friendly bit of man-chat about cars while Kirra made Geoff his very weak, very hot coffee, just the way he liked it. The three humans and one dog sat down at the dining table and enjoyed their coffees together, making inane chit-chat about the weather and when the bins went out next.

"Now you seem like a nice bloke Daveo, but you know our Kirra here's a very special girl," Geoff said, levelling David with a serious stare. "What are your intentions?"

"Jesus Geoff!" Kirra stared at him, gobsmacked. She looked over to David. This wasn't the sort of question someone you had been officially dating for all of twelve hours should be getting asked.

"To make her happy and look after her and Gus," David responded in a heartbeat, maintaining direct eye contact with the old man.

"Good answer, lad," Geoff winked. "Alright, I've given this guy the onceover and he seems alright, darl," he said to Kirra. "Me and my best mate will be off. You have a good day at work, and I'll see you tonight."

He hobbled over to David and shook his hand goodbye. After a "Nice meeting you, Daveo," he left, Gus totting off behind him.

Kirra looked to David

"Sorry about that, he's normally very chipper."

"Nothing at all to be sorry about, he loves you and Gus, so he's all good in my books."

***

"You two make me fucking sick," Paul whispered into Kirra's ear as she was making herself a cup of tea in the office kitchen later that morning.

She spun around, but he was decidedly not looking at her, fixing a cup for himself. She could see he was smirking.

"I have no idea what you're talking about."

"Mate," he replied with quiet exasperation, checking around the corner for any eavesdroppers before addressing Kirra directly. "Our new friend from down south, who is a lovely guy by the way, has been making goo-goo eyes at you since he arrived, even after you threw your toys out of the cot," he paused, checking around the corners again before continuing on in a rushed whisper. "But then again lots of dudes in this place do. Much to my confusion, because you're hideous."

Kirra snorted a laugh but was quickly growing panicked as to where Paul was going with this.

"So, imagine my shock and horror when I see YOU making goo-goo eyes BACK at him." He whisper-screamed his words for emphasis, undermining the purpose of whispering to begin with. Kirra gave him a moment to finish his tirade, sipping her tea and staring at him blankly.

"I know Kerry's already told you this, because she told me she told you" – God there are no secrets in this fucking place – "but be careful, mate."

"I will, Paul. I appreciate it. I don't know if I even want to stay here anymore. And if I do, anti-fraternisation clauses are notoriously hard to enforce."

Kirra had shared her displeasure with Kensington Menschel with Paul many times in the five years they had been working together, but she hadn't yet shared how serious she was about leaving this time. She still didn't know how serious she was. She and David hadn't discussed how they would handle being together while working for the same firm, but she knew they would eventually have to have this discussion. In the meantime, they had to be exceptionally careful.

"I'm not talking about that. Well, not just that."

"No? Then what?"

"The relationship."

She looked at him blankly.

Kirra had put a tick in the box next to resolution number one yesterday, just before David brought her pad thai. She had found someone. It was done. She was off the senseless hook-up merry-go-round.

"Real relationships aren't just going out to fancy dinners and great sex, he's going to want to know the real you, the bad and the good. All of it."

That made Kirra pause.

"If it's serious, you've got to let him in."

Chapter 36

Good news all round

David had wanted to have Kirra over for dinner at his apartment the following night, but she had already agreed to catch up with Dan after work. She had been close to cancelling, but she'd had so many friends drop her like a sack of potatoes at the faintest whiff of a new relationship only to be picked up again after it didn't work out. She had sworn she would never do that to someone else. She had never even considered ditching Dan for anyone else in the fourteen years they had been friends until tonight.

"I'm dating someone," Dan announced as they sat down at their favourite poké bowl restaurant.

"What, what!?" Kirra squealed, "Me too!"

Dan looked at her as if seeking clarification.

"Oh, David, I picked David!"

"So, wait, we both have boyfriends?"

"We both have boyfriends!"

They had reached an ear-splitting volume, and a head from the neighbouring booth had unsubtly popped over to see where the noise was coming from.

"Sorry – we've been single for ages and have both just started dating, it's momentous!" Dan told the young woman who had popped up. She gave a thumbs up and popped her head back down.

"Look I know we're not drinking, or drinking less or whatever, but we need bubbles," Dan announced, using the code on the table to order a bottle from his phone.

"Abso-fucking-lutely we do," Kirra concurred.

Bubbles half consumed, Kirra had been peppering Daniel with questions about his new beau.

Ned and Dan had been chatting on a dating app for months, the pair's schedules never aligning for a date, when lo and behold they bumped into each other in real life by complete chance.

"I thought they called my number at Maccas and grabbed this bag when this really hot, vaguely familiar guy stops me and accuses me of snatching his order."

"Oh my god, and it was him?!"

"Yeah, and get this – we'd both ordered the exact same thing."

Kirra knew Daniel's Maccas order off by heart: double cheeseburger, add bacon, add tomato, add lettuce, large fries with a sweet and sour sauce and a large cokie-no-sug-sug.

"Fuck off, he really ordered the *McFancy* too?"

"Yes, he somehow knew the secret recipe. I was shocked."

"And the sweet and sour?!"

"AND the sweet and sour!!" Dan was beaming.

"Daniel, this is like, the best meet-cute I've ever heard. I'm shaking." And she was. The idea of Dan finding a man to share his life with and being happy filled her with such jittery excitement that she could barely contain herself.

"We've gone on two dates, not including the one at Maccas – one on the weekend and then one last night."

"Aw, why were you waiting to tell me?! I was blabbing about my situation at dinner on Monday. I feel like a total dick now. You must have been itching to say something!"

"I was, I was – but Joel was too obsessed with that bracelet for me to get a word in, and I was also waiting to make sure I was sure about him. And I am sure now." Dan couldn't wipe the smile off his face. It made Kirra feel even more lightheaded than the bottle of bubbles they'd drained.

"But you picked David?" he asked. "And gave Ben the bracelet back?"

"Yep, I did."

Kirra had been trying not to think too much about Ben, and luckily hadn't been called in to do much more work with Guerír since returning the gift. When she was in on something, she was all in. But she had been contemplating Paul's warning about what being in a relationship really meant, letting your partner see *everything.*

Kirra didn't know what to expect with what she had begun with David. She knew she didn't want to feel as helplessly in love with David as she had with Him; how stupid that sort of love had made her. She wanted a relationship like what David had described, but she didn't want to lose herself like she had when she was younger.

That couldn't happen again.

That wouldn't happen again.

Chapter 37

Kirra, fifteen years old

Chris had gone cool on her, and Kirra was distraught.

Their conversations about what they 'were' to one another were never specific, just that he really liked her and she really liked him. She had maintained enough of her dignity not to tell him she loved him – yet.

He started replying slower, and he and Nick signed up for a gym so she couldn't watch them work out at her house anymore. One afternoon when Chris was dropping Nick back, they were propped on the bonnet of Chris' car, smoking and chatting. Kirra, to her shame, had snuck and hid behind her father's parked car in the carport to eavesdrop.

Nick asked Chris if he was going to message Sarah back, saying she had seemed really keen on him at the party they were at last night. Kirra was anticipating he would say no, that he was seeing someone, so when she heard him say, "Yeah maybe, she was pretty hot," she thought she might die. Nick said he should text her. They talked for a little while longer, then Chris drove off.

Kirra was infuriated and texted him immediately.

"Who the fuck is Sarah?"

"What?"

"Sarah, I heard you and Nick talking about a Sarah?"

"She's just a friend of ours don't stress baby"

"When am I going to see you again, it's been ages??"

"How about I come pick you up later tonight?"

Kirra's heart had slowed down a bit.

While his response about Sarah had been non-committal and vague, he wanted to see her *tonight*. Her heart had picked up its pace again over arranging the meetup. She had no alibi, and it would be a proper jailbreak from her house, which was incredibly risky. She thought it over for a grand total of forty-five seconds and texted him back

"Yeah ok, what time?"

Kirra slid into the passenger seat of his car at midnight. She had risked breaking her neck shimmying out of her second-storey window and onto the carport roof and made a hard landing on the ground that scraped up her shins. He leant over and kissed her, and all thoughts of Sarah evaporated from her mind.

He drove her to a bushland area a short drive from where she lived to 'show her the stars'.

They pulled up at a secluded lookout. He hopped out of the car and ran around to open her door, like a gentleman. The clearing was lit by the full moon, bright enough that their bodies cast shadows on the grassy hill. She hopped out, and he pulled back the soft cover of the tray of his ute. He had furnished it with blankets and pillows. There was a small esky in the corner that he opened and fished two cans of rum and cola out of.

They sat on the edge of the lowered tailgate and sipped their drinks while talking about the beautiful evening. The stars were twinkling, and the distant lights of the city on the horizon made the night feel magical. The rum, her first drink ever, was making Kirra feel lightheaded. She felt a warmth trickle over her as she rested her head on Chris' shoulder. She was the luckiest girl in the world – her friends at school were making out with pimply boys with Milo-stain moustaches down at the skate park while she was here, in the woods, staring up at the stars with a man.

"You still haven't got your period yet hey?"

The question jolted her back to Earth.

"Um, no, not yet – why?" She was perplexed – was he going to break up with her because she was too young, physically? She panicked. She should have just lied and said she had started.

"Well, it's just uh, I totally forgot to get condoms, been so busy with work – but I really want to fuck you." He bit his lip and looked her up and down, like she was a meal and he was starving. "If you haven't got your period yet, I can't get you pregnant, and I would pull out anyway." He trailed off, looking away. "Nah forget it, I'm sorry – I'll remember them next time." He leant away from her.

Without thinking any further, she stood up in the tray of the ute. He twisted to look up at her.

She shimmied out of her jeans, top, bra and underwear. She was completely naked. She stepped over him and sat down in his lap. He kissed her, and she felt him grow underneath her. He picked her up, turned her around and placed her flat on the tray of the ute. He took off his belt, jeans and briefs, leaving his shirt on as he climbed on top of her.

He looked into her eyes and asked her, "Are you sure?"

"Yes, I'm sure."

She didn't know what she was sure about anymore, but she was sure she didn't want to say no to him.

With that, he pushed himself in her, skin to skin for the first time. He groaned louder than she had ever heard him before.

"God Kiz, your pussy is unbelievable. Does my cock feel good?" He pushed all the way into her, and the familiar dull pain in her lower abdomen was there almost instantly. His foul language, being inside her, she couldn't think. She felt as if she was on autopilot, overwhelmed with sensations and emotions.

"Yes," she whispered, frozen.

He told her to roll over, so she did. She crawled further into the tray of the ute and rolled over onto her stomach. He roughly propped her hips up, her behind poking up in the night's air, and planted his knees on the outside of her thighs. He reached down and wrapped one big hand around her throat and placed the other down beside her head for balance. She was pinned down, unable to move. He took her hard, his hand applying enough pressure to her throat to make her feel giddy and drunker than she already was.

She was surprised when, seemingly out of nowhere, he swore loudly in her ear as she felt him exploding inside of her.

He collapsed on her, panting. After a while, he pulled out of her, and she felt some of what he had left in her trickle out.

"Fuck, I'm so sorry, I couldn't help myself," he said, rushing to the cab of his ute to get her some tissues while still naked from the waist down. She turned over and looked up at him as he returned, her cheeks flushed, both of them glistening with sweat. He handed her the tissues, and she attempted to clean herself up while he dressed himself.

He drove her home and told her that because she hadn't got her period yet there was no way she had to worry about getting pregnant and that he didn't 'have anything'. He said to be on the safe side, she should take a really hot shower, 'just in case'.

Kirra was in awe of how much he knew about, well, everything. Thoughts of Sarah from the Party couldn't be any further from her mind.

Kirra was a woman, in love with a man.

Chapter 38

Thursday night at The Wickham

Kirra and Dan had agreed to introduce each other to their new boyfriends at The Wickham for Trivia on Thursday. She had been dying of excitement at the prospect of meeting Ned, and of Dan meeting David. Kirra arrived as Dan and David texted that they were almost there, so she ordered the table some sangria jugs. As she was placing them down, a tall, tanned Greek-god-of-a-man cautiously approached her.

"Hi, you wouldn't be Kirra, would you?"

Kirra was gobsmacked by the piercing green eyes looking back at her from under thick, dark brows. "Ah, you must be Ned!" She reached out and shook his hand, not wanting to be too casual or familiar with a kiss on the cheek, but Ned wrapped her in a huge hug instead. Dan was a hugger too. He pulled away and smiled broadly. The guy had a jawline you could cut your finger on and the most perfectly manicured stubble she had ever seen. To put it lightly, he was fucking gorgeous.

"Dan's told me so much about you. I've been so keen to meet you."

"Same, Ned. Same."

Kirra's best friend and boyfriend arrived at the same time, chatting when they walked in. They had bumped into each other walking down the street and, upon recognising each other, walked the rest of the way together.

Kirra had forewarned David that Daniel was the most magnetic person in the world. If you had any secrets you wanted kept, avoid looking into his eyes; they were like kryptonite.

Daniel had one of those faces that made everyone spill their innermost fears and desires to him without realising or meaning to. Kirra had seen it a million times: gentle-giant Daniel cleaning a random girl's mascara up for her while consoling her about whatever it was she needed consoling about, three other tear-streaked females waiting their turn in line to be 'fixed' too. He never made you feel bad about it afterwards either.

Dan had fixed Kirra up about a four thousand times since 2011, at least.

True to form, when Daniel and David got to the table, Daniel was suggesting that David's sister might have borderline personality disorder. He said he should give her a break, even though it's hard, and that David shouldn't shy away from being involved in his nephew's lives just because of the challenges he has with their mother.

They had been talking for *five minutes*. Daniel has one of those faces.

Daniel and David joined Ned and Kirra, and the four of them got to the serious business of drinking their drinks and waiting for trivia to start.

Kirra, normally confident and chatty around people she knew, struggled with new people in general. She felt stuck between worlds – some groups struggled with how much she swore, whereas others found her topics of interest too stuck up. So, she had a system. She would normally observe for a while and insert herself in the conversation in a way that made her seem social enough without exposing her real personality, but that was an exhausting balancing act.

Hanging out together this evening, however, was instantly fun and easy. Ned was hilarious and David could talk to anyone, so the conversation flowed effortlessly between the two couples.

Dan and Kirra had boyfriends at the same time. The thought made her squeal internally.

"So is Ned short for Edward or Edmund?" Kirra asked Ned, who she had noted hadn't been able to keep his hands off Dan the entire time. He always had a hand on a shoulder or a leg, or he was leaning into him.

"Uh, Dan doesn't even know this – but it's actually short for Neptune."

"Fuck off, that's too cool! How am I only just hearing this now?" Dan was incredulous but smiling back at him. Goddamn they looked good together.

"It hadn't come up yet, I suppose. My brother Marty is actually Mars, and my sister Venny is Venus."

"Those are some *hectic* names," Kirra ventured in a slight accent, testing the waters.

"Fully hectic," Ned returned in a far less subtle accent, grinning.

Trivia was hosted by a fabulous queen who was inexplicably dressed as a huge, sequined turtle, and their table dominated. David had all the geography and sports questions covered; Ned, an avid reader, was across literature and world history; and Dan and Kirra handled all things entertainment with their encyclopaedic knowledge of pop culture.

The group handed their papers to the host and downed the last of their drinks.

David nestled in beside Kirra and kissed her neck. She leaned back into him, relishing the touch. She resisted the urge to breathe him in, as badly as she wanted to, or kiss him back. She didn't trust herself not to get carried away and wanted to maintain some semblance of decency in public. She thought the risk of being seen out at night with David at The Wickham was minimal, but then again, Brisbane was a very small place. Although who was she kidding? Blind Freddy could see that the four of them were clearly on a double date.

Ned and Dan popped up to the bar for more drinks, David and Kirra declining another round.

"I really like Dan. Ned seems great too," David said, face slightly flushed, his eyes roving over Kirra's face, from her eyes to her mouth and back again.

"It's kind of hard not to like Dan, and I agree. Ned seems lovely. I'm so happy for him. Both of them."

She was sure she was mirroring David's slightly drunk, hungry look back at him.

"Are you happy for yourself, Kirra McNamara?" he asked, tucking her hair back behind her ear.

"I'm very happy, D W," she trailed off, and he leant in and met her lips with his. She couldn't resist the pull any longer. He cradled her head with one of his hands and kissed her slowly. She moaned, unable to help herself.

"Get a room you two."

Kirra's eyes snapped open, and her heart plummeted. It wasn't Dan or Ned teasing them.

James, the receptionist from KM, smirked across the table at them, slinking away before either of them could say anything back. Knowing him, he had probably snapped a picture before he had announced his presence. The pair looked at each other, eyes wide with shock.

Ned and Daniel returned to the table.

"Jesus, what's wrong guys? Are you okay?" Dan plonked their drinks down and Ned mirrored his concerned look.

"James, the evil fucking twink from work, just busted David and I kissing. What the fuck!" Kirra had turned hysterical in an instant, words spilling out one after the other as they often did when she was spiralling.

This would be the third tantrum David had seen since she had met him less than three weeks ago. At least no one could accuse her of hiding her true colours.

"Kirra, relax, you're assuming he's going to report this, when he probably doesn't even care, he's not the anti-fraternisation police. It's going to be fine." David's voice was quiet and calm.

"You don't know him, David. He's vicious and thrives off the misery of others. This undergrad was doing work experience in our office, and he fished around her socials until he found a picture of her in this tiny bikini and sent it to Nathaniel. She had her placement finished, and it fucked her graduation date. She hadn't done anything to him! She was twenty! He's just a hateful bitch!"

Kirra had worked herself up. Her heart was pounding and her stomach churning. The warm buzz from the sangria and David's kiss had left her body and been replaced with icy dread.

She snapped down off her barstool and ran out of the pub. She dashed around the corner to the back street, which faced the loading zone of a supermarket. Kirra fished out her vape and started pacing along the narrow footpath.

She was aware of movement along the wall and saw David in her periphery, keeping his distance but close enough that she knew he was there. Great, now he knows I fucking vape too. She had been planning to quit before he knew she had the habit to begin with, but she supposed resolutions don't necessarily follow the order you make them in.

The path was otherwise empty, and it was quiet. She could hear her heartbeat in her eardrums and the sound of her feet scuffing along the ground. David stayed where he was as she started crying between drags on her pen.

"Fuck, fuck, fuck! He's going to tell Nathaniel, or worse, Ken. Nathaniel can obviously sack me, but he's too dumb to do it properly. Ken, on the other hand … he'll find a more sinister way of getting me out, finally." She was muttering to herself, sobbing, one hand on her pen, dragging on it incessantly, the other hand in a white-knuckled grip on the strap of her handbag. At the rate she was sucking on the vape, it would be empty in two minutes.

She hadn't looked up, instead focusing on the repetitive motion of her feet on the ground, the sound of her shoes, the drag on her pen, her grip on her handbag.

"Kirra," David quietly interrupted, but she kept pacing.

"I mean, I was going to leave anyway, maybe. Jeannine told me not to, but fuck that place. I wanted to leave on my terms, not after being blackmailed by some skinny little—"

"Kirra." David took her by both elbows. She was rigid, locked in place, feeling as though her head might burst.

Without speaking, David took the vape pen from Kirra's hand and put it in her bag, which he then slipped from her shoulder and placed against the wall. She was sobbing, gasping, overheated in the sticky late-January humidity. He tucked her hair behind her ears again, unsticking the loose strands that had plastered themselves to her sweaty forehead. He took her hands and wrapped them around his lower back, hugging himself with her arms.

He then wrapped his arms around her and gently kissed her forehead. His lips felt cool against her hot skin. His breathing was slow and steady, his heartbeat a consistent thud against her chest. She breathed him in out of habit, the sickly-sweet taste and smell of her pen replaced with David's cologne and his skin — that addictive combination.

In time, she copied his breathing, inhaling and exhaling when he did, her mouth closing so she could focus on regaining oxygen for her overworked, overstimulated brain. When she was able to breathe through her nose and her heart rate had slowed, he spoke.

"I'm not going to tell you it's going to be alright, but I can say that we're going to be alright. *You* will be alright, Kirra. I see you sorting shit out for other people every day, I mean, you just got Ned's tax lodged for him during trivia?"

She chuckled, sniffling.

Ned couldn't figure out how to get into his MyGov app and had accepted that he would get a fine for not doing his taxes, but Kirra had got him logged back in, checked over his details and lodged it for him while their trivia scores were being tallied up. They had won, too. Kirra had registered the bar tab coupons in Daniel's hand when he and Ned had returned to their table just after James had busted her and David.

"Kerry told me you helped get her dad into a better care facility after she couldn't manage it on her own. Paul told me you got a colleague compensation after they got injured on a work trip but were too embarrassed to tell anyone despite living in pain every day. You're so bloody smart, McNamara, but that's not why you're going to be okay."

Kirra looked into his eyes, trying to believe the beautiful words he was saying.

"You always show up for other people, and when you finally show up for yourself, nothing's going to stop you."

Chapter 39

Garden-variety blackmail

David hadn't stayed the night at hers.

He had gotten her back to Paddington and collected Gus from Geoff's while she showered, tucking them in and kissing them both goodnight. Kirra couldn't remember the last time someone had tucked her in, maybe her mum when she was in primary school. When she awoke the following morning, a plan started coalescing in her mind.

Kirra had been tempted to work from home to avoid James, but David's words from the night before buoyed her into the office not a minute before eight-thirty, several hours after she normally started. There was no getting past James; he sat sentinel on his throne in front of the elevator doors. After the lift slowed to a stop, the doors opened and she strode towards where he sat.

"Good morning, James. How are you on this beautiful Friday?" she beamed at him.

"Fine, thank you Jane, and yourself?" he offered in a most collegial tone, filing his nails. His platinum blond hair was perfectly styled as usual, swept up and off his face without a strand out of place. His flawless glass-looking skin shone under the downlights of reception as he fixed her with a knowing smirk.

"Great, thanks for asking. You have a super day."

***

"Hi Mary!" Kirra tapped on the HR manager's door.

Mary looked nervously to Kirra. "Oh, Jane, how can I help?" Most of Kirra's interactions with HR had been unpleasant. Every time Ken and Nathaniel had come for Kirra's conduct in the past, they had needed to involve HR, and each time Kirra had walked away without so much as a warning given her unrivalled knowledge of employment law, consistently high billings and positive performance reviews. If my performance is so bad, then why haven't I heard about it until just now?

Ultimately, unless she was accused of harming a colleague or not performing to the standard expected of her, it was hard to dole out any sort of disciplinary action. They had given up after a while. How many times can you be dragged in to a meeting with HR because some rodent dobbed on you for saying cunt in the lunchroom or heard you throw up in the bathroom, really?

Kirra knew she had been playing with fire recently with Ben and David. The steady increase in how much she partied since turning thirty had sometimes blurred the lines between her professional and personal life. She had often wondered when her luck was going to run out, but it sure as shit wasn't going to be today.

Kirra stepped into the office, closed the door behind her, and sat down opposite Mary.

"I need a favour."

Mary was immaculately groomed and in her mid-fifties with grown children. She was moderately competent, in Kirra's opinion. Kirra had overheard her on multiple occasions talking to Ken or Patrick about their investment properties and how much they'd increased their tenants' rent over the years and, obviously, stories of people they went to school with. High school. Still having that conversation in their fifties and sixties made Kirra's eyes roll all the way back in her head.

Mary had put her daughters through St Margaret's then 'college' at UQ. Living as a boarder at a university only a short City Cat ride from where their parents lived formed a big part of the culture of Brisbane's elite. Mary couldn't handle the thought of her beloved daughters being *day rats*, driving their VW Golfs to university then back home again that same evening.

Her mansion at Ascot had been paid off for years, and she held a Hermes scarf up to her mouth when Ryan, the high-vis clad gentleman that frequented the ground level of their building, offered her a copy of The Big Issue on her way into work.

All this was to say that Mary could go fuck herself.

"A favour?" Mary looked concerned, a slight tic in one corner of her forehead that the botox hadn't reached a clear tell of her anxiety at Kirra's willing presence in her office. She was normally hauled in like a prisoner.

"A favour," Kirra repeated, smiling as sweetly as she could. Her face was going to crack with all the fakeness. She didn't know how normal people did it. "I need Mark Woodroff's emergency contact information. His wife's number, please."

Mary's eyes bulged out of her head. "You know I can't give that to you. It would be immediate dismissal for me if I did, and it should be immediate dismissal for you just for asking."

Her pallid skin grew a shade redder. Kirra studied her closely. She had taken a huge risk asking for Mark's number, but she knew now without a doubt that her inkling was correct. Mary was fucking him.

"Well then, how am I going to let Mrs Woodroff know her husband is having a workplace affair? Mark's not on social media, and I can't find anyone by his wife's name either. I'm really worried about her, I value the sanctity of marriage so much—"

"What the fuck is this about, Kirra?" Mary snapped, calling Kirra by her actual name. She had access to Kirra's identity documents as part of her employment contract and knew Jane was a pseudonym.

"No need to swear, Mary, and I don't go by that name, thank you," Kirra replied calmly.

Mary was furious; Kirra could see a tendon bulging in her neck. This woman had the worst poker face Kirra had ever seen. She had her on the ropes.

"Okay, never mind. I don't need Mark Woodroff's emergency contact information, but I am going to need Tony's please."

Mary went from looking nervous to furious to completely baffled in a space of two minutes. At this rate, she'll need to bring her next botox injection forward a few weeks.

Kirra figured she was giving Mary a choice; deny her again and risk Kirra outright accusing her of having an affair with Mark, or being done with this interaction and giving her Tony's wife's number, violating privacy laws and risking dismissal. Kirra knew it was a long shot, her plan had a lot of moving parts and it was risky, but it was all she could come up with in the short time since James had busted her and David. She figured she had something on Mary and had to twist it to her advantage, otherwise it was just sitting and waiting for James to draw first blood. Kirra could see the cogs working in Mary's mind, weighing up what was more important: her marriage or her job.

Mary did the maths quickly. Her job was merely something to keep her busy, not a real means of income, her investment properties did that for her. But the loss of her marriage due to infidelity would result in the loss of something far greater – her social standing. She would never be able to set foot in Bistro C in Noosa again.

"Low-life fucking bitch." Mary lost her composure, unleashing on Kirra while she opened her laptop and typed in Tony D'Linio's personal details. "Scum, slut," she was hissing as she brought up the screen then grabbed a pen and Post-it note. "Piece of low-life fucking trash." She scribbled down the number and thrust it at Kirra, who didn't take it from her, peering at it instead.

"I'll need her first name, and that last digit is a little tricky to read. Could you write it again?"

Kirra stared coldly back at Mary.

The HR manager's words did nothing to her. That's the good part of having extended bouts of exceptionally low self-esteem – if someone says something foul to you that you've already said to yourself a thousand times, it doesn't sting as much. Hearing Ken had talked shit about her to David had hurt, as she was more concerned about David's opinion of her at that time. Mary calling her a slut was more amusing at this point. Kirra probably gave her husband a lap dance or two back in the day.

Mary's eye was twitching as she did what she was told, rewriting the number and putting 'Isabella' next to it.

"Mary, I honestly mean you no ill will. This won't get back to you, and I'll never ask for a favour like this again, I swear," Kirra said, her tone genuine. She took the Post-it, shoving it in her pocket as she stood. "Thanks."

"You're welcome." Mary glared up at Kirra from her desk.

Part two of Kirra's plan was a little trickier and required faith that another inkling she had was true. Mark and Tony were both senior partners at their firm and, from her years of observing them, she intuitively knew they were both unfaithful men.

Mark had three phones: one for work, his personal and another one. The phones were never together at the same time, but Kirra noticed everything. They were identical iPhones, all the same model and colour. His personal one had a case on it while his work one did not. In a briefing, Mark would take his phone out of his pocket and place it face down on the table. Kirra had noticed a prominent scratch on what she thought to be the work phone one day that had miraculously disappeared the next day then reappeared at different intervals.

The inconsistency had been bugging her. She noticed one day he was texting on the scratched work phone and saw Mary picking up her phone at around the same time. It was almost imperceptible, but she saw the look the pair exchanged. The scratched iPhone was his burner that he used to communicate with Mary. That's how she knew they were fucking.

While this was gross, Kirra wasn't going to do anything with the information. However, Mary had access to the phone number she actually needed. She needed to get in touch with Tony's wife directly and discreetly. It wasn't a scratch on a phone that had revealed Tony's infidelity; Kirra had sniffed it out, literally, another way.

Kirra bought a sim card, popped it in her phone and texted Isabella D'Linio the following:

Isabella, your husband has a sugar baby who he fucks on a Wednesday, pay close attention to him when he comes home next week and check his bank statements if you can – A Concerned Third Party.

She snapped the sim in half, not waiting on a reply.

She had done all she could do, and now she had to play the waiting game to see if Isabella would take the bait.

Kirra didn't feel good about what she had done, but she didn't feel entirely bad either. Mary, Mark and Tony were cheating on their spouses. Kirra had a temporary pang of remorse – maybe people who had been married a long time did this. She was thirty-four and in her first adult relationship, so maybe she was the misguided one and this is just what normal people did.

Her inner sense of justice ultimately prevailed. She felt like she had done the right thing, just maybe not for the right reasons.

Chapter 40

The Guide

The weekend was looming, her first full weekend with a boyfriend.

Boyfriend sounded too young, but partner was weird because that was her job title and manfriend sounded like she was paying an escort to keep her company. Boyfriend was the least gross out of all the options.

She had been debating whether to invite him to Bree's birthday down in Byron on Saturday.

While Kirra wanted to introduce David to Bree, Bree was unfortunately married to her brother. The idea of Nick saying something foul to David about Kirra so soon after they had started dating sent her mind racing. David had been nothing but upfront from the outset about his feelings for her, but if he received another warning about her, first Ken then Nick, could those feelings change? Her dad would be there too, so it would be a full *hey this is my boyfriend, David, we started dating officially on Monday* to her immediate, living family.

She wondered if David would find it flattering or desperate to meet them so soon.

"I'd love to come." David was thrilled at the invitation, beaming at her with a smile so wide Kirra wanted to reach out and touch the crinkled skin under his eyes. She delivered the invitation when he came to hers after work that afternoon, bringing with him pizza and red wine.

Kirra had offered to come to his, but his apartment complex didn't allow dogs, not even as visitors, and he wanted to see Gus too.

Kirra was instantly relieved. He didn't seem at all weirded out by the timing.

"Seems like a good time to mention I booked you a seat just in case for next weekend down to Sydney. It's my dad's 70th, and we're throwing him a party, I was hoping you'd want to come … if you didn't have anything else on."

Kirra's relief at David not thinking she was asking too much for this weekend was instantly replaced by apprehension about meeting his parents the following one. She clearly couldn't use the excuse that it was too soon as that was hypocrisy, but she didn't know if she was ready to meet any more new people, particularly people she desperately wanted to like her. Things had gone so well with Ned last night – she wasn't sure if she could expect a similarly warm reception from David's parents.

"They'll love you; you have nothing to be nervous about. I really want you to come," David said, his knowing eyes doing their normal MRI on her brain.

"Please stop reading my mind. I'm nervous they'll think I'm scum, but I'll come down anyway because I'm a big girl."

"Please stop calling yourself scum," David said calmly, sipping his wine.

"Trash, then," she said, taking a bite of pizza.

"Trash is slightly better than scum, I guess. Can I just say you're the most highly intelligent, stunningly beautiful, hilariously funny piece of trash I've ever met?"

She considered his words for a moment. It must be exhausting for David, and Dan too, hearing her talk so lowly of herself so often. She knew that if she were in their shoes, listening to either of them speak ill of themselves, she would want to slap them.

"Thanks D W, you're right. I am a highly impressive piece of trash." She smiled back at him. "I'll have to give you a briefing on Nick and Dad, and all of Nick's cockhead friends who'll be there too. I can't be bothered thinking about it tonight though. Remind me on the drive down."

"That won't be necessary – it's all in The Guide," David said in a matter-of-fact tone, refilling her glass.

Kirra paused, slice suspended in the air.

"The Guide?"

"The Guide," he repeated, screwing the lid back on the bottle.

"Ah, are you going to make me beg to know what The Guide is?"

"A guide Dan wrote for your future partner. He told me I could tell you about it but to keep it confidential as you're not the intended audience. He was going to explain it last night but didn't get a chance when the James thing happened."

Kirra was gobsmacked. A written guide, about her, by Dan, given to David.

"Is it like, a book – have you read it?" Kirra asked, still stunned.

"It's more of a pamphlet. I read it last night after putting you and Gus to bed." David scooped up the pizza box, the now empty bottle of wine and the plates and continued to Kirra's kitchen to clean up. Kirra followed him, glass of wine in hand.

"And?"

"It's great. I mean, I would have figured a lot of it out on my own in time, but I appreciate the background info and context."

He was cleaning the dishes, his back to Kirra, speaking as if The Guide was the most normal, everyday thing someone could be handed by their new partner's best friend upon meeting them for the first time.

"Can you tell me anything about it? What's it say?"

"I'm not meant to. Just tips and advice on how I can make you happy, what you need, things like that."

"Sounds like the instruction guide you get with a packet of Sea Monkeys. Does it have how often you're to feed me in there?"

"Every three to four hours, and not after midnight or you'll turn into a gremlin." David had cleaned the dishes and placed them in the rack to dry.

He turned around and leaned against the sink, gripping the edge of the bench. His eyes roved up and down Kirra in that piercing, hungry way that set her senses to high alert. Her thoughts of The Guide, the garden-variety blackmail she had engaged in at work, the incriminating knowledge James had, all of it faded away to nothing when David fixed her with that gaze.

"Put that glass of wine down and come here," he commanded, his eyes boring into hers without a hint of a smile on his face. Without hesitation, she did as he bade, placing the glass down and crossing in a few short steps to stand in front of him. He still had his hands on the bench, his eyes not leaving hers.

"Take your top off." He wasn't smiling, and his voice was stern, serious.

Kirra was entranced and, to her astonishment, turned on beyond words almost immediately. Just as it had happened on the phone, he instructed and she followed. It was significantly sexier in real life.

"Did The Guide tell you to boss me around?" she asked, a little breathlessly, pulling her top over her head and standing in front of David in her kitchen in her bra and tiny gym shorts.

"No, just had a hunch that you'd like it. Is it okay? Do you?" he asked in his normal voice. "I don't have like a domination kink or anything, so if you're not—"

"I like it, a lot," she cut him off. "Keep going." Her heart was fluttering.

He switched back to the role he was playing moments before, bringing his hand up to hold her firmly by the throat. He tilted her head back and stared down at her.

"Get on your knees, now," he said, suddenly letting her go and returning his hands to the edge of the bench. She slid to the floor immediately, looking up at him through her eyelashes.

"Take your bra off."

She couldn't really tell if he was getting as aroused as she was by this, and she honestly didn't care. She was wholly caught up in following his instructions, the incessant chatter in her head silenced as she removed her bra and awaited his next command.

"Squeeze your tits for me."

Kirra had never heard him say the word *tits* before, and her mouth went dry. She grabbed her breasts, massaging them when her eyes snagged on his growing erection.

"Keep your eyes up here," he snapped at her, and she gasped at his volume. His eyes quickly flared in alarm, and he whispered, "Sorry, is that oka—"

"Shut up, don't stop, please," she muttered urgently back up at him. The way David got her consent was sexy, checking in to make sure she was into everything he did, but this dominant version of him was sending her insane. She was sure she was panting. "I'll tell you no if I don't want to," she got out in a breathy whisper.

He got the message.

"Play with your nipples, and don't look away from me again," he ordered her, eyes roving over her face, her chest. She did as she was told, a little moan escaping from her throat as she rolled each of her nipples between her thumb and forefingers.

"Be quiet. I'll tell you when you can make a noise."

Kirra was sure she had soaked through her underwear and shorts; his voice was that fucking hot. She felt possessed. She silently played with her breasts and nipples, her pussy a steady throb, eagerly anticipating what he would make her do next.

"You've been a good girl. You can suck my cock now."

Kirra had to stifle her excitement at finally being able to touch him. She rose up higher while kneeling and took him out of his shorts. He was rock hard, and she hungrily lapped at the bead of precum before taking him into her mouth. He was just as aroused as she was, it would appear. Maybe he did have a domination kink after all and just couldn't admit it out loud. She held the base of his dick while she circled her tongue around the head of his cock.

"Put your hands behind your back, only use your mouth," he groaned, roughly gathering her hair in his hands. She did as she was told, grabbing her wrist with her other hand and placing them both behind her. He tugged firmly on her scalp, putting her head where he wanted her. The pressure he had on her hair was perfect, and she thought she could come right there and then.

He started thrusting, lightly at first, using her head for his own pleasure. She closed her eyes for a second before he barked at her to keep her eyes open, lightly pulling on her hair in warning.

His thrusts grew rougher and deeper, never quite choking her. She could feel how hard he was in her mouth, down her throat, and she thought she'd combust.

He suddenly withdrew, and she took down a gasp of air.

"Get up," he got out through gritted teeth, eyes glazed with lust. On shaky legs, she returned to where she had been standing a moment before. "Go and get a condom and come back here."

She all but ran to her room and was back before him in almost an instant, the packet in her trembling hands.

"Put it on me, take the rest of your clothes off, then put both your hands there." He gestured to the bench beside where he was leaning. She did exactly as she was told, ripping the condom out, rolling it onto him and throwing the wrapper on the floor. She shimmied out of her shorts and underwear, kicked them off and turned to grip the edge of the kitchen bench. He stood behind her and reached around her front and rubbed her clit, leaning down to whisper into her ear.

"Do you want me to fuck you from behind?" His voice was sinisterly quiet, and Kirra could barely form words. He slid his hands down further and dipped a single finger inside her. He quietly swore under his breath, losing his domineering façade for a moment. "Holy shit, you're dripping. You do really like this" he said, sounding mildly surprised.

"Yes, I want you to fuck me from behind," she choked out, his finger still inside her.

Not wanting to lose the momentum he'd gained, he switched his tone back to how it had been a moment before. He quickly added another finger, thrusting it into her, deep and slow. "Beg me," he whispered into her ear, pumping his fingers in and out of her.

She could hear how wet she was, feel how hard he was pushing into her back. "Please, David, please fuck me," she almost cried out. He withdrew his fingers, and seconds later ran his cock up and down her pussy, slowly inserting himself in her as she whimpered with pleasure.

"Oh fuck," he groaned as he was fully inside her.

He pushed her down on the bench so her breasts were flat against the countertop and hoisted one of her legs up to rest along the bench too. Her head was almost hitting the splashback, and he roughly grabbed both her arms and held them behind her back. She had one tiptoe holding her to the kitchen floor while she was spread, bent over and pinned down.

He started pumping slowly into her, one hand on her hip and the other pinning her arms together. Her eyes rolled back in her head as he set a slow, steady pace. She croaked out a "faster", and he squeezed tighter on her arms in warning.

"Don't speak unless I tell you to. I'll fuck you how you need to be fucked." The demanding tone in his voice wasn't as strong as it had been before, but he was still committed to the cause. Kirra let out a whimper of protest, and he slowed down even more as punishment.

"You think you want me to fuck you faster, but your body's telling me you want it slow and hard." He punctuated the last word with a deep thrust that had Kirra drooling on the bench top.

He withdrew almost all of the way out then pushed back into her deep and slow. She had to bite her lip to keep from screaming. She was completely powerless to stop him as he gained pace, angling himself to hit her G-spot perfectly. She couldn't tell if she was about to come or coming already; the waves of all-consuming pleasure combing over her body were growing increasingly close together and intensifying.

She felt the waves of pleasure crash together and her inner walls clench around him as she climaxed, the leg she had on the ground buckling. David caught her and supported her weight, both of his hands on her hips.

"Come for me, come all over my dick." His pounding turned vicious, uneven, and he slapped into her with everything he had. Kirra's body was limp and her mind was mush. Seemingly out of nowhere, another orgasm erupted out of her. She let out a cry as he pummelled into her, slapping her arse and squeezing her cheek hard enough to leave a bruise as he finished shortly after her.

She lay there, crumpled over the bench for a moment longer before she slowly regained control of her legs. He withdrew from her and lowered her down to the floor, turning her around as he did. When her eyes could focus again, she took in the expression on his face. It was a mixture of satisfaction and surprise.

"Alright Mr I-don't-have-a-domination-kink, what was that?" she joked, her voice trembling. Her legs were still shaky, and he held her in place by her upper arms.

He was drinking in the satisfied look on her face.

"I don't think that's my kink."

Kirra felt like she was looking at a different man, a different layer she'd excavated. She wondered if he was seeing a different layer of her too.

"I think my kink is giving you exactly what you need."

Chapter 41

Byron

Kirra was glad David was driving as she didn't trust herself enough to focus on the drive to her brother's house in Byron. She was talking incessantly, flicking back and forth between songs without letting one finish and asking David questions then interrupting him before he had the chance to reply. She was giving herself the shits but couldn't stop. David humoured her, clearly seeing she was panicked about him meeting her family.

"Did you already know you liked being dominated, or was that new last night?" David asked, eyes on the road in a perfectly conversational tone, interrupting Kirra's monologue.

She had been talking, ad nauseam, about the attention to detail the creator of Breaking Bad had put into the show. Apparently there had been an hour-long meeting with the crew discussing the exact shade of red Skylar's toenail polish had to be for just one scene. Kirra was silenced for a second, her mind cast back to the kitchen bench.

"Um, I don't know." She really liked how direct David was, it was one of her favourite things about him, but when she didn't feel 'on', it made her feel vulnerable to making a fool of herself, like she might not be able to respond as eloquently.

"I like it, you know, a little rough sometimes." She wanted to be this confident, sex-positive woman who could openly talk about pleasure, but her reality was that she still felt some shame around what she liked.

"Like being choked and spanked?" he asked, nodding along.

"Yeah, I guess." She was sweating like a whore in church. "Did you like it? Bossing me around?"

He considered the question a moment.

"I didn't like being rude to you. But, looking at you, how into it you were," he trailed off, looking over to her for a second before putting his focus back to driving, "I really, *really* liked that part. I would do anything to see you like that again. Knowing that I'm the only one you look at like that makes me feel like the luckiest guy in the world, like I've won a secret lottery."

Kirra swallowed; she could hear the shakiness in his voice. Giving her something she needed, badly, gave him what he needed. She hadn't planned on turning up to Bree's party horny, but here she was, five minutes from their front gate and ready to pounce on David. She tried to snap out of it.

"And you promise there wasn't any weird psychosexual shit in The Guide that gave you the idea?"

"No, nothing at all like that," David chuckled, shaking his head as if to clear the impure thoughts he'd just been having. "Dan just mentioned how in your head you get, which I'd already noticed. I see you spend all day telling people what to do and I wondered if you'd like a break from thinking to focus on just feeling."

Kirra sat quietly, thinking about how much he was trying to get to know her and figure out how she worked.

"Why don't you like the lift?" she blurted out.

"Huh?"

"The lift, at work, you don't like it. Are you afraid of heights?"

Kirra saw David's hands grip the steering wheel tighter as he faked a smile and gave a nonchalant shake of his head.

"I'm not a huge fan of enclosed spaces," he said.

Kirra wondered why he wasn't telling her the truth, but then again, she wasn't fully telling him the truth about everything yet either, she supposed.

She probably should have left it there.

"And Patrick, you don't like him." She registered an almost imperceptible flinch at the mention of the white-haired partner who floated alongside Ken like a dementor around the office.

"That's interesting you say that," David replied.

"Yeah, why's that?"

"Well, interesting you'd noticed, firstly, but interesting you interpreted whatever you saw as me not liking him."

"Maybe dislike isn't the right word. I can see that he," Kirra searched for the words, "disturbs your peace."

David was quiet for a moment.

"Patrick's known me a long time, since I was a kid actually. I went to school with his son."

"Oh yeah, you don't think he takes you seriously as an adult, is that it?" Kirra said.

"Yeah, maybe something like that."

Kirra could see that this conversation was done for today, and with good timing, as they were almost at her brother's house.

Nick's architect-designed home was nestled in the Byron hinterland on a compound of almost three acres. It was a gated fortress that backed on to a dense, green jungle atop even more acres of rolling green hills. Bree had poured her heart and soul into the landscaping and gardens and was constantly declining interviews with style magazines as she and Nick valued their privacy more than showing off.

David's Mercedes rolled up to the electric gates, which opened a moment later. David pulled up and ran around to Kirra's side to open her door before she'd had a chance to reach down and grab her handbag. After she was out, he ducked around to the boot and grabbed the drinks they had brought for the party so that Kirra's hands were free to carry Bree's gift.

Kirra's heart was pounding so hard she could almost hear it. She felt like she could faint at a moment's notice. She had imagined, in detail, the myriad of things Nick could say to David. He could humiliate and embarrass her so easily, and she would be backed into a corner with nowhere to run in his big, dumb, beautiful house.

They walked through the huge front double doors and followed the sounds of voices and music to the back patio, a sprawling undercover space where Bree entertained her guests. Kirra smiled at a few familiar faces, her lips trembling with nerves, when out from nowhere she was gripped from behind around her waist by two very tanned arms.

"Kizraaatttttt," Bree squealed, picking Kirra up off the ground and jumping up and down.

Bree was a few centimetres shorter than Kirra but crazy fit — in the useful way too, not just aesthetically. Kirra still held Bree's gift in her hand, and David stood off to the side, arms full. Bree put Kirra down, and she placed the gift on the nearby table before wrapping her arms tightly around her friend's petite frame.

"It's so good to see you, Cheesy." Kirra squeezed her tightly.

Bree stepped back and beamed at Kirra before acknowledging David.

"And who's this good-looking rooster?" Bree said, walking to David and jutting out her hand.

"I'm David. Nice to meet you, Bree. Kirra's told me so much about you." David rearranged the bottles in his arms so he could shake her hand then smiled his most charming smile.

"Not the bit about me shitting myself at Big Day Out, I hope," Bree grinned back at him.

David snorted a laugh, clearly taken aback.

"No, she hadn't mentioned that."

Bree was tiny and bronzed with flowing blonde hair and dressed entirely in white. She didn't exactly look like someone who shat themselves at festivals.

"You know our Kizzy's a one-of-a-kind girl here, and she's *never* brought a guy to meet us before. You must be special." Bree beamed at David, who looked over to Kirra briefly with a shy smile. "I like you already Daveo, come on, come meet everyone." She grabbed him by the arm and led him out further to the patio. Kirra nervously followed. She always knew Bree was going to give her new boyfriend a warm welcome.

Kirra, however, was still terrified.

She scanned the room and saw him leaning against a post, staring as the sun set over the beautiful landscape his wife had built for him. Nick was unusually alone, although Kirra eyed several of his mates spread around the patio, down near the pool and hanging around the bar.

Nick's normal black T-shirt and jeans were replaced with a white button-down shirt that was opened obscenely low, showing off his heavily tattooed flesh, and a pair of shorts that Kirra could only describe as slutty.

He turned around and noticed her just as David came to her side. Nick approached them, and as he got to within abuse-hurling range, David thrust the bottle of very expensive tequila he'd bought for the party into Nick's hands.

Nick instinctively grabbed the bottle and looked down at it for a split second. While distracted, David took a step closer and wrapped Nick in a hug.

Kirra thought her heart might burst from her chest and scurry off into the bushes, *Alien* style.

A fucking hug? David's hug pinned Nick's free arm at his side, his other clutching at the uniquely shaped bottle. It would have been a humorous sight to an outsider, given that Nick was close to a foot taller than David and much, much broader. David stepped back and smiled broadly at Nick.

"So nice to meet you, Nick. I'm David."

Nick was clearly taken aback. He'd just been handed a bottle of tequila worth over three hundred dollars and hugged by a stranger.

Nick wasn't a hugger.

"Nice to meet you too," Nick grunted back at him. Kirra hadn't seen Nick for months other than when he had dragged her out of the club a few weeks ago, and she hadn't really taken in his appearance then. He looked even bigger than last time and had a new tattoo along his hairline. He looked down at Kirra.

"He looks just like your type."

"And what's the meant to mean?"

"He's got a pulse."

Nick looked back to David, who instinctively stepped closer to Kirra, placing his hand on her lower back. She couldn't picture David getting physical with anyone, let alone Nick, but she knew if he so much as looked sideways at her brother, he would kill him. And if he didn't, one of his equally huge mates would.

Before Kirra or David could retort, Nick looked over her shoulder, and his face transformed. His furrowed brow and tense shoulders released, and the straight line of his unsmiling mouth curved into huge grin that spanned the whole of his bearded face. Even though she hated him, he was objectively a very good-looking man when he smiled.

And he only ever smiled for one person.

Bree bounded up to him and wrapped her arms around his waist, burying her face in his chest before spinning around and facing Kirra and David.

A human shield.

Smart and beautiful, Kirra thought.

"Look how happy Kirra looks with Daveo. We're so happy for them, hey?" She looked up at Nick, and he glared back at Kirra. Bree's tiny elbow thrust back into Nick's sternum in a quick yet ferocious movement, winding him temporarily.

"Yeah, so happy," he wheezed.

"Let's go make some margaritas with this fancy tequila they've brought us so Kirra can introduce David to your dad," Bree said, leading away her hulking husband and winking back at Kirra.

Kirra let out a breath and turned to David. As far as interactions with her brother went, that wasn't too bad.

"He seems nice," David offered with raised eyebrows. "Remember, you get to meet my charming sister next weekend."

David pecked Kirra on the forehead and lightly rubbed her lower back before looking out over the landscape Nick had been admiring minutes prior.

"This place is amazing," David said. "You said Nick was an electrician?"

"Yeah."

"Hmmmmm."

"What's hmmmm?"

"Nothing, let's go find your dad."

***

Steve McNamara was manning the barbecue after having out-dadded Bree's father for the honour. Kirra approached him, and he immediately handed the tongs to a bald gentleman with a completely tattooed scalp that he had been chatting to. The goon looked relieved to be done talking to Steve, who could talk underwater without really saying anything.

"Kizzy!" Steve beamed, kissing Kirra on the cheek. "So good you made the drive down. Traffic okay for you? Took me three and a half bloody hours, Bruce Highway then the Pac," he trailed off. "Who's this then?" he said, acknowledging David, who had been patiently waiting to be introduced.

"I'm David, nice to meet you Steve." Dave shook his hand, and Steve unsubtly looked him up and down.

"Lovely to meet you, mate. We don't often meet Kirra's uh, friends."

"I'm lucky then I guess." David smiled back at him.

"And you're friends? You know, like our lovely Dan?"

Are you gay?

"Christ Dad could you be any less subtle? These are the sorts of questions you ask after the event, not during." Kirra rolled her eyes.

"Kirra and I just started dating. We work together too," David said.

"Another lawyer! Well, you won't find many of your folks around here. As I'm sure Kirra will tell you, we're all tradies."

Steve was wearing an old faded polo shirt stuffed into jeans he'd had since the nineties, and a pair of thongs: the black-and-white kind you get for two dollars. This was his 'dressed up' as he had on 'a collar and long pants'. David was wearing olive-green chinos, a Ralph Lauren button-down and leather boots. Kirra had told him he didn't need to dress up, but he genuinely didn't think he had.

"Kirra mentioned you're a chippy, how's that going?" David engaged Steven in benign chit-chat, and Kirra thought it was safe to leave them alone for a minute. David was a chatty guy too. Kirra thought she was a talker more than a chatter. If she found someone that matched her freak, so to speak, she could speak for hours and often ended up the centre of the party. But if it was talking for the sake of talking, she couldn't do it. It made her feel like she needed to peel out of her skin when the conversation would turn to the weather and traffic.

She scurried away and found a quiet spot down the hill from the main party, grabbing a beer on her way and tucking in somewhere secluded to vape. She was glad she had made the trip for Bree, who she knew appreciated it, but she had been beside herself with anxiety for hours, which had birthed an almighty headache.

She reclined against a macadamia tree and enjoyed the last of the beautiful sunset as it receded over the hillside. David was up there with her dad, and she was hiding down here, like a scared rat, bumping alcohol and nicotine into her blood system to cope with social anxiety. Fuck she could be a loser sometimes.

Aware she was chastising herself, she made the conscious decision to stop and take a minute to count all that she was grateful for instead.

David.

She had decided to open herself up for a relationship and this was the first one she got: a thoughtful, kind, sexy, funny, smart man who seemed to be quite infatuated with her too.

Hattie's little friend Harrison seemed like a nice kid, and she needed to trust that her goddaughter could look after herself in matters of love.

Daniel had a gorgeous boyfriend who seemed totally into him too.

There was much to be grateful for.

She decided to trudge back up the hill and rejoin the party. David was still animatedly chatting with her dad when she was approached by someone she hadn't seen in person in years but had very recently seen on the other side of a laptop screen.

"Tim! You're back!"

Kirra hugged one of the few of Nick's moron friends she had something of a soft spot for. He was softly spoken and permanently sunburned and he helped her dad out a lot around his house. He was a good guy.

"All thanks to you Kiz, you saved my arse." He hugged her back. "Nick's so lucky to have you for a sister."

"You go tell him that – he hates my fucking guts."

"He doesn't Kiz, he really doesn't." He looked into her eyes, then around to make sure no one else was listening. "Nick's always got your back, even if it doesn't look that way, and we know you've got ours too."

Kirra was intrigued by the way Tim said 'we'.

She had helped out Nick's mates a few times over the years when there had been small misunderstandings here and there, but she wouldn't have said she 'had their backs' by any means. She was also perplexed as to how Nick supposedly had hers; all he ever seemed to do was ignore her, abuse the shit out of her or drag her out of a club unannounced. How is that having someone's back?

"Thanks again for getting me out of Bali. I really appreciate it." He squeezed her in a tight hug again before shooting in a different direction, away from the party.

Once Kirra had found David, they mingled with some of Bree and Nick's friends. It was nice having someone to do the mingling with. David was a natural; it was genuinely impressive how he found common ground quickly and effortlessly with almost everyone. Kirra had unfortunately found herself in a conversation about soccer, or football as the group of guys kept referring to it, and she zoned out.

Her eyes roved the party, and she saw Bree carrying one of her friend's newborn babies around. The friend was letting her hair down and smashing margaritas, leaving Bree to bottle-feed the little bundle.

Kirra watched and her heart ached for how much she wanted Bree's dream to come true.

Bree had been drinking tonight. Kirra always closely watched her at any social function to see if she declined a beer or wine in the hopes that a happy announcement was imminent, but it never happened. Bree's golden hair fell down in front of her pixie-like face as she stared at the baby sleepily taking their bottle, and the longing in her eyes was enough to break Kirra's heart. The world's not fair, mate.

David and Kirra decided to head home around ten, declining Bree's repeat offers to stay the night in one of their many guest bedrooms. Steven had already passed out in one of them, trying to keep up with shots Nick's friends had goaded him into doing. Nick even shook David's hand as they left and offered Kirra a surly nod.

They were on their way home, the pair deeming the night a success.

"I didn't know you'd spent so much on that wanky bottle of tequila! And going in with a hug, did The Guide tell you to do that?"

"Absolutely not, it actually told me to avoid Nick at all costs if I could. I decided to go a little off-script there." David grinned at Kirra from the driver's seat. "Your dad's a lovely guy too, really easy to talk to. I think you'll love my parents as well – they're the nicest people on Earth."

"Should I try and hug Catherine?"

"No way. I may have risked hugging Nick, but you'd lose an arm if you tried that with her. You're also not a hugger, so it'd be out of character."

"How do you know I'm not a hugger. I'm a hugger! I hug you!"

"You hug, yes, but you're not a *hugger*. I can't elaborate any further."

Kirra laughed. She compared the light feeling in her body to the immense dread she felt driving down and decided the worry really hadn't been worth it. It never was.

She searched around for her lip balm in her bag when she felt something brush up against her hand.

"What the fuck is th—" She felt a sticky, dense bundle of something and held it up to see it better. It was a fat wad of fifty-dollar notes almost too wide to hold in one hand, held together with rubber bands. She gasped.

"Christ," David took his eyes off the road for a split second to see what Kirra was holding.

Kirra's mind was racing, trying to make sense of it.

She never carried cash, it must be close to ten thousand dollars judging by the weight of the bundle, which meant someone must have put it there.

Who would have done it … was it some sort of setup? Was she about to be pulled over by police before re-entering Queensland and thrown in jail? Her mind raced, maybe James, the evil twink, was planning to get her. Then it dawned on her.

It wasn't a plant – it was a payment.

"Oh my god, I think Tim put this in my bag when I saw him earlier." Kirra was dumbfounded.

"Tim, the guy you helped when we were in Perth?"

"Yeah him, but I didn't do it for payment. How would he even have this much in cash, it …"

She went silent for a second. None of it made sense. She stared out the window as they got onto the highway heading back for Brisbane.

David broke through her swirling thoughts. "Kirra, I don't mean to be rude, but Nick isn't an electrician."

"Uh, yes he is. Why would you say he isn't?"

"Well, he might be an electrician, but he's not *just* an electrician, obviously," he said matter-of-factly.

"What do you mean *obviously*?" Kirra quickly grew irritated.

David took his eyes off the road to observe Kirra for a moment before he changed his tone.

"I'm sorry, I didn't mean to be condescending, but Kirra – you're a smart woman, I mean, you even have a criminology master's from Oxford. None of Nick's life adds up. That house we were just in must be worth six, seven million dollars, easily. Chris Hemsworth is one of his neighbours for fuck's sake!"

"What are you saying?" Kirra's heart was racing as she felt the crushing weight of a huge penny dropping on her blind, naïve head.

"Your brother is clearly into some highly profitable but very illegal shit."

218

Chapter 42

Not that nice

The rest of the ride home was tense.

David tried to talk to Kirra a few times, but she was silent. She wasn't mad at David, or even Nick. She was mad at herself. She was embarrassed at how everyone else seemed to be completely aware of Nick's actual job. If David knew after a single encounter, then Daniel obviously did too, probably Zoe – and Bree? Was she in on whatever he was doing too?

Kirra noticed everything – a scratch on a phone, a faint wedding ring tan at night – but she didn't notice her own brother's overt criminality. What a fool she'd been, just like Skylar in Breaking Bad.

No, worse, she was Hank.

"What do you think he does?" she asked David quietly as they were going through Eight Mile Plains.

"Drugs, probably, cocaine or steroids. Maybe he's affiliated with a bikie gang or something?"

"He doesn't have a bike though."

"Maybe you don't really need one to be in a gang. Maybe it's more of an aesthetic choice." David was trying to make light of it.

"Do you still want to be with me?" Kirra choked out, tears welling in her eyes.

"What?! Why would you say that?" David asked, sounding panicked, his eyes darting from the road and back again.

Kirra exploded.

"My brother's a crim and I've just been paid for legal work I did for one of his fucking crim mates in fucking cash!" she spat.

"You're this private school boy whose family all work in law, you went to this amazing school, you've got no baggage – why the fuck would you want to be with me? My family's trash and worse, I might even be liable for criminal charges. I could be struck off and have to leave the profession!"

"Kirra, you didn't know he was a crim—"

"You know I used to be a stripper too, when I was studying? Yeah, and, and…" she was working herself up into hysteria, getting close to telling him everything, when he interrupted her.

"It wasn't that nice of a school," he said quietly.

"Wha – what?" she paused her tirade.

"It wasn't that nice of a school."

She looked at him. His eyes were fixed on the road, and his knuckles were almost white on the steering wheel.

"I was abused there, in grade ten. Groomed and raped by the school's minister." He didn't look from the road.

Kirra's breath stole out of her.

"Oh my god, David. I'm so sorry. You don't need to tell me anything you don't want to, I'm—"

"No, I want to tell you. I was going to tell you anyway. My psych says it's good to share with people you care about, to let them in. I just wanted you to know that it wasn't *that* nice of a school and I do have baggage." He paused, swallowing. "I was also going to tell you that I'm in love with you."

Kirra stopped breathing. Her brain was overloading with information, but she was acutely fixated on David's profile as he stared at the road ahead. She was intent on hearing everything he was saying. If she breathed too loudly, she might miss something.

He went silent.

"But you're not going to tell me now, because I'm a strip—"

"I wanted to do it somewhere nice, make it special, but then you asked me if I still want to be with you. Of course I want to be with you. Even if your brother is a crim, it's got nothing to do with you. Donate the cash to a charity if you're worried about it," he paused, blinking back the tears that had formed. "I love you, Kirra." His voice broke, and she sat in silence. "You don't need to say it back to me right away, or say it back at all actually, but I wanted you to know."

She had no clue what to say. No one had ever said those words to her.

"I don't know what that kind of love feels like." She knew the words were serious and didn't want to throw them around without fully understanding what she was doing.

"You'll know it when you feel it. I've felt it since the moment I first saw you."

Kirra scoffed. "What, when I called you a cunt?"

"Yeah," he smiled, quickly looking at her for the first time since he had said he loved her.

His eyes glittered in the darkness with unshed tears. Kirra reached into her bag, past the huge wad of illegal cash, and got him a tissue. They were heading off the riverside expressway towards Milton, almost home. He dabbed at his eyes with one hand.

"Did you want to get a McFlurry?" she asked, completely out of the blue and not at all in keeping with the sombre mood of the car. It was the only way she knew how to communicate, it would seem.

"I'd love one, actually," he sniffed.

***

When they hopped into bed after eating their ice creams, it was almost one in the morning. They had been quiet the rest of the journey home. They lay there in silence for a while.

"I'm so sorry that happened to you." Kirra was stroking David's face in the dark.

"I appreciate that. I'll tell you more about it another time."

"Thank you for saying you think you're in love with me."

"I know I'm in love with you, and you're welcome, I guess?"

Kirra wished she could trust herself to say the words back to him. "I'm so into you. The most I've been into anyone, ever. I just —" Tears welled in her eyes again, and her throat closed up.

221

"You don't need to say it back to me right now. You'll know when it's right for you." He traced his hand across her face, wiping away her tears.

"Why are you so nice to me, so patient?" she croaked out. "I don't get it."

"Why are you so nice to me?" he responded.

She thought about it for a minute. "Because you are gentle and kind. You're clever, charming and really good in bed."

"Sorry, I missed that last part, you'll have to say it again."

She could hear the smile in his voice in the dark. "You're a good root, Daveo." She laughed. "You also smell *so* good and have the most beautiful smile I've ever seen. I also love the way you look at me, your eyes, and the way you make me feel. And you love my Gus," she finished. There was more she could say, but those were the main points.

"And I feel the same way about you too. All of it. Why's it so hard for you to think that I feel the same way about you as you do about me?"

"I don't know." She yawned. She was so exhausted and sick of crying.

"Good night, D W"

"Good night, Kirra."

As she drifted off to sleep, she remembered the situation loving someone had gotten her into last time. She wasn't sure she could handle being in love with someone again.

Chapter 43

Kirra, sixteen years old this week

It was Katie, the captain of the under-17s soccer club, who first noticed something was wrong with Kirra.

Kirra hadn't been feeling well and put it down to probably finally getting her period. Her boobs were aching, and she had been exhausted from the moment she woke up. She had been missing practices, and when she did show up, she knew she wasn't anywhere near as focused as she usually was.

Katie pulled Kirra aside after an evening's practice and offered to drive her home. Kirra was thrilled – she thought Katie was the coolest person alive (apart from Chris) and quickly texted her mum to tell her she would make her own way home. Kirra thought Katie knew where she lived as she had dropped her home before, but she took a different route. Kirra was about to correct her when they pulled up in front of a chemist.

"Kiz, I'm taking you inside to get a pregnancy test."

A fucking what? Kirra was gobsmacked – she just stared open-mouthed back at Katie.

"It's all good, mate. I'm not going to tell anyone anything – I'm worried about you. I've seen that guy in the Jumbuck around, Nick's mate or whatever. No one else has noticed or said anything, but I know what's going on."

Kirra sat in stunned silence, staring at Katie.

"My sister … you know Bec?"

Kirra nodded. Bec came to games all the time and was equally as cool as Katie. She had an adorable little four-year-old boy, Tristan – Katie's nephew, who loved hanging out with the 'big girls' after a game.

"Well, Bec started seeing this older guy. She was really sneaky about it, but Mum cottoned on and busted them one time. She chased him out, but by that point Bec was already pregnant with Tristan. She was only sixteen, Kiz. I was thirteen and I knew something was up then too. I wish I'd told Mum what I thought was happening sooner."

Kirra knew Bec had never finished school and was raising Tristan on her own with the help of her mother and sister.

Katie paused, looking at Kirra expectantly.

Kirra still didn't know what to say or do, so she numbly followed Katie into the chemist and they bought the test. They pulled around the corner to the nearest Maccas and Katie showed her what she needed to do, and she did the test in the toilets. Afterwards, Kirra looked down at the strip, not understanding what she was looking at.

She opened the cubicle door, and Katie looked down, then up at Kirra.

"Mate, you're pregnant."

Chapter 44

Scars

Kirra woke up on Sunday, later than usual, to David making her a coffee. He was dressed when he brought it in to her, leaning on her side of the bed and kissing her gently.

"Don't worry, I'm pissing off now – I know Sundays are sacred. The Guide told me that."

"They are, but please stay … if you don't have anything else on?"

The thought of David being alone so soon after he'd told her he loved her, and what had happened to him, made her feel sick.

"Are you sure?" He seemed pleased, snuggling back down into bed with her.

"Yes, we can self-care together."

They both walked Gus down to the markets, the early February sun beating down on them.

Kirra wasn't hungover, she'd only had a few drinks down in Byron, and was thrilled at the thought of a whole day of sunshine with David and nowhere else to be.

"What's that scar you have on your stomach?" he asked her while they walked. Kirra had been waiting for the question. She had been asked it before.

"I had my appendix removed when I was in high school. The surgery was harder than it usually is as I have endometriosis, so they thought I was just having a flare up. Turns out my appendix had ruptured and they ignored it for days," she lied, fluidly. He nodded.

"I've had mine out too, but the scar's so faint you've probably never noticed it. Yours is a lot lower down than mine, and bigger."

Kirra's heart skipped a beat, and the bottom of her stomach gave out, like when you miss the last step on a set of stairs.

"Must be different on women with endo," he added. She couldn't tell if he had bought her lie or just had the grace to move past being lied to. "You know that mate that I told you about, the one that took his own life?"

"Yes." Kirra was both stunned and relieved by the sudden topic change. The honesty he had shown her was something precious, and she wanted to be there for him no matter what he wanted to share. It was almost enough to make her tell him about her past, all of it.

Almost.

"He got abused by the same guy as I did, same time too. He never told anyone though, begged me to keep his secret. Which I have, until just now, I guess. I was the best man at his wedding, and he was my best friend until the day he died."

Kirra silently processed what he had said.

"Patrick's son was at your school when all this happened," Kirra added, quietly.

"He was, in the year above me. Patrick's never outright accused me of lying about what happened, but he was an old boy of the school too and couldn't stand how much press the whole thing got, the disrepute it brought to such a proud, long-standing institution. It obviously died away, like all of these things do. My nephews bloody go there, so if I ever want to see them play any of their games I have to go back to where it all happened."

"Fuck, seriously? Your sister sent her boys there after that happened to you?" Kirra was incredulous. "I mean, was she not concerned for their safety? Why would she do that?"

Kirra was going to have to stay away from this bitch next weekend. She already wanted to throat-punch her.

"Well, firstly, she's spiteful. When it all came out, she was in year twelve, and she was disgusted at the attention I received during *such* an important year for her. Secondly, she figures they caught the guy, so he wasn't a threat anymore. Which they did – he died in prison not too long ago actually. Thirdly, it's still the most prestigious school in Sydney so her sons *had* to go there, and only there. Anyway, enough about me, tell me about your stripping days."

Kirra choked on the smoothie they had bought from one of the market stands.

"Did you wear the big shoes?"

Kirra was in awe of how well-adjusted David seemed despite what had happened. He could talk about the horrors he had faced in broad daylight in a crowded market. She had never once seen a therapist, other than Dan, and even then Dan didn't know what had happened to her. He knew about her mum, but even then, only some of it.

Maybe David was what twenty years of therapy and having supportive parents looked like.

"Oh, those are called Pleasers, and no, I couldn't afford them. I just wore normal heels."

"Not to sound like a perv, but the thought of twenty-year-old Kirra on a pole is giving me impure thoughts." He looked down at Gus, patting him on the head. "Sorry Gus, must be hard having a hot mum."

They walked back home, David insisting on carrying both the shopping and Gus' lead.

"Does your claustrophobia come from what happened at school?" Kirra knew she was being insensitive, poking at a bruise, but she wanted the whole story. David stopped dead in his tracks, eyes fixed on the ground. He took a deep breath.

"Yes, but I can't talk about that yet," he gritted out before continuing their walk back up the hill.

"Okay, I'm sorry."

He was quiet for a while longer. Kirra regretted being so nosey. "My mum died six weeks after she was diagnosed with cancer, when I was in year twelve," she offered as a token of her apology and to practice a technique David had told her about: sharing things with people you care about.

"She was a primary school teacher, and she worked her guts out for the kids in her class. Always crafting some crazy shit for her classroom, putting all this work into making school so special for them. She knew she had a lump and ignored it for months. Even when she got worried about it, she still put off getting it checked." She had other things to deal with at the time.

"It was so quick, she went from this vibrant, healthy woman to this frail shell of who she was. I have nightmares where I watch her die again, then it's me in the hospital bed – both of my breasts removed, no nipples, a thick red scar from armpit to armpit, hair falling out in clumps – and dying anyway, despite the fight to survive."

David was quiet a moment before placing the shopping cart against a tree and wrapping Kirra in his arms.

"I'm so sorry you lost your mum, at that age too. That would have been horrific."

Kirra didn't cry, she couldn't cry over that, because if she started, she wouldn't stop. She placed the lid back on the memories of her mother. She had shared enough for now … enough for David to know she wasn't an insensitive brat with no problems of her own, hopefully.

Her heart still ached for what had happened to him and what had happened to his best friend, how even decades later it had caught up and beaten him.

"Well, aren't we a bucket of fucking laughs," she offered, wrapping one of her arms around David's lower back and continuing on home.

They spent rest of the day together, but David was ultimately banished back to his place in the evening so Kirra could complete the Everything Shower in solitude.

Chapter 45

Sugar baby

With the realisation her brother was more than likely involved in organised crime, Kirra had temporarily forgotten about her own recent illegal dealings. It was Thursday when the scene erupted.

Kirra was leading a client from one of their meeting rooms back to reception to sign out when an attractive, well-put-together woman in her early sixties stormed up to the reception desk.

"James?" She spoke down to him, hands gripping the raised edge of the bench, head cocked to the side like an eagle about to snap a mouse in half.

"Yes? And you are?"

"Isabella D'Linio." She glared at him.

James didn't so much as flinch. The client Kirra was signing out smirked at Kirra and clearly wanted to see what was about to unfold. They slowly keyed their phone number into the iPad at reception that tracked visitors, taking their sweet time. It also gave Kirra the excuse to stand around, metres from where Isabella was cornering James.

"Do you need to see Tony, Isabella? I can let you through if you—"

"No, I don't need to see Tony, I see him every night. Every night except Wednesday, when he sees his personal trainer."

Damn, this woman was cold. She was staring at James, waiting for him to sweat, admit something, but he was just as cold. Her words were slow and clear.

"I waited up for him on Wednesday and it was clear he'd had a workout, but not from lifting weights." She paused, waiting for him to interrupt her, but James looked wholly unbothered. "It just confirmed that whoever he's been spending thousands of dollars on Net-a-porter for was in fact giving him payment for the goods."

Kirra's client had dropped their phone then needed a drink of water all of a sudden. Kirra was politely standing behind them, waiting for them to leave, watching. She knew James could see her standing there too.

"So, my question to you, James, is how someone on your salary can afford that Vetements shirt and those Prada glasses you're wearing?" She punctuated each luxury item with a wave of her hand.

"That is such a rude question. I buy all these things myself and I don't appreciate what you're insinuating. I'm about to call security," James bit back, reaching for the phone.

"Oh, okay. I'm sorry for being rude. I'll go," Isabella made to leave, and James lowered the receiver, "but I do have one more question for you." She fished her phone out of her bag, unlocked it and brought up a video. She pressed play and shoved it in James' face.

Kirra and her client both heard the video but couldn't see it from where they were standing. The sound was telling enough. The colour drained from James' already pale face as he looked at the screen.

"Is letting an old man fuck you in his car really worth all the gifts, James Reynolds, whose face is clearly fucking visible in this video?" Isabella's calm composure had fractured, spit flying out of her mouth.

Kirra's client had finally finished signing out.

"Thanks again for your help, Jane," they offered, eyebrows raised and a smirk on their lips.

***

"So how did you know James was Tony's sugar baby?"

"I smelled it on them." Kirra and David were walking to lunch the following day. They had decided that never leaving the office together looked suspicious in itself, as lots of their colleagues would grab a coffee or food together.

"Smelled it on them?"

"James is so into fashion, brands, personal grooming, his skin, hair, fragrance. He looks runway-ready every single day. But then he came back from lunch one day and smelled like Joop."

"And?" David was clearly not following.

"James would die before he wore a fragrance that could be bought from Priceline. I knew something was up, so I sniffed a little further. I'd always been a little sus on him anyway – he only wears designer clothing. He'd be on a quarter of what I am, and I couldn't afford his wardrobe. I got the idea he might be a sugar baby from one of my mates who had a sugar daddy for a while, not that it's literally any of my business and I wouldn't judge—"

"So, you smelled Joop on Tony and—"

"Please, let me have my yarn, David," Kirra cautioned with a pointed finger. He put his hands up defensively then made a gesture that he was zipping his lips. "I smelled Joop on Tony, but that wasn't enough evidence, what actually closed the case was—"

"Wait, sorry to interrupt, but when did you do all this sleuthing?" David looked a little scared at having to stop his girlfriend mid-yarn, but the story did have some holes in it.

"The end of last year."

"So, you freaked out about James catching us kissing, but you already had this on him. Why the freak out when what you had on him is so much worse than us dating? Why the sleuthing to start with, either?"

"The sleuthing was because once I notice something that's not fully explained, it haunts my waking thoughts until I can make it make sense. James wearing Joop threw me big time, as did the expensive gear. Also, he hates me."

"Do you know that for a fact?"

"I know that for a fact. He got drunk at last year's Christmas party and said 'Jane, I fucking hate you'."

"Oh, that's charming."

"It is. As for the freak out, I didn't want to use it just because I had something on him. He's on less money than I am, he's in a marginalised group – I don't like punching down. I'm not a monster."

"To punch down, don't you need to think you're above someone though?"

"Oh, I absolutely do. Not because of his financial situation or sexual orientation though, but because he's a mean little bitch."

David was laughing, trying to let Kirra's meandering story come to its finale.

"Anyway." He gestured for her to go on.

"Anyway … James smelt like Tony, clearly had a sugar daddy, and Brisbane's a really small place, particularly if you're gay. James bragged to a friend about fleecing an old guy at work, and that friend told my friend."

"Oh."

"Oh?"

"Just, that's kind of an anti-climax, not a lot of sleuthing really, McNamara."

"There was a little sleuthing. So, I anonymously told his missus to look into her dodgy husband. She checked his bank transactions and probably saw all the Net-a-porter orders despite him wearing seriously out-of-date clothes, and then the old creep clearly filmed him and James going at it one time. The video probably backed up to their shared cloud drive or something."

Kirra had deliberately skirted around the details as to how she managed to get Tony's wife's number.

"Damn, busted for being bad at technology." David was smirking, clearly impressed by Kirra's cunning. "Such a closeted-boomer way to get done, really."

When the pair returned to their offices, reception was empty.

Chapter 46

Daniel and Kirra worked from home together at hers so he could help her pack for the weekend. She was so anxious not to look too slutty, too boring, too… *too*.

She also asked him if he thought Nick was a criminal, and he said he had been suspicious for a while but didn't know anything for sure. She asked him why he hadn't mentioned it to her, and he told her she would have eventually seen it for herself. Also, telling someone their brother might be a drug dealer or gang member isn't exactly good manners if you don't know it for a fact. The rest of the afternoon had been spent with Daniel trying to calm her down for her weekend away.

***

If she had been painful on the drive down to Byron, she was excruciating on the flight to Sydney.

David quietly held her hand on the flight, clearly sensing how frightened she was.

"I've booked us a room for both nights in the city. The party's at Iceberg's tomorrow night, but we don't have to have dinner at my parents' tonight if you're not feeling up to it."

David was trying to not make a big deal of it, but he had clearly told his parents he was bringing a woman with him, and they were desperate to have them over for dinner before the big night tomorrow. Kirra had overheard David on the phone saying "we'll see" and "I'm sure she'd love to, I'll get back to you" no less than five times when his mother had called him yesterday.

"No, look I'm really sorry I'm being such a dick about this. I just really want them to like me. They're going to be these super posh Sydneysiders and I'm just a—"

"Rhodes scholar and top billing partner in an international law firm," he interjected.

"A stripper from the 'hood," she corrected.

"Stop it with that shit, it's tiresome." His tone bordered on exasperated. Kirra hadn't heard that in his voice before. He realised it too.

"Fuck, sorry, that sounded awful. I'm not tired of you. I could never be tired of you." He squeezed her hand a little tighter, "Although you should stop doing that, really. I'm on edge at having to see Catherine again, to be honest." He looked over at Kirra, his expression drawn.

"You're right I do need to stop with it. I bore myself sometimes, even." Kirra added David to the list of straight men she had admitted were right about something. That list now had one name on it.

"And are you seriously telling me Catherine's going to be worse than Nick? My criminal brother who said my type is anyone with a pulse?"

"Genuinely and without exaggeration, yes."

Chapter 47

Girraween

Kirra felt close to vomiting, shitting herself and passing out on the cab ride to David's parent's house: the anxiety attack trifecta. She had deliberately left her vape in Brisbane. She wanted to make a good impression, and sucking on one of those things and smelling like fairy floss absolutely wasn't going to do that. She had expected a longer drive from the airport out to one of the nicer suburbs of Sydney but didn't know where they were headed. She looked out the window trying to take in some of her surroundings, but she was so lost in the swirling thoughts of impending embarrassment that she took no notice of where they were heading.

When she had imagined David growing up, she pictured him hopping on a bus in his private school blazer, mucking around with his friends on the ride in. The car slowed down to a stop and she took in where she was.

There was no fucking way he had ever once caught the bus.

Kirra stepped out and looked up at the sight before her, jaw slack and lost for words while David got their bags.

"You … grew up, here?"

"Yep," he raised his eyebrows at her. "Sorry, I know it's a bit of a dump."

Kirra was standing before two huge open black metal gates set into high sandstone walls that led to a grand walkway with a fountain in its centre. At each side of the walkway were immaculately kept lawns and hedges, the façade of a cream-coloured fortress looming behind it.

David led the way to the front doors, which were also open in anticipation of their arrival. Kirra ascended the sweeping steps into a marble-floored foyer, a cavernous space with high ceilings and chandelier. An actual chandelier.

"They'll be outside near the upper pool, I reckon. Let's put our bags down and go find them – are you alright?" David came to Kirra's side with a look of worry on his face.

"Um, David – what the actual fuck!?" she whispered, still deeply in shock.

He was shaking his head as if confused.

"What? I told you my family was well-off."

"Um, no – Nick's well-off. I'm well-off. This … this is a mansion." She spun around, taking in more of the old-world charm. She was waiting for the furniture to start singing a la Beauty and the Beast. "What suburb are we in?"

"Vaucluse. The house is called Girraween."

"How many bedrooms does this place have?"

"Seven."

"Bathrooms?"

"Thirteen."

Kirra wanted to run. She was going to make an absolute twat of herself in here, and David was going to realise they weren't at all compatible.

Girraween would have to be one of the most expensive houses in Sydney, the entire country. It made her feel small and dirty in comparison. People who walked through here worked in politics, went yachting, owned racehorses. She bailed suspected drug traffickers out of Balinese jails and drank warm Passion Pop with retired strippers. What the actual fuck was she even doing standing here like she had anything in common with these people, with David, even?

Sensing her stillness and silence, he dragged her by the arm up the stairs to a landing on the mezzanine level, their bags in his other arm. She went willingly, floating. He opened the door to a lush guest bedroom with a gigantic king bed tastefully decorated in muted blues. The harbour twinkled in the distance out of the balcony doors. He threw their bags down and steered Kirra to the edge of the bed, plonking her down before kneeling before her.

"Look at me." He had that demanding tone in his voice, the one that turned Kirra to goo in seconds. She snapped her eyes from the window and down into his icy blue stare. "I came home to this place after I'd been locked in a cupboard and raped by a seventy-eight-year-old paedophile." Kirra started trembling almost instantly. David glared at her without blinking. "It's a big fancy house, sure, but it's also the place I used to hang out with my best mate Harry, my mate who then went on to gas himself in his fucking garage while his wife was at work and his kids were at school."

Kirra had started crying, tears rolling silently down her cheeks, but she was fixated on his words. She couldn't look away from him.

"Years later, I wrote my own suicide note, in this exact room, before I swallowed a whole pack of sleeping pills and waited to die."

He paused, looking down at the carpet before looking back up at her. She wanted to stop him but also wanted him to keep going and tell her everything.

"I didn't die, or give myself brain damage, thankfully. I'm actually glad it got to that, to rock bottom. If things had have just kept plodding along the way they had, I would have found another way to kill myself, a longer but more successful way, like drinking, or smoking or working sixteen-hour days until my heart just gave out—"

"Karoshi," Kirra blurted out without thinking. David looked at her, puzzled. "Death from overwork, it's a Japanese term."

"Right, exactly."

While she wanted to slap herself for interrupting him, the break seemed to restore a bit of normalcy to David's tone and demeanour. He had been rigid, jaw tight, teeth almost grinding.

He went on. "Instead, I had one failed attempt. When I woke up in hospital, I was relieved. Relieved I hadn't ended up like

Harry, that I'd been given another chance. I decided I was going to sort my shit out, properly. Once I was well enough, sober, fitter, I moved up to Brisbane for a fresh start. I was going to work on myself, by myself." David had been speaking clearly, his eyes a determined stare, but his lip started to tremble and tears welled in his eyes. "But then, I met this woman, almost straight away. This beautiful, intelligent woman who called me a cunt straight to my face."

Kirra huffed out a laugh, her tears rolling even faster down her cheeks. She'd never heard him drop a c-bomb.

"She's talented, and funny, and has this really cute dog who I think would personally prefer to live with me, but whatever." She ran her hand down his cheeks where he knelt before her, wiping up some of his tears and tracing her thumb over where they had been. "When I told her I had feelings for her, she stripped in front of me and masturbated while I was on the phone to my boss, which was pretty awesome."

Jesus, Perth felt like a lifetime ago, but it hadn't even been a month. She couldn't help but smile through her tears.

"It's been so much fun getting to know her these past few weeks, the most fun I've had in, fuck, years. And now I'm in love with her." Kirra's heart jolted. He hadn't said 'I love you' since the car trip back from Byron almost a week ago.

"And now she's here, where I grew up, freaking out over a house."

"A mansion," Kirra sniffed. Her trembling had stopped, and she had David's face in both her hands. His tears had stopped falling too.

"Alright, a mansion. She's freaking out over some walls and a roof." He stood up, took a step back and wiped his face on the back of his sleeve. Then he levelled her with that look, the same one he had given her when he told her to put her glass of wine down and get on her knees.

"Stand up," he instructed.

Without thinking, she obeyed.

"Wipe your eyes."

She did.

"Does my makeup look—"

"Don't talk," he snapped, but then quietly added, "You look beautiful." The commanding tone came back when he said, "You're going to come downstairs and meet Evelyn and George Waters, who are dying to meet you. Are you ready?"

"I am."

And she was.

A few minutes later, the pair descended the stairs and travelled through several buildings connected by floor-to-ceiling glass hallways. David explained the land was bought as a compound of houses and had been renovated to connect them into one gigantic house, which explained the multi-levelled madness of the sprawling estate.

Kirra and David found Evelyn and George next to the upper pool, for there was another one on a lower level, sipping a drink and chatting. The minute Evelyn eyed them, she leapt up, slapping George to follow her as she trotted toward them.

"Helloooooo!"

Evelyn Waters was a tiny woman with a perfectly toned white bob wearing a flowing linen set of navy blue that offset the pale blue eyes she had passed down to her son. She bypassed David completely and wrapped Kirra in a hug tight enough that it hurt. Evelyn stepped back and looked up at Kirra.

"Sorry, we're huggers."

George, equally as well-put-together in dark linen, followed suit, shoving past his wife and embracing Kirra like he had known her for years. He shared the elegant bordering on sharp angles of David's face. When he let her go, she saw where David got his smile from.

"Kirra, we have been dying to meet you," Evelyn declared. "I'm Evelyn, but you can call me Ev, and the old man is George."

"It's lovely to meet you, Ev, George." Kirra couldn't stop the smile from spreading over her face, the intense anxiety she had felt moments before dissipating the minute she saw the Waters – their likeness to David and their seemingly genuine excitement to meet her as opposed to the scepticism or wariness she had expected.

See, nervous system, why do you do this every time? Most people are nice. Stop trying to kill me.

"Let me get you both a drink." George walked off to behind the bar built into the sandstone pergola that sat alongside the huge infinity pool. Ev waved at the pair to come and sit down. George joined them a moment later and handed them each a glass of wine.

"Kirra … well, Jane, I've heard a lot about you, and not just from David," George offered as an opening.

Kirra's stomach dropped. While David's father had retired and had done most of his work independent of the firm, he would of course have connections with Kensington Menschel all around Australia. He had worked there for decades. Kirra hadn't had much to do with the firm's branches in other states or countries, so her mind jumped to the only logical explanation; he already knew she was an unhinged slut because Nathaniel or Ken had told him so.

"Your billings basically keep the Queensland office open. They're very bloody lucky to have you!"

Jesus Christ fight or flight, switch off, for the love of all things holy, switch OFF.

"Oh, I don't know about that." She almost blushed.

She did know about that.

It gave her a certain sense of impenetrability when she had been caught, for example, vomiting in a bush on the way into work on a Monday. Maybe more than one Monday. Yes, I'm hungover, yes, I may have peed in my pants a little as well just now, but I bill almost ten times my base salary, so you can suck it.

"Would you ever go out on your own?" George asked. Kirra had been asked this same question a few times, and she had a pre-rehearsed answer that she almost believed.

"I might sometime down the track, but I enjoy being part of a team and my overheads being covered for now," she lied.

She would never go out on her own because while she may be competent and hungry enough, the fear of potential failure paralysed her. Failing and having to come crawling back would be a fate worse than death. Another firm maybe, but a solo career? Never. And then, if another firm, why not just stay at KM, they're all the same. She hated that cycle of thought. She used to do brave shit, and now she felt trapped, had done for a while.

"Honestly, you should." George gave Kirra a knowing look.

"How come you've never told me to go out on my own, Daddy?" David asked his father, deadpan.

"Did you know David never wanted to be a lawyer, Kirra?" Evelyn cut in, chuckling.

"No, I didn't know that," Kirra smiled at David.

If Nick or Steve spoke of her while she was around, it was generally derogatory on Nick's part and tone-deaf on her father's. When your dad innocently still uses the word 'poof', there's always a certain risk of a looming social faux pas in the air.

The air between David and his parents felt clear and light. It was pleasant to be around.

"I still don't know what I want to be when I grow up." David smiled back at Kirra.

God, he was so beautiful. She hadn't fully processed what he'd said in the guestroom: the horrors he'd endured as a boy and a man.

"You're a very good lawyer," Kirra said to David. She added to his parents, "He ran a case we had in Perth a few weeks ago and was amazing."

"David is amazing, isn't he?" came a lilting voice from behind Kirra. She twisted around to see where it had come from.

A beautiful woman in her mid-forties stood in a crisp white shift dress, pearls in her ears and blonde hair swept back into a low, sleek bun at the nape of her neck. She was skeletally thin with prominent cheekbones and those same pale blue eyes her mother and brother had. She smiled weakly down at Kirra, who stood up and extended a hand to who could only be David's sister Catherine.

Kirra's gesture was returned, loosely, Catherine barely closing her long thin fingers. Kirra noted Catherine was also wearing one of the bracelets Ben had gifted her, and the matching necklace. The size of the diamond on her left hand and the beautiful pearls in her ears had Kirra crunching the numbers mentally, using the bracelet as a starting point and scaling up. She had to be wearing close to two hundred thousand dollars' worth of jewels. To dinner at her parents' house. Kirra wondered what she would wear to the party tomorrow night.

"I'm Kirra, lovely to meet you." Kirra's ease at George and Ev's company was replaced with immediate tension as Catherine's glacial eyes bored into her.

"Keira? Like Knightly?" Catherine had her head cocked to the side, and her smile didn't reach her eyes or voice.

"No, Kirra like the beach on the Gold Coast, but I get Keira a lot." Kirra laughed awkwardly.

Catherine stared back at her, her eyes briefly flitting down and back up, taking her in. As if to thwart their daughter's mistreatment of their guest, Ev and George hugged Catherine from either side. Kirra stepped back, grateful for the distance. Catherine didn't hug her parents back, her arms instead hanging listlessly at her side.

"Uncle David!" A juvenile voice came from somewhere in the dark, and a boy of about twelve bounded up and piled on top of David as he attempted to get off the sofa. The kid was almost the same height as David and had a mop of platinum blond hair and a smattering of freckles across his nose.

"Eddy, how've you been mate?" David stood up and squeezed the boy.

"It's Edward," Catherine corrected him. Kirra saw David supress the urge to roll his eyes.

"Catherine, nice to see you," David offered curtly.

Damn, was this how rich people showed their disdain towards one another? It wasn't uncommon when Nick and Kirra had a fight that someone spat or threw a glass. This was way worse.

David looked past Catherine to another boy, an older one, emerging from the dark. The resemblance he had to his mother was striking: a similar angular face with a look of mild irritation painted across it. He looked like he was trying not to smile but couldn't help himself when he saw his uncle.

"George! Mate, you're officially taller than me now. When did that happen!?" David wrapped his older nephew in a hug. Kirra could sense the love David had for these two boys even with a human blackhole hovering less than a metre away attempting to drain the space of its oxygen and light. These boys clearly loved David back too; they couldn't wipe the smiles off their faces at seeing him again despite their initial efforts to appear aloof and cool. Kirra wanted to say something to Catherine about naming her son after her dad, something nice and benign as a way of conversation, but thought better of it.

After finishing their drinks, the seven of them walked inside and sat down to dinner. Kirra was completely gobsmacked by the meal Evelyn placed before her.

It was bangers and mash with frozen peas.

Catherine's husband Dylan sent his apologies for missing the dinner due to a migraine and passed along that he was looking forward to seeing the family tomorrow night at George Senior's party. Kirra wondered what the long-term side effects of living with an ice queen like Catherine would be: a migraine would be the least of it. Her presence was so unsettling – she seemed to darken the corner of the table she sat at and only opened her mouth to subtly criticise or nitpick.

The boys were very typical for their age. They were telling the table, with authority, about things everyone already knew about, and the adults humoured them. These boys were clearly used to being heard too, routinely talking over other people. It was already grating Kirra's nerves, but she couldn't hide her flinch when George Jr referred to a girl his friend had started dating as a fat bitch. David had cautioned him about his language, which had caused Catherine to tell David to mind his own business, which had caused Kirra to want to throw her wine at both Catherine and her son. She gripped her cutlery with all the strength she had and got her food down without causing a scene.

Chapter 48

Fatality

After dinner, Catherine skulked off somewhere in Giraween, and David helped his mum tidy up. Kirra and George talked shop for a while, which Kirra always enjoyed.

David's father had inherited his career from his father, the late Edward Waters (that explained Catherine's second son's name), but for the majority of his career had represented a select list of Australia's richest and wealthiest businesspeople and celebrities in all matters. He wanted to know all about her niche in healthcare and how she physically managed to do the work she did with the finite hours in a day. Kirra could see where David got his charm from. She wasn't one who normally felt comfortable speaking about herself to a relative stranger, but George seemed lovely and was very easy to talk to. Not once in the evening was she asked where she went to school.

Now that's properly classy.

George excused himself to take a phone call, but before he picked it up, he encouraged Kirra to go for a walk around the place and make herself at home.

She wandered through the cavernous hallways and ended up on a lower level overlooking the second pool. A small set of stairs led down to a sunken loungeroom where Edward and George II were playing video games. Their belongings were strewn about the room, and they were eating Doritos and wiping their neon orange fingers across a cream-coloured sofa that took up most of the space.

Pigs.

"Whatcha playing there, boys?"

Edward yelped in fright, and George spun around to look at her. They clearly weren't used to being interrupted. Edward regained his composure and answered Kirra, but George's eyes returned to the screen.

"Mortal Kombat, with a K, the latest version of it. It was a game from the eighties."

"Oh yeah, I've heard of it. It was turned into a cinematic masterpiece in 1995."

"The movie came out in 2021," George corrected her, eyes fixed on the screen.

"Would you believe there's more than one, and that one came out before you were born?"

Kirra couldn't help herself. He'd been allowed to talk shit all through dinner, clearly had a burgeoning dislike of women, but now he was simply *wrong*. His eyes briefly flitted up to her, then back down to the screen.

"Do you think I could have a round? I used to play Tekken on the PlayStation 2." Kirra had made her way down the stairs.

Edward handed her his controller, adding, "The controls would be nothing like what they used to be back then."

"X to kick, square to punch?"

"Uh, yeah, pretty much."

"Sweet, we're sorted then." Turns out mansplaining wasn't reserved for men, boys could do it too.

Kirra took the controller and used the joystick to select her fighter.

"Oooh she's hot," she said, earning a snort of laughter from Edward as she selected a busty fighter with two gnarly looking blades and a purple mask covering the lower half of her face. George silently selected Raiden, a guy in a funny hat with some lightning business going on.

Kirra thought this was a great way to chat with the boys, who David was clearly very fond of. It was a low stakes activity they enjoyed. Maybe she would even make George laugh by the time she left this evening. She really wanted them to like her.

She looked down at the controller briefly to figure out if the symbols were still in the same place as they had been when she was a kid and figured she could get a kick or two in on George before he would inevitably flog her.

A booming voice intoned FIGHT, at which point muscle memory she didn't know was there kicked in.

Without looking back down at the controller, Kirra executed a series of commands that had George's character airborne and getting kicked around like a hacky sack. She timed her strikes perfectly – each time Raiden fell back down she had him back in the air, unable to retaliate.

By the time George realised he was getting his bread buttered, it was too late. He ineffectively mashed at the buttons in retaliation, but the gameplay had already slowed to a cut scene. Kirra's character stabbed George's, spinning him around and taking several gruesome bites out of the top of his head before an obscenely long tongue licked what was left of the gore off her fingers. Yikes. That same booming voice announced *Fatality, Mileena wins, flawless victory*.

Kirra turned to look at George who was glaring at her, his face red and lips thin. The shade of puce his formerly smug face had turned made his platinum blond hair look even lighter.

Edward was on the floor wheezing with laughter.

"You cheated. My controller glitched!" George spat, his voice breaking with rage. Oh no, a sore loser and a cry-baby.

Kirra couldn't help herself.

"Which was it Georgie, did I cheat or did your controller glitch?"

This was not going how she wanted it to at all, but she'd had more entitlement and smugness out of this little prick than she could handle.

"Both! And don't call me Georgie!" he spat back at her.

Edward had regained his breath. "Fuck, she smoked you!" he finally got out.

George continued to glare at Kirra.

"Okay, how about we switch controllers and you select my fighter for me for a rematch," Kirra offered.

She still didn't really know how she knew what she was doing. Maybe she had just gotten lucky with that fighter and George could kick her arse fair and square the second time. Then her plan of making the kids like her would be back on track.

George's face had returned to its normal pallor, and he handed her his controller. For Kirra, he selected a dude with a moustache and a cape who looked like a newer character, and he picked a more traditional looking fighter with long hair and glowing eyes for himself. Maybe he thought picking a fighter that wasn't in the older versions of the game would throw her.

They played again, and somehow her hands took over while her mind went blank, ending in her character holding George's aloft while a moving train tore him to shreds.

George threw the controller and spun on Kirra.

"Why are you acting like you've never played this game?"

Edward had lost his mind and was twerking in the corner, seriously enjoying his older brother getting shown a thing or two.

"Honestly, George, I've never played this game. I have trouble sleeping and sometimes will end up on these YouTube wormholes for hours before drifting off. I must have watched some videos on this and forgotten about it."

"Forgotten about it? All of those combos? For two different characters?" He was indignant.

"She's not lying. I've seen her do the same thing with multiple languages too, mate," David's voice came from the upper level.

Kirra was immediately embarrassed. She had hoped she would have time to smooth it over with the boys before David found her. This bonding experience had not gone as she had hoped.

"Marry her, Uncle David," Edward shouted up at him, giving Kirra the thumbs up.

Okay, maybe her plan had worked for one nephew and backfired completely with the other. Better than them both hating her, she supposed.

David had made his way down and extended a hand to Kirra.

"Kirra and I are going now, boys, but we'll see you tomorrow night at Grandad's party."

Edward ran up and squeezed his uncle in a hug and proceeded to show Kirra how to dap someone up. She didn't know if that was a boy thing or a Sydney thing, as Hattie hadn't shown her it before. Regardless, she dapped up one of David's nephews and got a slight nod as a goodbye from the other.

Mum and Dad – check, Catherine – work in progress and maybe a lost cause, Edward – check, George – failure.

If she kept these odds up after tomorrow night, maybe she did deserve to be David Water's girlfriend.

Chapter 49

A sure thing

Catherine hadn't resurfaced after dinner, much to Kirra's relief. She didn't want to face her again so soon after making her eldest son spit with rage over a videogame. David had found the whole interaction with his nephews hilarious, much to her relief, as she filled him in on the details on their way back into the centre of the city. Kirra was content, relaxed and lightly warmed from the wine David's parents kept plying her with, enjoying the passing twinkling lights of the city from the backseat window of their Uber.

"Honestly, I'm glad you got to see that. George takes after Catherine a lot more than Eddie does, but they can both be little shits. Love them to death, but spoilt little pricks."

"Are you one to call someone spoilt though? I mean, look at where you grew up."

"Yeah, maybe I was. It didn't really feel like that at the time. Dad made me get a part-time job delivering papers when I was in year eleven, and they kicked me out when I got back from Europe, so I worked at Maccas while I was at uni to afford rent."

"No way, really?"

"Really."

"Shit, I cannot imagine you in the uniform."

"We can't all work a pole to make ends meet, McNamara. Some of us had to mop floors." He levelled her with a serious look across the darkened back seat of the car.

"You could have stripped – Ev showed me some photos of you in your early twenties. Bring back that eyebrow ring, I say." Kirra fanned herself with her hand, tongue lolling.

The car pulled up, and a concierge came to greet them and take their bags. In keeping with the lifestyle he had grown up with, which Kirra was quickly becoming accustomed to, they were staying at one of the nicest hotels Kirra had ever laid eyes on.

"I appreciate this whole seduction thing you've got going on here but let me give you a tip – I'm a sure thing." Kirra quoted Pretty Woman in her best American accent, and David took her by the hand as they sauntered into the beautiful lobby.

"Thank god. I know how much you bill for thirteen minutes; I don't think I could have afforded a whole night."

***

The suite David had booked was complete with a loungeroom and a fireplace that Kirra was tempted to light despite it being the middle of summer. She wandered around, enjoying being in the beautiful space, each room nicer than the last one. The bathroom was white marble with gold finishings, and a vase filled with freshly cut roses scented the room. She found her way back to the kitchen where David was drinking a glass of water and staring out towards the bay. Kirra snuck up behind him and wrapped her arms around his waist, resting her ear to his back and listening for his heartbeat.

"Your mum and dad are lovely," she sighed into him, enjoying the stunning apartment, being alone with him, the relief of one social event being done.

"I'm sorry I dumped all of that on you just before you met them." He turned around and wrapped his arms around her, nuzzling into her neck.

"You don't need to be sorry. I like that you've told me everything. I appreciate it so much." She felt guilty as the words left her mouth, knowing she wouldn't do the same for him.

"I get it though, if it's a bit much. I know this is moving pretty quickly."

"Is it?"

251

"Yeah, it probably is. I figure if it feels right, go with it. I'm old enough to know what I want. I figure you are too." David ran his hands down Kirra's back and rested them on her behind. "Have a shower with me?" he asked, kissing Kirra on the neck and massaging her arse.

She sighed at the feeling and melted into it. After the emotional rollercoaster of anticipation, relief, reignited anxiety at meeting Catherine and her kids, and brief relief again only to be replaced by more building anxiety and anticipation at tomorrow night, Kirra wanted to stop thinking.

She let him walk her to the gorgeous bathroom and undress her. He wasn't doing his dominating bit, but he was leading the way. After he removed her top and bra, he knelt down, kissing her breasts and stomach as he undid her jeans and slipped them to the floor. He shimmied her underwear down and kissed back and forth across her hips before dragging a whisper of his tongue down her pussy. Her knees buckled almost instantly at his touch, and she let out a small laugh of surprise.

"Later, when you can't fall over and crack your head open on the tiles." He smiled up at her, and her breath caught in her throat at the sight.

"You are so beautiful, David." She had her hand on his face while he knelt before her for the second time that evening.

He stood up and she unbuttoned his shirt, pulling it down over his arms. She paused for a moment and kissed across his chest, his collarbones, his shoulders. His eyes closed and he groaned as she kissed down his neck. She could sense his relief at being alone with her again too.

Kirra undid his pants and let them fall to the floor, rubbing his growing erection through his briefs.

"I thought we were having a shower?" he smirked, looking down to watch her work him before his eyes returned back up to hers.

She could only imagine how she looked right now. She was so hungry for him that she had to bite her lip to stop from leaning forward and biting him. The urge to have him inside her was so strong she could barely think.

"I got an STD check just before we started seeing each other." Her GP must be so sick of her requesting a check every few months, but she routinely had one at the same time she would get checked for lumps in her breasts. Those were at least two elements of her health she'd always looked after.

"Yeah, I had one before I came up to Brissy. I'm all clear too," David returned, eyelids heavy with lust as she stroked him faster. "Are you saying—"

"Fuck me without a condom, I'm on the pill." Kirra was sure she was snarling like an animal as she tugged down his underwear.

David's throat bobbed before he nodded.

She took her hand off him and stepped inside the huge shower, turning on the water. Before she could turn back around, he was behind her, under the steady stream of hot water, rubbing her breasts and pushing his erection up against her arse and lower back.

"Christ, I want you so bad," he murmured into her neck. The welcome warmth of the shower, his unrestrained arousal, how good his hands felt on her, it was too much. The steady throb that had been building between her legs since she walked in the hotel suite was driving her mad. He rolled her nipples between his fingers and lightly bit her neck.

She turned around and gripped him in one hand, grabbing the ledge behind her with the other hand for balance. She lifted her leg and rested on his shoulder.

You can take the girl out of the strip club, but she'll always be able to do the splits.

She ran the tip of his cock up and down her opening.

"God that feels good," he gritted out, gripping the leg on his shoulder as he held the side of her face with his other. "Are you sure about this?"

"I'm sure," she let out on a breathy moan.

He took her in a slow, deep kiss and pushed into her. Kirra was soaking wet, and he slid in without any resistance. He groaned into her mouth, gripping the leg on his shoulder even tighter.

Kirra wrapped her free arm around the back of his neck for support while he slowly pumped into her. He broke the kiss to stare into her eyes.

"You feel so," he pulled almost entirely out of her before pushing back in slowly, "fucking good. Do you like that?" He was staring down it to her eyes, dripping wet, and her mind emptied with how perfect it felt.

"Yes, I'm already close," she whimpered, biting down on his shoulder to stop from screaming.

She bit him hard enough she could almost taste him, and he started thrusting up and into her even harder in response, anticipating what she wanted. The angle had him hitting her G-spot perfectly, and the pressure to come had already built up to an almost painful level.

His thrusting grew faster, both hands grabbing her tightly by the hips so he could pull her down on to him as he thrust up into her.

"Kirra, I'm close," he whispered across her lips before he kissed down her neck.

"Me too, come in me. I want you to, please," she moaned into his neck. She didn't want him to stop, no matter what.

"Are you sure?" His head snapped up to look at her without breaking his pace.

"Yes, please." Her last vowel extended with a guttural moan as she exploded around him, head rolling back on her shoulders and feeling like she might black out, her legs buckling.

He rearranged her legs so both were wrapped around his lower back and gripped her arse with both hands to support her weight. He slammed into her with everything he had left, pushing her against the wall of the shower. His breathing stilled for a moment, and he groaned into her mouth as he came inside of her.

They stayed there like that for a few minutes, him inside of her, her clinging to him. David gently lowered her and withdrew, making sure she could stand, a gush escaping her and running down her thighs.

They stood in the shower, looking at each other in silence for a while longer, enveloped in hot water and steam.

"That was unbelievable." David ran his hands gently up and down Kirra's soaking wet body, looking into her eyes.

She was beyond words and could only nod.

The night didn't end there.

Maybe it was being back in his hometown, his joy at having his parents and girlfriend get on so well or wanting to make the most of the lush suite costing him almost two thousand dollars a night, but David not only backed up his efforts from the shower but also went for round three. Unheard of for someone whose doctor had recommended he start screening for bowel cancer annually.

Having desecrated every polished and padded surface in the suite with their loud lovemaking then devouring cheeseburgers from room service, the pair fell into a sweaty heap in the gigantic cloud of a bed, utterly spent.

***

The light from a beautiful Saturday morning filtered into their room.

She looked over to David, who was still peacefully asleep, head on the huge fluffy pillow with one of his arms over his forehead. Kirra traced the lines of his jaw down his throat and rested her hand on his chest, feeling his heartbeat through her palm.

She had such intense feelings towards him right at this moment that she decided she would just tell him she loved him and stop debating whether she did or didn't. She would just say the words. If what she felt towards this man wasn't love, then she wasn't capable of feeling it towards anyone. Kirra opened her mouth and took a breath.

She would say it quietly out loud while he was asleep, then do it properly once he was awake.

He dragged his arm from his face and opened his eyes, squinting at Kirra in the dappled sunlight. Her words snagged on her tongue.

"I morning," she blurted out.

"I morning to you too," he groaned back at her, grabbing his glasses from the bedside table.

"Shall we go down and get some breakfast?" she offered, quickly looking for something to say.

"Yeah, sounds good. You might have to carry me though – my back's fucked."

***

Kirra piled her plate up high with a variety of breakfast delicacies then procured coffees, smoothies and juices of all varieties. She was ravenous. David looked over at her haul and quietly chuckled.

"Hungry after a big night with this stud?" he gestured to himself, gingerly sipping on his coffee. "I feel like I've been hit by a bus."

"I tend to have that effect on men." She grinned at him before shoving waffles and bacon into her mouth.

"You've got to remember I'm older than you, not some young buck you can use as a chew toy." He pulled at the collar of his shirt and revealed teeth marks Kirra had left on him.

"Whoops, sorry,"

"I'm kidding, obviously. Last night was the best night of my life. The hotel in Perth is the second best." He smiled at her warmly.

"Can we go back up after breakfast for another round?" Kirra was still exceptionally horny; last night had stoked the fire rather than smothered it.

"I think I need at least a 48-hour recovery window, McNamara. I'll lay you down on that sofa near the fireplace and eat your pussy though."

A small cough sounded from behind him as a waiter offered to refill their coffees. Kirra busied herself with her smoothie to avoid any eye contact and stifle her laughter. David looked mortified and declined a refill.

Kirra smirked at him once the waiter had walked away. "You've caught foot-in-mouth disease from me. Sorry, they can't test for that."

They spent the morning in the gym and pool and walking around the grounds of the hotel. David had booked Kirra in for a facial at the spa in the afternoon. She could definitely get used to this princess treatment.

She emerged from her treatment relaxed, refreshed and feeling well and truly ready to face the evening with David's family and friends. She had agonised for hours with Dan as to what she should wear tonight. They'd come to a unanimous agreement that the silky aqua-green shift dress with the pointy silver kitten heels was the best choice.

She pulled her dark hair back in a slick low bun and was adventurous enough to attempt a smoky eye. Her skin was glowing with layers upon layers of expensive products from her afternoon at the spa.

She felt beautiful.

When she emerged from the room, David was reclined on a day bed, looking out towards the city. He'd put his contacts in and was wearing a dark, collared shirt with light-coloured pants. He was freshly showered, styled and immaculately dressed – Kirra wanted to leave more teeth marks on him right now.

"Fucking hell, you look good," she almost growled at him. He turned to look at her, that beautiful smile shining back at her as he took her in.

"God, so do you." He stood up and wrapped her in a hug, turning her around so that they could both look over towards the harbour, the sinking sun making the ocean glitter.

"Sydney is alright," she offered sarcastically.

It was bloody gorgeous, particularly this time of day. While people from down south had always rubbed her the wrong way for coming off as superior, it was an undeniably stunning location for a major city.

"That's why we got the Olympics thirty-two years before Brissy," he quipped.

Chapter 50

Icebergs

Kirra was the only person wearing colour in the whole place.
All the men wore some iteration of David's cream/white and navy/black, and the women were all in sleek ensembles of white or beige. She felt awkward and exposed in her mini shift. While she was always keen to show off the legs she broke her back in the gym to achieve, she couldn't see a single other set of knees in the place.

Kirra fought the urge to round her shoulders, to make herself smaller. She'd had enough of that for the weekend. She took control of her spiralling thoughts, straightened her spine and gladly accepted a glass of champagne from a passing waiter.

"Can I introduce you to some people? I'm a bit keen to show you off." He planted a kiss on her neck, one arm around her lower back and the other holding his own glass of champagne. The kiss made her tingle, and the first sip of champagne loosened her shoulders some more.

"By all means, David," she offered in her most regal accent.

David, the most charming man in the world, mingled with his father's friends, extended family and old mates with polished ease.

Kirra was always in awe of how well he handled all social interactions he was placed in. All the hands Kirra shook were of very friendly, kind people who all wanted to learn more about her, tell harmless jokes about David and include her in the conversation. Kirra was reevaluating her preconceived ideas on people who were born rich. They did seem to have an easy breezy friendliness about them in general, which was hard to dislike.

Maybe she wouldn't eat them when the class war broke out.

Almost as if sensing her brother's excitement and Kirra's comfort, Catherine showed up, a fair-haired freckly man of about fifty closely on her heels. David turned to address his sister.

"Ah Catherine, you look beautiful." He leant forward and gave her a peck on the cheek. She allowed him to without so much as smiling or inclining her body towards him in return. He turned to her companion.

"Dylan! You son of a bitch!" David had put on the *worst* Schwarzenegger accent Kirra had ever heard as he clasped his brother-in-law's hand in a mid-air arm wrestle.

"What's the matter, the CIA got you pushing too many pencils?"

Dylan was grinning back at David, the strain of trying to win their game evident on his pale face. He gave up after a moment or so and clapped David on the shoulder.

"Good to see you again, mate." He grinned at David, then at Kirra.

"I'm Dylan. You must be Kirra – lovely to meet you." He leant in for a kiss on the cheek and smiled warmly at her.

"Nice to meet you, Dylan. Good to see you again, Catherine." She nodded at David's sister, deciding against any kind of physical greeting.

The boys came over and shook David's hand, foregoing their usual hug as a greeting with the extra eyes in the room. There must have been close to a hundred people milling about, laughing loudly and sipping expensive champagne.

"Eddie was telling me you flogged George in Mortal Kombat last night. I was sorry to have missed it!" Dylan chuckled, Edward grinning at Kirra and George giving her absolutely nothing. Catherine gave her husband an irritated look. The woman looked in desperate need of an orgasm and a cheeseburger.

"Oh my god, did he? That wasn't really the first impression I was trying to make." Kirra blushed a little bit, looking away from Catherine's husband.

"What kind of first impression did you want to make?" Catherine cut in, levelling Kirra with a withering look.

It baffled Kirra how two siblings with the same pale blue eyes could use their stare for such different purposes. One set made you feel seen and heard, like you were the most important person in the world, while the other's turned you to stone.

"Uh, I don't know, a good one?" Kirra offered ineptly.

"Well, you've made a great impression on Dad – he hasn't shut up about you since last night." Catherine gestured towards where George Senior was holding court, chatting to a bunch of people who stood around him.

Catherine's tone wasn't aggressive enough to be taken as instigative, but it was unsettling and cold enough to know she wasn't just making chit-chat. Kirra knew she was in trouble. David had said she had been upset at the attention he got when he had been abused at school, which was foul and ridiculous.

This was positive attention, from their dad. She was absolutely fucked.

David instinctively moved closer to Kirra, wrapping his arm more tightly around her.

"That's a bit of an exaggeration, Catherine," David returned, his voice lowering in warning.

"Oh look, there's Jez. We haven't seen him since our wedding, babe," Dylan mirrored David's posture and ushered Catherine towards the opposite end of the restaurant. She shot one final glare at Kirra before being led away by her husband.

"Fuck, what's her problem?" Kirra muttered under her breath.

"Once you figure that out, you let me know," David replied, draining the rest of his glass.

Kirra was rattled, but things went smoothly otherwise.

They eventually made their way over to George and Evelyn, who welcomed them warmly and excitedly like they hadn't seen them less than 24 hours ago. Kirra chatted, and drank, and chatted and drank some more. The champagne was crisp with the perfect amount of fizz and was going down easily. David subtly handed Kirra a glass of water which she gulped down before accepting a pale-yellow cocktail served in a martini glass from the next passing waiter.

David and Kirra were talking with some of David's acquaintances from the Sydney branch of the firm when they were approached by a beautiful blonde woman maybe a few years older than Kirra.

"David, hi!" She had a news presenter's voice, a little husky, that carried across the room. As she leant into kiss David on the cheek in greeting, Kirra noticed they were almost the same height. She was wearing the same billowy beige ensemble as the rest of the people at the party. She was fucking beautiful.

"Mel, lovely to see you again." David's eyes darted quickly to Kirra, then back to Mel.

Her stomach dropped with immediate understanding as she read that look. Mel was his ex. The ex. The one that wanted a ring. The one he'd run away from.

"Mel, this is my girlfriend, Kirra."

If he had introduced her with anything else other than that title, she would have vomited right there on Mel's tailored white pants.

"Kirra! I love that name." She extended her perfectly manicured hand and shook Kirra's firmly. Kirra felt numb, like all the champagne she'd consumed had hit her at once.

"Thanks, Mel," Kirra could feel her lips moving and the vibration of noise coming out of her throat but couldn't really hear her own words as they left her.

"So nice of your dad to invite me. He still plays golf with my dad every Sunday."

Kirra looked to David, who looked slightly panicked.

"Yeah, your dad's here too?" David's throat bobbed.

Kirra was looking on like a statue. She couldn't believe David had left her – she was physically perfect and exuded confidence and elegance. Kirra wondered if David's attempt on his own life coincided with the end of his and Mel's relationship.

She couldn't stand it a moment longer.

"I'll leave you guys to catch up. I'm just going to go get some fresh air," she interrupted, earning a worried look from David. "I'll be right back."

She leant in and planted a quick kiss on David's neck as she pushed passed him and headed to the balcony. He lightly grabbed at her elbow, but she kept moving. Her ears were ringing and the normal urges to run, explode or numb were crippling her.

She got to the balcony, the sticky ocean air welcome on her overheated skin. She slid the door shut behind her to drown at the clamour inside and moved as far away into the corner as she could. Kirra closed her eyes and worked on steadying her breath. She would do anything for a cigarette, a bump, something to quiet her racing thoughts. She wasn't sure if it was even jealousy doing this to her or just embarrassment at having no clue how to act around their partner's stunning ex-girlfriend – an invited guest and family friend.

She was running away, again.

"Getting some fresh air, Jane?" A familiar voice came from behind her, his face obscured by the light streaming out on to the darkened balcony.

As if this night couldn't get any worse.

She knew who it was before she saw his face. It seemed she wasn't the only Brisbane-based guest who had been invited to George's birthday celebrations.

"Ken, what a pleasure," she offered, plastering on her fakest smile. "I didn't expect you down here."

"George and I go way back," he drawled, moving closer to Kirra. He was tall and thin, his grey hair more telling of his age than his smooth, lineless face. "So, what are you doing here? I wasn't aware you had any dealings with the Sydney office or George Waters."

Kirra was cornered, literally and metaphorically. It was a private party with no more than 100 guests. There was no way she could lie her way out of the question.

"I'm David Waters' plus one."

She'd been busted. She was fucked.

"Oh, is that so." Ken had closed the distance between them and leant on the railing beside Kirra, looking out over the Pacific Ocean alongside her. She was readying herself to be told that she had broken her employment contract by dating a coworker and that she could pack her bags come Monday.

"Smart move on your part. His family is worth millions."

She felt her throat close in rage. She wondered whether, if she wheelbarrowed the old cunt over the balcony, she could convince the rest of the party he had fallen. Not only would she not be sacked, she would like coming to work more. Murder lingered on her mind for a heartbeat or two.

"I'm surprised though. I thought you were fucking Ben Andrews from Guérir." He levelled his cold eyes on her.

He was close enough that she could smell the whiskey on his breath and notice that his eyes were slightly unfocused, even through her own drunkenness. His wife would be inside, clutching at her pearls and squawking with the other old partners' wives.

"He could barely contain himself when he whisked you out of the office the other day." Ken looked at her with disgust and something else.

"What can I say, I'm irresistible to men in their fifties and sixties." She turned and straightened up, taking a step closer to him in defiance.

"Well of course you are. They're old enough to know an easy root when they see one, aren't they?"

"If I'm such an easy root, then why haven't you had a turn, Ken? Are you mad I've fucked half of Brisbane and you still didn't make the cut?"

Kirra was seeing red.

"I almost did though, didn't I?"

Chapter 51

Kirra's first free-flowing function

When Kirra had been a first-year graduate, there had been a function.

It was a function with free-flowing alcohol, senior partners and cocaine. She hadn't touched drugs since getting back from Oxford. When she had gone out with Tamika and Zoe and found out just how expensive they were in Brisbane, she had stuck to Passion Pop. But at this function, some of the senior partners, including Ken, had invited a very drunk Kirra into an office at the back of the restaurant.

Ken had racked up three lines on the polished hardwood desk and done one in front of her, offering her the rolled up hundred-dollar note that had just been stuffed up his nose. Without thinking, she had leant forward and bumped the second before another one of the older male partners did the third.

She remembered the feeling vividly, like it had happened yesterday and not almost twelve years ago. She had been twenty-three, and Ken fifty, at the time.

"You want another, Kirra Jane?" He had gripped her by her chin and looked down into her face.

"Yeah, I do," she had giggled back.

The memory came crashing in on her as she stood there with a now grey-haired Ken. It still brought shame. She had been so foolish.

Ken lined up thousands of dollars worth of blow on that desk. He had bent Kirra over at the waist, tightly wrapping her hair around his hand and holding it back while she snorted line after line.

He ground into her from behind, making lewd comments to the other man in the room about how wet the drugs were making her, how she would do anything for another line. He wasn't entirely wrong either – she was already drunk and high, wanting more of something she couldn't have afforded on her own.

After they had finished all of his coke, Ken picked her up and placed her on the edge of the desk. He kissed her, his thin lips slobbering over hers and his stubble brushing up against her skin. Her lips and throat were numb. She didn't kiss him back, but she didn't push him away either. She was propped on the edge of the desk like a mannequin.

While he kissed her, he reached up her skirt, pulled her underwear to the side and roughly pushed two fingers into her. The memory of that evening had been diluted by hundreds of nights of drinks, drugs and running away, but it hadn't been forgotten entirely.

She remembered the other guy, whoever he was, asking Ken how wet she was for him. Ken had laughed into Kirra's mouth and said she was soaked. But she wasn't, she was dry, it hurt, it burned. *Burned.* As if brought back to her senses, Kirra had shoved Ken back, jumped down off the desk and run back to the function. As soon as she had rejoined the party, Jeannine had grabbed her by the elbow.

"I've been looking everywhere for you. We're going." She had ushered Kirra out of the venue and safely home, where no questions were asked and it was never spoken of again.

Chapter 52

Dumb and drunk then, dumb and drunk now

Kirra recalled it all in vivid detail as he stood there before her now, the same nasty prick he was all those years ago. He was still an entitled, arrogant arsehole who thought so little of her despite how hard she had worked to prove that she wasn't just some bogan, druggie slut.

"You sexually assaulted me that night. I was twenty-three."

"Plenty old enough to know what you were doing," he countered quickly, like he had justified his actions to himself countless times before.

"It wasn't my age, it was the age difference, the power imbalance. You plied with me drugs and penetrated me without my consent."

"Your memory of that evening is inaccurate. You were fully consenting. You were loving the attention and the free coke – you grabbed my hand and shoved it up your skirt."

"No, I fucking didn't." Her memory may be hazy, but she remembered that part crystal clear.

"Yes, you fucking did." He was standing over her, but her back was straight despite her trembling hands and pounding heart.

"How about I go in there and tell Mrs Maunsell that you fingered someone half your age?"

"By all means, go for it. Go in there and embarrass David and his father by causing a scene, something you're an expert in." He sneered down at her.

Kirra couldn't handle it any longer. Her ears were ringing, heart pounding, vision blurring. She pushed past him and dashed through the event without looking up to see where David was. She made her way through the crowd, out of the restaurant, and ran. After a few paces in her shoes, she pulled them off, tucked them under her arm and ran some more. The bitumen cut and pulled at her feet, but she didn't stop. The sticky night's air sawed in and out of her lungs as she ran unseeing.

She made her way down to the dark beach where she sat, shaking. Wrapping her arms around her legs and burying her head between her knees, she wept.

Taking in great big bucketfuls of salty sea air, she let it all come out. Her throat strained and her eyes streamed, the grip she had on each of her elbows threatening to pull them out of their sockets.

She was just as stupid now, at almost thirty-five, as she had been at twenty-three … as she had been at fifteen. All that time and she hadn't learned a fucking thing. She hadn't learned how to deal with people like Ken, predators above reproach. She hadn't learned how to play nice with others, live and let live, make less of a spectacle of herself. And, most importantly, she hadn't learned how to let someone as perfect as David love her, all of her. She hadn't learned how to love someone back, either.

Kirra sat there, crying, wallowing, the sounds of the waves drowning out her pitiful sobs.

He hadn't announced his arrival with words, but she knew he was there, sitting in the sand silently beside her. He lightly placed a hand on her back, and she felt its warmth through her dress.

The salty scent of the beach at night mixed with the smell of his cologne, and she felt his calming presence bring her out of her head and back to reality. She unlocked her head from between her knees and looked ahead into the ocean.

She wanted to commit to David, properly, but she couldn't do that without telling him how things had ended with Him, why she was so irreparably fucked up.

So she took a deep breath and told him.

All of it.

Chapter 53

Kirra, almost sixteen years old

Kirra had found a place she could get her pregnancy terminated and was booked in for the procedure on Friday – three days away. Happy fucking birthday. Katie, the living legend, had loaned her the few hundred dollars it cost to get the procedure performed at a not-for-profit organisation that promised safety and discretion to girls and women in need.

As it turned out, Kirra had been pregnant for a while and had missed the window to address her situation with medication, so she needed a surgical termination instead. Turns out you can get pregnant without actually having menstruated. Chris was misinformed on that front. She was set on her decision to terminate the pregnancy but still wanted to tell Chris what had happened.

She was going to tell him the news, let him know she was booked in for Friday, and that she would get an IUD inserted at the same time so it wouldn't happen again. She thought everything could continue on as it had been with the two of them.

He came in, and they sat on the lounge. He immediately pushed her down and started kissing her, but Kirra pushed him off her and spoke.

"Chris, even though I haven't got my period yet, I'm somehow pregnant."

He looked at her, shock contorting his features in an instant. She didn't want to allow a second to pass without telling him she had already made plans to remedy the situation. "I'm already booked for a—"

"You lying fucking cunt! You clearly had your period and were trying to fucking trap me!" he bellowed, the words spilling out of him in a torrent. He stood up and paced the room, running hands through his hair. "Desperate fucking bitch," he was muttering to himself without looking at Kirra.

She was indignant and stunned silent for a moment too long at his reaction – rage, which had been lying dormant for months now, built up in her. She stood up too.

"I wasn't! I'm not! You were the one who said we'd be fine!"

She gathered her senses. She needed him to know she was going to fix it, that they could stay together. He was mad, but they'd get over this.

"It doesn't matter anyway because—"

In a heartbeat, he had stopped pacing and was in front of her.

Her stomach heaved, bile surging up in her throat. A splitting pain tore up from her navel and into her chest. The pain wrapped around her spine and made her blind in an instant. Her mind quickly made up a reason as to the source of the agony. *Don't worry about the termination, you're having a miscarriage, Katie said this could happen.*

There was no way her mind could reconcile what was happening until Chris drew his fist back and swung another bone-crunching punch into her stomach.

Maybe there's a fly on me, and he's trying to swat it – she remembers, years later, that was her next thought. It wasn't the punches themselves but where her mind went – *a fly, that has to be it, he loves me, he wouldn't, this makes no sense* – even after it was clear he was attacking her.

Whenever she woke up sweating, panicked in the middle of the night, it was the shame of that first ridiculous thought that haunted her, not the memory of the physical pain.

She fell to the ground in agony. She hadn't seen his face since she had told him she was pregnant, hadn't had the chance to finish saying she was getting a termination, and now she was on the floor, white crowding out the corners her vision as she felt something hard connect with her side again and again.

She came to a moment later and felt the pressure, the tightness on her throat and the blurred sight of his face above her, drool spilling out his mouth in rage and his empty eyes staring into her while his thumbs sank into the middle of her throat.

She couldn't speak, couldn't scream for help. Her arms hung lank at her sides.

The boy she loved was killing her.

She sank into darkness, the pain and pressure receding as she lost consciousness.

Chapter 54

Beeping

The first sign that she was still alive was the beeping.

There was an insistent chime on a nearby monitor, and a different bell ringing further in the distance. The sounds grew louder, and she realised she was still hearing. If she was still hearing, then that meant she may still be alive. She willed her eyes open.

A dimly lit room came into view. She saw a TV suspended from a white-panelled roof, and behind the TV was a metal rod supporting a blue-green curtain. Without moving her head, she turned her eyes left and right. To her right she could see a small grey box with a black screen lit up with numbers, above which a bag of clear fluid hung from a thin metal rod. To her left, another monitor and a chair.

A chair with a slumped figure in it.

If she could hear and see, she must be alive. If she was alive, she could speak. She opened her mouth, but her lips were crusted together and stung when she tried. She moved her tongue around in her dry mouth and tried to say something, but her voice wasn't there. In a moment, she was panicked.

The monitor's beeping quickened, which seemed to jolt the sleeping figure awake.

It was her dad. Startled, he looked at her. Realising she was looking back at him, he immediately pushed a button above her head. A little light lit up and there was a different beeping sound. So many different beeps, she thought absentmindedly.

It's so loud in here.

I'm hearing, I'm seeing, I'm breathing.

I'm alive.

"Kirra, Kirra sweetie, you're okay, you're safe." Her dad took her face in both hands and looked into her eyes, which she could feel burning with tears. Her dad's eyes were swollen and red. He started crying even though he was smiling, his relief mixing with his despair. Kirra got her lips working and tried to speak again. A raspy, windy noise escaped where her voice would have normally.

"Don't try and speak sweetie, your uh, your…" He looked down at the floor, clearly unsure of what to say. "You need to heal darling, it's okay darl. It's okay," he said, more to himself than her, stroking her hair.

The nurse arrived at the call signal Kirra's dad had triggered. She looked between patient and parent. "I'll get the doctors. It's great she's awake and alert. She's pulled through," she said to Kirra's father.

It was all too much, the beeping, her dad's puffy face, the odd upright angle of the bed, the sterile smells. She quickly let darkness take her, and she was asleep again.

Kirra's sweet sixteenth was spent in the Royal Brisbane and Women's Hospital in and out of consciousness.

***

Chris had nearly killed her, and he would have had Nick and her dad not come home when they did. Nick had pulled Chris off Kirra, and Kirra's dad had rushed to help her, calling an ambulance when he took in how badly injured she was. Whatever Nick had done to Chris had landed Chris in hospital, in a similar condition to the one he had put Kirra in, with Nick in police custody.

Kirra's injuries were extensive.

She had burst vessels in her eyes and severe bruising around her neck from where Chris had choked her, but her windpipe hadn't been completely crushed so she had kept on breathing. The worst of the injuries had been to her organs, where he had punched and repeatedly kicked her with steel-capped boots. She

273

had required an emergency laparotomy after first attenders suspected she was haemorrhaging internally. Several of her organs had been perforated, including her spleen and liver, which were hurriedly repaired by surgeons. The surgery had left her with a crooked, rushed incision, but it had saved her life. Her ribs were broken, much of her body was bloodied and bruised.

She was no longer pregnant.

Her father didn't leave her side that first day, and he was quickly joined by Kirra's mother after Nick had been released from custody. Kirra saw Nick once in the hospital in the days she was there. He acknowledged her, but no words were exchanged, and she didn't see him again until they were home.

Kirra spent most of her September holidays at home, neither of her parents leaving her side. Being young, Kirra recovered well from the surgery and her injuries and was able to return to school two weeks into her last term of year eleven.

She dropped out of her soccer team completely, telling her coaches she wanted to focus on year twelve, but in truth she didn't want to run into Katie again. Katie had contacted Kirra's mother when she couldn't find her to take her to the appointment. Katie had invented a story about a soccer tournament, and her mother had invented a story in response about Kirra being inexplicably unwell and having a short stay in the hospital. Katie had texted Kirra but they went unanswered while she was recovering, and when Kirra finally texted her back, she made up a story about losing the baby naturally. So many made-up stories, no one telling the truth, no one talking to each other.

Katie was a good friend, but Kirra couldn't tell her what had really happened. She couldn't tell anyone what had really happened. Her parents never asked her. Police and lawyers did, but not her parents, and she never offered details. To the family, life went on as if the whole thing had never happened. If she didn't have the wound on her abdomen where she had been cut open and put back together, she could even trick herself into thinking it was all a dream, or a nightmare.

It took Chris longer to get out of hospital. When he did, he was charged.

Chris' defence relied heavily on the fact he hadn't intended to kill her when he went to the house, that he had an otherwise clean record, and that he was experiencing a mental health crisis at the time of the attack. All of these things were true, but the irrefutable evidence of his grooming a child and attempting to murder her, which resulted in significant, lifelong injuries, landed him a life imprisonment with the possibility of parole in twenty years.

Twenty years. Chris would be thirty-nine years old when he came out. The number rolled around in her head. He would go in a boy, a teenager, and come out a man almost in his forties. Would he ever get married, have kids? Is thirty-nine too old for that sort of thing?

Kirra didn't have to attend the proceedings, but she wanted to. It wasn't to see justice being served – she had just wanted to see him one more time. It was another memory that haunted her; she wanted to say goodbye to him, even after he had tried to kill her.

She was numb and didn't know how to feel. In the courtroom, Kirra could feel a pair of eyes boring into her, and she looked up and into his face for the first time since the day he had almost killed her.

She was shocked at what stared back at her.

Nick had caved in most of the left side of Chris' face. His lower eyelid hung loose in its socket with his eye pointing out at an odd angle. His hair sat unevenly on his scalp where his skull had been battered. He hadn't had the teeth Nick had knocked out replaced, so his lips curled in on one another, making him look much older than he was. His mouth was closed into a tight, crooked line.

He looked out into the crowd at Kirra with the one beautiful brown eye that still pointed in the right direction.

Nick had mutilated him.

Chris was no longer beautiful and may never be again. Kirra looked back at him. She hadn't processed any of it, hadn't said a word of what happened to anyone other than the police, and couldn't put words to what she felt in that moment.

She was there when they passed down the verdict.

Nick had his own trial. The attack landed him with an intensive corrections order which had him regularly report to a community corrections officer. It stopped him from leaving the state of Queensland for a year, and he had to see a counsellor for intense therapy until it was determined he wasn't capable of hurting someone as badly as he had hurt Chris again. Nick complied with the order, did all he was mandated to do, but was still left with a permanent record at age seventeen.

Chris went to jail, Kirra finished her penultimate year of high school, Nick finished school and none of it was ever discussed ever again.

Until just now.

Chapter 55

Confessions

David had shuffled closer to Kirra and wrapped his arm around her while she told him everything. He hadn't interrupted or asked questions, just listened until she was done.

"He's due out next year." David cut the silence, having done the maths of how long Chris' sentence was.

"Yeah, I don't know how these things work, but he went away just after I turned sixteen." Her voice was strained from talking. She wasn't aware of everything she had said and wondered how much detail she had gone into. Judging by how cold the night had gotten and how sore her legs were from sitting in the same position, she figured they had been there for hours.

"Kirra, I'm so sorry that happened to you, I mean – fuck, you almost died." David's voice broke.

"Nick almost killed him, too."

"Then your mum died the following year?"

"Yeah, she did. Chris almost killed me in September of 2006, and Mum died in May 2007."

"You don't think they knew you were pregnant?"

"Honestly, I don't know. Even when Mum was around, we weren't talkers, not like your family."

"And you and Nick, what was that like after everything that happened?"

"Different, I can't really explain it, but Nick just …" Kirra started crying again.

Nick had never been the same, really. He had been coarse and blunt his whole life, but after he had that assault on his permanent record, after he'd almost killed his best friend, who had almost killed his sister, an impenetrable wall had been placed between him and Kirra. A huge, unspoken divide had opened up and was further widened when they lost their mother.

"Kirra." David kissed her hair, softly saying her name against her scalp.

She nestled into the side of him, the chill of the night's air cutting through the heat on her skin. She placed her face into his neck and took in one big lungful of him. He tilted his head to let her get closer.

She straightened up to see him. The moonlight and the ambient light from the street outlined his face, and Kirra was again struck by how very lovely he was to look at.

"I love you, David," she admitted. "I've loved you since I found you in the hammock with Gus."

David's face broke into a smile.

"Oh yeah, that's cool," he said, smirking, but the glistening of his eyes told her what she already knew.

"You're fucking kidding me," Kirra laughed, sniffing.

He leant forward and kissed her, and it was different. She felt an ache in her chest like her heart was both being torn apart and put together at the same time. It was both beautiful and terrifying.

"I love you too, Kirra Jane McNamara. I've loved you since the moment I first saw you."

"When I called you a cunt." She remembered the ride back from Byron when he told her he loved her. She should have told him then.

"A bit before that, actually. Nathaniel was introducing me to the office, and I saw you in the crowd sharing an evil-looking joke with Paul. I thought you were the most beautiful woman I'd ever laid eyes on." He traced his hand over her face, eyes scanning all her features as if he was seeing her for the first time. "And *then* you called me a cunt."

Kirra and David didn't return to the party, electing to go straight back to their hotel. They had a bath together, in silence, in the dark. It was exactly what Kirra needed after the overstimulation of the party, meeting David's ex-girlfriend, the confrontation with Ken, the confession about Chris, telling David she loved him. She was spent, utterly spent.

She was gritty too. For someone named after a beach, she hated the sand.

David towelled her off, wrapped her in a lush hotel robe and carried her back to their freshly made bed.

It felt so good to be clean and having shared her secret with the man she loved.

Chapter 56

Kirra insisted they swing by Girraween before their mid-morning flight to say goodbye to David's parents. They had an early flight back to Brisbane so Kirra would be back in time to see Hattie's dance performance. Hattie had been working so hard on it for months, and there was no way Kirra would break her unblemished record as her goddaughter's cheerleader in the crowd.

A bright and chipper Evelyn and a severely hungover George greeted them and made them coffee which they enjoyed in one of the estate's many sitting rooms, chatting about how the party had gone. George needed David to help him move something, and Kirra was left alone with Evelyn.

"Kirra, thank you," she said, completely unprompted, the minute George and David were out of earshot.

"Oh, um, of course. I felt bad about the Irish goodbye, but I couldn't possibly go back to Brisbane without seeing you guys again."

"No, not that. Well, I mean, not just that." She looked over her shoulder to make sure her son and husband hadn't returned yet, "I haven't seen David this happy in forever."

"Since Mel?" Kirra regretted the petty, insecure words the moment they broke free from her mouth.

Evelyn smiled and shook her head.

"No, I mean forever. Mel's a lovely girl, but she was more of a family friend who just happened to date David for a while. Probably a while too long, to be honest. But this," she gestured to Kirra and then in the direction the men had walked off in, "is different. I hope he's making you as happy as I can see you're making him." Ev had the suggestion of tears in her eyes.

Kirra couldn't imagine what this woman had endured, knowing what had been done to her son in a place that was meant to keep him safe, to see how it had tormented him for years and taken one of his closest friends. Ugly things still happen in beautiful places.

"He is, he's perfect." Kirra smiled, on the verge of tears herself.

David and his father returned and, after much hugging and a promise to come up to visit in Easter, the pair set back for Brisbane.

Chapter 57

So sweet and scarlet and free

Hattie looked so beautiful on stage.

Kirra managed to peel her eyes away for a moment to observe the crowd, and they were just as transfixed by her. Hattie's solo performance had just finished to a standing ovation and the obscene screaming of her mother and godmother, the ultimate hype girls ever since Hattie had taken her first steps.

"Fuck Zo, she's brilliant." Kirra's face felt like it was about to split from how hard she was smiling. She could see in the darkness that Zoe's mascara was smudged and running. Hattie would be so embarrassed to see the state both women were in.

Her performance with Harrison was next, a contemporary number that Zoe had warned Kirra was a bit 'out there'. The curtains drew back to the mournful opening bars of 'Where the Wild Roses Grow'.

The routine started as an elegant waltz. Harrison led Hattie around the stage, him dressed in black and her in red, the pair looking longingly at each other. Hattie's expression was peaceful and happy, but there was something else there – fear or apprehension, like she knew there was something about Harrison's character she couldn't trust. She was wary but still let him lead her around the stage, carrying her gently like a delicate flower, freshly picked, that could fall apart at any moment.

The song built to its crescendo. Hattie knelt, wistfully looking into what the audience was to believe was the river, the one Harrison's character had been taking her to every day of their courtship. She turned at the last moment to see him strike her from behind. She fell on the stage floor, some clever lighting making the whole space turn red as Harrison performed his solo for the end of the song, and then the curtains were drawn. There was reverent silence in the hall for a moment before rapturous applause rang out all around Kirra. People on either side of her, including Zoe, were on their feet, whistling, screaming, cheering.

Kirra was frozen, immobilised.

Zoe noticed and knelt down, shaking her by the arm.

"Kiz, Kiz!"

She was snapped out of her reverie.

"What's wrong, mate. Are you okay?" Zoe looked panicked. Kirra felt how wet her cheeks were, how tight her jaw was from clenching it the entire song.

"Zoe," she whispered, the crowds around them still going wild. "That happened to me," she mumbled. "The first guy I loved, he tried to kill me."

***

Zoe and Kirra shared a cigarette in the carpark waiting for Hattie to be done.

While her performances were finished for the night, she had to stay there and watch her fellow dancers from the wings. Kirra had filled Zoe in on Chris and decided she would let Dan know too when she saw him next. Her loved ones had every right to know what she had been through and share it with her. Just like after she had told David the night before, telling Zoe made her feel even lighter and somehow closer to one of her oldest friends.

Kirra changed the topic and gushed at her goddaughter's performance. "Hattie was so beautiful. She knew he was bad news, but she still went off alone with him." The way she was able to show such nuance with her facial expressions and her body – she truly was doing what she was put on this Earth to do.

"Kiz, you were fifteen and in love with a nineteen-year-old boy. You weren't to know he was capable of what he did to you." Zoe had picked up on what had left Kirra so devastated by Hattie's dance.

"That's the thing, Zo. I kind of did. I'd seen him and Nick get into a punch-up before, a serious one. They beat the shit out of each other in the backyard one time over something, and when I asked Chris about it, he said they were just mucking around. Then there was this other time."

Kirra couldn't say these memories were being unlocked, they had always been there. She had thought that never reliving them would starve them of their oxygen and eventually kill them. Instead, they had festered and mutated, becoming even worse over time.

"I saw him kill a brush turkey with a nail gun."

Zoe gasped in shock. "Oh fuck."

Kirra recalled it vividly as she said it out loud. She had been standing on that same balcony she had dropped her Doritos off, hidden from view.

"Yeah, it was making its nest in our front yard. Dad went inside to grab something, and I saw Chris plug the gun into an outlet in the carport. He lined the poor thing up and shot a few nails into its head and body then kicked the leaves over it. Then he just unplugged the gun, put it back in the tray of the ute and hopped back into the cab as Dad came out with his lunch or whatever he'd forgotten." Kirra gazed up at the night sky, letting the smoke from her Winfield Blue pass over her lips. "Like it was nothing. Like stepping on an ant."

"Mate, that's fucked, but how were you to know he was capable of being that violent with a human? With you?"

"I wasn't, I guess." She still wasn't ready to absolve herself of Chris' crime completely.

"You weren't, so you need to stop blaming yourself, immediately." Zoe wrapped Kirra in her arms and squeezed her tightly. It felt so nice, closer, like all the hugs before that had been through a jacket and this one was skin to skin.

Kirra had been there with Zoe when she had dealt with an unplanned pregnancy: broke, young and vulnerable. She had held Hattie hours after she was born, the most perfect little bundle of life wrapped up and looking around her new world. She had held

Zoe and stroked her hair as she battled post-natal depression, weeping openly as the reality of her new life as an unprepared mum crashed in on her.

Now it felt good to be held by someone she loved so dearly, to feel and accept Zoe's love in return.

Over Zoe's shoulder, Kirra saw some movement from the back of the hall and heard giggling. A pair of kids had escaped the performance to make out near the overflowing skip bins. How romantic, good for them.

Zoe checked her phone and figured the performance would be close to being over, and they started to head back inside. The closer they got to the doors, the better Kirra heard the giggling and was hit with an icy wave of recognition. Without announcing her hunch to Zoe, she shot off down the side of the hall, Zoe skidding behind, shouting after her.

The flood lights pointed towards the carpark, shrouding the pair huddled up against the wall of the building in darkness, and she whirled on them when she thought she was close enough. She shone the torch from her phone, intent on busting Harrison and Hattie making out when they were supposedly 'just friends'. Her arse they were. She saw how he looked at her on stage – it wasn't a fucking act and Harrison was bad news. She knew it.

The light caught Hattie's eyes first. She threw her hands up to shield them, but it wasn't Harrison quickly withdrawing his hand from down the front of her leotard. It was a different boy, a taller one. The door at the side of the hall opened, flooding the space with light, making her phone's torch redundant.

Kirra took in the piece of shit who had just been groping her goddaughter. He had one of those dumb fucking broccoli haircuts every boy his age seemed to have these days. But what age was that? Kirra's eyes adjusted, and she took in what he was wearing – one of the senior's jerseys from Hattie's school, Class of 2026 on his collar.

This kid was turning seventeen, or maybe eighteen this year. Hattie had just turned fourteen, she was in year eight.

Kirra's hands moved before her brain had a chance to stop them. She shoved with all her might into the boy's chest and sent him flying back into the brick wall, hearing the satisfying *whump* of the air leaving his lungs. She was aware of a shrill noise to her left but couldn't make out what it was or who was making it. The boy put his hands up defensively, but Kirra swung with all her body weight into the side of his face with a closed fist, not registering any pain in her hand or the contact with his head.

The next sensation she registered was at least two pairs of hands dragging her backwards. She was off balance but managed to stay on her feet.

She regained some awareness and took in the shrill sound as Hattie and Zoe screamed at her to stop. The boy was still standing, luckily, bleeding from his lip, looking at Kirra in horror. She realised what she had done too late – there was a crowd forming, drawn in by the screams of her friend and goddaughter.

For the second time that weekend, Kirra turned and ran away.

Chapter 58

The wheels fall off

Kirra routinely showed up hungover or even still a bit drunk to Kensington Menschel of a Monday, but she always showed up. Today, for the first Monday in almost thirteen years, she didn't.

Her phone hadn't stopped buzzing all night and into the wee hours of the morning, probably Zoe, but she had left it on the other side of her room, choosing to stare at it rather than answer it. She had somehow gotten home from where Hattie's performance had been, but the specifics eluded her. Her hand throbbed from where she had hit the bastard who was feeling up Hattie. *The child she had assaulted.*

Kirra didn't have the energy to fret; she was beyond caring. If the police knocked on her door right now to arrest her, she deserved it. If Nathaniel sacked her for having a relationship with a coworker and missing work, so-fucking-be-it. Her body felt like it was lead – heavy and numb – the only sensation she felt was the steady throb of her busted knuckles and a deep, deep exhaustion.

Fuck, she was tired. So, so fucking tired.

She had been run down, dehydrated, overworked, stressed and overwhelmed for many years, but this was a new type of tired. It wasn't just being tired of your job, tired of your surroundings, tired from needing a good night's sleep. It was being tired of everything – tired of life itself. For wherever Kirra went, be it a mansion in Vaucluse, a renovated cottage in Paddington or a strip club in the Valley, there she was.

And she was fucking tired of being her.

She had hit a child, openly picked a fight with Ken, was dating a coworker.

Christ, David.

Kirra had wanted a relationship, or thought she had, and now she had fallen in love with him. She had met his parents, he'd met hers, she'd told him about Chris. She had met him five weeks ago and now look where she was … about to get fired, charged with assault, struck off and liable to have her heart broken.

If he thought he was in love with her before, he wouldn't be now. She still didn't really believe he was to begin with. He was clearly unwell himself – growing this attached to her in such a short space of time was a huge red flag that should have been obvious before now.

There was a knock at the door, but Kirra ignored it. The police could kick her door in if they wanted her so badly. Another knock. She could hear Gus skidding across the hardwood floor and jumping up at the door.

"Kiz, darl?" Geoff called through the window. "I'm here to get Gussy, you alright?"

Of course, it's Monday.

She willed herself up, pulling her body to the front door, ignoring Gus' excitement at seeing her upright. She snapped on his leash and opened the door just wide enough to let him pass through. She went to slam the door shut, and Geoff put his hand in the frame to stop it.

"Kiz sweetie, what's wrong?"

"I've got gastro, Geoff. Don't want you to get it."

He slowly took his hand away.

"You call me if you need anything, love. I'll have Gus as long as you need. Get better."

Another person who thought more highly of her than they had any right to. She would need to sell this place once she was struck off and unable to work, and move somewhere cheaper. Geoff can babysit the new owner's dogs or kids. They could take his bins out for him.

She shuffled back to her room, picked up her phone and threw it down the hallway, then drew her curtains and hid back under her covers.

***

When she woke up, it was dark.

For a blissful moment, she thought it must be Saturday night, that she had slept the day away again, but the pain in her hand reminded her of where she was. Kirra switched on her bedside lamp and looked down at her fist. Her fingers were red and her knuckles blue-black and fat, the gaps between them almost gone. The pain radiated up to her elbow and made her feel sick to her stomach. She must have hit him hard to have damaged her hand this badly. Kirra pulled herself from her bed and into the shower where she attempted to make herself feel better, cleaner.

She had completely missed Self-Care Sunday.

She tried to wash her hair in the shower, but the task was near impossible without the use of her right hand. It must have taken her close to an hour. She shrugged into some trackpants and a T-shirt and skulked out to the loungeroom, retrieving her phone.

She had cracked the screen badly when she had thrown it. She saw several notifications that she couldn't check, the glass failing to respond to her touch.

There was a bang at the door.

Geoff returning Gus. She grabbed a medical mask from her cabinet to make a show of not wanting to get Geoff sick, adding some plausibility to her story, and then made for the front door.

She opened the door a crack, anticipating Gus skidding inside so she could then quickly shut the door in Geoff's face before she had to deal with him. Instead, the door was grabbed and swung open with force.

Kirra stepped back in shock.

A tall figure stood on her deck, shrouded in darkness and obscured by the light streaming out of her house. It stood there, arms at its side and motionless, staring at her. She was frozen, squinting to make out who it was, before her heart plummeted and she took a step back in horror.

One dark brown eye pointing towards her, the other turned outwards, looked down the hallway behind her. Lips pulled back in a snarl exposed several gaps where the teeth her brother smashed in were never replaced.

It was *Him*. He had been let out early.

He was here.

She willed her legs to move, her voice to scream for help, but it was as if she was concreted in place. No, no, she couldn't go like this. Not while Hattie still needed to be protected from seventeen-year-old creeps, while Gus still needed someone to take him for a walk every day, while David …

She was going to die, and David was going to be alone again.

The figure stepped over the threshold of her house, the downlights from her hallway illuminating his face fully.

Where she had seen a crooked brown eye and a toothless snarl seconds prior, she saw dark grey eyes, similar to her own, looking back down at her.

A beard, a tattooed hairline, a black T-shirt.

"Kiz?" Nick sounded panicked. He rushed to her, held her by both arms and lowered himself to her eye level. "Kiz, are you alright? Tell me you're alright." His voice cracked. He gently turned her head to check her over.

She tried to take her mask off with her right hand then winced, removing it with her left instead. Her vocal cords finally cooperated enough to speak.

"Nick, I … I thought you were …" she let out in a choked whisper before her vision blurred and she felt her legs buckle underneath her.

Chapter 59

Not an electrician

Kirra woke up on her lounge. She looked down to an icepack wrapped around her hand. Nick was perched in a lounge chair opposite her, leaning forward and looking at her. Gus was curled up at her feet, fast asleep. She remembered what had happened.

"Thanks for getting Gus for me," she croaked.

"All good, your neighbour shit himself when he answered the door. Refused to hand him over, didn't believe I was your brother."

"How'd you get him then? You didn't kill him, did you Nick?" Kirra said, attempting humour but also a little wary. Her brother snorted a laugh. Kirra could count on one broken hand how many times she had heard Nick laugh since they were adults.

"I showed him a picture from my wedding, the one of us and Dad." He smiled sadly at her. A laugh and a smile? Maybe this was Chris just about to yank a Scooby-Doo-style mask off over his head and finish what he had started twenty years ago.

"Then I pulled a sawn-off shotgun out and told him to give me the fucking Staffy or I'd blow a hole in him," he deadpanned.

"That's more believable." She smiled back at him.

Nick was here, had put an ice pack on her hand and draped a blanket over her, collected her dog. Unusual didn't even begin to describe this evening, this weekend, this whole year – come to think of it.

"What do you do for work, Nick?" Kirra ventured, wiggling her broken fingers a little bit. The ice had taken some of the pain away, but it still throbbed badly.

"Electrician."

"An electrician who lives next door to Chris Hemsworth," she challenged.

"Yeah well, you know, the mining boom—"

"Right place, right time," she cut him off.

He levelled her with a serious look. "Right place, right time," he returned, nodding.

"You know, I really had no idea. Everyone else did, but I genuinely didn't until Tim put ten thousand dollars in my bag at Bree's party."

Nick's eyes flared.

"To pay for bailing him out of Bali."

"Thanks for that, by the way." Nick should have gone into law, or politics, the way he skirted around direct questions without denying them outright.

"So, what is it, Nick? Drugs? Is that why I couldn't score anything when you popped up in that club, other dealers close shop when you come to town?"

Nick looked down at the floor then out her window, biting the inside of his cheek. "It's honestly better you don't know, Kiz."

Kirra scoffed in disbelief.

"But Dad knows, and Bree?" The numbness she had been feeling for the last day was making way for panic and rage, more familiar feelings.

Nick just shook his head again. "You don't need to know anything. It's better you don't, with your job."

"Which I'm about to lose. I punched a child hard enough to break my hand."

"Yeah, I heard."

"From who?"

"Bree, think Zoe must have told her. The kid's not going to press charges, so you don't need to worry about that."

"How do you know that, Nick?"

"You don't need to know that, either."

"Fuck, Nick, you didn't—"

"Christ, Kiz. No, I didn't kill a fucking kid. Are you out of your mind? I just found him this arvo and had a little chat, that's all." Nick smiled at Kirra, but it wasn't kind like the one from before – it didn't reach his eyes. "He's staying away from Hattie, and he's not pressing charges. If he does either of those things, he's going to have a bunch of cunts that look like me pulling up at his school just after three tomorrow."

Kirra closed her eyes, a headache blooming behind them.

Hattie was going to hate her even more now. If anyone had come between her and Chris back in the day, she would have killed them. Kirra had not only made a huge scene, struck her boyfriend or whatever she thought he was to her, but now Nick had threatened him. What a nightmare.

Still, she struggled to fight the smile that was spreading over her lips.

"Was he scared?" Kirra asked, biting her bottom lip to stop the grin from erupting any further.

"Shit scared. Think he pissed himself a little bit." Nick grinned back at her, a gold tooth glinting from the back of his top row of teeth. Another detail she had never noticed.

"Good." Kirra couldn't help but laugh, and Nick joined her.

They were cackling loudly enough that Gus woke up, spun around and licked Kirra furiously. She kissed his muzzle, took a deep whiff of his musky smell and held tight onto his nuggety little frame while his tail whipped her through the blanket Nick had wrapped her in.

The pair regained their composure.

"You called me Chris." Nick couldn't meet Kirra's eyes as he said the name out loud.

"Did I?" Kirra had lost consciousness after she realised who was actually at her door. She hadn't eaten or drunk all day, the adrenaline tearing through the last of her energy. Nick must have grabbed her before she hit the floor as she didn't have any new injuries.

"Yeah, you did. You looked terrified when you saw me." Nick looked up at her. His eyes were sad, his mouth a straight line under his beard. Kirra looked back at him.

"I'm sorry," she croaked out, eyes welling.

"What? What for?" He looked confused.

"I'm sorry." She took a deep breath, all these confessions in one weekend … she felt like she couldn't stop them now. She didn't want to stop them. "I'm sorry I got myself in that situation and how it impacted you. I know you've hated me ever since because I put your best mate in jail and got you a permanent record. I get it, I get why you hate me."

Kirra let the tears fall down her cheeks, snuggling into Gus for warmth and comfort. She was greeted with silence for a few long moments.

"I don't hate you," Nick said through clenched teeth. "I hate him. And I hate myself for what he did to you."

Kirra was stunned. She had expected Nick to lay into her, to call her a slut like he always did. "How was it your fault?"

Nick's eyes were down at the floor. He was hunched forward and clenching his huge hands together between his knees. "I knew what was going on. Well, at least I thought I did. I never outright accused him of anything, but he made a comment about you one time, and I kicked his arse. He said he got the message, but I knew he hadn't. I should have intervened, but he was helping Dad out so much at work, and …" Nick looked up at Kirra. "Honestly, if I'd have told you I knew, asked you to break it off, run Chris off, beaten him up again, would you have? Would you have let him go?"

Kirra stayed silent for a minute, pretending to think it over, but she had known the answer instantly. "No, I wouldn't have stopped. I was completely obsessed with him," she answered honestly, breaking into tears again.

Nick left the chair he was sitting in and crouched down next to Kirra, running a hand through her hair.

"Why are you such a cunt to me then, Nick? If you don't blame me, then why?" She was sobbing. She let him stroke the hair out of her face. It was such an unusual scene, hulking Nick patting her like she was a child or a dog.

"I don't mean to be, I just," he sighed, pinching the bridge of his nose. "I don't want you mixed up in my shit. You're too good for it."

"You think I'm a stuck-up bitch," she sniffed.

"No, I don't think that. You *are* too good for it. You're the smartest person I know by a long way, not that that's saying much as you know most of my mates."

Kirra snorted, wiping at her nose with the back of her sleeve.

"And you've worked your fucking arse off to get what you've got. I figure if you hate me, if I make you hate me, there's less chance you'll want to hang around with me and the boys, less chance I'll taint your credible, legitimate life," he finished.

Kirra paused, taking it all in. "I didn't know you knew any four-syllable words."

"Oh, fuck you, actually." Nick laughed. He stood up and made for the kitchen to get her a glass of water.

Kirra got off the lounge, and Gus totted off to sniff around Nick's feet. "I wish this had happened sooner. It's a shame I had to smash a kid, then my phone, for you to tell me all this."

"Yeah, sorry about that." Nick handed her a glass of water and bent down to scratch Gus under the chin. "You know the McNamara's aren't really talkers." Nick chanced a smile at his sister. "Bree's been on me for years to talk to you. She's right, obviously."

"Does Bree know what happened to me?"

Nick nodded. Kirra felt an odd mix of relief and jealousy. Relief at not needing to tell Bree the story, and jealousy that Nick had been the one to tell it. She supposed Nick had his own response to what had happened – he was allowed to tell people.

"Does Bree know what you do for work?" Kirra wanted to try her luck one more time, but Nick just raised his eyebrows and shrugged.

Fucking hell, she really was the absolute last person to know, and even then, she still didn't.

"I messaged Dan to let him know you're alright, and he said he let your work know you were just really sick too." Oh fuck, work. That's right. She might not be struck off for assault, but Ken still knew about her and David.

David. He would be so worried.

"Your fella's on his way over here now, too,"

"Oh?"

"Yeah, he was desperate to talk to you. Dan gave him my number, and I had a quick chat with him while you were out too." Nick paused and fished around for his keys in his back pocket in a gesture that he was on his way out. "He's a good bloke, David. I can see that. And as for the other guy ..." His look turned serious. "If you don't want him to get out, which he's due to next year, say the word and he stays inside."

Kirra looked at Nick in disbelief while she thought about his offer.

"He can come out – he's done his time." Kirra was obviously anxious about Chris' release, but she figured the law was the law. A judge had determined a sentence of twenty years fit the crime he had committed, and that sentence had almost been served.

Nick nodded in understanding. "You've done your time too. You need to move on, be happy." Nick jangled his keys, swinging them around his finger once. "Alright, I'm off."

He made to turn and leave, and Kirra pounced on him with a hug, wrapping her arms around his, pinning them to his sides. He reached up and patted her awkwardly on the arm. "I love you, Dickolas," she said into his huge chest.

"Yep, back at ya, Kiz." Nick broke the embrace, nodded at her again then turned and left.

She watched him descend her front steps and hop into his car, a matte black SL class Mercedes. Of course he was never an electrician. She really was Hank Schraeder from Breaking Bad. It was so painfully obvious, and she could only laugh at herself now.

Kirra waved at him as he drove off up her street just as another, less-expensive Mercedes pulled up to take its place.

Her heart skipped a beat.

She ran down the stairs as David hopped out of the driver's door and ran to meet her in the street, wrapping both arms around her. His embrace, his warmth, his scent – a sense of being in the exact right place with the exact right person settled in and around her.

"Christ, Kirra, I've been beside myself all day. I was stuck in court and didn't know you hadn't shown up at work until a few hours ago," he spoke quickly into her hair.

He pulled back to look at her.

"Are you alright?"

"No, not really, but I'll be better now you're here."

Chapter 60

All good things come to an end

Kirra rocked up to work on Tuesday as if nothing had happened. If Nathaniel wanted to reprimand her for having a day off without telling anyone, he could come to her office himself. She wasn't going to prostrate herself before him. She got to work even earlier than usual, before the sun had risen, leaving David asleep at hers to sneak out and get a head start on her day alone. David had taken her to the Royal last night where she was informed she had fractured her pinkie, a 'boxer's fracture'. When the doctor had asked how she had injured herself, she said she'd lost a week's rent on the pokies so she had punched a hole in the wall – in the most bogan accent she could muster.

The doctor had quickly looked at a very well-dressed David, then back to Kirra, hair matted and wearing trackpants and thongs, before deciding not to ask any further questions. She had been put in a wrist brace that splinted her pinkie and ring fingers together and given some ibuprofen.

"That was some good acting," David chuckled, finally releasing the laugh he had been stifling since Kirra had spoken to the doctor.

"It wasn't acting. The voice I normally talk to you in is the fake one."

The day was almost over with no meeting request notification from Nathaniel, no knock at her door from HR, no sight of Ken. She was almost disappointed; she had been ready to tell them they could shove their job up their arses.

She was having dinner with Dan. He had agreed, under duress, to provide her with a copy of The Guide. She was desperate to see him and debrief him on all that had happened over the weekend: the Chris story, Sydney, the assault of a minor.

The minute she saw him already seated in the restaurant, she felt that familiar sense of warmth and comfort radiate from her scalp to her toes. He took her in one of those bear hugs, and when he pulled back, she was already crying.

"God, that bad huh?" he smiled at her, pointing to her busted hand then her tear-streamed face.

"Um, yeah, it's fine, but I'm good actually, like – really good."

Kirra had so many things to tell Dan, but she first needed to know how his weekend had gone.

In a most serendipitous turn of events, Dan had also travelled to meet Ned's family in Melbourne while Kirra had been meeting David's in Sydney. Things were moving just as fast in his new relationship as hers.

"Kiz, they were the best, like funny, loving … and the food – holy shit, I thought my family could put on a feast, but it was next level. Ned's sister reminds me so much of you – she was a scream, and his yia yia…."

Dan went on, and Kirra was so bloody happy for him. After he was finished, Kirra spilled everything about her weekend as well as her past, about Chris, Ken, David, Nick, Hattie and the kid she had punched in the face. All of it.

"Now seems like a good time to give you this, then," Dan said, sliding a tri-folded handout to Kirra after their mutual debriefs had concluded.

"Oh my god, The Guide," Kirra gasped, looking at the title. "Daniel, really?"

"What? You haven't even opened it yet?" he gaped at her in mock outrage.

"This is in comic sans, the least serious font," Kirra shook her head. "I'm an Arial or a Garamond girlie, surely." She opened the pamphlet and silently read the first few lines.

"Daniel," she intoned seriously for a second time.

"Yes?"

"This reads like the DSM-5-TR, what are all these acronyms? How many mental illnesses have you diagnosed me with?!"

"A few but keep reading." Dan was grinning.

Kirra had almost finished when she got to the closing notes on the back page.

Kirra Jane McNamara has been my closest friend for fourteen years, and I hope this guide helps you understand and love her just as much as I do. She's going to make your life amazing in so many ways, and it is your duty, Guide Receiver, to do the same for her. Take care of my Kizrat.

Sincerely, Dr Daniel K Manaaki, FRANZCP

"Dan, it's beautiful."

"So, did I give The Guide to the right guy?" Dan asked, his big dark eyes focusing intently on Kirra.

"Yeah, you did. David said it's been helpful too." Kirra hadn't stopped smiling through her tears this whole dinner, she was an open wound, bleeding everywhere at this point.

To anyone in the restaurant, it must have looked like Dan had just broken up with her.

"Kiz, I'm moving to Victoria."

He *was* breaking up with her.

Chapter 61

Not great, thanks for asking

Kirra had not taken the news well at all.

Daniel had explained he was taking a senior leadership role with an online counselling service that he had been volunteering with for years. It was a massive promotion for him, and he was going to be doing meaningful, rewarding work for an organisation he was already working with for free; a dream come true. It also coincided with a new job for Ned, who had jumped at the opportunity to move back down and be closer to his dad who had recently been diagnosed with early onset dementia. The weekend's trip had been a mix of business and pleasure. Ned and Dan had signed a lease on a townhouse in Fitzroy North.

Kirra felt like her heart had been ripped out of her chest.

She couldn't deny that Dan deserved the job, one that he wouldn't be likely to find up here in Queensland. She was gutted, but she got it. Daniel had found his Mr Right, and the once-in-a-lifetime opportunity was the cherry on top. They had ended the dinner with a hug and more tears, but the drive home left Kirra feeling numb.

What was she going to do without him?

He was set to leave for Melbourne within a fortnight. As if organising the custody arrangements of a child, Dan had referred her to a psychologist he knew and trusted and made sure David nagged her to go to her appointments. After she had spilled everything about what had happened to her in her teens, both Dan and David had encouraged her to speak to a professional who could help her process her trauma.

"I did the same thing once," David had offered when Kirra had explained what she had done to Hattie's groper, "when George was about four and Ed was just a toddler. We were at a park and this old bloke walked up to George and started talking to him, on his own, while I was chasing Ed. I saw it out of the corner of my eye, and before I knew what I was doing, I had him by the front of his shirt. Anything that reminds you of what you went through can be really triggering, sometimes things that don't even seem related might set you off if you've got CPTSD. My psych's been amazing at helping me figure all that out."

***

On top of Dan's imminent departure, Hattie was still ignoring Kirra's messages weeks after the incident.

Zoe, on the other hand, wasn't and understood where Kirra's attack had come from. She said she would have done it herself had she had gotten to them first. Zoe had also been ignorant of Hattie's crush on this older boy, Jayden, and after the attack had demanded Hattie turn over her phone.

Zoe told Kirra that it was bad. Not as bad as Kirra's vivid imagination may have thought, but still bad. There were messages upon messages from him begging for nudes, telling her she was the most beautiful girl in the world, how he wouldn't show anyone, he was just desperate to see how good she looked. In response to his persistent requests, Hattie had sent him some, at fucking fourteen years old. She had sworn to Zoe she was still a virgin, and it was just flirting, sexting and what Kirra had busted them doing at the dance recital. The photos didn't contain Hattie's face, but who was to know how many people Jayden had shown them to.

Kirra was prepared to take Nick up on his potentially real offer of having the boy entombed in the concrete slab of a construction site, but Zoe had said she had it under control and that wasn't necessary.

Not at this stage, anyway.

Kirra needed to let Hattie's mum be her mum, and she needed to get back in her box as cool, cashed-up Aunty Kiz. Someone who bought their goddaughter Gucci shoes and took her friends to the movies, not a psychopath with smeared mascara beating up teenagers. It was hard, but she trusted Zoe to keep Hattie safe. She had no choice but to trust her.

Kirra just wanted her Hattie back: to pick her up from school and take her to get her nails done, to sit next to her in a dingy Chinese restaurant in the Valley, to film a stupid TikTok dance with her. She missed her so much it physically hurt.

Work had been much the same, but Kirra was sure her luck was about to run out at any moment. She could sense it.

Ken knew about her and David and also had unconfirmed suspicions she had slept with Ben, which meant Nathaniel probably knew both of those things too. The Ben thing wasn't as damning as her current relationship with David as it had happened before she worked with him, but it still added to the picture that Kirra was unprofessional and unpredictable. James and Tony had been dismissed after the scene at reception, and she was waiting for Mary from HR to out her as the person responsible for causing it.

Kirra knew where James did Pilates and had managed to slip the huge wad of illegal cash Tim had given her into his gym bag while he was working out. It alleviated some of the guilt she'd had about getting him fired, but she had also heard he had found a job within a few weeks of being let go from Kensington Menschel. In the end, it hadn't been as much of a disaster for him as she had feared it would be.

Tony was yet to reappear at another firm.

She hadn't been able to shake the bone-deep exhaustion she had been feeling for months, and her stomach issues had even forced her to lower her caffeine and alcohol consumption as a matter of necessity. She even had her first oat-milk iced latte. Just one, maybe not enough to classify the resolution complete, but it was a start.

Rather than go to the GP, which David had been begging her to, she threw herself into work even harder than before. She busied herself in favour of looking after herself.

Chapter 62

Patek

She had been feeling like garbage, preoccupied with Hattie still hating her guts and desperately missing Dan, so David had organised a date night for the two of them at the restaurant where they'd had their first date to cheer her up. It was early April, and Brisbane was feeling the first chill of Autumn.

It was a beautiful evening, and the twinkling fairy lights wrapped around the large fig tree in New Farm filled her with a previously unfelt whimsy and nostalgia, like she was seeing it for the first time. David was driving, and she was enjoying being a passenger princess, relaxed and greedily drinking in the sight of him while he drove her around.

"Even your wrists are good-looking," she said. "Who has good-looking wrists?"

They entered the restaurant, which was unusually dim and quiet. It was a random Wednesday evening, so she had expected it wouldn't be as busy as it would be on a Friday, but it was almost empty. A waiter led them to their table, which was lit by candles that seemed brighter given the lower lighting.

"Can your mate not afford his electricity bills anymore?" Kirra asked David off-handedly, sitting down to peruse the menu. "I'm starving. I could eat the arse out of a low-flying duck."

She decided what she was going to have, then placed her menu down, looking across the table to David, but he wasn't there.

Seconds later, she realised he was kneeling down beside her chair.

"Are you okay, did you fall?"

"Kirra, I'm okay." David chuckled then opened a black box in front of her.

Her heart, prone to launching into fight or flight over anything, seemed to cease beating altogether once she realised what was happening.

David was down on one knee. His hands were trembling as he held the ring up to her.

She squinted in the candlelight and realised it wasn't a ring; it was a watch.

A cream-coloured lining revealed the small oblong dial of a deep sapphire blue set with four diamond markers; the bezel and clasp were white gold and set with more diamonds that glittered, even in the low light. It wasn't at all like the watches she normally wore, which were larger and busier, but it was somehow still very *her*.

Temporarily mesmerised by the details of the beautiful watch, she forgot why she was looking at it.

She looked down into David's eyes.

"Kirra Jane McNamara, will you marry me?"

For once in her life, she didn't need to have a discussion with Daniel or Jeannine before making a big decision. There was no second guessing or any question about what she wanted. She had no reservations.

She wanted that watch, and the man who was giving it to her, forever.

"Of course I will, Daveo." She smiled back at him.

David slipped the watch she was wearing off her wrist and replaced it with the slim black leather strap of the new one, his hands trembling, to the rapturous applause of the restaurant's staff who had been hiding in the shadows, eagerly awaiting Kirra's response.

David rose to his feet, and Kirra wrapped her arms around him tightly, burying her face into his neck and letting his warmth, scent and heartbeat soak into her.

"I think I'm going to pass out. I've never been so nervous in my life," David huffed into her hair, still shaking.

"Did you think I would say no?" She pulled back to observe him, to read the look on his face.

"I don't know. You're the most perfect woman on Earth. It'd be arrogant if I thought you saying yes was a sure thing."

They sat back down. Kirra was vibrating with excitement and shock.

"Why a watch?" She could have phrased it better, but she knew David would be able to fill in the blanks, the fluff; *this is the most stunning watch that was ever created, it's perfect and I never want to take it off. What made you want to propose to me with a watch and not a ring as per traditional norms, you beautiful man?*

"I've never seen you wear a ring, but you always wear a watch, so it was practical. I figure you might want a wedding band when we get married, but two rings would annoy you."

This was true. Kirra would routinely fidget with hair-ties, earrings, buckles and laces on shoes, pulling them on and off throughout the day. Watches were the only accessory she managed to keep on for any period of time. Of course he had noticed that.

"It was my dad's twentieth wedding anniversary gift to my mum. It's a Patek from the early 2000s. I collected it when we were down in Sydney. I thought it would suit you – the dial's a similar blue to your eyes." He paused a moment, looking at Kirra's wrist, her lips, her eyes. "I knew I wanted to marry you after that night on the beach."

Kirra's heart ached with how much she loved him, how much thought and effort had gone into this evening and how stunningly beautiful the watch was. "After I ran out of your dad's party and spilled my darkest secrets to you?"

"No, not then. Afterwards. When you let me bathe you and put you to bed. I laid you down and watched you go to sleep, and I thought I want to do this forever. I want to put you to bed when you've had a shit day, to look after you, and to lay down next to you every night until the day I die."

Kirra was lost for words. Her brain could retain languages, thousands upon thousands of clauses and caveats, multi-step combinations for a videogame she had seen once on a YouTube video. Surely it could recite something beautiful and poignant she'd read or heard somewhere.

Once her brain reconnected to her mouth, she would tell him she felt such a deep and unwavering love for him, and that love had in turn made her love herself for the first time in her entire adult life. She would tell him that he deserved nothing but happiness for the rest of his days, and that she would honour and cherish him until her heart stopped beating.

"Samesies," she replied, instead.

Chapter 63

Wonderful young woman

Hattie finally texted Kirra back after she messaged her a snap of her wrist telling her she was engaged.

"To a guy you've been with for three months?" Hattie responded.

Shots fired.

"Things move quickly when you're an old woman, Harriet," Kirra had responded.

Even though her goddaughter was throwing shade, she was happy to catch it. She had desperately wanted to talk directly to Hattie – Zoe could only feed her so much second-hand information as to how she was going. "Your dance with Harrison was beautiful. Your mum and I were crying the whole time," she added.

"Thanks." Dots appeared, disappeared, reappeared. "Mum's being a stinge and won't give me money to get my nails done. Take me after school?"

***

Kirra was parked in the carpark of Hattie's high school waiting for three o'clock. She happened to look up from her phone just as Jayden skulked to the lowered old WRX she was parked next to. She fought the urge to hop out and smack him again and, for a change, was successful in controlling herself. She instead imagined, in vivid detail, slicing his head off with a samurai sword, blood squirting vertically from his neck, which gave her burning rage a small outlet.

Once his shitbox had loudly pulled out of the carpark, his aftermarket muffler cracking and popping as it left, Hattie slid into the passenger seat of Kirra's coupé. She looked over at Kirra warily. Without hesitating, Kirra leapt out of her seat and wrapped her arms around Hattie, who fervently squeezed her back. They sat like that for a moment in silence, Kirra relishing having Hattie back in her arms, not being shoved away.

"I'm so sorry I beat up Jayden, Hatts. I'm a psycho," Kirra huffed into Hattie's hair.

Hattie's slim shoulders started shaking. "It's okay." She pulled back, crying, "He was a jerk, I didn't realise it at the time."

God, she was so much smarter than Kirra was at her age. Hattie wiped at her eyes and smiled at Kirra, and she was sure her heart would burst. She had only been wanting to see that smile for a few weeks, but it had felt like a lifetime.

Kirra took them to the nearest shopping centre and got them both a bubble tea, then they sat down to get their nails done. Hattie picked a ridiculously long set that Zoe would be disgusted by, as per her and Kirra's tradition. The smell of the chemicals in the salon mixed with the lumpy sweet beverage had Kirra feeling nauseous, but she rallied to chat with Hattie.

"I got myself into trouble when I was fifteen. I don't know if your mum told you," Kirra offered.

"No, what happened?" Hattie angled her head to look at Kirra, bending down to slurp up her tea as she did so.

"My dad had this apprentice, Chris, he was really good friends with Nick—"

"Who threatened to bash Jayden," Hattie interrupted with raised eyebrows.

"Yes, that Nick," Kirra returned with her eyebrows raised in challenge, "and I was absolutely obsessed with him, like a crush but a million times more intense. I literally couldn't think about anything but him, ever." Kirra paused to look over at Hattie, who was looking down at her hands as they were pulled and filed by the manicurist.

She wondered if she was thinking about Jayden right now.

"It was great at the start, he was smoking hot, lovely to me, made me feel special and beautiful. But he—" Kirra's throat closed. She didn't know if she really should share everything with Hattie, she was only fourteen. But maybe that's not that young, considering what she had caught her doing, the photos she'd already sent. If she'd had someone share a story like this with her when she was her age, would she have been a bit warier of Chris?

"He got me pregnant, and when I told him, he almost beat me to death. Nick and Dad pulled him off me, and Nick fucked him up. He went to jail and gets out sometime next year," Kirra finished quickly.

She felt the familiar churning of her stomach but couldn't help but feel proud of telling her story, out loud, in broad daylight. It wasn't kept in a box anymore, it was a part of her history, and it was important Hattie knew how bad these things could go so she wouldn't fall in love as blindly as her godmother had.

Hopefully.

Hattie looked horrified, her eyes growing wide with shock.

"I'm so sorry about flipping out at your recital. I just saw that kid and …" Kirra trailed off, looking out the shop window at the passing shoppers.

"I get it, I do," Hattie said quietly. "I was so stupid, Auntie Kiz, sending him photos."

"No. You are not stupid, Hatts. He was pressuring you and giving you attention, making you feel special. He knew what he was doing. I feel so sorry for you girls now. If I'd been able to send photos on my junky old phone back when I was your age, I would have gotten myself into even more trouble than I did."

They sat together in silence, their nails nearly finished.

Kirra hadn't had her nails done in years after being told they weren't in keeping with the dress code of Kensington Menschel. Her set wasn't as long as Hattie's, but they were pointy and light purple with a glittery love heart design on each ring fingernail. Jeannine wouldn't approve at all.

"You were smart to not include your face, too. Did he send you anything back?"

Hattie blushed and looked away.

"Yeah, he did." Hattie bit her lip and tried not to laugh. "Not that I'd ever seen one, but I could tell his was really small, like it barely made it out over the fly of his jeans."

Kirra snorted out a laugh.

"Of course it's tiny. I heard how loud his stupid fucking car was. Definitely compensating for something," Kirra wiggled a pointed pinkie nail at Hattie to the admonishment of the manicurist, who angrily tapped the curing lamp with a nail file, telling Kirra to return her hand underneath it.

Hattie was giggling, still Kirra's absolute favourite noise in the world.

"Why were you making out with him then, Hatts, letting him put his hands on you? Did you even like him that much?" Kirra thought she shouldn't push it too much, but she wanted to know what was going on in Hattie's world, to try and understand it from her perspective.

Hattie shrugged. "I don't know. My friend Penny has been doing *stuff* with boys the past few months and all our friends are like obsessed with it, hearing all her stories. It made her seem so cool and mature, like she's in grade eleven or something. Jayden had been rizzing me up for months, and I just wanted to see if I could be cool like Penny, I guess."

"He'd been what-ing you up for months?"

Hattie rolled her eyes and laughed. "Rizz! Like chatting to me, telling me I'm pretty."

"Fuck me, what was wrong with the word flirting." Kirra shook her head, exasperated.

She was relieved to know Hattie wasn't lying about not being into the kid she had bashed. She remembered what it was like to be a teenager. There was always that one friend who snuck some of their mum's smokes to school, wore a push-up bra or watched an R18 horror movie – doing something earlier than your peers made you inherently cooler. Kirra was so proud of Hattie, her self-awareness and ability to reflect on her actions at such a young age, graciously accepting Kirra's apology for doing something probably unforgivable.

She truly was a wonderful young woman.

"Aunty Kiz, stop looking at me like that," Hattie cautioned her.

Kirra started ugly crying. "I just love you so fucking much, Hattie."

"Love you too, but please stop making a scene, you're embarrassing me in front of the nail ladies."

Chapter 64

HR

"Jane."

A voice at Kirra's office startled her from the email she was drafting. She spun around and saw Mary from HR.

"Can you please come to my office? It's urgent."

Oh fuck.

Even though Kirra had been anticipating this day since she had returned from Sydney, she was still filled with lead. Dragging her feet to Mary's office, she saw Paul. His eyes flared with alarm, mouthing the words *what's going on?* but she just shrugged and dutifully followed the executioner to the gallows.

It was the longest walk of her entire life.

She slid into the office and, as expected, Ken and Nathaniel were there, but her heart fell into her stomach when she saw that David had also been called in. He quickly offered Kirra a small polite smile but then looked back down at his hands that were clasped together in his lap.

Her mind raced. In all the scenarios she had anticipated, she figured she would bear the brunt of all the accusations of inappropriate workplace behaviour and that David would merely receive a caution given that he hadn't upset them previously. It always happened that way when someone was already being 'managed out'. It didn't matter what other people were involved in the misdemeanour – if you were on their shit list and your co-conspirators weren't, they got off scot-free and you got shit canned.

All of it was inevitable, and probably even fair, to a degree. She was engaged to her coworker, and they knew they had been living on borrowed time. She was surprised it had taken them this long to pounce.

"Jane, David, it's come to our attention that you are in a romantic relationship," Ken began, but Kirra cut him off.

"Shouldn't Nathaniel or Mary lead this meeting, Ken? Why are you even here? You aren't our manager."

"No but I'm an equity partner who has a vested interest in making sure—"

"I'm basically an equity partner with how rich my billings keep you all," Kirra cut him off.

Nathaniel remained silent and looked uneasy. He wasn't very good with conflicts despite being in an industry that ran on them.

Mary stepped in, deciding to do her job. "Jane, how long have you and David been in a romantic relationship?"

"We decided to see each other exclusively as of this weekend. We were coming to disclose the relationship to you today." Kirra didn't so much as blink.

"She's fucking lying!" Ken let out in an exasperated bark. "She was with him at a party more than six weeks ago in Sydney, I saw her there." His normally calm façade had broken, a vein in his temple bulging.

"Is there really a need for language, Ken?" she replied cooly, riling him up further.

"That's funny, from you," Nathaniel offered awkwardly, chuckling. "You called Mr Waters a most offensive name not too long ago."

"Is that true, Jane?" Mary intervened, ignoring Ken and Nathaniel. "We have a policy that states workplace relationships must be confidentially disclosed to HR as soon as practicable to ensure there aren't any conflicts of interest, and then we ensure all parties are aware of what acceptable workplace behaviour is as per our code of conduct. If you delayed in disclosing your relationship with David, that would constitute a breach of—"

"I didn't delay, I'd like to disclose it now. David and I won't let our relationship become a problem for the firm or any of our colleagues."

"She is absolutely lying about the length of her relationship with David Waters. She was at his father's birthday party, look …" He had taken his phone out of his pocket and found a photo from Icebergs. David had his arm around Kirra's lower back, the pair talking to another guest. Ken had clearly spotted her before she had realised he was there and taken the picture. The lengths he would go to oust her still astounded her, even after everything.

"Jane and David, how do you explain this?" Mary asked.

Kirra spoke before David had a chance. "Oh, silly me. Yes, now I think of it, I was at that party with David."

Ken had allowed a smug smirk to spread over his cruel mouth.

Kirra slipped her phone out from her pocket, placed it next to Ken's and played a video for the room. It was Ken, on the balcony of Icebergs, from the perspective of a low coffee table that Kirra had placed her phone down on just before she had hit record when they'd had their little chat.

"You sexually assaulted me that night, I was twenty-four."

"Plenty old enough to know what you were doing,"

"It's not my age, it was the age difference, the power imbalance. You plied with me drugs and penetrated me without my consent."

"Your memory of that evening is inaccurate. You were fully consenting. You were loving the attention and the free coke, you grabbed my hand and shoved it up your skirt."

David's eyes flared with rage, and his jaw clenched. Kirra hadn't told him about what Ken had done to her all those years ago. He looked liable to rip Ken's head off.

Ken had gone red, and Mary and Nathaniel looked deeply shocked, staring down at the phone then back to Ken. He opened and closed his mouth like a fish gasping for air.

No one had said anything.

Yes, he had a picture of David and Kirra at a party, but she had a video of him confessing to doing drugs and fingering her.

Fatality – Kirra wins.

"She fucked Ben Andrews from Guérir!" He had spittle clinging to the corner of his mouth as he pointed a shaking finger at Kirra. Her stomach dropped. Another thing she hadn't got around to telling David about.

She looked to David. He looked furious. She desperately wanted to know what he was the most mad about: her having slept with Ben or the fact that Ken had touched her, that she had let him touch her. His mouth was a thin line and his brow furrowed, staring down at the floor, his jaw clenched so tight it looked like he might explode.

Ken wasn't just trying to get her fired, he was trying to hurt her, to hurt David. He was faced with undeniable evidence of his assault and he refused to go down without dragging her along with him.

"Ken, did you touch Jane?" Mary asked, finally able to form words.

"No!"

"That video, which clearly has your face in it, shows you admitting to having your hand up her skirt and—"

"Enough!" David shouted.

Kirra looked at him pleadingly. He looked devastated.

"This meeting is unnecessary as the relationship won't be a problem to anyone here anymore," David announced.

Kirra felt her heart breaking in her chest. She knew it was all too good to be true, the perfect man wanting to be with her forever. How was it ever true?

It was over, done.

"I'm quitting. Mary, you'll have my letter of resignation within the hour."

With that, he stormed out of the office.

Chapter 65

The body keeps the score

Kirra had run out after David. It took her a while to find the direction he had set off in, and she found him crossing the street a block away.

"David!" she called out after him, but he kept walking, either unhearing or ignoring her.

She ran, almost rolling her ankle in her heels, and finally made her way to him. She grabbed him by the arm. He spun around and looked at her, breathing harshly.

"David, I'm so sorry I didn't tell you about Ben. It happened before you and I met and—"

"Kirra, it's not that," he managed to choke out, turning to face her properly in the middle of the pathway. "I can't believe Ken did that to you." His hands were balled up in fists.

"So, you're not dumping me – we're still together?"

"Of course we are. I love you, Kirra." He kissed her, her heart slowing down a fraction. His kiss relayed everything she needed to know. *I don't care about the other guy, I know you're with me, we're getting married, it's going to be okay.* He broke the kiss to look at her.

"You're not really going to quit, are you?" She was unusually out of breath. She routinely ran ten kilometres without breaking a sweat and had only trotted a few short steps to reach David. Her heart was still jackhammering in her chest, even though she knew David wasn't breaking up with her.

"I am, it's the right thing to do. I should have done it weeks ago."

"What – why?"

"You are so good at your job, and you deserve to be there. You've worked so hard for it. Not that I understand how you can work with that animal, but if you want to, then fine. I'm not kidding myself into thinking I'm a great lawyer, or that I deserve to be in a firm like KM. If I'm there and they know we're together, they'll just keep coming for you." He kissed her on the forehead, his lips cold on her overheated skin. "I'm also going to kick Ken's wrinkly old arse when he leaves the office for the day, Patrick's too for good measure. I would have got sacked and maybe struck off the roll for assault anyway," he attempted to smile at her.

She felt weak and exhausted after the interaction in Mary's office, and the thought of not having David at KM with her made her feel sick to her stomach. Her heart was still beating from running. She felt clammy despite the beautiful crisp day, and her head began to throb. Her vision was blurring.

"Kirra, are you okay?" David grabbed her by the sides of the face, and she registered his beautiful eyes as spots of white crowded out her vision and she felt the Earth go sideways beneath her.

***

Beeping.

An insistent chime on a nearby monitor, and a different bell ringing further in the distance.

Kirra forced her eyes open, gripped with fear, a vice crushing her heart in an instant.

She was dying, just like her mum. The beeping, the smells, she was in hospital and dying.

David's face appeared over hers. She struggled to speak, her voice catching in her throat.

"You're okay, you just passed out. We're at the private hospital in Spring Hill." He held her head in his hands. He looked relieved, just like her dad had looked all those years ago. It was all so familiar.

319

"They took some blood while you were out. They said you were dehydrated and hooked you up with an IV." He gestured to the bag swinging above her. "Kirra, you haven't been yourself for weeks now. I wish you'd gone to the GP sooner. We'll get some answers while we're here." He clutched her hand, running his finger back over the wrist band of the watch he had given her when he asked her to marry him.

Kirra couldn't stand it, the drip in her hand, the beeping, David's relieved face.

She knew it wasn't just dehydration.

"David, I know it's going to be bad." Kirra's lip quivered. "I've treated my body like absolute shit my whole adult life, and cancer runs in my family. I fucking smoked and vaped for so long." She was hyperventilating. It was all too good to be true, keeping her job, keeping her man.

Something had to give and it was this: her health, her life.

"Kirra, we don't know anything. You've had genetic testing, you haven't vaped in weeks, and you are one of the fittest people I know – it's going to be okay." He was trying to calm her, but there was no use. She had been aching, sore and tired for weeks now.

A doctor entered the room, a kind looking middle-aged woman with greying hair and glasses.

"Kirra, I'm Dr de Silva. Do you know why you're here?"

"Um, I passed out in the street." Kirra's eyes were focused on the clipboard in Dr de Silva's hands. She wanted her to hurry up and spit out what the tests had said, tell her she had an abnormal blood count, that her white blood cells were through the roof and they were going to rush her for a scan for tumours.

She remembered how quick it had gone with her mother. From start to finish, it was less than three months. Her mother who had never smoked, drunk or done drugs. How long would she have, would it be weeks?

"Great news. Your complete blood count was all within the normal range, and your hCG levels were nice and high."

Kirra didn't know what that meant – why would you want to have 'nice' high levels of cancer markers?

"You're about eight weeks along, judging by these levels. How long have you been trying for a baby?" Dr de Silva beamed at the pair.

The smile quickly slipped off her face when she registered Kirra's shocked expression.

"Oh, I'm sorry. I just presumed, given your age, you might have been trying to …" she trailed off, looking down at her clipboard. "I'll let you two, um …" and she shuffled away, leaving the clipboard at the end of Kirra's bed.

Kirra finally looked at David, who was staring at her. He looked just as shocked as she felt.

"I'm… I'm on the pill," she managed to spit out.

She and David had only known each other a few months. They had never talked about kids. She was sure she never wanted to be a mother. After the surgery she'd had to repair her damaged organs in her teens, her endometriosis, her age and her lifestyle, she didn't think she would be able to get pregnant anyway.

She knew she would need to tell David at some point before they got married, but had been putting off having that conversation, worried that telling him her wishes would be an end to their relationship if he wanted kids.

She looked to David, who was doing his best to be unreadable.

"What are you feeling?" she asked him.

He considered her question a moment longer, staring into her eyes, searching and scanning her face intently. "I don't want to say. I want to know how you're feeling."

"I … I don't know," she stammered. "Please tell me – what are you thinking?"

"I'm thinking," he swallowed. His voice broke when he spoke. "I'm thinking that's the best fucking news I've ever heard in my life. I never thought I was going to be happy again, after everything that happened in the past, that at best I could just get by and survive."

Kirra squeezed his hand, rolled over in her bed and ran her other hand down his face.

"Then I fell in love with you, and you loved me back, and I thought – I'm finally happy. It can't get any better than this – I get to be with you forever." He ran his finger over the watch he had given her. "But now, I just …" his words escaped him.

Kirra held him.

"I'm just, really fucking scared, but somehow even happier than I was a minute ago. I want a baby with you, very much."

Kirra tried to make sense of the news, to realise how it made her feel, and think about what she was going to do. She was in her mid-thirties and had been spending her entire adult life avoiding this exact situation. She was terrified. The fear gripped her suddenly and with a force so tight she thought her heart would cease to beat.

Her thoughts swirled. She looked inward and realised what was really terrifying her. It wasn't being pregnant; she had known that fear before.

It was the fear of losing the baby she had only just learned about.

"I'm shit scared, but I want to have a baby with you too," she let out on a whisper.

David beamed at her with his gorgeous, whole-face smile, and her cheeks hurt with the smile that had erupted on her face too. He leant over her and wrapped his arms around her, kissing her hair before standing up to look down at her, her belly.

The way he was looking at her was different than before. His gaze always made her feel beautiful, seen, special; but this – this was something else altogether. He was looking at her like a miracle, like she had just walked on water. Down to her belly, then back to her eyes.

She huffed out a laugh of disbelief before she spoke again.

"Things are moving rather quickly, aren't they?"

They were, she was in shock, but she knew she would handle whatever was going to happen.

Just like she always did.

Kirra and David will return in Kizrat II

Acknowledgements

Much like Kirra, I have an amazing inner circle of people who have supported me in my journey in getting Kizrat out into the world, but I shall save acknowledging them for book two. As for this book, I am only acknowledging myself.

Why, isn't that a bit self-absorbed? A bit full of myself? A little bit who-does-she-think-she-is? And in rebuttal to that, I'd like to quote the Barbie movie; "I worked very hard, so I deserve it".

I've always wanted to be an author but never thought I could be one. When I pictured an 'author', I pictured someone who already had a tonne of money and spare time to fritter about with. They had a slick laptop, their own writing space like a cute office overlooking a quaint garden. They quietly click-clacked away at their keyboard until they wistfully closed its lid to call their publisher and tell them that they were 'done'. Hallmark movie type shit.

Meanwhile, in the real world, I have two little kids, a full-time job and no desk. All I had was a busted old Lenovo laptop that weighs five kilos that's missing the "Q" key, and some stolen hours in the evening after my spawn were asleep (Dad's putting you to bed tonight kids; Mum's writing a sex scene).

I curled over my laptop with the posture of a prawn and got it all out of my head and into words. I surprised myself with a complete narrative. I got it professionally edited and a cover made for it, and the result is an actual BOOK. I did that shit.

Me.

No one else.

And now **you** have read it?? WHAT THE FUCK!

I am honoured that you committed your precious time and attention to reading Kizrat, thank you **so** very much.

I have a fancier laptop now to write the sequel on, but still no desk.

I can't wait to continue Kirra's story.